"MAKE YOUR FRIEND HERE WANT IT," BILL SAID.

"What?" Dani murmured, swimming in a blood haze. She could feel her wolflike incisors starting to extend, and she began to panic.

Her girlfriend was quivering like a frightened animal. "Dani, please help me."

Dani shook and kicked in Bill's arms, but he held her effortlessly and seductively kissed her neck. He was easing his desire into her, she realized. "Let the victim be afraid, but make it so she needs it," Bill said coarsely.

"Stop it," Dani whispered, "I can't do this. Not yet."

"If you love me, then do it!" Bill demanded, pulling Dani back to him, then plunging his ivory teeth into her bared neck.

Suddenly, as Dani felt the pain, then the orgasmic fugue-state overcome her, she was blind to her girlfriend's pleas, blind to everything but her own need. This is what she must do to be loved and wanted, to finally belong . . .

THE VAMPIRE ODYSSEY

SCOTT CIENCIN

ZEBRA BOOKS
KENSINGTON PUBLISHING CORP.

ZEBRA BOOKS

are published by

Kensington Publishing Corp.
475 Park Avenue South
New York, NY 10016

First printing: August, 1992

Printed in the United States of America

ACKNOWLEDGMENTS

This book is dedicated to Alice Alfonsi Kane, a magnificent friend and a phenomenal editor.

Special thanks to Michele Nicholas and Liz Detrich for technical advice, friendship and support.

"No cord nor cable can so forcibly draw, or hold so fast, as love can do with a twined thread."

> Burton
> *Anatomy of Melancholy*

"I have
      Immortal longings in me."

> Shakespeare
> *Antony and Cleopatra*

Prologue

Tampa, Florida. 1974.

Whoever was on the other side of the door had been pounding away as if they were attempting to lose skin in the bargain. Samantha Walthers had been lacing up her running shoes when the slamming had begun. It was just after five-thirty in the morning and it was still dark outside. The tall, attractive brunette had already changed into her gray baggy sweats which had been left over from her police academy days. The park where she performed her daily three-mile run beckoned in her mind. From memory she could smell the freshly cut grass and feel the hard earth beneath her feet. The moment she heard the frantic banging at the front door to her cheap, rented apartment in one of the worst sections of downtown Tampa, she knew that her cherished routine was going to be broken.

"I'm coming!" she hollered as she finished tying the knot on her left sneaker and bounded to the door, snatching her handbag containing her car keys and weapon from the table beside the door. A quick peek through the peephole revealed an overweight Spanish woman in a bathrobe. She recognized the woman as one of the neighbors who never deigned to speak to the *gringa* who wore pants like a man. She opened the door, one hand inside her bag, fingers touching the gun, in case the woman was not alone. The neighborhood was a bad one, but it was all Sam could afford. She was recovering from two years spent living on credit cards to support her ex-husband. The responsibility of paying back her consolidation loan on a rookie's salary dictated her living arrangements.

"¡Venga conmigo! ¡Venga conmigo!" the woman said frantically as she grasped Sam's arm and tugged at her to follow. She led the twenty-year-old policewoman into the hallway of the two-story frame Victorian house, then dragged her down the dimly lit stairs and outside to the veranda. The house had been built around the turn of the century and subdivided into four apartments within the last twenty years. There were smaller dwellings on the same street that usually housed more than one family. Immigrants and those seeking cheap rents and stylish architecture were drawn to the neighborhood.

They followed the small dirt road that ran from the street to behind the house and came to a garage that had once been a converted stable. Beside a smaller house in the back that had once been the servant's quarters lay a pea-green Dempsey dumpster. Gathered before the open trash bin was a circle of neighbors, more than a dozen in all.

The thin, morning air carried with it several unpleasant odors from the garbage dumpster where flies circled and buzzed excitedly. A yellow-orange bulb mounted like a street light gave the only illumination. Nearly all those gathered before the large green bin were clothed in pajamas and bathrobes. A few wore baggy boxer shorts and T-shirts. All were at least twice the age of the young woman who was pulled through the crowd by the older Spanish woman.

The woman, Ruisa, if Sam remembered correctly, had been repeating the same two words from the moment Sam had opened her door. She pointed at a

10

small bundle lying on the dirty ground before the trash bin. Her finger stabbed the air as she gestured at the tiny white hand protruding from the worn, khaki blanket.

"¡Ahí! ¡Ahí!"

Sam's heart nearly stopped as she registered that she was looking at an abandoned infant. A bloated, green Glad bag rested beside the leg of one of the sunburned men staring down at the discarded child. She guessed that he had been the one who had found the baby. Setting her bag on the ground to one side of the child, Sam peeled back the corners of the bundle and found herself staring at the baby's bluish-white face. The infant was a little girl with a wisp of black hair. She was not breathing. Sam's head snapped around and her gaze bore into the eyes of the man with the trash bag as she asked him in Spanish how long it had been since he first found the child.

"A few — a few minutes," he said nervously.

Judging from the number of people who were gathered here, Sam did not believe him. At least he spoke English.

"Did you call 911?" she asked as she examined the infant. She pulled the child's eyelids back and saw only white. The baby's eyes had rolled back into her skull. The man did not respond and she said, "Did anyone call for an ambulance?"

Murmurs greeted her, shamed tones.

"Someone do it now!" she screamed as she lowered herself to the child's face, placed her lips over the infant's nose and mouth, and blew fresh air into the baby's lungs. Forcing away her panic that she might crack the baby's ribs, Sam relied on her training and administered infant CPR. Almost a minute passed as she switched between forcing air into the child and massaging the baby's heart. Suddenly she heard the harsh tearing of breath sounds. Sweat poured into her eyes as she heard her neighbors sigh adoringly at

11

the infant and applaud her actions. Her patience with these imbeciles was almost at an end. "911," she screamed. "Did *anyone* call for help, goddamnit!?"

She did a quick head count. No one had left the scene. They had not wanted to miss the action. "Bastards!" she shouted as she threw her bag over her shoulder, scooped up the child, and ran for her car. The car was a dented white Karmann Ghia VW hardtop left to her by her ex-husband. Her divorce from Eugene had become final the same day she graduated from the academy and Sam knew enough not to question that kind of synchronicity.

Balancing the child in the crook of her arm, Sam fished in her bag for the keys. They seemed to be stuck beneath her gun. She screamed in frustration.

"Dámela a mí."

Sam looked over to see Ruisa standing by with her arms outstretched. The older woman repeated the phrase and Sam needed no further urging. Ruisa carefully took the child and hurried around to the passenger door as Sam yanked her car keys from her bag and unlocked the door. In seconds, Ruisa was sitting beside Sam in the car and Sam was pulling the seat belt around the woman's pudgy arm, helping to anchor her hold on the baby. The twenty-year-old policewoman yanked her flasher from the glove compartment, plugged one end into the cigarette holder, slammed the rotating blue light onto the roof with a loud clank, and turned her key in the ignition. The motor rolled over without hesitation. Sam glanced at Ruisa with desperate eyes. The older Spanish woman placed her free arm around the infant and nodded with a single, sharp motion. Sam threw the car in gear and tore out of the drive, making a left onto Florabraska.

Ruisa squealed and shut her eyes as they came to Florida Avenue, their first light. Samantha jammed the car through the red light, turned right onto the larger road, and merged with traffic. A bloodred

Chevette nearly sideswiped them as she frantically changed lanes, her attention divided between the road and the slight rise and fall of the baby's chest beneath the blanket. The Karmann Ghia barreled past Buffalo, again running a red light. Three cars came to screeching halts to allow her to pass.

"*¡Mas despacio, por favor!*" Ruisa urged.

The streets of Tampa were already filling up. When they reached Hillsborough, traffic was thick in every lane. Sam let out the clutch and gunned the car into fifth as they came to yet another red light.

"We can't slow down!" Sam shouted as she bolted into the intersection, narrowly avoiding an oncoming diesel truck.

"*¡Es un milagro!*" Ruisa said as she rocked the child in her arms.

Sam smiled inwardly. Ruisa was correct. This child was a miracle.

"*¡Es un milagro que no nos ah matado!*"

Frowning, Sam disregarded the slight, though it was true—the way she was driving, it was a miracle she hadn't gotten them killed.

In less than a minute they were before St. Joseph's Hospital, and Sam was gunning the car to the double doors of the emergency entrance. She looked over in shock and realized that Ruisa was crying. The baby was no longer breathing.

For a moment the world seemed to shut down for Samantha. The opening of the emergency room doors was a distant noise, the shouts of the two nurses who came out to greet her a slight whisper. For an instant she heard the beating of a human heart and did not know if it belonged to the child or herself. She pulled the baby from Ruisa's hands and left the car, glancing at her watch. Four minutes from her apartment to the hospital. The nurses guided her into the emergency room, past two bays that were already occupied with low priority cases, to a stretcher beneath a glaring white light. She laid the child on the stretcher and reluctantly backed away as a bearded doctor, an intern, and both nurses descended on the baby. The nurse skillfully cut away the blanket. The doctor called code blue. A third nurse arrived seconds later with a crash cart. One of the nurses turned to Sam and told her she would have to leave.

"Like hell," she said.

The nurse, a blonde in her late twenties with a round face and pockmarked skin, frowned, then moved Sam back a few paces so that she would be out of the way. Sam watched, feeling helpless, as IVs were run into the baby's tiny arm and the doctors attempted to revive her.

The world fell away for the second time that morning and she thought of nothing but her desire for this child to live. All that mattered in the world was this baby, even her own life was expendable if she could just see the infant take a breath, then another.

Sam was shocked by the depth of feeling that this little girl had awakened in her. Had these feelings been with her all her life?

Certainly *compassion* had been a part of her job, a part of her existence, one of the reasons why she had decided to become a cop. But there were limits to be observed. Compassion was acceptable only within certain *limits*. In her brief tenure as a police officer, she had encountered heart-wrenching domestic situations, she had comforted people who had suffered losses, she had even held the hands of the dying after terrible highway accidents. She knew that it was all right to feel, but not to be sucked in by those feelings. The rule was to stay outside the event. If you didn't, you could get sloppy. You could make mistakes. People could die.

Sam looked at the baby. She knew what this girl's life was going to be like: The girl would be shuffled from one agency to another, placed with people who had their own agendas and didn't actually care about

14

her.

No, Sam. That's your life, a taunting, long-forgotten voice called in her mind. It's different for infants. She'll be in high demand. You were eight years old when *your* mother left you.

My mother didn't leave me, Sam thought as she identified the voice in her mind. It belonged to Vera Midian, the director of the orphanage where Sam had spent most of her childhood. She railed against the voice: My mother got sick and she died! She didn't leave me!

Sick in the head, maybe, stark raving looney. And what else do you call it then, if she didn't leave you? She went away, didn't she?

Shut up! Sam wanted to scream. She didn't want to go, the disease made her.

The voice was stilled. Nevertheless, its words continued to mock her. She *had* been alone since she was eight, and throughout her life she had been a problem for everyone who tried to help her. She had run away from foster homes, or acted up until she was sent back to face Ms. Midian's scornful glances. *No one will ever want you. You're a terrible girl.*

Labels had been attached to her. She was rebellious, angry, unwilling to trust, unwilling to give. Even her ex-husband said that about her. In a way, it was true. She let no one in completely. And when she had trusted someone, when she was on the verge of loving them, she found that she was terrified. Ten minutes after she was out of their company she was struck down with fear, fear that they would leave her, fear that they would hurt her. And so she would hurt them first.

Now she was on her own. That was how she liked it.

But in the single, startling instant when she had seen the baby laying on the ground, helpless, Sam knew that it had all been a lie. There had been a need in her that was so wide, so all encompassing, that it

15

had swallowed her up without her being consciously aware of its existence. A need to love and to give love in return. A need to fill the great, yearning chasm of loss that had been opened when her mother had died.

This little girl needed her in a way that no one had ever needed her before. When she heard the child's first, tentative gasps, Sam had felt the darkness that had weighed her down for the past dozen years suddenly lift. For the first time in her adult life she felt as if her life meant something, as if she mattered. Because without her, this little girl would not be alive. She might not have given birth to this baby, but she *had* given her life. She could not bear the thought of seeing that gift rejected. If this child died, then Sam's heart would die in the same terrible moment.

In the emergency room, staring at the baby girl, Sam felt a sudden weakness, as if some nebulous *thing* had latched onto her. She ignored the sensation and instead focused all of her will, the sum of her raging strength, on the baby girl who was suffering the necessarily harsh treatment of the physicians.

All for you, Sam thought. All I am, all I have in the world, it's yours, honey, just breathe, just don't leave me.

Suddenly she felt as if a huge, invisible hand had closed over her chest, squeezing her heart. The pain caused her to gasp, but the sound she made was overshadowed by the first deep breath that the baby had taken. The pressure in her chest eased and Sam looked down to see the infant's head loll to one side, to Sam's side.

The eyes of the child opened dreamily, revealing grayish-black pupils with beautiful golden flecks. Those eyes were the most magnificent sight that Samantha Walthers had ever witnessed.

"You're mine," Samantha whispered.

One of the doctors stepped between Sam and the infant. In the single moment before the curtain was drawn, Sam was certain that she saw the little girl smile.

Three nights later, Sam was maintaining her vigil outside the maternity ward. She was still wearing her gray sweats. Her long brunette hair was tangled and matted to one side of her face. A young nurse stood beside her.

Sam hugged herself and said, "She knows I'm here."

The nurse, Carlotta Evans, gave a deep sigh. She had been trying to talk Sam into going home for the past ten minutes. Sam had refused. Carlotta had made it clear that the baby was out of any danger, that she would be fine.

"She needs me," was Sam's only response.

Carlotta shook her head. She had light almond-colored skin, dark eyes, curly black hair, and a brilliant white smile. She had been concerned that Sam would topple over at any moment. The young police-woman had been at the hospital from the moment she delivered the baby to the emergency room and had refused to leave. As far as the nurse was aware, Sam had not bothered to sleep in the last three days either.

The rescue of the baby had been picked up by all the Tampa newspapers and television stations. The national NBC news bureau was desperately in need of a "feel good" story to close out their broadcast and the story was sent out to the entire nation at eleven twenty-eight that night. But now the press had moved on, Sam's superiors had stopped coming by to tell her what a fine job she had done, and the doctors had lost all patience with the rookie cop who absolutely refused to leave the baby's sight for more than a few minutes at a time. If it hadn't been for her occasional need to visit the ladies' room, the nurse would have begun to wonder if Sam were even human; the notion that this young woman was obsessed could not be argued.

At a quarter past nine, as Carlotta gently coaxed Sam to go home, the police officer's knees finally gave out. Carlotta picked Sam off the floor and deposited her in a wheelchair. Hoping that Sam was actually asleep, the nurse attempted to wheel the chair away from the ward. Suddenly, the red-eyed policewoman grabbed the wheels with both hands and nearly toppled forward, out of the chair. Carlotta chose to wheel Sam back to the window, where the officer gazed reverently at the golden-eyed child. Sam had told the press that she would do everything in her power to adopt and raise the girl as her own daughter.

"She *is* beautiful," Carlotta said at last.

Sam nodded, her shoulders sagging slightly, the tension beginning to drain.

"Have you picked out a name for her already?" Carlotta asked.

"Danielle. That was my mother's name. She died when I was eight."

"Your dad took care of you?"

Sam shook her head. "Ran off before I was born. No other relatives. Ward of the state." Her gaze did not leave the child. "That's *not* going to happen to her."

Carlotta understood. Samantha was worried that the child might be transferred to another hospital, taken away the moment her back was turned.

"Did you see that bitch HRS sent over?" Sam said in a half-delirious tone. "She said that it wasn't *healthy* for me to get too attached to the kid; that there were forms and procedures, and no guarantee I'll be able to adopt her. Like she gave a shit about my health. Or Dani's."

Carlotta knelt down beside the wheelchair. "Sam, I'll make a deal with you. We've got a spare bed just down the hall. Get a few hours sleep, at least, or else

18

you're not going to be any good fighting these bastards. You won't be able to protect your little girl."

A shudder raced through Samantha. "But—"

"I'll keep an eye out. If anything that even smells like Health and Rehabilitative Services comes into this wing I come get you."

"You'd do that for me? Why?"

Carlotta smiled. "Because I have two *bambinas* of my own at home, and if they ever get into trouble, I want someone with nuts like ball bearings to be on my side. Deal?"

A slight laugh escaped Samantha as she placed her hand in Carlotta's. "Okay, deal."

Carlotta rose and allowed Sam one more look at her daughter before she wheeled her down the hall, into the private room she had set aside for this purpose.

Within the maternity ward, more than two dozen infants slept peacefully. Suddenly, the eyes of a single child flashed open, revealing bright gold pupils. In some instinctive manner, the child knew that her mother was no longer close and she began to wail at the top of her lungs. Before a minute had passed, every child was awake; the infectious screams of the golden-eyed baby spreading throughout the ward. Soon close to half the children were wailing in mortal terror.

It wasn't until every single baby was crying in primal fear that the golden-eyed infant was able to stop her screaming, smile a warm, gentle smile, and settle into a deep, comfortable sleep, the screaming of the other babies a lullaby that she found indescribably sweet.

One

Beverly Hills, California. 1992.

The slender eighteen-year-old stood before the partially open drapes in the living room of her new home, looking down at the sloping front yard and the pair of white cars parked in the drive. One of the cars was a 1970 Karmann Ghia VW hardtop. The other was a leased Toyota Corolla GT-S brand new from the factory. The house was a recently constructed single-story dwelling with a pool and a Jacuzzi; the former owner was an actor who had, in a flurry of press conferences, announced his intentions to give up the movie business and move back to New York to appear in stage plays. *People* magazine had aptly reported that he was desperately striving for legitimacy in *Death of a Salesman* because his latest movie crossed the hundred million dollar mark and didn't net him an Oscar nod.

It was a few minutes after eight in the morning. The harsh sunlight pouring in from the east made the golden slivers in the girl's eyes shine like a Hollywood special effect. Everything about this place had a story-book quality for the young woman. She took a step back from the window and caught her reflection in the mirrored paneling to her left. Studying her own image, she decided that she'd found the one thing in this house that was perfectly ordinary. In this she displayed a rare talent for self-deception, as her beauty was evident to any who cared to look for it.

Aside from her unusual, gold-flecked eyes, she had deep brown, almost black hair cut in bangs above her eyebrows. Her thick lustrous hair cascaded past her shoulders and soft curls framed her face. She possessed perfectly sculpted features, cheekbones that were high and strong, and flesh that was luminous and soft. Her glistening lips were bright red even without lipstick. She wore a bulky gray sweatshirt that served to hide her large but perfectly proportioned breasts and flat stomach. Her tight red shorts revealed her statuesque legs.

Suddenly aware of the approach of another figure in the mirror, she turned her gaze back to the view of the hills from their living room window. "This is really happening, isn't it?" Dani said as if she were awakening from a dream. "We're actually here."

Her mother came up from behind her and gave her a hug, wrapping her arms around the girl's slight waist. Samantha Walthers kissed her daughter's cheek and smiled in the early morning sunlight. "I know what you mean. I keep expecting Robin Leach or Rod Serling to come out from behind the curtains and say, 'Sorry, just kidding.' But considering the pain in the ass unpacking has been for the last week, I'd say it's a safe bet that we're going to be here awhile."

"I love it already. I really do."

"I can tell," Sam said as she rubbed her daughter's back then went deep into the spacious living room, hunting for her purse. In a futile effort she checked the love seat, couch, and the cabinet that housed the home entertainment center.

Dani turned from the window and crossed her arms over her breasts. "So, are you going to meet this Allen Halpern guy any time soon?"

Her mother frowned as she scanned the room once again. "Eventually, I guess. He's kind of betting the

22

farm with the money he's laying out to set us up like this, so I expect that he'll stop by the office sometime or another."

"Don't worry about his money," Dani said. "I read that Halpern and Weiss is the second largest insurance firm in the world. They have assets like over a hundred *billion* dollars. They could have *bought* this house and the car for us and they wouldn't have felt a thing."

Sam was busy hunting between the pillows of their obscenely large couch when Dani picked up her mother's purse from the small table beside the door and handed it to her. Shoulders slumping in embarrassed defeat, Sam took the purse, checked for her keys and weapon, and grinned at her daughter. "Someone as intelligent as you should be off planning for her college education, you know?"

Dani leaped back into the soft love seat, landing on the balls of her feet with the grace of a cat. She rested her chin on her knee. "And someone as pretty as you should be posing for the cover of *Cosmo,* not working as a private investigator for corporate America."

Sam shook her head. She had never known how to receive a compliment and had never truly felt deserving of them. She was not totally oblivious of her physical appearance: at thirty-eight she could still pass for ten years younger. Her figure was kept in perfect shape by her daily routine and the physical nature of her job. She had quit the Tampa police five years ago to become a private investigator. Over the past two years she had been involved in three high-profile cases that had received national attention.

In the most recent of these cases, Sam had managed to prove that a wealthy businessman had faked his own death in a boating accident; his company had been on the brink of ruin and he had absconded with millions that he had embezzled over the years. The man's grief-stricken wife had hired Sam to find her beloved husband and had unwittingly delivered the man into the hands of prosecuters for his crimes, which included the murder of a company officer who knew his secret and could have exposed him.

Before that, Sam had been hired by a young woman who had been raped and beaten in the back room of a pool hall in Tampa by a man who had become a Presidential candidate. Supporters within his party had defended him at first, even going so far as to make offers to buy off Sam and the girl, then resorting to threats when that didn't work. Sam proved the victim's allegations, the case went to trial, and the candidate was ostracized by his party. Ironically, several party members were so impressed by Sam's prowess that they later hired her for private security contracts.

But the most tragic of the cases that Sam had handled which received national attention had been the first, and it had been a case that had struck close to home. It had been two years ago and one of the twin daughters belonging to her old friend, Carlotta Evans, had been murdered by a trapper who had tortured and raped the child repeatedly before killing her. Dani had been best friends with the girls.

Standing in the living room of her Beverly Hills home, Sam tried to turn her thoughts away from the incident. She knew where such thoughts led and did not want to picture her daughter alone and frightened in the killer's lair, where she had been found with a dead man.

But the memory would not be denied. With perfect clarity she could see Dani huddled in a ball in the corner of the damp, filthy, reconverted bomb shelter the killer had owned. Blood and brains had covered Dani's face and her body had shook as if she'd had palsy. Sam had been closing in on the killer and in return, the murderer had been stalking her daughter. He had taken Dani a few blocks from their home and had held the girl hostage for twelve horrible hours.

Dani was later found by a neighbor in the killer's basement, physically unhurt. The trapper was dead. The official verdict was that he had shot himself. Dani couldn't say what had actually happened. The police investigation revealed the man's death to be a suicide. Dani had been unable to remember anything that happened for the twelve hours she had spent with the killer. Psychiatrists and hypnotists had been unable to unlock the secret of those twelve hours.

Breaking from the memory, Sam suddenly embraced her daughter, holding her as tight as she could. "I love you, honey."

Dani drew back and caressed her mother's hair. "You too, mom."

Sam could not erase the terrible image from her mind. Her concern for her daughter's well-being was painfully evident in her expression, along with her guilt. Sam had always felt that she had failed her daughter miserably. Sam should have been able to protect her daughter from that monster.

Dani recognized her mother's train of thought. "I'm all right, Mom. You're going to have to get over this."

Staring into her daughter's face, Sam wondered if she ever would. Dani had always been a loner who never had an easy time making friends, despite her beauty. She had only been close with Jami and Lisa, Carlotta's daughters. After Jami's death, Lisa and Dani drifted apart. Dani became increasingly withdrawn, rarely leaving the house except to go to school and return. The only activities in which she participated were those that she was forced into by Samantha. When the job offer came from California, Dani had been thrilled at the prospect of leaving Tampa, the home of all her wretched memories.

"It's just like you told me, Mom. This is our chance to start over. A house in Beverly Hills with a pool and a maid that comes in twice a week—

there are worse ways of starting over, you know?"

Sam was silent.

"For instance, two months ago you wouldn't have been wearing an outfit like *that* to work."

Sam was dressed in her daughter's favorite colors. Her outfit consisted of a deep red skirt and jacket, expensive, matching shoes, a lacy white blouse, and designer sunglasses. Sam's high-profile cases had netted her the attention of Allen Halpern. Halpern had hired Sam sight unseen for a staggering yearly salary and assigned her to their Beverly Hills office. For the first time in her life she did not have to think about money. Her wardrobe, insisted upon by Halpern and paid for with a company credit card, reflected that lack of concern.

"Cut it out. We're not talking about me," Sam said.

Dani threw open her arms in an exaggerated motion. With a perfect preppie overbite she said, "I'm sorry, Mother, but I'm going to be the absolute first to say that you look *fabulous,* and you're just going to have to accept it."

Sam laughed. The move had begun to give Sam back her daughter. The sadness had left Dani's eyes, replaced with an excitement her mother had rarely glimpsed. She leaned down and kissed her girl. "I've gotta get to the office. Look, why don't you take the Karmann Ghia and go into town. Just relax and have fun, okay? You deserve it."

"I dunno," Dani said. "We'll see. I think I might want to hang around so I can see how it feels to give orders to the hired help."

Placing one hand on her hip, Sam said, "You *are* a lazy thing."

"That I am," Dani said as she eased herself back into the soft couch.

Sam was at the door when she turned and said, "Well, don't get too comfortable. By the end of the summer you're going to have to de-

26

cide, college or a full-time job."

"I don't suppose I could think about what's behind door number three?"

"So *lazy.*" Sam growled lovingly as she told her daughter that she would be home by six and closed the door.

An hour and ten minutes later, Samantha Walthers was bolting from the elevator into the main lobby of Halpern and Weiss's twelfth-floor offices. The security guard on the ground level had given her a temporary ID badge and had nodded sympathetically as she complained about the gridlock traffic that no one had warned her about.

On the twelfth floor, the receptionist guided her down a teal corridor to the conference room where a dozen people were already gathered. There were eight men and four women seated uncomfortably in the windowless room, three blacks, one Hispanic, one Asian. The remaining seven men and women looked as if they worshiped the same mousse and hair dryer her new supervisor, Pete Martell, had evidently made love to every morning. All but two of them eyed her suspiciously.

"Sorry I'm late," she said as she took the only unoccupied chair and found herself sitting at the opposite end of the long conference table from Martell, a deceptively attractive and soft-spoken man who had revealed himself to be a consummate hard-ass in their first meeting, last Friday. Allen Halpern had hired Sam and assigned her to this office without consulting Martell first and her new supervisor had not appreciated the move.

"That's all right," Pete said with his soft, well-oiled delivery. "We just thought you might still be running on Florida time. People from the deep South have a tendency to take their time over their *chitlins* and *grits* in the morning, or so I've come to understand."

Samantha smiled and contemplated giving the officious little prick an anatomy lesson. She would wager that he did not know how many bones there were to be broken in the human body.

"I've never actually had grits, you'll have to tell me what they're like some time," she said. "The only appetite I have is for hard work. What do you have for me?"

Martell laughed. Turning his attention away from Sam, he retrieved a stack of files from the counter behind the long conference table where the staff supervisors had been gathered. As Martell slammed the folders onto the table to get everyone's attention, Sam wondered how long it would be before the predator's waltz would begin. Obviously, several people were in line for the job she had taken and resentment was running high. Backbiting in-house politics were never her favorite pastime, but she could cover her ass with the best of them, if it came to it.

"First up," Martell said, "I'd like everyone to greet our new staff member, Samantha Walthers. I'm sure everyone has been briefed on Ms. Walther's position and responsibilities. Put simply, my friends, today we leap blindly into hell, and Samantha here is our point man."

With an experienced flip of the wrist Martell sent a single file skidding across the table to the far end where Sam had taken residence. She opened the file as he went on.

"Mark Smith, thirty-four. He claims that his wife was murdered by intruders who struck him down and left him for dead. The police are satisfied with his story. We are not. The investigator's report is somewhat spotty for my tastes."

"I'll get right on it," Sam said.

"Before you do, let me make a few things clear, Miss Walthers. This office is under extreme scrutiny right now due to piss-poor management by the old regime. Claims that first graders wouldn't have approved were passed on without a word, and investigations, if you can call them that, were sloppy. I was transferred to this office three months ago for quality control. We have had sixteen layoffs in that time. The sad truth is that I expect that we will have more. In your spare time I want you to work with my people downtown on preparing reports for continued cost-cutting efforts. Overstaffing has always been a problem with this company, and I intend to utilize your *talents* to the fullest."

Sam felt the full weight of a dozen cold stares. You son of a bitch, she thought. You're trying to turn me into a complete pariah in this office. Now everyone is going to go out of their way to make my job as difficult as they can.

She could only think of one way to make the situation tolerable, and it was very dangerous. The last thing she wanted was to tell Dani that she had been fired on her first day and they were moving back to Florida. But this situation had to be brought under control.

Sam rose from the table and said, "Absolutely not. With all due respect, I was *not* hired to be a corporate headhunter. That is not covered under the title of Chief Claims Investigator. That is not the job that Mr. Halpern hired me to perform. If you want to change the parameters of my job description, I suggest you take it up with him."

Martell was speechless. Someone would have to tell him that it was all right to close his jaw again. Several of the supervisors grinned broadly. Calmly retrieving the Smith file from the table, Sam slipped on her sunglasses for added effect and said, "Now if you'll excuse me, I have a claim to investigate."

She walked out of the conference room without looking back. When she reached the downstairs lobby, she frantically slid a quarter in the nearest pay phone and dialed the private number Halpern had given to her. She knew that it was a matter of who

29

managed to get to Halpern first, her or Martell. In seconds she heard the familiar voice of her unseen benefactor. Halpern listened to her story and promised that she had nothing to worry about. Martell had always been a bit full of himself and he would be dealt with. The man stayed on the phone an additional three minutes discussing ways of beating the traffic before he cordially said goodbye.

Sam stopped at a coffee shop to review the Smith file. She was on her second cup of coffee when she attempted to familiarize herself with Smith's address and its map coordinates. Getting around in Los Angeles had proven to be an adventure and she was certain that she would get lost unless she dutifully studied the map.

Two hours later, after getting lost more times than she would ever care to admit, she found Smith's home almost by accident. The house was a modest two story on a residential street in West Beverly. The mailbox door hung open and what appeared to be several days accumulation of mail had been crammed into the plastic box. The car in the driveway had been Smith's Pontiac.

She walked up the stone path and was about to knock on the front door when she realized that it was slightly ajar. The horrible, unmistakable stench of death drifted to her from inside the house and she automatically drew her handgun. Cautiously cracking the door another few inches, Sam peered inside and saw blood splattered on the white walls of the living room.

Shock assailed her and she forced herself to remain calm. She knew that the proper course of action was to back off and have one of the neighbors call the police. But, if what she suspected were true, those few minutes could cost an innocent life. Without making a sound she shoved the door all the way open and dropped into a crouch, weapon ready. There was no hint of movement. The stairs to the second floor were directly ahead of her. She slipped inside, checking her danger zone, and saw no one. The old fear was back. She forced herself to focus on the task at hand, but that did not keep the sting of sweat from her eyes or the bitter taste of blood from her tongue as she bit down hard on her lip; she felt as if she were swallowing iodine.

Next to the stairs was a den. An assailant could have been waiting there, ready to take her from behind when she entered the blood-spattered living room. She checked it quickly and was relieved that it contained no closets or other hiding places. Back in the hallway, she heard a sound from the far end of the house. A slight hiss, a crackle. The rustle of pots and pans. Someone was in the kitchen.

Stepping into the bloody living room, Sam looked back at the stairs again, then turned her attention to the doorway to the next room. That room had been darkened, the shades drawn. In it, she could see the edge of a dining room table, no chairs. Crossing the length of the living room to the doorway, she pressed her back against the jamb and cautiously peered into the dining room. Two people were propped up at the opposite end of the table. Both had been hacked to death, stripped of clothing, and skinned. Dinner plates filled with chunks of human flesh sat before the corpses. The bodies were duct-taped to the chairs, their hands clenched in fists from which knives and forks protruded. Their jaws were open wide in soundless screams, their tongues already removed.

Sam trembled as the first wave of nausea struck her and she forced down the heavy bile. She could feel the weight in her stomach of the two cups of coffee that she had consumed, and regretted the stop she had made.

She heard the sound again. Meat sizzling on a

31

grill. Someone started to whistle. It was the tune from the Disney version of Snow White, "Whistle While You Work." She felt the blood drain from her head and her toes went numb. In another moment vertigo would set in. She forced herself to think of Dani and knew that she would not be alive for her daughter if she allowed herself to be overcome.

The kitchen was visible above and below two slatted barroom-style doors. She could see a man's bare feet as he moved back and forth in the kitchen. Easing the safety from her weapon, Sam forced herself to move on, staying close to the wall where antique china was displayed in an oak cabinet. She had to pass directly behind the bodies to reach the well-lit kitchen and stay out of visual range from the doorway. The button from her sleeve caught in the matted hair of the first corpse, which had been a woman. Tugging slightly caused the head to flop up and down, the upper and lower jaws clattering slightly. With a sharp pull Sam freed her sleeve, but the force of her motion caused the chair to move slightly, groaning against the hard wood floor.

The whistling stopped and she froze, her gun trained at the door. She cut a glance back in the other direction, worried that the killer might have an accomplice. There was no one behind her. After a moment the whistling resumed, and Sam felt her heart thundering painfully as her entire body began to quake. Force the fear away, she thought, stay focused, dammit, focused!

Her flesh was clammy and the grip on her gun was becoming slippery. She had to go now. There was no way that she would last more than an additional few seconds in the dining room with the bodies. Drawing in a deep breath, she turned, shoved her body against the right-hand door and screamed, "Freeze, you fucking son of a bitch!"

The man standing above the grill in his underwear dropped his skillet and peed in his shorts. She recognized Mark Smith from his photograph, tall, soft around the middle, hair bleached yellow from the sun, reddish skin, a stubbly beard and mustache.

"Get down on the floor!" she commanded. "Now! Hands behind your head, fingers locked. Do it now!"

Smith did not argue. He seemed terrified. Sam could smell his urine over the pungent odor of cooked human flesh on the grill as he went to the floor and began to beg for his life. She glanced back to check her danger zone once again and the breath nearly left her body.

The bodies were gone. The dining room was brightly lit and the plates were missing. The pools of blood on the floor and the streaks of blood against the glass windows and the oak cabinet were no longer in evidence. She looked back to the kitchen and Smith was still on the floor, his entire body shaking. The meat on the grill was hamburger.

"Please, please, I'm sorry, I'll give you anything, don't shoot me, please, I don't want to die," he whimpered.

"Stop it," she said softly, and he immediately fell silent. Sam looked back to the kitchen. The carnage, which had rivaled the horror she had walked into when she had finally located the house where her daughter was being held two years earlier, had vanished. The house was normal. Even the smell of death had gone.

With startling clarity she realized that she had imagined all of it.

"Okay, get up," Sam said in a hoarse whisper.

Smith did not move. Tears were streaming down his face.

"I said, you can get up. It's okay. Just, uh—"

What? she thought. A misunderstanding? Get a grip, Samantha. Both of you can't be hysterical. But the temptation's there, isn't it?

"Please get up," she said, her words clipped. Smith slowly rose to his feet, his legs wobbly beneath him.

33

He looked like a fawn attempting its first awkward steps.

"Don't shoot me, please," he cried.

Suddenly aware of the gun that was still trained on his chest, Samantha slipped the weapon into her purse and held her hands out, palms open. Smith relaxed slightly and dropped into one of two chairs that had been taken from the dining room.

Just proceed, business as usual, Sam. Tell him who you are and what you want, she thought. Then she considered an alternative: run like hell before he could establish a clear mental picture of her. But she was not a criminal and she would not behave as one. Wrong, kiddo. Unlawful entry, brandishing a firearm, threatening an unarmed man. You won't need Martell to destroy your career, you're doing a fine job on your own.

"My name is Samantha Walthers. I'm with Halpern and Weiss."

"Christ, I paid my fucking premium, okay?" he said with a weak attempt at a smile. He was recovering from the initial shock far more quickly than she had anticipated.

Sam did not share in his recuperative abilities. She felt weak and drained. "I had, uh, I had some questions." Her heart was still racing. "This is a bad time. I can come back again."

"No!" he said. "Now's fine. Don't come back."

"I could call you on the phone."

"No, ask me now." He crossed his legs to cover the wet spot on his shorts.

Sam glanced back at the dining room. Nothing. Swallowing hard she said, "Look, you have every right to call the police and report what just happened. I promise, you're perfectly safe. I'll sit here and you can swear out any complaint you want."

"No, no," he said, his brown eyes glazing over. "I've had enough of the police. Just ask your questions."

34

She reached into her purse and he froze at the sight of her pocket tape recorder.

"None of that," he said. "I'll tell you what you want to know but I don't want to be taped."

Sam was not about to argue with him. Allowing the recorder to slide back inside her purse, she removed a small notepad and came to her first question. Inside of five minutes, the interview was finished. Acutely aware of the smell of urine, Sam had wondered why he did not at least take the time to clean himself up before she questioned him. Then she realized that he must have been afraid to turn his back on her.

He walked her to the door and she said, "I really can't apologize enough for this. I know it's hard to explain. But I really am sorry." She thrust her hand into her purse. "Let me give you one of my cards—"

"That's all right," he said as he glanced at her handbag in mortal terror. The gun, she realized, then withdrew her empty hand slowly.

Yes, it's all right, just go, stupid.

Moments later, she sat behind the wheel of her luxurious company car. Smith's living room curtains occasionally moved and she saw a figure looking out. She knew that he wasn't going to relax until she was gone. Reaching for the ignition, hands trembling, Sam wished that there was some way of convincing him that he was not the only one who was terrified.

Two

Dani Walthers had *suspected* that she had been thrust into a fairy-tale existence; but after driving along Rodeo Drive, she became convinced of that fact. She had never seen so much money in her entire life. Stopping at a light, she glanced over at the car in the turn lane and saw a thoroughly gorgeous man talking on the cel phone of his red sports car. The top was down and the man looked over at Dani and smiled. She looked away, thoroughly embarrassed, and almost forgot to keep her foot on the clutch as the light turned green. The Karmann Ghia lurched forward as she stole a final glance at the man. He winked at her as he made his turn and quickly vanished from sight.

Rodeo Drive was only a few blocks long, and finding a parking space was impossible. Dani had been reminded of stories she had read in school about the Knights of the Round Table and their quest for the grail. After driving up and down the stretch several times, Dani finally gave up and found an expensive parking lot several blocks away.

So much for my spending money, she thought, looking at the posted prices. Out of habit she rolled up the windows and locked the car before she went out to explore. She felt foolish for a moment, then reminded herself of the statistics for car theft in California. If anything happened to her mother's car she would never forgive herself. Perhaps now they would be able to place a security system in the car.

Stepping away from the curb, she took in the overwhelming sight of window shopper's heaven. Ignoring the lure of Gucci and Diamonds on Rodeo, Dani drifted toward a clothing shop that displayed a startlingly beautiful red and black dress that instantly caught her attention. She stood before the window for over a minute before she made her decision.

Entering the dress shop, Dani suddenly became extremely conscious of the clothing she wore. She had changed into a faded pair of blue jeans and an "Aztecs rule!" T-shirt that Jami had purchased for her when Carlotta took her children to Mexico to visit her distant relatives. Her feet were bare except for a pair of sandals. Mirrored sunglasses protected her from the initial double take usually brought on by her strange, gold flecked eyes, which seemed to take on more of an ordinary brown cast when not accentuated by sunlight. One of the children who took on the holy crusade of torturing her in grade school had named her "headlights." A few years later, when her ample figure began to show itself, the nickname took on an even more demeaning connotation.

Shit, Dani, this is a second chance. Stop thinking about that crap.

A pretty saleswoman in a soft pink dress suddenly made her presence known. Her smile was warm and friendly and she did not seem bothered in the least by Dani's casual wear.

"May I help you?" the woman asked.

"I was just, um, I was just looking."

"Is there anything in particular you wanted to see?"

Dani thought of the dress in the window. She knew that she could never afford to buy the dress, but there was no harm in trying it on. When she suggested that particular item the saleswoman turned with an enthusiastic bounce in her step. Dani had the feeling that the woman's excitement level was in direct proportion to the price of the dress. She was surprised that she had not attempted to steer Dani to the bargain racks. Then looking around the shop, she realized that there were no bargain racks here—and probably no bargain racks in all of Beverly Hills. She guessed that her grungy appearance was not that uncommon. Maybe she could pretend to be a movie star incognito. Then she remembered the sunglasses that would have to come off in a moment and thought to herself that she wouldn't stand a chance of pulling off that deception.

The saleswoman returned with the dress and shepherded Dani to the changing room. Moments later, Dani emerged, transformed, and stared at herself in the mirror. The dress was black with red trim folding out from the bosom. The strapless cut of the dress showed off her soft, creamy shoulders and the sensuous V of her throat. It was cut deep to reveal the tops of her breasts and gathered tightly around her small waist to descend in cascading folds. The front was open just enough to expose the occasional tantalizing view of her magnificent legs.

"Unbelievable."

The saleswoman had gone. In her place stood a considerably more attractive girl with sleek, blunt-cut jet-black hair, piercing green eyes, and a figure identical to Dani's. She was dressed in an understated black and white print jacket with a white blouse and a black leather skirt.

"You have to own this," the young woman said.

Dani flushed with excitement at the thought. Then reality set in. She had to find a way to get out of the dress and the situation into which she had just dug herself.

"I'm not sure that it's me," she said. Lame, girl. Really lame. Even her ridiculously poor self-image could not override the evidence of her senses which

38

told her that she had never looked so beautiful in her entire life.

"Well, we'd have to accessorize, but now that I've seen you in this dress, I can't imagine you not taking it home."

Terrific. She could tell that the words "no sale" were not in this girl's vocabulary.

"By the way, my name's Madison." The young woman held out her hand. Dani took it and was surprised by the incredible flash of heat she felt at the contact. The sensation started in her heart and rose up to stitch across her entire body in seconds.

"I'm Dani."

Madison was staring at her eyes. She had finally noticed. Dani turned away slightly and Madison stopped her with a touch. Again, the strange and beautiful rush of warmth spread through her.

"Your eyes are the most gorgeous thing I've ever seen," Madison said in complete awe. Her tone was convincing, the compliment was sincere, not manufactured.

Dani could not lie to the girl; she felt terrible at the thought of leading her on for another second. "I'm sorry, but I can't really afford this dress."

Madison smiled. "Well, I'll buy it, then."

Confused, Dani said, "I thought you worked here."

"I wish," Madison said with a laugh. "With the amount of money I spend here, an employee's discount would really come in handy."

"I should get changed before the saleswoman gets back."

"Don't worry about it. She's ringing up my stuff. It's going to take her a while." Madison looked down, surveyed the cut of the dress once more, then shook her head in amazement. "I'm serious. This dress is perfect for you, and I've got the ideal place for you to wear it. There's a party at my house to-night. Beautiful people, gorgeous guys. Enough money and debauchery to make Gaius Caligula blush, if he were around today."

"Um, it sounds great, but—"

"Okay, I know. How about this. I'll buy the dress for myself and you can borrow it for the party. I guarantee that if you show up wearing this dress you won't be going home alone. In fact, considering how big my place is, you may not need to go home at all. What do you say?"

"I'm—I'm *really* flattered," Dani said. "But I just wouldn't feel right. I'm sorry. Can you excuse me?"

Disappointed, Madison took a step back and let her arms fall loosely to her sides. "If that's what you want. Everybody makes choices."

"Yeah, I guess," Dani said as she retreated into the changing room without looking back.

When she emerged again, Madison had already left the shop and the saleswoman had returned.

"Oh, I'm sorry," the woman said. "I was hoping to see you in that dress. I had the feeling it was you."

"I'm not sure," Dani said, adjusting her sunglasses. "I'm going to have to think about it."

"Well, you take your time, hon."

Dani left the dress shop, amazed that the saleswoman did not try to make her feel guilty about the dress. As she walked down the street, pausing briefly to look in the windows of the jewelry shops, she felt a pang of guilt that had nothing to do with the saleswoman. She felt miserable about the way she had treated Madison. The girl was only trying to be friendly and she obviously had more money than she knew what to do with. Dani was certain that she was not consciously trying to buy her friendship with the dress and wondered if perhaps Madison had come from a poor background like hers. She knew almost nothing about the girl except that for the first time in a long time she felt absolutely comfortable with someone other than her mother. If only she had learned the location of the party, she could have stopped by and spoken with her for a time.

No, Dani. You know damn well that you never would have gone. You never take advantage when you have the opportunity to meet new people, you always shy away.

Walking back to her car she felt totally disgusted with herself. Dani knew that she was adopted. A part of her had always felt inadequate. Her need to apologize for her very existence often rose to the surface when she met new people. Her feelings certainly did not stem from a lack of love and encouragement when she had been growing up. Despite Samantha's impossible schedule, she was always there for her daughter.

Dani had read all the newspaper accounts of the bitter fight her mother had waged to gain custody of her and had seen the television footage of her mom when she was only two years older than Dani was today.

A particular memory came to her: Dani had been ten years old and Sam was barely making enough money to keep them ahead of her debts. It had been Halloween and Sam had helped her to create her daughter's costume. Dani was going to be a fairy-tale princess. The motion picture *The Terminator* had just been released, and the girl who had dubbed Dani "headlights" had already seen the movie. She had been making rude comments about Dani's gold-flecked eyes, comparing them to Arnold's glowing red eyes in the movie, and Dani was terrified of the ridicule that she might face if she showed up in school wearing her costume. She had attended her classes in the morning and then her teacher had sent the children home to change for the Halloween parade, where all the kids would be shepherded through the streets in their costumes.

Sam had come home on her lunch break and Dani pretended to be violently ill. Her mother stayed home with her and an hour later Dani was staring out the

41

window as the parade went past. She never knew what the other children would have thought of her costume and all her life that memory had remained to sum up her existence.

Every time she thought she was past all that, something would happen to remind her that she was still, in many ways, that same ten-year-old girl afraid to reach out and embrace life.

She crossed the street and stopped dead before the Karmann Ghia, her key ready to enter the lock. Sitting in the passenger seat was a large package from the dress shop that she had visited a half hour before. Her windows were still rolled up, the doors were locked. Cautiously, Dani entered the car and examined the box. Slipping the ribbon off the side, Dani peaked into the red and black box, certain that she would see the dress she had tried on. The dress was there, along with a handbag and shoes that were, amazingly, the correct size.

Beneath the box, lying on the seat, was a note with the directions to Madison's beach house in Malibu and the time of the party. Dani stared at the note for a long time, her hand inside the box, touching the delicate fabric of the dress as if she were handling magic incarnate. After a few moments she began to cry, though she was not certain why she should have this reaction. After the tears ran their course, Dani cranked the ignition and pulled out onto Rodeo Drive.

On the way home she decided that she would have to go to Madison's party, if only to return the dress. When she pulled into the drive, another car was already there. She went inside, introduced herself to the cleaning woman, then found that she could not suppress her urge to try on the dress a second time while she had someone else to appreciate its beauty.

The cleaning woman said very little, but her expression was all the approval Dani needed. She took off the dress and hung it up in the bathroom. Over

42

the course of the next few hours she devised nineteen excuses to visit the dress. Each time she found herself staring at it with the love of a woman who had found the key to her second chance. All she needed now was the courage to unlock the door and step into her new life.

Dani thought of the monster who abducted her two years ago. She had never remembered any more than the first moments when he had appeared and chloroformed her, then the endless stretch of time when she woke to learn that it was dark outside and the killer was dead, apparently by his own hand. If she had the courage in her heart to face that nightmare and survive, she could certainly manage to attend a party and make a few new friends.

With a joyous shout, Dani snatched the dress from the hanger, leaped to her bed, and hugged it close as her laughter gave way to tears of pure bliss.

Three

At ten minutes after two in the afternoon, Samantha Walthers returned to her office. She had spent the last several hours driving through the city, making a conscious effort to familiarize herself with the streets and the fine art of highway driving in California. In truth, she was simply attempting not to dwell on what had happened at Mark Smith's house that morning.

Sam stopped at the front desk for her messages and was greeted by Rosalind, the firm's forty-five-year-old receptionist. A freckled, pale-skinned redhead who wore slightly oversized glasses, Rosalind had a stylishly saucy appeal; and her age was only revealed by the deepening laugh lines around her eyes and mouth. With a resigned and sympathetic smile, Rosalind looked up from the wildly flashing yellow lights of her switchboard and alerted Sam that Martell was looking for her.

Sam had assumed that a confrontation was inevitable, considering her actions in the staff meeting. He had every justification to fire her for insubordination. Her only hope of saving her job had been the intervention of her guardian angel, Allen Halpern. She wondered how much support she would get from him if he were to learn about her actions this morning.

Unexpectedly, Rosalind leaned forward and whispered, "He's such a damn dickweed, don't you think?"

Sam grinned. Apparently word had circulated of her confrontation with Martell in the staff meeting. She had sized up their coming battle as a war of attrition; turnover in his position was statistically much higher than in her own. All she had to do was survive the next few months and Martell would certainly be rotated to yet another system to spread his personal warmth.

"That's an understatement," Sam told the woman as she proceeded directly to his office. The best way to deal with unpleasantness was to get it out of the way quickly, she had always told herself. As his secretary buzzed her in, Sam wondered if this job was going to amount to anything but unpleasantness.

Martell was sitting behind his black marble desk, going over a report, grinding his teeth in his perfectly straight jaw. He did not look up when Sam entered, he merely gestured at the empty chair before the desk. She set her purse and valise on the floor beside her right leg and waited for him to address her.

"I've received two phone calls regarding you today," he said as he finally looked up and set his report to one side of the desk. "The first was from Mr. Halpern. It seems he supports your actions this morning fully. Consider my knuckles slapped, Ms. Walthers. Round one goes to you."

The man was smiling the most weasellike smile Sam had ever seen. He hesitated, rocking back and forth in his chair, milking the moment for all that it was worth. "The second call . . ."

Martell shook his head and poured a cup of coffee from the pitcher on the other side of his desk. He took a long sip, smacked his lips, then began to strum his fingers against the ceramic cup.

Sam was absolutely certain that she had not betrayed any visible reaction to his primitive scare tactics. He was waiting for her to *ask* for the killing blow. That wasn't going to happen. Sam waited patiently.

Martell raised an eyebrow. "The second call was from the police."

She flinched, even though she had already guessed what was coming. Smith had changed his mind and decided to press charges. "I thought it best for the company to keep this quiet," she said softly. She understood that she was about to lose her job on her first day; even Allen Halpern's generosity would have limits.

Martell's reaction had not been what she had expected. He seemed perplexed by what she had said. "You walked into a murder scene, found *three* dead bodies, and decided that it was best not to say anything?"

She flinched again. "What are you talking about?"

Running his fingers through his perfectly groomed hair, the edge of Martell's lip curled slightly as he said, "At eleven o'clock this morning, you went to Mark Smith's house, is that correct?"

"Yes," she said, her anxiety showing itself for the first time.

"Your card was found at the premises. A neighbor saw you enter and noticed the company car."

"Someone was *dead?*" She recalled the corpses at the dining room table. Hallucinations. But what had caused her to have delusions in the first place?

"Three people," he repeated slowly, as if he were talking to an ignorant child.

"It must have happened after I left," she said. "I interviewed Smith." She was about to reach into her purse for her pocket tape recorder when she remembered that he had not allowed her to tape him.

"Walthers, the only reason why the police aren't crawling all over this office is because the time of death had been established as more than thirty-six hours ago. It must have been awfully goddamned

46

rank in that place. To be honest, I can smell some of it on you."

"That's ridiculous," Sam said as she gestured with her palms open wide. Martell gasped the same time that she did. There was blood on her palms.

"Jesus Christ," he said as he turned away and began to gag. After a moment he calmed enough to order her to take a cab to the precinct house. Then he gave her the name of the officer who wished to interview her.

She rose from the chair, gathered her purse and valise, and fought away the temptation to rush into the ladies' room and scrub her hands to remove the blood, which would have amounted to tampering with evidence. Calling a cab from her office, Sam waited for it downstairs. The security officer who supplied her with her temporary pass, a black man named Roger, asked her if her day was getting any better.

"It can't get much worse," she said as she saw the taxi pull up in front of the building. The ride to the station house seemed to take forever, and her driver, intrigued by her silence, tried to guess her life's story. She paid him without answering even one of his long list of questions.

At the police station, she was surprised at the speed and efficiency with which she was processed. Inside of five minutes she was sitting before the desk of the investigating officer, Detective Sergeant Edward Pullman. At his command, one of his subordinates had taken a sample of the blood from her palms. After she was allowed to clean herself up, the detective proceeded to lead her to an interrogation room. The room was bare except for the table, a mirror that was certainly two-way glass, and a window that seemed to capture the glaring mid-afternoon sunlight and force it to nova before it reached her eyes. There she was put through the most

47

polite inquisition that she had ever encountered.

Pullman was fifty-eight, the same age her father would be now, assuming the man who had run off after impregnating her mother was still alive. As they spoke, he smiled at her with a decidedly loopy grin, and frequently brushed back the wisp of white hair that still grew from the top of his sunburned scalp. Normally she would have looked at his bulk and considered a barrage of donut insults. Strangely, she found herself enjoying his company, and she worked especially hard to tell him everything she could remember of the incident.

Pullman never once intimated that she was losing her grip on reality. Nor did he act the least bit relieved when the police psychologist, a woman ten years younger than Sam, entered the small room. She set her notebook on the table and asked the detective to give them a few minutes. He shrugged and left the room. Sam knew that Pullman would be close, monitoring their conversation through the two-way mirror. His presence behind the glass, real or imagined, helped to calm her as the dark-haired woman began her interview.

After two hours of discussion, the psychologist, Mary Ephraim, suggested an explanation for what Sam had experienced earlier that day: "You were obviously scarred more deeply than you knew two years ago, when your daughter was taken hostage by a serial murderer. You entered several crime scenes in your investigation of that killer and encountered bodies that had been horribly butchered. My guess is that when you entered the Smith residence and discovered the first two bodies, the mental trauma was too much for you to bear. Just before you found Smith in the kitchen, your mind created the fantasy of the house restored to normal, Smith alive and well, the bodies and any evidence of foul play completely gone. At a very deep level, your mind edited the input that you were receiving and switched it out for something that was considerably easier for you to deal with."

"You're saying that I sat in that kitchen and had a conversation with a dead man?"

"Essentially, yes. That's why the Smith that you remember would not allow you to tape his voice. You would have played back the tape and realized that you were the only one speaking. Then the fantasy would have been shattered, defeating the whole purpose of its creation."

Sam rested her head in her hands. "So I'm totally unglued and I can no longer trust my own senses. Is that what you're telling me?"

"No. What happened, I believe, was an isolated incident. 'Unglued' is a term that should only be used if you want to beat up on yourself, which I am not going to encourage you to do."

The detective returned to the interrogation room and Ephraim briefed him on her findings. She meticulously extracted the word "unglued" from their conversation.

"There is one thing, though," she said with grave concern as she turned back to Sam. "Are you still carrying your weapon?"

Sam let out a deep breath as she removed her gun from her purse and placed it on the bare wood table. Pullman was very sweet as he brought out the forms to suspend her license temporarily, pending a later review by his superiors. She felt naked as she left the precinct without her gun.

Just before five o'clock, another taxi dropped Sam off at the Halpern building. She breezed past Roger with a weak smile, half-expecting him to stop her and tell her that her clearance had been revoked. Instead, he simply tipped his hat to her as she walked by his desk.

On the elevator ride up to the twelfth floor, Sam made the conscious decision that she was going to accept the verdict laid down by Dr. Ephraim. Although she was not yet convinced that her sanity and her grip on reality were not in jeopardy, the doctor's words made sense, and she would cling to them for the sake of her daughter. No matter what life had thrown at her, she had to remain strong for Dani's sake.

The elevator doors opened and she was surprised to see Martell and a handsome white-haired man standing before the main reception desk. The older man turned and gave her a generous smile. She recognized his bold, Roman-style features instantly; she had seen his photographs in several business magazines. Allen Halpern walked up to her and held out his hand.

"Samantha Walthers," he said in his larger than life voice. She found herself wondering if he had ever trained as an actor as he went on to say, "I'll consider this an honor and a privilege."

She took his hand. It was red hot, as if it burned with his legendary inner fires. She immediately felt at ease with the man. Pete Martell frowned at her as soon as Halpern's back was turned.

The expression of the attractive, white-haired man became compassionate without a trace of condescension. "I understand that you've had a rather trying first day."

"Yes, sir," she said, trying to maintain her equilibrium; she felt as if she were going to fall flat at any moment.

"Please, call me Allen," he said. "I hope that you don't feel that I was intruding, but I made a phone call to detective Pullman and he gave me the rundown on their findings. I know that you had a terrible experience today, and if you need someone to talk to, I'll be available."

"That's very kind of you," she said. "Allen."

"I wish that I had more time to talk, but I have a meeting at five-thirty. Perhaps we could have lunch in the next week or two, after you settle in."

"Yes," she said. "That would be wonderful."

"Call my secretary, she'll make the arrangements. Have you been to Spagos?"

Samantha shook her head as he moved past her and touched the button for the elevator.

"It will be a new experience for you. We can make fun of everyone who's pretending to have a power lunch."

She laughed and told him that it would be a delight. A soft bell announced the arrival of the elevator and beside her the double doors opened. Halpern told Martell that he would be in touch, then hurried into the elevator and punched the button for the lobby as the doors hissed shut.

Pete Martell was leaning against the reception desk with his arms crossed over his chest. His lips were pulled back in an expression of consummate distaste and he laughed as if the word smug had been invented solely to justify his existence. "Now I get it," he said as she turned to face him. "He just wants to fuck you."

Sam remained silent. The thought had occurred to her, also, but she was not about to admit it. Martell did not seem to notice as she slipped her hand into her purse and gently touched the red button on her pocket tape recorder.

"What did you say to me?" she prompted.

"I said, the lecherous old fart obviously just wants to pop you. He wants to get his salami wet. He must have seen your picture in *People* magazine and has probably been whacking to it every night for the past six months." Martell sighed. "Well, at least that makes sense. I was beginning to think I was missing something here."

Behind him, Rosalind stabbed at the air behind his back with a letter opener then smiled pleasantly as he glanced in her direction. "I'll tell ya, Walthers, you are one lucky psycho. Play your cards right, you can probably marry the limp-dicked old geezer. I bet you wouldn't have to do more than give him a blow job every couple of months to keep him happy. It could be a good career move for you."

"You think so," she said. "So you don't think Mr. Halpern is capable of making responsible business decisions anymore?"

Martell laughed. "Look, Walthers, of course, he *has* to back you if he doesn't want to look like a fuck-up in front of his conference room buddies. That doesn't mean he isn't plotting the course of this company with his dick. I'll tell you what. Everyone should do what they do best. If you think you can perform your job better laying on your back, I'd be happy to arrange for a steady supply of customers for you. You might want to get in some practice before you have to do him under the table at Spagos."

Sam remained absolutely still. Martell took her silence as a sign of defeat and took a few steps toward her. "I'll have you out of this office inside of a month. We don't need you here and we don't want you here. Got it?"

"I understand," she said without emotion.

"Good. As long as we're clear."

With that, Martell strutted down the hallway to his office. Once Sam heard his door shut, she reached into her purse, withdrew her recorder, and ejected the micro-cassette.

"Rosalind, do you think I can ask a favor?"

The receptionist removed her glasses as she gingerly plucked the tape from Samantha's hand and gave it a kiss. "I'll have it hand delivered to Mr. Halpern first thing in the morning."

"That would be wonderful," Sam told her as she backed away and stabbed at the button for the elevator. As she waited for the doors to open, Sam looked back at Rosalind, who was busy slipping the micro-cassette into her purse. She wondered exactly how many bootlegged copies the receptionist was going to make before she sent the tape on in the morning.

Several, she hoped.

The deceptively quiet bell sounded and she heard the hiss of the elevator doors. Before she entered the elevator, Rosalind said, "Hey, Sam, you want to go have a drink?"

Samantha laughed. "Why don't we wait until tomorrow, so we can celebrate?"

Rosalind winked. Sam stepped inside the elevator and punched the button for the lobby. After a hellish start, the day was actually beginning to look up.

An hour and a half later, while fighting the traffic gridlock, Sam decided she had to try to solve the double mystery if she was to justify the trust her sponsor had placed in her. Did Mark Smith kill his wife? And who in turn killed him? She thought of the corpses in the dining room and the maniac she had encountered two years earlier who had tried to take Dani away from her. She was deeply troubled when she walked into the living room of her new home and found Dani wearing the most spectacular dress she had ever seen on the girl. Dani had avoided her high school prom. Looking at her in the strapless black and red gown, Sam realized the effect her daughter would have had on the male portion of her graduating class. For the first time she felt a slight relief that the girl had avoided that particular function. In some ways, Dani was all grown up; in others, she was still a child.

"Where did that come from?" Sam asked.

Thoroughly embarrassed, Dani rushed into her bedroom and struggled out of the dress. Her mother followed her and tried to help. After a few minutes, Dani told her mother the entire story. Sam did not share her own wretched experiences from the day; she had rarely seen her daughter so enthusiastic about meeting new people and she didn't want to bring her down. Even so, parts of Dani's story nagged at the investigator in Sam. "You're sure the car was locked?"

"Well, I thought I was. I must have left the passenger side open or else she wouldn't have been able to get in."

"Uh-huh. Look, do you really think it's *normal* for someone you've just met to buy you a gift like this?"

"What do you mean?" Dani said innocently. The same thought had occurred to her several times during the day and she had done her best to force it away. Madison was different, that's all. And this was Beverly Hills.

Sam frowned. "It just strikes me as odd, that's all. Why don't we do this: Give me a few minutes, I'll take a shower, then I'll drive you up to the party. That way you can give Madison the dress back and—"

"No. *Absolutely* not."

Sam was stunned by her daughter's forceful delivery. "Honey, you don't know what these people can be like."

"No, and I'm not going to find out if I keep hiding behind you every time I get a little afraid to do something."

Sam sat down hard on the edge of her daughter's bed. She felt as if she had been struck. Despite her statements to the contrary, she was desperately afraid to let Dani go and have a life of her own. For the past eighteen years her own life had been consumed by two overriding passions: ensuring the safety and happiness of her daughter and becoming the best that she could become at her work. There had been men, but no decent ones; none that would have measured up as a father for Dani. With Dani gone and her work going to hell, she would be left with nothing. But that should not have mattered. She knew she had to think about what was best for her daughter. The child needed a life.

Dani sat beside her mother on the bed and set her head on Sam's shoulder. The move always softened the woman up, no matter how hard she clung to her anger or hurt. Sam grinned, wondering how her

54

daughter had become so talented at pushing all the right buttons.

"You keep saying you want me to grow up and do things for myself," Dani said. "Let me do this. I promise you won't regret it."

Sam put her arm around her daughter and hugged her tight. "I know, honey," she said. "Just be careful."

Dani pulled away and laughed. "I'm just going to a party. What could possibly happen?"

Sam smiled and somehow managed to keep herself from listing the endless possibilities that were floating through her mind.

Four

Dani was forced to park half a mile from the address Madison had left for her. Though she had been driving at night, she had no difficulty finding the house. The tree-lined embankment was clogged with Porsches, Rangers, and cherry-red Mustang 5.0s. A seemingly endless dance mix of C & C Music Factory's latest drifted lazily to the vacant clump where she had stopped to gather her courage. Dani sat in the Ghia, clutching the steering wheel until the blood drained from her knuckles. She took a deep breath, collected the package containing the dress, and left the car, stepping into the night. She wore a loose fitting blouse over her button-fly jeans.

I'm doing this, I'm actually going to *do* this, she thought as she walked along the shoulder of the road, feeling vulnerable and afraid. Suddenly she realized that she had left Madison's note home. She had read it so many times that the directions were chiseled in her memory. Images came to her of burly private security officers working the door, demanding crossly to see her forgotten invitation. Holding the box tightly against her breasts, Dani pressed on. The worst that could happen was Madison being summoned to the door, where Dani would pass the box to her and run for her life. She certainly wasn't going to leave it with strangers.

The bravado she had felt when she'd stood up to

56

her mother faded the moment she had entered Malibu. Studying the vast estates of the wealthy, the famous, and the infamous, Dani finally understood the kind of people she was dealing with. Saddened, she had realized how absurd it was to think that they would welcome her as one of their own.

Madison's two-story house was an elegantly designed Victorian wreathed by masses of deep green palm fronds—a green curtain of mystery hiding what lay beyond the house from casual observers. Bronze lions sat on either side of the marble walkway. Dani resisted the urge to touch one of them as she walked to the door, which had been ajar. She stood before the door, her fingers curling into a fist, debating on whether or not to knock. The volume level of the dance music was such that she doubted anyone would hear her. She considered simply walking in, but a fantasy of the music stopping and a hundred party-goers suddenly stopping and staring at the plainly dressed golden-eyed teenager flashed into her mind. Digging her hand into her pocket, she retrieved her mirrored sunglasses and quickly put them on.

She took a deep breath and thought, you're an idiot. What the hell were you thinking, coming here? This isn't for you.

She turned away from the door and was confronted by a couple who appeared to have been torn from the covers of *GQ* and *Vogue*. They seemed oblivious to her. Attempting to back out of their way, Dani felt the door against her shoulder and suddenly she was swept inside as the couple entered the house. She was overcome by the explosion of life that greeted her. At least one hundred stylishly dressed people were crammed into the reception area. Some danced on the gray marble floor while others rested against the teal marble walls. Any furniture had been cleared for the party. The music caused her eardrums to shudder. People shouted good-naturedly to make themselves heard, while others found excuses to stare at their reflections in the exquisitely wrought silver-framed mirrors lining the walls and ceilings.

No one was staring at her. She felt at once relieved and disappointed. A couple brushed against her, holding each other and swaying to the music as they kissed openmouthed. A flush of embarrassment raced through Dani and she shied away from them, issuing a slight cry of apology. The couple had not even noticed her. As she passed through the gauntlet of amazingly beautiful people, Dani's thoughts began to wander.

In high school, Dani never had a steady boyfriend. Her romantic experiences had been limited to double dates that Lisa had set up for them. A few of the boys she had gone out with had been anxious to bury their hands in her jeans or underneath her T-shirt, but not one of them had been interested in her, in what made her special. She had shut them down without regret.

Inevitably, after one of her rare dates, her tormentors seized the moment. Taped to her locker, for all the world to see, she would find pages torn from Harlequin romances or hard-core porn novels. Passages concerning heaving breasts and savage violations of trembling womanhood were usually highlighted. Angrily, she would tear them down. What kind of statement were her tormentors making, she wondered. Was she bringing down the average by remaining a virgin? Or was it just that they always knew exactly how to get to her?

To hell with them, she would decide. *Her* breasts had never heaved as far as she knew and *her* trembling womanhood wasn't about to be savaged until she was damn well ready for it.

What affected her most deeply about this particular tack that her tormentors had chosen was that they had struck so close to home for Dani. She *had* been curious about sex. If curiosity could be viewed on the same terms as hunger, she was ravenous for knowl-

58

edge. But she was also terrified of making a mistake, of giving in to her hunger simply because she felt she had to, or because the darker sides of her personality wished her to. She had forced down her wants and needs many times, and she was determined that her first time would be special, that the man she gave herself to would be in it for more than her body, that he would love her and want to be with her.

Still, her curiosity was not completely powerless, and a few of the clippings had been kept.

A familiar voice shattered her revery: "There you are!"

Dani looked up, dazed, and saw Madison standing directly before her. Madison wore a sleek black jacket unbuttoned to reveal her black, lacy bra. Her skirt was very short and she wore black stiletto heels.

"Come with me, come on, come on," Madison said as she took Dani's free hand and led her away from the receiving hall. They passed a large glass window that revealed a pool of epic proportions, went through a comfortable living room with an adjacent bar, entered a chamber that was covered with thousands of photographs, then scampered up a flight of stairs where they ended up in a bedroom that Madison had to unlock. They entered and the raven-haired girl threw on a light. Dani followed her, realizing that she had not said a word to her new friend.

"Okay," Madison said as she flipped on the adjoining bathroom's light, "you can change in here. Lock it up when you're done or else the orgiers will mess up the sheets. I'll be downstairs. See ya!"

Before Dani could say a word, Madison had sailed out of the room, her hair flowing behind her, and closed the door.

"What?" Dani finally said, but there was no one in the room to answer.

Finally, Dani decided that she had only two options: leave the dress in the locked room and get out of the house while attempting to avoid Madison, or put the damned thing on and get it over with. There really was no choice.

Oh my God, she thought as she stripped out of her clothes and laid her sunglasses on the nightstand beside the bed, I'm really going to do this.

As before, the dress had been a revelation. Having left her purse in the car, she took her keys from the pocket of her jeans and slipped them into the matching handbag that had come with the dress. She knew that she should have left them in the locked room with the rest of her clothing, but she would have felt silly walking around with an empty handbag.

Downstairs, the music had softened to one of Enya's slow, lacy, new-age ballads.

The hallway lights had been shut off. Dani descended the stairs carefully, following a flickering orange glow from below. She came to the room crammed with photographs and paused for a moment as she looked through the doorway into the main body of the house and saw that all the lights had been turned off. Everywhere she looked, ornate candelabras held collections of wonderfully crafted, lit candles. By the soft, passionate candlelight, couples held each other tight, dancing, murmuring seductively.

The memory room, as she thought of it, was miraculously unoccupied. Still not quite ready to mingle with the other guests, Dani felt her discomfort and nervousness momentarily abate as she paused to examine a few of the photos.

Each was blown up to exactly the same size and framed in an identical silver frame. The room itself was a photo album. Dani recognized celebrities, actors, and politicians. In almost every shot she saw a couple that she assumed to be Madison's parents, though Madison was not in any of the photographs.

She turned away from the photos and stopped suddenly as she noticed a department store stand-up of

60

Vanna White in the corner. Taped to the woman's outstretched hand was a box of Trojan condoms. Dani blanched. Turning, she nearly screamed as she suddenly registered the presence of a tall, brooding man beside her. His unwashed black hair descended halfway down the length of his back and his pock-marked face was unshaven. For the amount of chains that hung from his leather jacket and pants, he could have passed for a heavy-metal rock star.

"I would have been insulted that they didn't leave the extra large ones," he muttered, more to himself than to her.

A slight smile flashed across Dani's face and she backed out of the room before the man could truly notice her. She did not want to be trapped with such a creature.

"Careful," someone whispered, and Dani turned to see that she was near the small alcove of a bar where a dozen people had gathered. Several of them stared at her in slack-jawed wonder and Dani felt herself straighten slightly, only now realizing that she had been slumping a bit.

"Hi, I'm Ted and this is Alicia," a blond-haired man in a white, camel-hair suit said as he extended his hand. The woman beside him could have passed for a young and stunningly made up Eva Braun. Together they were an Aryan's fantasy come to life. Dani shook each of their hands and smiled. The yellow light from the candles flickered in their eyes. Dani glanced around and saw that it was the same for everyone. Her own strange eyes seemed perfectly natural in this environment. Dani wondered if Madison had set this scene with that thought in mind, then told herself that she was being ridiculous. Madison barely knew her.

A second couple introduced themselves to Ted and Alicia, and before they could draw Dani into their circle, where she was afraid she would remain for most of the evening, Dani slipped away. Soon she was

61

entrenched in the crowd gathered near the doors to the pool. The admiring, wondrous looks she received from dozens of men and women had an intoxicating effect on the young woman.

Was this a joke? she thought with a degree of schoolgirl giddiness. A setup of some kind? Could Madison have convinced all these people to go along with her plan?

Breezing onto the walkway surrounding the pool, Dani found herself moving with an ease and confidence that she had never before possessed. Women complimented her. Men stared at her. People treated her as if she were a goddess, ethereal, something beyond their comprehension.

A young, buxom waitress approached, bearing a tray filled with drinks. The woman was dressed in a style similar to all the help, a tuxedo top, stockings, bursting white blouse, heels. A magician's assistant. Appropriate.

Dani looked around and felt as if magic had taken her this night. She felt as if she had been transported to another realm and made into a creature that was worthy of existing in that realm.

Without a second glance she took a wine glass from the tray and turned from the serving girl to explore. She felt as if she were on a soundstage. The pool looked like a matte painting from a *Batman* movie. It extended so far that Dani was certain she would walk into the wall it was painted on at any moment. Track lighting adorned the rim of the pool, a collection of small colored lights that winked on and off, creating patterns and sometimes the illusion of movement. Dani laughed as two separate bursts of light issued from the center of the rectangular pool's bottom edge and raced away from one another. Gold, green, blue, and red lights fired then faded, the steadily rising twin flares of illumination starting at the bottom, then racing up the sides like brilliantly lit falling dominoes, until they met at the middle of the top, and sped past each other to race back down the opposite sides and culminate at the bottom. She shook her head and absently rested her hand on the head of a statue, suddenly noticing the array of ceramic cherubs and angels that spouted fresh water into the pool.

At the far end of the pool, on the opposite side, Dani saw a face that made her heart feel as if it was about to explode. It was a man; a *beautiful* man. Dani was instantly captivated, she could not tear her gaze from him. The man had been talking to someone, a woman in a red dress, and he slowly turned his gaze directly upon her, as if he had been able to sense her staring.

Dani did not look away. She felt as if a pair of invisible hands had reached across the distance separating them and gently cupped her face between them, keeping her attention riveted upon the man. Dani had considered herself immune to this type of thing. The entire evening, she had been absolutely certain that if movie icons like Christian Slater and Keanu Reeves approached her at this party she could play it cool, pretend she was unimpressed.

Well, she thought she could, anyway.

This man, however, had overwhelmed her. He held himself with a matchless grace, a quiet dignity, and an unbelievable confidence she found incredibly exciting.

He'd be obnoxious to talk to, she told herself, trying desperately to hold onto reason. I bet he's some male model with an ego the size of his bank account.

But there was something self-deprecating in his manner and his smile, some unknowable quality that chased away such knee-jerk evaluations as quickly as they arrived. Though he appeared only a few years older than herself, this man radiated an unearthly, larger than life quality. He possessed what the film magazines referred to as true presence, a quality Dani had never before seen in person, only at the movies.

63

More than anything, she had been captured by his eyes. They were a luminous silver-blue, the eyes of a glorious wolf running wild in a frozen paradise. They held her and whispered forgotten secrets into her mind.

God, Dani, get a grip, she thought, hugging herself tight. She tried to look at him objectively. Aside from his luscious eyes, he had short, perfectly styled black hair that shined brightly in the moonlight. His features were classically styled, Japanese-American. The suit he wore was smoke gray. A black T-shirt set it off in contrast. He was the most exquisite being she had ever seen in her life.

She turned away in embarrassment, and when she chanced a look back, he had been swallowed up by the crowd.

"I see you're making an impression."

Dani did not jump at the sound of Madison's voice, though the sight of the beautiful man had wired her more tightly than she had been the entire evening.

"It's the dress," Dani said, downturning her eyes.

Madison stepped before her and set one hand on her hip as she evaluated Dani. "I don't think so, girlfriend. And you know what?"

"What?"

"Neither do you."

Dani smiled. Madison was right. She suddenly noticed the two women standing next to Madison. Sensing the girl's discovery, Madison introduced her friends, Angel and Isabella. Angel was a platinum blonde who wore a daring, see-through outfit laced with gold lamé. Isabella's dress was bloodred, matching her crimson lips. Her long, lustrous brunette hair had been curled off her face and hung to the midpoint of her back. The bright red straps of the dress called attention to her creamy shoulders. Her bodice dipped low to show off ample cleavage. Her eyes were oddly dark with shining slivers of deep blue.

She radiated a deep, piercing intelligence along with European beauty. Neither woman looked older than twenty, but Isabella somehow appeared to be much older.

"Let us show you off," Isabella said in a rich, sensuous voice as she took Dani's hand and led her back inside. Angel followed, Madison remaining behind.

The magic that had permeated the evening continued to hold as Isabella and Angel lived up to the dark-eyed woman's promise, displaying Dani as if she were their prized discovery. Dani's tension returned at one point as she spoke with a handful of college students. She felt inadequate and thought she should lie about her age, pretend that she was also a student, that her family was rich. Then she thought of all her mother had sacrificed for her and decided that she was not ashamed of who she was and where she came from. She told the others the truth and no one seemed to think less of her for her answers.

Sometime later, in the vast receiving hall, Angel and Isabella drifted away for a few moments and a man in his mid-thirties with a receding hairline and a ponytail approached Dani.

"So how old are you?" he asked, sporting a grin that did nothing to mask his desire. "You look like legal tender to me. Nice and young. Good and tender. But are you legal?"

Dani tensed. She knew that this could be classified as a harmless come-on, if such a thing existed. Yet this man made her terribly uncomfortable.

Suddenly, Isabella was at her side, eyes blazing with rage. The man's face paled as he saw her.

"Richard," she said, "haven't I warned you about this before?"

The muscles in his cheeks twitched. "I'm sorry," he said, unable to meet her gaze. He lowered his head and hurried away.

"Are you all right?" Isabella asked.

"I'm fine," Dani said, noting the tremor in her

voice. Then she saw something else that caused her concern: Angel was standing very close to another woman. They were holding hands. Angel whispered something in the woman's ear, kissing her on the cheek and then on the mouth. Their lips lingered a moment too long.

My God, Dani thought, do these women want to sleep with me? Is *that* what this is all about?

She had always considered herself very liberal, and completely tolerant of other people's preferences. You want to smoke and drink? Fine, you do it. Drugs? No thanks, help yourself, screw up your own life if you want, just leave me out of it. Sex? Whatever — everyone's entitled to their own choices.

Suddenly she felt like a raging hypocrite. Beside her, Isabella seemed to sense the change that had come over her.

"Here's Madison," she said, "and she's brought someone who wants to meet you."

Dani tore her gaze from Angel and the other woman long enough to see Madison leading the dark-haired Japanese-American she had seen earlier through the crowded receiving room. All of her concerns fell away. The world fell away. She saw his bright silver-blue eyes, and she was lost.

"Hi," he said, reaching out for her hand. She allowed him to take it and was stunned when he leaned down and kissed it.

"I'm Dani," she said breathlessly. His smile was dazzling. She anticipated a dark, exotic name for him, something to match his flawless looks.

As if sensing her thoughts, he winked and said, "I'm Bill."

Five

Bill Yoshino was a god. There was no other way that Dani could describe him. There was no other way that she would *want* to describe him. Dani did not consider herself easily impressed. After all, there were dozens of absolutely gorgeous men at the party, a few of which she was convinced were actual celebrities. Somehow, none of that had mattered. Despite the compliments she had been given and the looks of desire and envy that she had received, she had continued to feel separate from these people. Even Madison and Isabella had been unable to set her completely at ease.

When she had seen Bill Yoshino, however, her tension had been washed away by the silver-blue, crashing waves she saw in his eyes. She was suddenly too excited to be nervous. Her body was awash in anticipation, though of what she was not certain. All that mattered to her suddenly was the way he looked at her, what he said, and whether he was going to touch her again. The feel of his lips on her hand had sent a tingling current through her body. She had even felt it in her toes, causing her to wonder if other clichés such as the hair rising on the nape of one's neck actually had basis in fact. No matter, the sensation had been wonderful and unique.

The music had turned back to a loud, thumping dance mix. The candles had remained, but a series of colored, strobing lights had been turned on to accompany them, and Dani had worried that Bill was going to ask her to dance. She had always been too self-conscious about her body to enjoy herself on the dance floor, and she was afraid of doing anything that would shatter the image that he held of her.

When he leaned close and spoke into her ear, his lips nearly touching her skin, she had begun to tremble. Her legs turned to water at the feel of his hot, sweet breath upon her neck.

"Why don't we go outside?" he asked.

Before she could answer, he took her hand and led her through the crowded receiving chamber. She held on to his hand a bit too tightly as they navigated through the house. The sting of a thousand tiny needles raced across her flesh whenever her bare shoulder brushed against him. The heat spread to her breasts and to the suddenly moist area between her legs, and she felt embarrassed by her reaction to this man. She had never experienced this before.

The voices of her former schoolmates whispered in her mind. Dani could picture them sizing up Bill Yoshino.

Do you believe in love at first sight?

No. but I believe in lust *at first sight.*

Dani and Bill made it to the back of the house, passing through the kitchen, and came to a small porch. She was surprised to see the sandy white beach and the rolling waves in the distance. Now she knew what the palms had been hiding.

They removed their shoes and carried them. The feel of the smooth white sand was cool and refreshing on their bare feet. The moon was almost full. They were alone on the beach.

Dani continued to feel as if she were in a movie. Nothing like this had ever happened to her before. Suddenly she realized that since they had left the party, Bill had been very quiet. Too quiet, perhaps. A flash of tension exploded within her, a sudden burst of emotions that she managed to suppress. Panic rushed through her. He was expecting her to say something, he was expecting her to do something, he was expecting her to make some kind of move. What was she supposed to do? God, she had no idea.

Suddenly, she felt an indescribable tug, as if a fisherman's net had been thrown over her fears, and gently they were torn away.

"This is a beautiful night," he whispered. "Madison told me that you almost didn't come. I'm glad you did."

Watch how you phrase that, Dani thought, then chided herself for her wicked response to his innocent statement. The flush of excitement returned to Dani. "Me too."

They walked along in silence, a bemused smile playing across Bill's face as he turned his head up to the moonlight and allowed it to wash over him. Dani had never seen anything half as sexy as the way he moved, the way he carried himself. If he had turned and tried to kiss her, if he had attempted any of the things that her dates had tried to get her to go along with in the past, she would not have refused. In that moment, she could refuse him nothing.

His smile changed to one of satisfaction, and Dani was suddenly hungry to be the one who brought about that smile. She pictured his naked body, imagined what she would do to him.

"Tell me about yourself," he said in his rich dulcet voice.

The question made her uneasy, and she had to fight the urge to wring her hands. "I don't know. My life is pretty boring. I'm just your everyday, average—"

"That's not true. There's nothing about you that's average. You're extraordinary."

I'm glad you think so, she thought. You're about the only one. Unusual, weird, a freak—sure. But extraordinary? You must have me confused with someone else.

She stayed silent, neither refusing or rebuking the

69

compliment. They had each been carrying their shoes on the outside of their bodies, leaving their inner hands free to occasionally graze one another. Unexpectedly, Bill took her hand. Dani felt the tingling sensation once again, her nipples suddenly growing so hard and tight that they became painful. She wondered if he could see the signs of her excitement through the dress.

On one weird level Dani couldn't understand her reaction. So little was actually happening, and yet so much was happening, particularly inside her. She felt that same, strange tug on her emotions, calming her, soothing her. His touch held a raw dangerous power over her, she realized, and she welcomed it.

"You can tell me anything," he said softly. "You know that, don't you?"

Somehow she *did* know that and under other circumstances, that knowledge might have frightened her. But she was no longer afraid. There was an air of excitement that passed between them as they reached the water and listened to the roaring waves. As they walked, holding hands, she found herself revealing everything about herself. It was as if Bill had draped a magic canopy over her and she felt safe under it — safe enough to tell him anything. She explained how she had been found in a garbage dumpster, and her adopted mother had saved her life. She told him of the teasing she had endured because of her strange eyes, and of the Halloween march she had missed when she was a little girl. Then, finally, she told him all she remembered of the events two years in the past, when the trapper killed her best friend, then abducted her.

"See, he wasn't really a trapper," she explained, "Mom and I just thought of him that way because he was able to trap *me,* because trapping people is what he did. But that's not really what they call it. I mean, technically, a trapper doesn't like to get blood on his hands. They suffocate a victim, poison them, or use lethal injection — anything that doesn't cause a lot of

70

blood. But Willis, that bastard, he really enjoyed it. What he did to Jami . . ."

"Don't stop," Bill said as he took her into a warm, comforting embrace. "Let it all out, it's all right."

Dani became aware that she was crying. The feel of Bill's strong arms around her was a ward against evil, shelter from the storm that had been those twelve terrible hours that she could not remember. She told him what her mother found, Willis dead, apparently by his own hand. There was no evidence that she had been raped or tortured.

"Are you sorry he's dead?" Bill whispered.

"No," Dani said in a feral growl. "I'm glad."

"I am, too."

He held her, caressing her hair, her back, rocking her. When her crying had run its course, Dani found the strength to pull away from him and raise her hands to wipe away the tears. He caught her hands and said, "Wait."

She looked up at him with uncertainty as he released her hands. They fell to her sides.

"Close your eyes," he said.

Lips trembling, Dani closed her eyes. Bill ran his hands through her hair and eased her head back, tilting her face upward. Her features and her long, elegant neck were pale in the moonlight. He leaned in close and kissed her cheek. Then he kissed close to her right eye, then her left.

Dani shook as Bill kissed her tears away. Her lips parted slightly as she waited for him to kiss her there, but he never did. Instead, when he was finished, he drew her into his embrace.

She opened her eyes and felt slightly disappointed. His kisses had been rapture. She had wanted to taste his lips. Why had he pulled away, what had he seen?

Dani decided not to torture herself when she saw the confused mix of emotions playing out on his face. Her heart sank as she said, "There's someone else, isn't there?"

71

"No," he said without hesitation. He went no further in explaining his abrupt withdrawal.

Then it's me, I did something, she thought. Anger sliced through her with the force of a blade, sudden awareness glinting off its serrated edge. Then she saw something in his beautiful silver-blue eyes, something soft and vulnerable, some terrific need that he wanted desperately to satisfy, but wouldn't. Maybe he wasn't rejecting her, maybe he didn't want to take advantage of her.

My god, she thought, he's being a gentleman. It was a phenomenon she had never before witnessed, outside of old Laurence Olivier movies.

"I should get going," Dani whispered, hoping that Bill would give her a reason to stay.

"All right."

"My Mom is going to be worried."

"No problem. You shouldn't make her worry."

God, she thought. He was so sweet. She desperately wanted to make love to him. The feeling crashed over her like an ocean wave.

"I'll walk you back," he said tonelessly, stretching his hand before him to indicate that she should go first.

Dani smiled nervously. She didn't like the change in his voice — the cold distance. What had happened, and what could she do to bring his warmth back?

She was about to turn from him when she suddenly decided to rush forward and kiss him hungrily. He caught her and edged back. Suddenly, the dark, beautiful, romantic man that she had first glimpsed across the pool had returned. He smiled, his touch causing unbearable heat to flare in her most sensitive regions.

"Not yet," he said. But his silver-blue eyes seemed to be making a promise to her — a promise that her deep, unfulfilled needs would soon be satiated. Dani felt at ease again.

They walked back, holding hands silently. No words were necessary.

Inside the house, the party was beginning to thin out. They met up with Madison, who was flanked by Isabella and Angel. Dani observed Angel closely, looking for any indications that the platinum blonde had designs on her. Angel seemed as innocent as her name would suggest.

All four walked Dani to the door. They stepped outside together and Dani finally realized that she had been holding on to Bill's hand, holding on tight, and she would now have to let him go. She didn't want to. She wanted nothing more than to take him with her or to go wherever he was going. In his eyes, she saw the same promise that she had seen before, that she would see him again.

Secure in that knowledge, she kissed him on the cheek. Waving to Madison and her companions, Dani walked down the marble stairs and vanished into the night.

Moments later, when the night's shadows had completely engulfed Dani's slinky black form, Bill spoke. "Do you think she'll be back?"

Isabella wrapped her arms around him from behind. One hand slid beneath his jacket. The other lightly brushed over the crotch of his pants before it came to rest on his thigh. She kissed the back of his neck, biting slightly.

"I wouldn't worry," she said.

Madison crossed her arms. "Hell no, Sugar. Believe me, any woman who's lucky enough to get a taste of you is gonna come back for more."

Her eyes narrowed into slits as Angel moved beside her and embraced her. Madison gasped as Angel plunged her tongue into her ear and gave her breast a painful squeeze. Her eyelids fluttered in rapture.

"In fact," she murmured, "I guarantee it. Now let's get rid of these people so we can go upstairs. . . ."

Six

Sam sat alone, curled up on the vast living room couch, staring at the clock. It was a small, rectangular clock with a blue digital read-out. She couldn't see the seconds passing. That was probably just as well. The minutes moved as sluggishly as hours. It was just after eleven o'clock at night.

What are you doing? she asked herself. You wouldn't like it if someone treated you like this. You wanted your daughter to have a life, so let her have a life.

She heard a knock at the door and every muscle in her body sizzled with activity. The knock came again. Dani had her own set of keys. No one here knew them. Who in hell would be knocking at the door. She rose from the couch. Instinct sent her to her handbag and she sank her hand into its recesses, where her gun waited. Only cold leather greeted her fingers. She had given up her gun.

She thought of Dani again and an icy-cold realization struck her in the stomach like a fist. She pictured two police officers, their faces set in sympathetic expressions. *Ma'am, there's been an accident, we'll need you to come down and identify the—*

Unwilling to wait even the few seconds it would take to gaze through the peephole, Sam tore open the door.

Carlotta Evans was standing before her.

"Do you have any idea how difficult it was to find this place?" the woman said, brushing past Sam as she entered the house, not bothering to wait for an invitation.

74

"Carlotta?" Sam asked, dumbfounded.

"No, hon. I'm a figment of your imagination. Fuck, it's cold out there. No one told me that it gets cold out here at night. I thought it would be like Florida, you know? You get maybe three days in the year when it's actually chilly and that's it."

"Carlotta?" Sam asked, a smile forcing itself upon her.

The woman rubbed at her bare arms. She wore a teal, sleeveless blouse and a black skirt. She was a year older than Sam, and still very attractive.

"Carlotta?" Sam asked for the third and final time.

"Duh," was Carlotta's reaction. "Come on, I know this is a surprise, but snap out of it!"

Carlotta snapped her fingers several times next to Sam's ears. The former police officer stared into her friend's eyes, then suddenly embraced the woman. Sam held on to her as if they were standing in the eye of a violent hurricane, the only objects that had not been ripped from their foundations.

"Hold on, hold on, you're gonna choke me," Carlotta said with a laugh. But Sam did not lessen her grip.

"Oh God, I'm glad to see you," Sam whispered in a tremulous voice.

"Yeah, I can tell," Carlotta said as she patted Sam's back and gently detached herself from the other woman.

Sam shook her head. "What are you doing here?"

"I have relatives in Mexico," Carlotta said, pronouncing the word meh-hee-ko. "My grandparents moved to Mazatlán. They bought this villa next to the ocean for a song and invited Lisa and me to come down."

"Yeah, I hear it's beautiful," Sam said absently, recalling a reference to Mazatlán as a poor man's Acapulco.

"It's been years since I saw them. Besides, I thought you might be feeling a little *displacement anxiety,* and my connecting flight ran through LAX, so I thought I'd leave early, spend some time with you, then take the second leg down south in a couple days."

"Displacement anxiety, huh?" Sam asked. Carlotta was taking courses to eventually qualify as a therapist.

75

"Yeah, babe. That's what I learned in school this week. Classes are out for now, seemed like a good time to visit. But I can't stay too long. Lisa's at the hotel, jet-lagged. I'll bring her by tomorrow so she and Dani can visit."

"That'd be good." Sam gestured at the couch. "Look, why don't you sit down? I'll get us something to drink."

Carlotta sank into the couch, issuing a cry of delight. "Sam, I don't believe this place. I swear to God, I was gonna drive right past it. I'm walking up the drive and I'm figuring that you've got a little efficiency in the back or something."

Sam had cracked open the liquor cabinet, a small, disguised alcove, and had finished off Carlotta's drink. She made a scotch on the rocks for herself.

"Tequila, no worm," Sam said as she handed the glass to Carlotta. "This is Beverly Hills, after all."

"I see."

Sam sat next to Carlotta on the couch. They both sipped at their drinks, then set them on the low, glass table before them. "That warm you up?"

"Oh, yeah."

"I just can't believe you're here."

"Well, I wanted it to be a surprise."

Sam nodded. "Okay, surprise me again. Tell me why you're *really* here."

Carlotta raised a single eyebrow. She reached down, took her drink, and this time she held on to it, nursing it as she spoke. "Lisa's been having the dreams again."

"Oh shit," Sam whispered fearfully. "I thought she was over that."

"So did I. Don't take this the wrong way, all right?"

"Sure."

"You're my friend and I love you."

"This is going to be really bad, isn't it?"

"It's just that a part of me thought that when Dani was all the way out of Lisa's life, that she might finally begin to get over what happened. But last week, it started up again. She claims she walked into her classroom at New

College and saw Jami sitting there, waiting for class to start."

"My God," Sam muttered.

"She says that she's been seeing Jami all over the place. Then later she finds out that she did things, or that things happened that aren't the way she remembers them."

Sam felt thunderstruck, but she hid any visible reaction. "What does her doctor say?"

"Separation anxiety."

The two women stared at each other.

"But Lisa and Dani weren't that close after what happened," Sam argued.

"I know, but Dani was always there. Now, all of a sudden, she isn't anymore. I mean, Lisa's no child. Consciously, she understands the difference between what happened to Jami and Dani's moving away, they're both eighteen, and everything, but —"

"No, I get it," Sam said. "All right. So the doctors think it would be good for Lisa to see where Dani's living, that she's okay, that nothing bad's happened to her."

"That's right."

Sam tensed. She felt as if she were going to cry. Carlotta moved close and put her hand on Sam's arm as she set down her drink.

"Sam? What is it? What's wrong?"

"I think something bad's happening to *me*."

With a bit of coaxing, Carlotta was able to drag the story of what had happened at the Smith house from Sam. The similarities in the incidents could not be ignored.

"What the hell's going on?" Sam asked.

"I don't know," Carlotta replied, stroking her friend's arm.

Sam shuddered as she thought about what had happened to her mother. She had only been eight, barely able to comprehend what had occurred. The woman had been ravaged by a sickness that took her sanity, and eventually her life.

That's not happening to me, Sam reminded herself.

77

"What are you thinking?" Carlotta asked.

Sam surprised herself by telling Carlotta everything about her mother's illness. She had told no one about what had happened, not even Dani. For the most part, she convinced herself that it had happened to someone else, not her mother. She preferred to remember the decent times she had with the woman, not the unpredictable rages or the delusional behavior that wracked her.

"And you think that's what's happening to you?" Carlotta asked gravely.

"Pretty stupid, huh?"

Sam heard a noise at the door. A key in the lock. She stood up and turned to the door.

Behind her, Carlotta said, "Not really, you fucking lunatic."

Sam spun in horrible surprise at her friend's devastatingly unkind words and nearly lost her breath. Carlotta was not sitting on the couch. Her drink sat on the table before the couch, untouched.

"Oh shit." Sam's breath came in ragged gasps. "This is not happening."

The door opened. She whirled to see Dani entering the house. She was wearing the dress that she had gone to Madison's house to return.

"What is it?" Dani asked, frozen in the doorway.

"Come inside, close the door."

Nodding, Dani did as her mother requested. She watched, perplexed, as Sam carried on a systematic search of the entire house. Her mother refused to say what she was looking for.

"Are you okay?" Dani asked.

Sam stifled the small, wounded cry that wanted desperately to spring from her lips. No, I'm not okay. I'm definitely not okay. That's one *fucking* word that does not apply to situations like this.

Should she tell her? She needed desperately to tell her. What had happened tonight had proved to her that there was no one else she could trust.

"I need to make a phone call," Sam said. Turning her

back on her daughter, Sam picked up the phone and dialed a number long distance.

"Hello?" the voice on the other end responded.

"Carlotta?"

"Sam?"

"Yeah, it's me."

Sam hung up the phone. With trembling hands, she rifled through her bag and found her address book. Then she looked up a number she had dialed more times than she could remember. Slowly, methodically, she dialed the number again.

"Hello?"

Carlotta's voice.

In Florida.

Where it belonged.

"Hello? Sam?"

"Yes," Sam replied. She could feel ice-cold fingers scrambling over her body, her mother's dead hands, calling her home, calling her to Hell.

"Did we get cut off?"

Sam did not answer. She was too busy shaking as if she had frostbite. Her throat constricted.

"What's the matter, Sam?"

"I really can't talk."

"But you called —"

Sam hung up the phone.

"Mom?"

"I gotta go!" Sam cried, rushing past her daughter.

Dani stood alone as she heard the door to Sam's bedroom slam shut, the lock clicking in place. She shuddered, then quietly went to the door and knocked softly. She called to her mother, and when there was no reply, she said, "I had a good night. The party was good. Really good."

No reply.

"Are you upset with me?" she asked.

"No, sweetheart," a small voice said from inside the locked room. "I'm just really tired."

"Okay," Dani said as she turned from the door and

moved down the hallway to her own room, where she retired for the night. As she undressed for bed, she realized that she had left her own clothes at Madison's house. She smiled. At least it was an excuse to go back.

Thoughts of Bill's wondrous touch mingled with images of the terror she had glimpsed in her mother's eyes. Unable to sleep, she went back to her mother's door, expecting to hear sobbing, or something equally disturbing. She could sense her mother's fear. It called to her.

There was no sound at all. The woman had obviously been stressed out from her first day on the new job and needed some time to herself.

God, Dani, it's not like the whole world revolves around you, you know, she thought.

"Sweet dreams," she said, then she went back to her room and shut the door.

Huddled in the corner of her room, Sam cleared her mind. She had practiced a series of exercises that were meant to drive away fear. In the process, she had endured a series of violent tremors as her emotions threatened to overwhelm her.

She was not losing her mind. She was not becoming her mother. Everything would be all right in the morning.

In her head, she repeated those words, an overworked mantra, a fractured lullaby. But she knew that the fear had not left her; it had simply been placed under control.

Sam's thoughts latched on to another time when she had lost control of her life. Shortly after graduating from high school, on her eighteenth birthday, she had been married. The marriage had immediately proven to be a mistake, despite the two-year courtship she had shared with her husband. They were divorced two weeks before she turned nineteen. He skipped town — and the bill collectors — leaving her severely in debt. She kept up a brave front, but she was alone and frightened.

She went to work for a local bank and moved into an

apartment in a section of Tampa that had once been one of the most glorious neighborhoods in America. Everywhere she turned, there were the smells of home cooking, the comforting sight of clothes on the line, and the blanketing shade provided by the beautiful, lush branches of one-hundred-and-fifty-year-old trees. She enjoyed the inviting reaches of brick-paved streets, the solitude of a park a half block away, and the sparkling beauty of a lake with swans gliding upon the waters. Her rent was only ninety-five dollars a month and for that she received a huge, beautifully furnished apartment that was filled with Victorian antiques and was close to her job.

For the first time in her life she was entering a community, something she had never before known. There was a heavy black populace, but there were also several elderly white couples who couldn't afford to go anywhere else, poor immigrant families, Cubans, and southeast Asian refugees. For a time she was able to fit in, but then the robberies began.

The first break-in occurred early one evening when she had been washing her hair. Someone got into her bedroom, stole her purse, rifled through some of her things, and escaped out the window. She didn't see or hear anything. That was not the case on the second occasion. There had been a storage room near the front of the house. She heard sounds and discovered four black teenagers, all about fifteen or sixteen, in the process of breaking in. One of them was all the way in, the rest were waiting outside, prepared to follow. Sam came running at them, screaming, a butcher knife held high. They dove back out the window and all four ran, screaming about the crazy bitch who was going to cut them all. At that moment, she probably would have, too. They were destroying the dream she had clung to all her life, to have a safe place where she belonged, where she would find acceptance. She phoned the police, only to have them arrive three hours later.

Her coworkers would ask why she stayed in that horrible place, and she would flippantly reply that as long as she was only robbed once a month, she could remain ahead—provided she didn't get hurt. And by that time she had begun to feel that it was her neighborhood. She didn't like the idea of some damn punks making her leave her neighborhood. If anyone was going to leave, it was going to be the punks.

Finally, she was robbed at knifepoint by a black man wearing a stocking mask. She had been on the first step of her back porch and it had been close to nine-thirty at night. In her mind, Sam had measured the distance between herself and the door, trying to find ways to get away, thinking strategy the entire time, but it was simply not possible. The knife was at her throat. There had been no threat of rape, but when it was over, she felt violated nonetheless.

She felt challenged and anger replaced her fear. It had been humiliating to have this stranger put a knife to her neck and force her to hand over her wallet, give up her license, checks, everything. Some items could not be replaced. She had lost a cheap necklace and a set of earrings—costume jewelry of little monetary value—that had once belonged to her mother. She treasured them. That's why she carried them in her purse. Now they were gone.

Sam had expected her decision to purchase a gun to be a terrible struggle. She'd held a very strong belief in gun control. But her need to take control of a real situation outweighed her abstract moral qualms. She sought advice from the security guard at the bank where she worked. He was an ex-police officer.

She went to the gun shop and picked out the weapon that met her specifications. It was a nickel-plated .38 long. She wanted it to be seen so she might not be forced to use it. They asked her if she had a criminal record, she told them that she did not. No one investigated, no one asked for an ID. She was advised that she would have to go through a three-day "cooling off" period and so she left without the weapon. She was mugged again the next night, during the waiting period.

It had been the same man as before. She had been very wary when she'd arrived home that night. It was about the same time as the first mugging. She'd waited in her car a moment, looked around cautiously, and was certain that she was safe before she stepped out. She was two steps to the door when he melted out of the shadows and placed his knife to her throat. It was dark and he wore a stocking mask. He was young with a sizable athletic build. His manner of speech indicated that he had been educated. Brimming with confidence, he had threatened her life and she was certain that if she put up any resistance he would have killed her and thought very little of it. She had been terrified. When he left her, he walked with a strut. He had gotten a charge out of the humiliation.

Two days later, she collected the gun.

The security guard from work took her to the firing range the first time. The range had been run by the police, who were very security conscious. She either had to enter with the gun holstered or broken open. The guard who accompanied her insisted that she fire his gun first, a weighty magnum. He told her that if she could get used to firing that weapon, any other gun would be easy for her. They wore ear protectors, though many of the men at the range left theirs off — apparently to seem macho. Even with the ear protectors on, the sound of the gun had been the loudest noise she had ever heard, uncomfortable loud, *nasty* loud. Though it had made a hell of a noise and jerked her hand back, she had no real accuracy with it. She had struck the target at fifty feet and it took a chunk out of the post.

When she fired her own weapon for the first time she had expected it to jerk her hand, but all it did was make a loud noise. She placed the bullet the first time. There were round targets made of paper, similar to archery targets, but not as large. They also had targets in the shape of men, black silhouettes against white backgrounds. These were only used for the longer distances and very few people used these targets. The different caliber weapons made distinctive sounds; and after a time, she could tell what weapons were being fired by their auditory signature. The bigger the gun, the lower the pitch.

The security guard was impressed by her approach and her skill. He told her she was a natural. But Sam didn't feel like a "natural." She didn't like holding the weapon and she didn't enjoy firing it. Neither did she like the type of people she met at the range. Mostly they were swaggering, cocky types who reminded her of her assailant. There were perhaps three other women at the range. They were being taught by their husbands or boyfriends.

The security guard told her that she could easily get into the Tampa police academy. He liked the fact that she wasn't a hot shot. She went at it very calmly, very maturely. She found out on the news that the police had begun a nationwide effort to actively recruit women in answer to charges of discrimination. The Tampa police department had one of the best training programs in the country; graduates from their program could be hired practically anywhere they wanted to go.

At first she did nothing about his offer. She got the gun to feel safe in the neighborhood, but ironically it was the gun that stopped her from fitting in. Her life began to change. A lot of kids in that neighborhood had been friendly, but they stopped being friendly after she got the gun. She carried the gun in her hand when she left her house and crossed to the car, keeping the gun in her hand at all times. She took the garbage out with the gun in her hand, went shopping with the gun in her hand, and came back from shopping with the gun in her hand. The nickel plating made it very bright, very obvious. She was constantly worried about being startled and accidentally firing on an innocent.

She received a sense of power from the gun. She was taking action, she was doing *something* to protect herself. Up until that point she had been a victim; now she was able to do something about it. Despite the worried, resentful glances she received from some of her neighbors, she found that many of the people on her street appreciated what she was doing. Some even told her that they felt safer with her around. Finally, she took the exam and entered the academy.

All of this had happened in a very short period of time. It had been at once frightening and exhilarating. She was a rookie cop when she had found Dani and saved her life. From that point on, the oath she had taken to protect and serve had a new and more pertinent meaning.

Breaking from the revery, she forced herself to get up and go into her daughter's room. Dani was already asleep. She had a warm, contented smile.

"I love you, baby," Sam whispered. "And I won't ever leave you the way my mommy left me. You can count on it."

Dani murmured, " 'night," and rolled over. Sam went back to her room and climbed under the covers. With sleep came nightmares from which she could not wake. She screamed twice during the night.

In the other bedroom, Dani writhed in her sleep. There was a delicious smile on her lips as she felt waves of pleasure wash over her.

She hadn't slept like this in *years*.

In her dreams, she lay in bed with Bill, consuming delicacies that had been created only for them. Her hunger had shocked and delighted both of them.

As the night wore on, she found that she could not get enough.

She never heard her mother's screams.

Seven

Dani had not realized how easily she had acclimated to life in Beverly Hills until the blaring car horn woke her from a sound sleep. In Tampa, she could have slept through a terrorist attack. But when the perfect tranquility of the morning was shattered by the insistent sound of someone leaning all their weight into their car horn, Dani was awake in an instant. She woke to find herself naked, her nightdress laying in a heap beside the bed. She stared at it and for an instant recalled her dream of Bill stealing into her room and slowly removing the garment as he covered her body with kisses. The position of the nightdress made her wonder if the dream had been something other than her subconscious lustfully fantasizing.

Outside, the car horn did not let up.

"All right, already, I'm coming!"

She was wide awake, not at all submerged in the languid, early morning haze that normally took several minutes to shake off. Grabbing a robe from the closet, she slipped it on and went to the window, wondering why her mother hadn't also responded to the sound. On the way to the window she noticed the time. It was after eleven o'clock in the morning. She felt incredibly decadent to have slept so long.

Opening the window, Dani stuck her head outside and hollered, "Cut it out!"

The noise stopped and Dani saw a bright red sports

car with the top down. Madison sat behind the wheel. She held up a pile of clothing that Dani dimly recalled. Suddenly, with a profound twist of embarrassment, Dani realized that she had left her real clothing in the bedroom upstairs in Madison's house.

"I'll be right down," Dani shouted. She felt her heart sink. Madison was angry at her. She wanted the dress back. That had to be it.

She collected the dress and went downstairs. Her mother had left for work hours ago and she was alone in the house. Opening the door, Dani was surprised as Madison greeted her with a hug and a kiss on the cheek.

"Good morning, sweetheart!" Madison cried, then brushed past her and entered the house. "Oh, this is gorgeous!"

"It's just rented," Dani said apologetically. "Mom's company put us up here. I guess it's not much compared to —"

"It's plenty, believe me," Madison said. "My place is rented, too."

Dani felt herself relax. She thought of the walk-in photo gallery at Madison's house. The girl was not in any of the pictures. Dani should have guessed then and there.

For a moment, Dani convinced herself that this put them on more equal footing. Then she realized the kind of money it would take to rent a beach house in Malibu and her ebullience faded.

"What's that?" Madison said in a mockingly cross voice. She was pointing at the dress in Dani's hands.

"I'm sorry, I shouldn't have worn it out last night, you must think I'm a total airhead."

She held the dress out to Madison. The girl frowned, placed one arm around Dani, and led her to the couch, where they both sat down.

"Let me explain something to you," Madison said. "The dress is no big deal. I wanted you to have it. Consider it a 'welcome to Beverly Hills' gift."

"I know how expensive it was."

Madison rolled her eyes, snatched a pillow from the couch, and buried her face in it as she screamed in exasperation. She slammed the pillow back into place and turned to face Dani.

"Here's how it works: When I first came here, I didn't have much. I wasn't broke, but I wasn't rich either. I met some people who helped me out and because of them, I'm doing all right. So I don't see anything wrong with spreading it around if I feel like."

"Fine, but I don't want to be a charity case—"

The pillow was back in Madison's hands. This time her shriek was even louder. She withdrew the pillow and made a slashing motion with her hand. "I'm gonna give you a patented Miss Piggy karate chop, I swear I am—haiiii-ya!"

The blow came nowhere near Dani. Considering the training the girl had received from her mother, that was just as well.

Dani realized that Madison had not brought Dani's clothes in with her and mentioned it to the girl.

"Well, I'm going to need some help with this stuff," Madison said, tugging at Dani's arm. She led Dani outside, to the sports car. "Prepare to be really *offended.*"

Before Dani could ask what Madison was talking about, she saw that the entire backseat was loaded with expensive outfits. Her clothes were piled on top.

"I can't take this stuff," Dani said. "It wouldn't be right."

"Fine. Get dressed, you can come to Goodwill with me and we'll dump this stuff off before we have lunch."

Dani recognized a few strategically placed designer labels and estimated that Madison had spent thousands on what was laying in the back.

"Fine," she said, deciding to call the other girl's bluff. These clothes weren't really going to Goodwill and they both knew it.

"This too," Madison said, snatching the black dress from Dani's hands. Dani felt as if a part of her had been torn away as Madison threw the dress in the back. The dress had become an object of magic and wonder. To see it treated in such a manner was disheartening, to say the least.

An hour later, they were in Los Angeles, pulling into a parking lot with a Goodwill truck. Madison had scooped up the clothing and had reached the first step of the small stepladder leading to the open door of the trailer when Dani finally stopped her and dragged her back to the car. She could not bear to see her black dress given away as if it was nothing but a used-up old rag.

"All right, all right, I'll take it," Dani said, biting her lip in excitement. "I'll take all this stuff. God, you're hard."

"You know it," Madison said, licking her lips in triumph. "By the way, I forgot your sunglasses. The mirrored ones? I think they're still up in the guest bedroom. But we're going back up there anyway, so remind me."

"Sure."

In moments they were back on Santa Monica Boulevard, the clothes safely locked in the trunk as they cruised the city. Madison explained that she usually wore a new dress only a few times before she discarded it and she preferred that someone she knew and cared about could have a crack at them first.

Dani thought of Angel and Isabella and tried to imagine either of them needing hand-me-downs. The idea was incongruous. She thought of Angel kissing the other girl, but she felt too ashamed to ask Madison about it. Then her thoughts shifted to Bill Yoshino and her discomfort fell away.

"You know what we're going to have to do tonight?" Madison asked. "The Third Street Festival. You'll love it."

"Okay." Dani paused. "What's that?"

"You'll love it, don't worry. Let it be a surprise."

Dani nodded. She twisted uncomfortably in her seat as they passed a bar with several people gathered outside. One of the men wore a sailor's suit with the cheeks of his ass cut out. He carried an inflatable sex doll and strutted as if he had a purpose. Many of the women wore clothing that would have caused her mother's vice department buddies to keep a close watch on them.

A car that looked exactly like something out of an L.A. gang movie cut them off. Madison hung back, allowing the low-slung, orange four door plenty of space. Rap music burst from the car's open windows, and the backseat was filled to bursting with young men in jackets, a few wearing bandannas.

"Fuck, those assholes cut me off . . ." Madison turned to Dani. "Want to have some fun?"

Before Dani could reply, Madison snapped her car out of traffic and pulled along the left side of the orange car. Dani found herself staring into the face of a teenaged black youth. She pulled back, frightened. She'd heard too much about L.A. gangs and drive-by shootings for kicks. Part of her felt like a jerk for her automatic recoiling. But then her views on tolerance stemmed from the rule of not getting in anyone's face, and Madison was violating that edict with considerable enthusiasm.

"Hey boys!" Madison said as she lifted her top, exposing her naked breasts, "how would you like to get a taste of what I got?"

"Holy shit!" Dani shouted, reaching over and yanking Madison's designer T-shirt back in place. "What the fuck are you trying to do, get us killed?"

"Yo, chill baby!" the driver in the next car said, laughing.

Dani saw that they were coming up to a light. If they were forced to stop, they could be dragged from the car, kidnapped, raped, maybe even killed. Images of her abduction two years ago cut across the landscape of her consciousness like shooting stars. This was not a game. This was not *fun*.

"Hey," Madison called leaning over Dani and shouting across to them, "is it true what I hear about black men?"

"Why don't you stop the car and find out, baby?" the man shouted.

Madison winked and said, "You mean you're gonna whip it out and show me how *small* it is right here on the street?"

The man's expression changed suddenly, as if a door had been slammed shut and a well-lit room had been thrown into darkness. Laughter sounded from the other men in the car.

" 'Course the rest of you boys probably can't even get it up, isn't that right?" Madison called.

"Get it out, get it out and give it to me!" the driver shouted. A flurry of activity consumed the passengers as they scrambled to hand an automatic weapon to the driver.

Dani watched the scene unfold in horror, her heart thundering. She shrunk into her seat and fear coursed through her.

Her voice was tense with panic as she cried, "Madison, what the hell are you doing, get us out of here!"

"I don't *think* so," Madison said in a singsong voice.

Dani saw that they were on top of the light, it was changing to red, and she knew that she was going to die.

Madison did not slow. She bolted through the intersection. Car horns blared. In the lane to their right, the orange car kept pace. Dani looked over. The muzzle of the gun was pointed at them.

She was going to die because of her friend's stupidity. In that moment, she hated Madison and she hated the driver of the car. She was consumed by a rage that was so palpable she felt as if she could reach out with it and use it against the driver like a weapon.

"Hey, bitches, we got somethin' for you!" The man's

finger was closing over the trigger when his expression changed. He appeared perplexed. The gun lowered slightly. His expression changed again, this time to an instantly recognizable emotion: Fear.

Dani was consumed by it. The sounds of the road, the shouts of the other gang members — all of those noises fell away. Silence closed over her, silence that was broken only by the harsh, ragged gasps of the driver. She tasted the powerful, shuddering current of fear that flowed between them and found it delicious. For a moment she was drunk on it.

Shoot yourself, you bastard, she thought. *Or do you still think you can shoot me, you fuck? Put the gun to your head and shoot yourself. Do it, go on!*

He angled the weapon until it nudged the underside of his jaw. When Dani saw this, she snapped out of her trancelike state and shuddered. The bond between them — if such a thing had actually existed — suddenly fell away and the sounds of the road came crashing back.

"Do her man, do her, whatchu waitin' for?" a voice called out from the backseat of the orange car.

"Bitch got devil eyes. Shoot that fucking bitch. Put one in each of those fucking devil eyes!"

Dani realized that the gold flecks in her eyes must have been shining like torches in the sunlight. Maybe that's what the driver had seen, maybe that's what had caused him to spare her life. The driver shook, his terror still evident, and forced himself to raise the gun. Before he could fire, he became aware of the traffic ahead of him, which had come to a dead stop.

"Shit!" he cried as he turned his attention to the road, slamming on the brakes.

Madison cut the wheel sharply to the left and made a squealing U-turn around the divider in the road. The screams of burning tires and the shouts of outrage from the youths in the orange car fell away as Madison let out a howl and floored the sports car, speeding away in the other direction. Despite her seat belt Dani was thrown around; but when she looked back, she was able to see the traffic close around the orange car like an angry fist.

Dani was silent as Madison turned off Santa Monica and followed a maze of streets until they were far away from the intersection where they had left the gang members. They pulled into the parking lot of an exclusive restaurant and Madison winked at the handsome young valet who opened the door for her and handed her a claim ticket.

"Nice tush, huh?" Madison said as she took Dani's arm and led her inside. Dani's legs felt unsteady.

Once they were inside and seated, Dani recovered enough to speak. "Promise me that you will never do anything so stupid ever again!"

"Not unless you want me to," Madison said.

Dani shuddered. She knew that she should have been angry with Madison — furious, in fact. What she had done was reckless and stupid. They both could have died.

But she was not angry. In truth, she shared the other girl's exhilaration. Something had happened when the driver of the orange car had aimed his gun at Dani. Whatever it had been, Dani had found it incredibly exciting.

"So, let's order," Madison said. "I just love this place. Here, let me show you what's good. . . ."

As they ate, Dani found Madison's earlier response echoing in her mind: *Not unless you want me to.*

Why in the hell would she say such a thing, Dani wondered. No sane person would ever want to experience an incident like that again. Or would they?

After lunch, they cruised the city. Dani had been worried about running into the driver of the orange car, so Madison took them back to Rodeo Drive. The rest of the afternoon was devoted to shopping. Madison spent close to three thousand dollars by the end of the day. She even convinced Dani to take one pair of a matching set of highly expensive sunglasses as an apology gift for the incident on Santa Monica.

Dani decided that she would let what happened remain in the past. Madison was wild, reckless, and very passionate. The exact way that Dani secretly wanted to be. She wasn't going to give up their friendship over something that was over and done with, something that would never happen again.

Not unless you want it to.

They stopped off at Dani's house around six. Her mother was not home. They packed the clothes into Dani's closet and Dani recorded a new outgoing message for her mother, pressing the answering machine's memo button when she was finished.

The drive to Malibu was uneventful, and Dani found herself thinking about Bill Yoshino. He had been in her thoughts all day, but she hadn't brought him up.

At the beach house, Madison checked her answering machine, then fixed ice tea and insisted that they go outside to watch the sunset.

Wearing their matching sunglasses, they sat on the beach, staring up at the bloodred sky as the burning, orange ball of the sun descended on the horizon.

"I'm sorry I scared you today," Madison said. "I dunno. It seems like every time things are going really well for me I do something stupid to fuck it up. Are you mad at me?"

Dani thought about the gun that had been aimed at her head. "Well, I was pretty pissed. That *was* a goddamned stupid thing to do. I just sat there thinking, 'how fucking stupid is this person and why the hell did I get in the car with her?' "

Madison frowned. "Don't hold back, girlfriend. Tell me how you really feel."

"Well, I was scared."

"I'm sorry. Forgive me?"

"Yeah, sure. I guess. But no more of that shit, all right?"

Madison shrugged. "What can I do to make it up to

94

you?"

Dani ran her hand over her neck. "Well . . ."

"You want me to tell you about Bill?"

Looking away in embarrassment, Dani wondered if she had been that obvious or if Madison was unusually perceptive. She decided it was probably a little of both.

"Come on," Madison prompted, "you haven't said a word about him all day, and I've been noticing those glassy stares you've been giving everything today, especially when we were in the jewelry shops. I know what's going on."

You know more than I do, Dani was about to say, but she decided not to b.s. Madison. The girl would see right through her embarrassed, schoolgirl lies.

"He and I used to be together," Madison said.

Dani looked at her sharply.

"Used to be. We broke up over a year ago."

"Oh," Dani said, suddenly not quite sure of what she was supposed to feel, let alone what she was supposed to say. She wondered if Madison was going to warn her off. It was possible that she wanted to get back with Bill.

"Really, we're just friends," Madison said forcefully.

"Uh-huh."

"Well, I suppose I should tell you everything. I'm getting an idea of how your suspicious mind works."

Dani lowered her head like a dog who had just been reprimanded.

"Cut that out," Madison said, reaching over and lightly slapping Dani on the arm.

"I didn't do anything."

"Yes, you did. You were Dani-bashing, I could see it. That is not allowed."

Dani opened her hands in uncertainty. "I don't know —"

"I'm going to be totally honest with you. Bill thought a lot of you. He'd like to see you again. You're all he talked about last night."

Dani sat at attention. "Are you serious?"

"Am I serious?" Madison shook her head. "Why do you think you don't deserve things? You're bright, you're beautiful, and I think that you can be a really good friend."

"I'm not that good looking," Dani said.

"You're a natural beauty. That's rare out here."

"What are you talking about?"

Madison rolled her eyes. "What you have is real. That's more than I can say."

Dani tried not to look at the other woman's breasts, but her gaze drifted in that direction anyway.

"It's all right, you can look," Madison said as she raised her T-shirt again. "See the tiny scars on the underside? Surefire giveaway. You watch enough pornos and you can learn to spot these a mile off."

Madison lowered the T-shirt and pointed at her nose. "This, too. And the mouth, cheekbones, teeth capped, you name it."

Dani shuddered. The reference to the porn industry had brought back thoughts of Madison's seemingly inexhaustible supply of money. Is that how she made her living? On her back, with a dozen sweaty, horny technicians watching her make love to strangers?

Dani felt ashamed at her suspicions, and uncomfortable with the heat that had risen in her as she had imagined Madison performing sexual acts for the camera.

I didn't have anything and some people helped me.

Dani shuddered, putting the thoughts out of her mind. "How old are you?"

"Nineteen. It's no big deal. Lots of girls get jobs done on them when they're still in high school. They're worried that they're going to start sagging and shit. Me, I just wanted to get laid. I wanted to get noticed."

"I don't think you've got any problem in that department," Dani said. She immediately wished that she had kept her mouth shut. Why was she acting like this? She usually didn't use swear words, but today she had issued a steady stream of them. And she was taking shots at Madison, who was revealing herself to be a very insecure, very needy person.

"Okay," Madison said.

"I'm sorry. I don't know what's gotten into me."

"I know what you'd *like* to get into you. Or should I say *who?*"

"Madison!" Dani said in genuine embarrassment.

"Let me tell you the rest. Bill and I were an item for a while, but we knew that it wasn't going to last. So we started seeing other people, but we stayed friends. We're still real close, but I know that I'm not what he's looking for."

"You wanted to check me out," Dani said.

"Yeah. See, he got hurt really bad about six months ago. He really trusted this girl and she just used him. I don't like to see someone I care about get hurt like that. I wanted to make sure you and Tory weren't anything alike."

"So what'd you decide?"

Madison smiled. "Well, sweetheart, I decided that I'm going to call Bill and see if he can join us for dinner. How does that sound?"

"Sounds wonderful," Dani said, disbelievingly.

"Then it's a date. But I want to see this first."

They sat together, watching the magnificent sunset. Madison removed her sunglasses and stared directly into the face of the sun, an odd expression on her face. To Dani, it seemed as if she was watching the fleeting sunlight, as if she were saying goodbye to a lover. A sense of mourning surrounded Madison, oddly coupled with a breathless excitement about what might come next.

Dani studied her carefully, and a bizarre thought occurred to her: Madison was staring at the sunset as if she was taking photographs with her eyes.

Eight

Sam had arrived at work purposefully late that morning, hoping to avoid a direct confrontation with Pete Martell. As it turned out, she had no reason for concern. She blew in at nine-thirty and found that Martell had been called downtown to Halpern's office. Rosalind gave her this information with no small amount of glee.

A half hour before lunch, Rosalind reported that Martell's secretary received a call from him, canceling all of his appointments for the day. Rosalind and a half-dozen other workers from the office insisted on taking Sam to lunch. Though she was still very shaken from the events of the previous day, she knew that it would be career suicide to refuse.

She had spent most of the day huddled in her office, reviewing outstanding files. Her horrible first day on the job had begun to seem like a distant nightmare. She had tried not to think of the events at Smith's house or at her own, and there had been no unpleasant reminders. She buried herself in the work, had a wonderful lunch, made some new friends, and filled out the rest of the day culling the files for incongruities, trying to find leads that might help her cut through some of her department's caseload.

She knew that this wonderful peace she was experiencing was only temporary. It was possible that

Halpern would fire Martell on the basis of the tape Rosalind had delivered; however, the man's skills could not be argued and it was just as likely that Halpern might keep him around so that he could see the man squirm for a time. Sam had not wanted to think about Martell and so she had put him out of her mind and continued on with the work.

Feeling guilty about coming in late, even though she was a salaried employee, Sam stayed an extra half hour and left her office at five-thirty. The building's parking garage was an adjacent structure, five levels high. Sam had been given a reserved spot on the first level.

She approached the GT-S, admiring the way its lines gleamed in the fluorescents, and found herself missing the Ghia. At least in the Ghia she didn't feel like a pretender. And she didn't feel that all this could be taken away from her at a moment's notice—which *was* the honest to God truth.

Sam had retrieved her keys and was about to deactivate the personal alarm on the GT-S when she heard the telltale echo of footfalls from somewhere close. She spun, digging her hand back into the purse. Nothing there. Again, she had forgotten her gun was gone.

She looked up and for a moment her mind refused to register the identity of the shape approaching her. The form seemed to be draped in shadows that quickly parted to reveal Dani, her beautiful, golden-eyed daughter.

"Honey, what are you doing here?" Sam asked.

"Oh, a friend of mine dropped me off. I wanted to see the new office."

"You should have called. You almost missed me." Sam dropped her keys back into her purse and suddenly realized that this was wrong, very wrong, though she had no idea why. Then it came to her: The clothing that Dani was wearing; she had never seen the girl in these clothes. "What's that you've got on?"

"I went shopping," Dani replied, nonplussed.

How much is this going to cost me, Sam thought.

Then she reminded herself that it didn't matter, she actually could afford it.

"Well, that's nice," Sam said lovingly. "You found some things you like."

"Um-hmm."

"Good." God, this new life was going to take some getting used to. "We can go to the office if you want to, but everyone's gone."

"That's all right. I just want to see all your new toys."

Sam shrugged and led her daughter to the elevators. "There's a covered walkway from the fifth floor to the main building, another security checkpoint there. This place is great. You don't have to worry about anything."

"Glad to hear it," Dani said flatly.

"You know, we have this guy, Alex Wren. None of us are supposed to admit to this, but he's got the codes to hack into every local and federal data base there is. Half the secretaries hit on him so that he'll pull up the guys they're dating on the Social Security d-base and find out what they're making."

"That *is* great," Dani said.

Sam sighed. Why in the hell was she feeling so awkward with Dani, she wondered. She was being paranoid, she knew, but something was wrong with the way Dani was reacting. Her responses seemed programmed. A scene from *The Terminator* flashed through Sam's mind of Arnold's landlord banging at the door and a data list appearing before his eyes. The half-human half-mechanical assassin had to choose from the list of all possible responses to the landlord, including, "fuck you, asshole."

They reached the elevators and Sam absently noticed the bank of security monitors above the elevator doors. There was a camera mounted nearby. The television screens changed views every few seconds. As they waited for the doors to open, Sam saw the middle screen display the view from the camera pointed directly at her and Dani.

On the monitor, the girl standing beside Sam was not her daughter. Sam looked at Dani sharply, and saw the golden-eyed girl she had raised. Then she cut a glance back to the monitor and saw a thin young woman wearing torn jeans and a halter top. The girl on the television had straggly hair and a small, pointed face twisted in a feral expression.

Jesus Christ, Sam thought. It's not Dani.

The taunting voice of her mother suddenly appeared in Sam's mind, a searing, unwelcome presence. *What's that you say? Not Dani? Of course, it's Dani. Who else would it be?* A cruel, terrible laugh erupted. *Face it kiddo, you're losing your mind, same way I did.*

That's not what's happening, Sam protested in the confines of her thoughts.

Then why don't you look at her? the voice of Sam's mother coaxed.

Stop it! Sam shrieked. I'm not like you! I've never been like you! Get out of my head, Mommy. I don't want to see you like this! This isn't you! Stop it!

The voice retreated, leaving the brief echo of mad laughter before it faded into oblivion.

Look at her, the voice had urged. But Sam did not *have* to look at the girl beside her to know what she would see. It would be Dani. What her all too human eyes saw and what the cold lens of the camera took in were two very different things. Staring at the monitors, Sam looked into a face that seemed to be hatred incarnate.

It's not Dani. I can see that much. So what the hell *is* it? Have I been hypnotized? Is that it? This thing next to me's some kind of psychotic Uri Geller? But as powerful as its mind control is, it can't fool the cameras.

A fairy tale Sam had read when she had been a child came to her. It told of a demonic creature that stole the identities of others and committed mischief and murder in their names. It was called a *doppelganger.* That seemed as good a name as any for this creature. Whatever she did, she could not allow herself to think of it as Dani. She didn't even want to think of it as human, considering the conclusion she had suddenly reached.

It's you or me, she thought as she stared at the twisted, murderous face on the monitors, isn't it?

She looked away quickly, praying that the doppelganger would not notice the television screen. Absently, she reached into her purse and drew out her keys.

"So how was your day?"

"Pretty uneventful," Sam replied truthfully as she watched the rapidly descending numbers. The elevator was on the third floor, coming down. Sam understood that whatever this thing was beside her, she had encountered it twice before. Impossible as it was to believe, the girl was not her daughter any more than it had been Mark Smith or Carlotta Evans. It could influence the manner in which it was perceived.

Later, Sam decided, should she survive, she would have a very deep argument with the logical part of her mind that was sleeping on the job, allowing her to believe such a fanciful concept as the doppelganger, but for now, she had to concentrate on overcoming it. She would only have one chance to take it by surprise.

The elevator had moved to the second floor and stopped. Someone was getting on. Shit.

Sam had no doubt that this time the doppelganger was going to kill her. It had committed the murder of Smith and his companions. She had taken it by surprise. The creature had not wanted to attack a victim who was armed. It had come to the house last night posing as Carlotta, hoping to find out what Sam had told the police. It was evidently weighing the necessity of killing her when Dani came home. For some reason it had not wished to kill her then. It might not have been very strong, it may have depended on the element of surprise. In any case, it had changed its mind and decided to kill Sam tonight. It would lure her to the deserted offices, overcome her, perhaps make her

102

death look like a suicide.

To do that, it would need a gun. Shit, she thought, the fucking thing was armed.

There were two other problems that Sam had to consider as the elevator touched down on the first floor, the light blinking on: First, whatever it was, it had chosen to look exactly like Dani. Second, if she was wrong and what she had seen in the television monitor was a delusion, she was about to attack her own daughter.

She heard the elevator settle and glanced up at the monitor once again. The wild-haired creature was grinning broadly. Sam knew there was no more time for thought. She had to act now.

Dani turned to her and Sam grabbed her by the arm and slammed her, face forward, into the elevator doors. The girl's head collided with the reinforced metal and she shuddered like a professional wrestler who had just been thrown into the corner block. The doppelganger released her grip on the small handbag she had been carrying and it fell to the ground. The doors hissed open and Sam saw that it was empty after all. Whoever had called the elevator had evidently gotten tired of waiting and instead took the stairs.

Thank God for the little things, she thought as she hurled the doppelganger into the elevator, then followed her inside. The creature that had been posing as Dani had not yet recovered from Sam's attack, and she struck the far wall of the elevator with a resounding thud. Sam knelt down, hoping to retrieve the gun from the creature's handbag before it could regain its senses. Working the snap, she saw that she had been correct in her assumption that the doppelganger had been carrying a weapon. Suddenly, an inhuman scream forced Sam to tear her attention from the bag and look up at her daughter's hate-filled face as it lunged at her.

Sam knew that she could not allow the doppelganger to escape. If it got past her, it would be able to approach her another time, wearing yet another guise. She would not be able to trust anyone. Cursing, she dropped the handbag and threw herself forward, tackling the creature and driving it back as the doors of the elevator hissed shut behind her.

The bag had fallen on the outside of the elevator. The gun was out of their reach. Sam felt the uncomfortable sensation of the elevator releasing its hold on the first floor and jerking slightly as it prepared to rise. She had fallen onto the creature and was attempting to hold it down when the doppelganger pounded its fist into her face. The blow was a tight, powerful snap of otherworldly strength. Sam was rocked back far enough for the doppelganger to shove her away. The creature scrambled to her feet in the confined space and nearly lost her balance as the elevator lurched and started to rise.

Lying on the floor of the elevator, Sam lashed out with a kick to the back of the doppelganger's knee, collapsing the creature's leg and causing it to fall. The look of surprise and betrayal in the eyes of her "daughter" as she collapsed was almost too much for Sam. She had to end this quickly.

The elevator was on the rise. As the doppelganger fell back a second time, Sam realized dully that she had not given up hold of her own key ring, two of her fingers pushed through and curled around the wide, silver ring. Closing her hand over the keys, Sam made a fist and allowed several of the keys to poke out from the slight cracks between her fingers. The doppelganger was on its side, starting to rise. Sam once again looked into the face of her daughter. She thought of the scars and punctures the keys would leave upon the creature's face. She could not picture her daughter's face cut and bleeding.

What if it's Dani? What if I'm crazy? I'll hurt my baby!

Sam hesitated, and the doppelganger attacked. It flung itself at her, catching her hand containing the key ring by the wrist and driving it back, against the far wall. An explosion of pain registered in Sam's hand as

104

it struck the wall, but she refused to give up her grip on the key ring. Sam was on her back, the doppelganger straddling her. The creature took hold of Sam's other wrist, yanking it forward. Then she pinned Sam's arm with her knee and reached up for the call box below the elevator's small bank of floor buttons. She ripped the door open and yanked out the bloodred phone. The line snapped, leaving the receiver and three feet of cord dangling from the creature's hand. The doppelganger looked at this and seemed to be debating how to use the weapon. She had the option of strangling Sam with the line or bludgeoning her with the phone.

The doppelganger smiled and sank her teeth into the line just below the receiver, shredding it with a feral turn of her head. She hefted the receiver in her hand and whispered, "Stupid bitch, I could have made this easy for you. It was supposed to look like suicide. But right now I don't give a fuck, you pissed me off."

It was Dani's voice, Sam thought, God help me, it's still using Dani's voice.

The creature grinned, seemingly well aware of the mental agony it was inflicting on Sam. Its eyelids fluttered in near-sexual transcendence, then it shuddered and concentrated on the task at hand. It raised the receiver over its head and prepared to bring it down with enough force to shatter Sam's skull.

I'm not going to die here, Sam thought. My little girl needs me, she still needs me, and I'm not going to die like this. Goddamn you, I'm going to kick your fucking ass, you bitch!

As if sensing her thoughts, the creature bristled, her expression changing to one of uncertainty. The bright, golden fear of her victim was gone, replaced with a powerful hatred.

The elevator lurched to a stop, the sudden shock of displacement intensified for the two women due to their positions on the elevator's floor. Sam felt a terrible wave of sickness wash through her, but she fought to hold on.

"Shit!" the creature howled as it reached up for the "emergency stop" button.

Sam knew that the creature needed to seal them off from curious eyes. The doppelganger had to strain in her effort to reach the button. Her knee eased from Sam's left hand for an instant as she hit the button. Sam yanked her hand loose, threw her keys from her right hand, which was still pinned by the doppelganger, to her left. She caught the keys and jammed them upward, into the creature's face, tearing open a gash in the creature's cheek. A puff of blood burst from her flesh and the doppelganger floundered for an instant, her hand once again brushing the "elevator stop" button, this time releasing it. She brought her hands to her face and cried out in shock. The moment was long enough for Sam to shift her weight and throw the doppelganger from her.

The elevator doors hissed open and Sam hoped that whoever had called the elevator would rush in to help her.

Once again, there was no one there. Sam was on her own. She briefly considered running from the elevator, but then she would have been the prey once more. It had to end here.

Punching the button for the first floor, she realized that the doppelganger was on her feet, swinging the phone at her. The receiver connected with the side of Sam's head as the elevator doors hissed shut. A searing flash of pain erupted in her skull and the impact drove her into the corner. This time, the creature did not relent. She brought the receiver down a second and third time on the back of Sam's head, the hairline cracks that had been wrought in its plastic surface from the previous blows widening.

Sam was driven to her knees, facing the corner. She looked as if she were about to give confession. The image was not lost on the doppelganger. "You'd better confess your sins, bitch, 'cause you're going straight to Hell!"

The receiver came crashing down a final time, but it did not connect with Sam. The investigator ducked and the receiver smashed against the wall, where it flew into pieces. Sam slipped past the doppelganger, the bright red cord from the telephone in her hands. As the creature turned, Sam slipped the plastic cord around its neck and drove her knee into the creature's back as she yanked with all her strength.

Sam was vaguely aware of the elevator's descent. They had risen to the fourth floor and were dropping rapidly to the first. The doppelganger struggled, attempting to tear at Sam's hands, but the woman held on tight. Sam hoped that she could render the creature unconscious and knew that she could crush the doppelganger's windpipe or choke her to death just as easily. She would have preferred a choke hold, but that technique was just as deadly and uncertain.

The doppelganger planted one leg on the door of the elevator and kicked hard, driving Sam back against the wall. The metal hand rail slammed into the small of Sam's back and her head snapped back, into the wall. The impact raised the same pain as the doppelganger's earlier blows and Sam felt nauseous and dizzy. She held on, anyway.

The doppelganger drove one of her elbows back into Sam's ribs and the woman's grip lessened. Suddenly the elevator lurched to a stop and the doors hissed open. The doppelganger wrenched herself free and stumbled out of the elevator, clutching at her throat as she gasped for breath.

Sam saw the creature go directly past the spot where its handbag had fallen. She dove for the bag, snatching it as the creature turned. This time her hand made it into the bag and she brought the weapon up, leveling it at the creature's chest. She could not bear the thought of aiming a gun at her daughter's stolen face.

"Freeze, Goddamn you!" Sam shouted.

The creature did not move. Its golden eyes, so much like Dani's, sparkled in the dim light of the parking garage. Her expression softened and she raised her hands to her mouth in the same little girl gesture that had always preceded a crying fit when Dani had been a little girl. Tears ran down her face as she shook her head and cried, "Mommy, don't, please, why are you doing this to me, don't hurt me!"

"Shut up," Sam growled. The elevator doors hissed shut behind her. Sam wondered why the security officer watching the monitors hadn't sent for help. Then she considered the possibility that the doppelganger had already gotten to the watchman. She wouldn't have killed him, she would have altered his perceptions.

Sweat poured into Sam's eyes. The doppelganger was continuing its litany: "Oh god, Mommy, I'm sorry, I didn't do anything, why are you so mad at me? Don't hurt me!"

"Shut up," Sam cried, "you're not my daughter!"

The wounded expression that Sam had always dreaded spread across Dani's face. "But you said I'd always be your little girl. You said it didn't matter that you found me."

Fuck, it's playing with me, it's just playing with me, it's not real.

Then why did its words hurt so goddamn much?

Because it knows your secrets. It knows what's in your head. It knows how to get at you. Where you're weak.

Where you're afraid.

Sam felt the sting of sweat in her eyes and her vision took on a reddish hue. Blood, she thought. Oh, Christ.

"I want you — I want you down on the ground, right now!"

"Mommy, please, don't!"

Stop it, stop it, shut up!

Dani's image was becoming dark, blurred. Sam

raised her hand and wiped the blood from her eyes. Her eyes were shut for a second, no more, but when she looked up again, the doppelganger was gone.

Sam kept the gun trained directly before her. The creature could not have escaped. There was nowhere for it to run. Sam turned constantly, checking her safety zone, certain that the doppelganger was still in the garage, that it might have been directly before her, and it had used its power to blot out her ability to see the creature. That seemed crazy, of course, but no crazier than any other task it was capable of performing.

The monitors, she thought. It can't fool the monitors.

She risked a glance to the bank of black and white televisions and saw nothing on their changing views. It was gone without a trace. Her fears from the previous night returned. She wondered if she was going insane, if she had hallucinated the entire incident.

Finally she saw footsteps and saw a couple approaching. Sam slid the gun in her handbag and turned away, slinking into the shadows. She had no idea what she looked like, but if she was bleeding, she was going to draw attention.

The woman was young, attractive, wearing a black leather outfit complete with a pair of boots that looked like a Paris import. The man wore a double-breasted blazer. Armani, from the look of it. The woman walked over the spot where the doppelganger had been standing and slipped. The man caught her. Neither looked down to see what the woman had slipped on. She was too embarrassed by her clumsiness, he was only too delighted to play the gentleman and rescue her.

Where were you people a few minutes ago, Sam thought. When the couple had left the garage, Sam examined the spot where the woman had almost fallen. The floor was slick with blood.

It hadn't been a hallucination. She wasn't going mad. The doppelganger was real. A terrible thought occurred to her as she walked to her car, checking it thoroughly — even the trunk — before she got in: If the doppelganger was after her, it might do what the trapper had done two years ago, and try to strike at her through Dani, or use Dani to draw her out.

She got in the vehicle, punched the button on the auto-dialer for her new home. The line rang four times, then she heard the answering machine pick up. The outgoing message had been rerecorded:

"Mom, hi, this is Dani. I'm going to be out tonight, Madison's taking me to dinner. If anything comes up, here's the number you can reach me at. Ready? It's 310-555-2329. Love you. Bye."

Sam punched the number and waited impatiently. The line rang for what seemed like an eternity before another machine picked up and she heard a beep. There had been no outgoing message. Sam began to speak, hoping that Dani's friend was screening her calls and would pick up. When she realized that no one was going to answer, Sam disconnected the line and re-entered the building. She scrubbed herself in the executive washroom, found that her cuts, though bloody, had been superficial, nothing but smoke and whisper unless she had a concussion, or was in shock. Right now, she didn't care.

She went into Alex Wren's computer, brought up the telephone company's data base, and fed it Madison's phone number. It was unlisted, and the address file refused to give her any further information unless she had the proper passwords. She dialed Alex's home number. There was no answer.

Cursing, Sam realized that she could not risk going home. The doppelganger wasn't finished with her yet, and it knew where she lived. She went through the yellow pages, chose a hotel at random, and made reservations under an assumed name. Then she went to an auto-teller, fed in one of her company credit cards, and drew three hundred dollars, the largest cash advance possible. She didn't want to leave a credit-card trail, cash was always safer.

Sam rejoined the congested lanes of rush-hour, downtown L.A. traffic. As she sat waiting in traffic, her frustration and fear mounting, she heard the doppelganger's words:

But you said I'd always be your little girl. You said it didn't matter that you found me.

Dani's voice. She trembled and fought back the tears.

Mommy, don't, please, why are you doing this to me, don't hurt me!

I wouldn't hurt you, baby, I could never hurt you. Never. I'd give up anything for you. I'd die for you.

As the traffic slowly edged forward, Samantha Walthers began to cry, because somehow, deep down, she knew that it might come to that, and she was not altogether certain that she was as brave as she would have liked to have thought.

Nine

It was still early when Madison and Dani left the Malibu house, and so Madison decided to give Dani "a taste of L.A. proper." They stopped at several of the more "touristy" attractions, such as Mann's Chinese Theater, where Dani and Madison compared their hands and feet to those of the stars. Then Madison talked Dani into going through the Fredrick's of Hollywood Lingerie Museum.

After being pelted by bustiers that could have put their eyes out, Dani retaliated by dragging Madison into the L. Ron Hubbard's Scientology "clubhouse," where a host of far-too-friendly staffers attempted to persuade them to sign up for a "reading." Several gullible, aimless types were already seated at stations in the adjacent room, being told what was wrong with their lives by strangers.

They escaped and ended up in a sex shop where the entire second floor was devoted to pretty pink neon signs and elegant glass cases containing custom-made whips, handcuffs, riding crops, and leather wear. A young, attractive couple stood before one of the cases. The man was blond, well groomed, and appeared to work out. The girl with him was a pretty blond cheerleader type with a broken leg who hobbled along enthusiastically on crutches. Dani had tried not to think of how she might have broken the leg.

Soon, they arrived at the Third Street Festival,

where the streets had been sealed off to traffic and performers clogged the asphalt. As they walked along, Dani saw acrobats, street musicians, and performance artists. They stopped at a few shops along the way, including one that was a veritable cornucopia of rare delights, such as an antique "three-D" viewing device, vintage pinball machines, and cartoon cels from *Fantasia* and other animated classics.

Finally, they came to the outdoor café where Bill had promised to meet them, and found him waiting. Dani looked into his glittering silver-blue eyes and decided that he was even more attractive than she had remembered.

"I hope we didn't keep you waiting," Madison said in a cheerful voice that had only a touch of sarcasm.

"Your timing's perfect," Bill said. "I just got here myself."

Madison winked at Dani then leaned over and said, "Consider yourself flattered. He's never on time, let alone early."

"Tonight's special," Bill said as he stared directly into Dani's eyes. "This means a lot to me."

"Me too," Dani whispered, raising her hand to her lips. She suddenly realized that it was trembling and she slid her hands into her lap, beneath the table.

"I'll get us some cappuccino. Does that work for everybody?" he asked.

"Sure." Dani shifted uncomfortably. Fine, she was a child. Fine, she was ignorant. But what exactly was in a "capa-chino"?

"I think I'd rather have a hot chocolate," Madison said.

"Yeah, me too," Dani added swiftly.

"No problem." Bill got up and took his bemused smile into the café.

"You're shaking," Madison said.

"It's a little cold."

"No it isn't." She looked back and watched Bill's rear as he took his place on line. "I'd say its pretty hot."

113

"Madison." Dani shook her head in embarrassment.

Bill returned with his cappuccino and the hot chocolates for the girls. They sat around, sipping their drinks, talking about nothing in particular, when the topic drifted to old movies, which Bill knew quite a lot about. Dani admitted that she used to rent an incredible amount of tapes, and stopped short of revealing that she had learned more about life from the movies than she had from experience.

"Yeah, I'll take Laurence Olivier in almost anything," Dani said.

"Heathcliff," Bill muttered in a Monty Pythonesque voice. "Heeeaath-clefff!" He sighed. "That's what's wrong with this city. There aren't any moors."

"What about *Rebecca?*" asked Dani.

"That's my favorite film."

"Come on."

"No, really. It was a shame about Dame Judith Anderson. Wasn't she *evil* in that picture?"

"Tell me about it," Dani said. "It was great."

"And Olivier. There's something about him all the way through that's not quite right but you keep hoping maybe he *isn't* some kind of psychotic."

"Exactly. Then when you find out what happened. God."

"Uh-huh. Well, I think as a race, we've always been fascinated with evil. I mean look at all the classic villains, right? They're only bad because they're operating on a value system that's different from what you and I think is acceptable. Or what society *tells* us is acceptable. But so long as they're consistent, so long as they remain true to their own version of right or wrong, we flock to them.

"Take *Silence of the Lambs* for example. Who's the most memorable character? Who do people talk about? Clarice Starling or Hannibal Lector?"

"Well," Dani said shyly, "yeah." It was obvious to Dani that Bill Yoshino was pretty bright. She tried not to feel self-conscious. Come on Dani, you can keep up with him.

"I think people really *want* to be bad, they're just afraid to let go and do what they want," continued Bill. "It takes a really good villain, a good symbol of evil, to allow us to live our fantasies. We don't do what we want to do. We don't take what we want when we see it, because society tells us that's wrong."

"I don't know if I agree with that," Dani said, deciding to rise to the challenge. "Don't you think society is right most of the time? I mean, you can't glorify what we're brought up to think of as evil."

"I'm not glorifying it."

"I mean, I'll admit, some of it's bullshit." Dani bit her lip, not believing that the word had left her mouth. Then she decided to go on. Bill was certainly not offended, and Madison barely seemed to be listening. "For instance, my mom was a cop all through when I was growing up. Her friends were all cops, they hung out. All I'd ever hear about was perps and code numbers for crimes. But a lot of times it didn't really seem to be about getting the bad guy, about doing the right thing, it was just, you know, get through the day and don't get shot. It was – I dunno – "

"They depersonalize it," Bill said. "It's like, if you're in a hostage situation and you get a sheet thrown over you, that's a really bad sign, because that means they're probably getting ready to kill you and they don't want to see you as a person anymore."

Dani blanched at the reference. She thought of the man who had taken her two years ago. If Bill thought there was something admirable in the behavior of psychopaths and killers, then he wasn't the person she thought he was. The thought that she had been deluding herself about him left her feeling cold. But then, how well did she really know him? Now that she thought about it, he had barely spoken the night before, and she didn't like what she was hearing from him tonight. And yet, she still felt incredibly drawn to him, incredibly excited by the conversation. Boys rarely allowed her to challenge them. Whether she agreed with Bill or not, spending time with this guy *was* exciting.

"Look, I've seen some really bad things up close," Dani said. "You're not going to change my mind."

"I'm not trying to," he said. "No, obviously, I think that certain things are wrong. I'm just saying that movies are heightened reality. We tend to admire the bad guys because they're being true to themselves, they're acting out their impulses, they're living their desires, and they're not worried about what might happen because of it. That's attractive to most people. Not the acts of violence, not the bad things, but just being free to do what you want. To be the one that's in control of the fear, not the one who's a slave to it."

Dani wondered why he was so passionate about this. Their time up to this point had been so laid-back.

As if reading her thoughts, Madison leaned forward and said, "Bill wants to be a big-time producer some day. He's got this script making the rounds that's kind of a modern day . . . What didya say it was like?"

"Faust," said Bill.

"Yeah, well, it's like sell your soul to the devil and shit."

"Have you read it?" Dani asked, excited. Bill smiled.

"Oh, yeah. It sucks. So what, though. That's never stopped a movie from getting made in this town. He's trying to get Michael Keaton or someone like that interested in it."

"Michael Douglas," Bill said, correcting her.

"Yeah, whoever."

"And thank you for the kind words."

"Don't mention it."

Dani smiled. Suddenly it all made sense. Of course these people were in "the business." Was there anybody out here who wasn't, or didn't want to be?

Bill frowned. "It's a double standard, in the movies. We want to see the bad guy get it in the end. We live vicariously through them, then we feel bad about the feelings that have been woken up inside of us. So when the villain gets killed, we feel purged. I don't know. Are you religious? I don't want to offend you."

"Pure pagan. Go ahead," Dani whispered, wondering which of his parents was Japanese, which American.

"It's like being a complete bastard six days a week, then going into a confessional on Sundays and feeling that you're forgiven, everything's okay and you can keep on treating people like shit because you've been given *executive clemency*. That's just wrong, as far as I'm concerned. I think people should be true to who and what they are."

"You don't like hypocrites," she said, sensing the underlying meaning of his words, understanding why he had been pounding this tack into the ground. He was nervous, too.

"No. Hypocrites drive me crazy."

"So if you wanted something, you would just go for it."

"Pretty much."

They stared at each other. The desire that passed between them hung heavily in the air.

"Provided the time was right," he added. "Provided the other person was ready."

Dani was stunned to feel her tongue graze the inside of her upper lip. Her entire body was tingling. She pressed her legs together and crossed her arms over her breasts, hugging herself tightly. Though it had not been phrased as such, he had just asked her a question, one that she had no answer for.

Madison, all but forgotten, sighed, fanned herself, and stood up. "Look guys, you left me in the dust about ten minutes ago."

Dani's heart sank. "I'm sorry," she said with genuine concern. Bill did not seem worried, however, and that calmed her.

"No, no, no." Madison leaned down and hugged Dani. She leaned close and whispered, "I'm going to

117

be out *all* night. Use the house as if it were yours, okay?"

"You mean that?" Dani asked hesitantly.

"Change the sheets."

"God!" Dani said, slapping the girl's arm. Madison waved to Bill, then quickly lost herself in the crowd.

"So what do you want to do tonight?" Bill asked. "What do you want to see?"

She thought of several responses, some sarcastic, others provocative. Then she decided to simply tell the truth: "You. All of you."

He pursed his lips, thinking about it. Suddenly, she felt like an idiot. Before she could tense up completely, he reached over and took her hand. An electrical charge seemed to flow between them.

"Are you sure you want to do this? Sex can be very addictive."

Dani straightened up and smiled. "You must think a lot of yourself."

Grinning, he said, "Let's go."

On the drive to the beach house, Dani was so nervous that she barely said a word to Bill. Occasionally he looked over at her, his serious expression fading to be replaced by a confident smile. At one stoplight he saw that she was shaking. Leaning over he made a "talking too much" gesture with his hand, his thumb flapping against his rigidly set fingers.

"Chee-burger!"

She smiled, despite herself. The reference was to the Cronenberg movie, *The Fly*, which they had both seen and admired, despite how disgusting it had been in the end. She had told him earlier how much that line had cracked her up.

"You're a jerk," she said. But she was smiling.

When they arrived at the beach house, Dani wondered briefly why they didn't go to Bill's place, but then her nervousness and her excitement flared once

118

again and she decided that it didn't matter. He opened the door of his classic black Mustang for her and took her hand as they went up the marble walkway, passing the bronze lions.

She shuddered as he punched a code into the key pad beside the door. With a click the lock disengaged. Dani's hand grazed one of the lions and she said, "I heard gargoyles are making a comeback. I read that in a magazine. I bet we'll start seeing them all over the place. They're supposed to frighten away evil spirits and terrify people into keeping on the straight and narrow."

Christ, she was babbling and she couldn't stop. "You know, I took this course once, and my teacher said —"

Bill turned suddenly, moving faster than she would have believed possible. He gathered her into his arms and pressed his lips against hers. All rational thought fled from her as they shared their first kiss. He tasted sweet and she did not resist the light flickering of his tongue. His lips were powerful, but he was not as aggressive as he could have been. As they kissed, he overwhelmed her with his restraint. With each kiss, with each touch, came the promise of so much more.

Always leave them wanting more, isn't that what they said in the industry? God, he knew exactly what he was doing, she thought. She felt a burst of sensations, a rush of pleasure so rich and pure that it was almost not to be believed. For an embarrassing moment she thought that she was going to have an orgasm. Her nipples were hard and erect, straining against her bra and blouse. She couldn't believe what she was experiencing. She laughed with delight as he scooped her up and carried her into the house. They stopped only to kick the door closed behind them.

She rested her head against her chest, amazed that she was allowing this guy to take total control of her. All her life she had done the right thing, she had been a good girl. No one had taken advantage of her; a part

119

of her knew that for reasons she would not admit to herself, no one could.

"Face it, honey. You're smarter than the average bear," her mother had told her when she was little. "You're special, Dani. You're not like anyone else and you know what? You don't have to be."

No, Mom, I don't have to be, but I want to be. God, how I want that.

Down deep inside she felt that Bill was like her, in whatever ways that meant. He was special, too. She could feel it. They belonged together.

They passed through the photo album room and found the staircase. Dani reveled in the comfort of Bill's arms as he effortlessly carried her up the stairs. Dani had changed into a tight fitting blouse and a short skirt, and she could feel his hands through the thin fabric. They came to the guest bedroom at the top of the stairs. The door was open, the lights off. Soft, blue-white moonlight filtered in through the open window. The leaves of a tree from outside created ragged patterns of light that shifted with the movements of the branches in the slight breeze. On a table beside the bed Dani noticed the mirrored sunglasses that she had used to cover her strange eyes — to hide behind. Dully, she realized that neither she nor Madison had remembered to collect them earlier. They sat alone, the moonlight glinting off the reflective lenses, and they looked to Dani like the skeletal remains of what was rapidly becoming her former life.

Bill laid her down on the bed, and Dani struggled to brush away all cautious thoughts — thoughts that reminded her she had met these people only yesterday. But then Bill began to kiss and touch her and the burning hot sensations returned overwhelming all rational thought. Dani barely restrained herself from writhing.

God, I'm such a slut, she thought. I'm really doing this.

She saw his smile and suddenly felt reassured. *He* didn't see her in those terms. She was certain of that.

120

Why should she feel that she was doing something wrong?

Bill withdrew, keeping one knee on the bed. He stripped off his jacket and dropped it to the floor. Dani felt her apprehension return and she awkwardly placed her hands on her stomach, one on top of the other. He smiled and she marveled at the beautiful patterns of light that were being cast upon him. She reached over and touched his leg.

His smile broadened. It seemed to say, I know you're afraid, but there's nothing to be afraid of.

Her fear turned to excitement once more as he stripped off his shirt and she saw his lean, heavily muscled chest. It seemed to have been waxed smooth. His body was perfect. Grinning, he kicked off his shoes, then leaned down and gently slid her shoes off, as well.

She wanted to touch his perfect chest, to breathe in his scent. When she realized that she could, she nearly passed out from excitement. He reached down and kissed her, and her hands caressed his chest, tracing the lines of his hard, perfect muscles.

In her thoughts, she was skimming over a beautiful lake of calm waters. Anything I want, she thought. I can do anything I want, I can *have* anything I want.

She wanted everything and she wanted it right away.

"Can I lie next to you?" he asked in his amazingly resonant and sensual voice. She nodded. He eased down beside her and urged her to turn away slightly. She moved so that she was lying on her side. He pressed himself against her back, wrapping one arm around her waist as he brushed the hair from her neck with his free hand and leaned in to blow on her neck. She gasped and he plunged his tongue in her ear.

Her fears continued to evaporate, washed away by her lust for this man she barely knew. Where had these overwhelming feelings come from, she wondered. It was as if a dark veil had fallen upon her, shadowing her reason. She felt a strange, amorphous presence in her

121

mind, releasing her desire. The experience was exciting, liberating. Then her thoughts fled as his hips gently rotated against her ass and she felt him through his pants, hard and straining. Suddenly she felt like an animal who wanted to be fucked, nothing more.

"May I touch you?" he asked.

"Hurry," she cried. *"Hurry."*

But he did not hurry. The movement of his fingers as they stole across her body was unmercifully slow. His caresses were gentle at first, teasing. He moved with a seamless elegance that aroused her even further. She couldn't wait to get undressed and feel the friction of their bare skin. Dani strained against him, kissing his mouth greedily as he caressed her legs, pushing her skirt up only an inch or so with his languid motions.

His hand finally closed over her breast, touching her so lightly she wanted to scream. His fingers moved in concentric circles, each smaller then the last, until finally he squeezed her nipple. Bill's touch was so gentle that she had to whisper, "It's alright. Harder is okay. A little bit."

He kissed her and complied. She loved the feeling of power, of being in control, and yet also experiencing a degree of surrender.

Reaching down, she hurriedly unbuttoned her blouse. Then she tugged at the snap at the front of her bra—she had never worn a bra like this, but Madison had several. She sat up and shrugged off her blouse and bra, enjoying the slight sway of her heavy, but perfectly shaped breasts, then settled back on the bed. Bill lowered his face to her bare breasts, kissing and biting them as his hand moved between her legs. She gasped, then settled back as he expertly manipulated her.

Her hand went to the front of his pants and she began to caress him. In seconds their movements were in perfect synch. He knew precisely where to touch her, his hands moving over her body, soothing and caressing her, his lips delivering kisses that made her moan and cry for him. He slipped her skirt off, then her panties. When he finally covered her sex with his mouth, she quivered and told him what she wanted, how she needed to be touched. The sensations soon became unbearable. She took his head in both of her hands and held his face tightly to her as an orgasm ripped through her. Her mind went blank and she surrendered to the pleasure. He eased off as she rode the wave, delighting in her shudders and ragged, passionate gasps. He stood for a moment and removed his trousers as she caught her breath.

Dani watched him as he finished undressing. He stood before the bed, his sex jutting straight out from his body.

It's so damn big, she thought. This is not going to be possible, sorry, no thanks.

He grinned, seeming to sense her thoughts. "That's what you do to me."

Her brow furrowed and she bit her lip. It was her decision. Hers entirely. She leaned forward, kissing his lips, then his nipples, and took him in both her hands. Years of unfulfilled curiosity overcame her. She had never touched a man like this, and was surprised at how silky and smooth he was. Her heart thundered and she took pleasure in the moan her touch elicited from him.

She had read about doing things like this in those *terrible* books her tormentors used to tease her with in school. Though she had pictured herself in scenes like this a thousand times, the reality was far different from the fantasy, grittier, but more exciting.

My God, what is this, what *am* I that I could do this, she thought. Then she felt the familiar haze fall over her consciousness. The haunting, fiery sexual demon that had been released inside her brain spoke to her:

This is who you are. This is what you are. You love it, don't you?

Yes, she thought, so very much. God help me, I do.

Dani did not resist as he forced her back on the bed roughly. She spread her legs and hooked them over his

123

shoulders as he anchored his strong arms on either side of her ribs. She gripped his upper arms hard enough to leave bruises.

This is it, she thought. This is the moment. She winced as she felt him brush against the lips of her sex. And this is going to hurt like hell.

But there was something else, something more important that she was forgetting, that the presence in her mind was making her forget. And there *was* another entity inside her, something alien and unknowable. It burned away her fears and doubts, leaving only her desires. She felt him throb against her and forgot all else.

Smiling lovingly, he lowered his head and kissed her, then eased himself forward, into her. She felt an explosion of pleasure as he slowly moved inside her, pushing deeper. She was dimly aware of resistance, of something tearing within her, but she felt no pain. The shadowy, loving entity that was making love to her mind as Bill Yoshino made love to her body would not let her feel anything but ecstasy.

She knew this wasn't normal, she understood that losing one's virginity was supposed to be a painful, frightening process, but right now, none of that mattered. She had been planning this. She had been expecting this. She had *wanted* this.

Dani did not feel awkward. With his indulgence and encouragement, she felt like a seasoned performer in a sexual ballet. Grabbing her by the arms, he pulled her up, allowing her to take command of their union. She laughed with pleasure and excitement, teasing him, then went wild until she could take no more. She toppled from him, lying flat on the bed, only dimly aware that he was not done with her yet.

Dani felt his hands scoop her up and did not resist as he placed her in a kneeling position and took her from behind. Suddenly, he exploded, triggering a bizarre, fugue state in her mind. She released her last vestiges of resistance to the welcome invader that had slipped into her mind with the grace and power that Bill had entered her body, and she felt as if she were experiencing life as only a god could imagine.

She felt him release his passion, felt her muscles closing over him, but in her mind, she was beyond the physical realm of pleasure. The sensations became too great for her mind to comprehend. Suddenly she was able to drink in a multitude of life experiences, see through a thousand eyes at once on all bands of the spectrum, breathe in the desires of others, breathe out their fears, and die a tiny death.

She was a hundred different people, young, old, male, female — anything, everything. She experienced their emotions, their dreams, their fears, and she delighted in the taste as she consumed what she encountered. Their fear was the most succulent. She collapsed on the bed, Bill falling on top of her, still embedded in her warmth, still hard and moving with short, gentle strokes.

She hugged the pillow to her face as he cupped her breasts and rested his mouth near her ear. She delighted in the exhausted gasps that came from him.

With an evil laugh she murmured, "I never thought it'd be *that* good."

Bill laughed with her. After a time, Dani fell asleep, her lover buried deep inside her body and her mind.

Later that evening Dani woke alone and felt a rush of panic. She checked the time and was relieved that it was only quarter after ten.

Where was Bill?

Horrified at the idea that he had abandoned her, that he had cruelly used her then left, Dani felt the calming presence of the entity that had made its presence known as Bill made love to her, and she was drawn to the open window. Looking out, she saw the beach. She giggled as she realized that Bill was surfing!

She watched his graceful motions as he mounted the

125

waves as expertly as he had mounted her and realized that he was naked. Her hand brushed a silk robe lying on a chair near the window and she decided to leave it behind. Glancing at the bed, she saw that there was no blood, no moist spot. Somehow he had changed the sheets while she was asleep.

She didn't want to think about it, and so she left the bedroom. Dani walked through the house, then down to the beach, her pale, naked skin glistening from the sweat of their previous exertions, despite the chill in the air. She emerged from the back door and once again saw Bill riding the waves.

Dani recalled an article she had read after learning she would be moving to Beverly Hills. She would sit in their cramped, Tampa apartment, fantasizing about lying on the beach or surfing in the California waves. The article said there were no waves for surfing in Malibu. As she watched her lover, the waters churned and rose in unnatural force only around him. She would have found it easy to believe that they were responding to his incredible, personal magnetism, just as she had, but such things were impossible.

Bill saw her and came in from the waves. She walked into the waters, thigh deep, expecting them to be ice cold. Images of men in thermal wetsuits tackling the beaches at night came to her, but to her flesh, the waters were warm and inviting. Bill threw the board to one side and tackled her, forcing her down into the waters. They played for a time, Dani holding his head under the water for what seemed like an impossible amount of time, then he lifted her out of the waves and carried her to the beach, where they sat, watching the tide.

"I love you," she said.

Smiling, he kissed her full on the mouth, then withdrew gently. "You have to go home. Your mother will be worried."

"She's a big girl."

"Do you want to call her?"

Worried that this was a test of some sort, she answered far too quickly, "No, not at all."

He laughed. She clearly wanted to call. The sound of the phone ringing trickled down from the beach house. She was looking at his naked body and saw that he had become erect as he had stared at her face and swaying breasts. Her own heat rose up, the demon took control. She kissed him greedily, then hissed, "The machine will get it, right?"

In response, he pulled her down to the sand and made love to her again, this time beneath the full moon. She was amazed as the psychedelic haze returned. The vast tapestry of fear she sensed earlier was within her grasp, the banquet from her dreams. She consumed it greedily and wanted more. Suddenly, Bill Yoshino pushed her over the edge with his fingers, his tongue, and his mind.

When they finally made it back to the house, Bill touched the playback button on the answering machine. Dani heard her mother's frantic voice on two separate messages, and realized that the first had been left before they arrived at the beach house. On the second, Sam demanded that Dani meet her at the lobby of a hotel in Los Angeles. She warned Dani not to go home, come straight to the hotel. "This is bad, so don't question, just do what I say. I love you."

"This time you better go," Bill told her as he walked her upstairs and helped her to collect her clothing. They dressed and he walked her to the Ghia. She kissed him deeply, caressing the front of his pants as he lightly felt her breasts.

She tore herself away and shuddered. "You weren't kidding about the addictive part."

She was in the driver's seat when he leaned down, kissed her again, and said, "there *will* be time for us. All the time in the world."

Feeling like the luckiest woman in the world, Dani drove off.

* * *

Bill Yoshino watched Dani drive away. Then he hurried inside and made a phone call. The sound of Samantha Walthers' voice on the answering machine had rankled him. It should not have been possible for her to call here; it should not have been possible for her to call anywhere, ever again.

When he heard the familiar, young, female voice on the other end of the phone, he snarled, "So what went wrong?"

Then he listened.

And planned.

Ten

From the hotel lobby, Sam had called the beach house every thirty minutes and had received no response. She had tried to keep the growing hysteria from her voice on the messages she left, but she knew that she had failed.

At eleven-thirty, Sam leaped to her feet as she saw her daughter finally walk through the doors of the hotel. Before the girl could ask what was happening, Sam dragged her before a security camera and checked the image in the monitor. It was Dani, not the doppelganger. She grabbed her daughter and held her in a frantic embrace.

"Where were you?" Sam asked as they rushed to the elevator. "Why didn't you pick up?"

"We were on the beach and couldn't hear the phone."

"Who's we?"

"Mother, I'm not a child anymore—"

Sam could see it in her eyes. "Oh shit. You slept with some guy. Oh God, honey, I thought we were going to talk about this first. Did you at least use protection?"

Dani gave her mother a cold stare. She seemed to be unplugging from the conversation, though, in truth, she realized that this was the item of deadly importance that the demon had kept her from thinking about. "Yes."

Sam turned away from her daughter as the elevator doors hissed open. She could tell when Dani was lying. They rode upward in silence, Sam cutting anxious glances at her daughter. It had only been a few hours since her dangerous elevator ride with the creature wearing Dani's face, and she was still nervous.

Sam had taken a two-bedroom suite, the only availability in the hotel. The rooms were elegant and spacious, but Sam barely noticed. Dani wanted to know why she couldn't go home and what they were doing here. Sam sat her down on the edge of the bed. In a low, halting voice, she explained all that had happened and offered her explanation:

"Whatever this thing is, I walked in on it at Mark Smith's house. For whatever reason, it decided not to kill me there. I dunno, maybe I intrigued it, or got it amused, I can't say. But now it's playing some kind of game, trying to make me think I'm crazy. I'm not. That thing tried to kill me tonight and it looked just like you. It can make itself look like anyone or anything it wants to."

Dani regarded her as if she were a stranger. "You're kidding me, right?"

Sam stared into her daughter's brilliant, gold-flecked eyes. "This is real, honey. This is really happening. I know it's hard for you to believe — "

"Pretty fucking impossible, actually," Dani said with a nasty, half-laugh.

"Don't talk to me like that."

Dani shrugged. "You want me to lie to you, I'll lie to you. I don't care." She smiled as she licked her lips and realized that she could still taste Bill.

The smile disturbed Sam. "I'm not making this up."

"Fine."

Frowning, Sam realized that she would have to address the other issue. "Who is this guy? How old is he?"

Dani tilted her head slightly and realized that she really didn't want to tell her mother anything about Bill. She didn't want to share him and she didn't want the magic of what they'd found together to be spoiled by a pragmatic look behind the curtains.

"You'll meet him," Dani said elusively.

Sam was not willing to give up so easily. "Do you love

130

this man? Is he in love with you? Did he say that?"

Dani's mood darkened. She was in love with Bill Yoshino, and had told him so, but his response had been physical, not verbal.

Do you believe in love at first sight?

No, but I believe in lust at first sight.

Of course he loved her. It would take him time to say it, that's all.

"Is that how he got you?" Sam asked crossly, frustrated with her daughter's lack of response.

"Christ, Mom, if you think I'm stupid, or you think I'm some little whore, why don't you just say it?"

Sam had to restrain her impulse to strike the girl. She had never felt that urge before. She forced herself to remain calm. "I don't think either of those things. But this is pretty sudden."

"Well, Mom, I'm growing up. Things happen." Dani's eyes seemed to blaze. "You wanted me to get a life, well now I've got one. I'm sorry you can't be happy for me, but you must have known that this was going to happen eventually. Or did you think I was going to be your little girl forever?"

Sam felt crushed. "Where in the hell do you get off talking to me that way? I love you Dani. I've been there for you. I've always been—"

"Maybe that's the problem. You've always been there. I could never do anything on my own."

Shit, Sam thought. This was going nowhere. Or maybe it was heading toward something that she never wanted to face. Maybe it was barreling straight toward that brick wall that has *I don't need you anymore, get your own life and stop living through me* written on it.

What are you going to do then, Sam? You're thirty-eight, you're alone. What are you going to do then?

Sam tore herself from her fear-drenched thoughts and saw Dani licking her lips as if she had just sampled an unexpectedly sweet wine.

"Look," Sam said, chest heaving, "we've got a situation that goes beyond all of this. We're not going to solve

131

it if we're at each other's throats. You honestly think this boy is something special."

"I do."

"So, for now, I'll have to trust your judgment."

"Gee, thanks."

"Dani—"

"All right."

Sam shuddered. She had never seen Dani like this before. "But you have to promise me one thing. No matter what he tells you, use protection. Always."

"Yeah, of course," Dani muttered, embarrassed into silence by her shame over neglecting such a dreadfully important aspect of lovemaking.

Sam surprised her daughter by taking her into an embrace. The girl was stiff and unresponsive at first, and Sam could smell a man's after-shave on her, along with the pungent odors of sex, but she said nothing. Dani relaxed and finally melted into her mother's arms.

"Let's get some sleep. We can talk about this in the morning."

"Okay, Mom."

Sam didn't tell Dani that she'd asked the front desk for a wake-up call at four in the morning. Considering the battle she had just faced, she felt it would be better for both of them to get a few hours rest before she informed her daughter that they were about to go running for their lives before dawn broke. The freeway would be congested in the morning, and Sam wanted to make sure they had an early start.

Sam had never before run from anything; but neither had she faced anything like the killer of Mark Smith and his companions. She decided to head south, then make it up as they went along.

Sam knew she would have to lie to Dani about some of what was happening. If the girl knew that she might never see her lover again, she would never agree to go with her mother on their dark odyssey.

They undressed and Sam insisted that they sleep in the same bed, side-by-side. Dani was uncomfortable with this for a number of reasons, not the least of which the memories that the familiar position recalled, but she chose not to argue with her mother. She'd never seen the woman like this before and it frightened her.

After clicking off the bedside lamp, Sam immediately dropped into a deep sleep. Dani shifted uncomfortably and found that she was too energized; she just couldn't relax enough to sleep. Sand clung to her from her encounter with Bill on the beach, and patches of her skin were sticky, while others were dried and cracking. She loathed the idea of washing away Bill's luscious scent, but parts of her stank like holy hell and she knew that her mother could tell everything that had happened simply from the smells. That thought bothered her above all else, because this moment, this night, was meant to have been private, shared by only two people.

After an hour, she gave up on sleep and decided to take a shower. The moment she rose from the bed, her mother's serene expression changed, and she began to toss and turn, as if her idyllic dream was becoming a nightmare. Dani had a strange, irrational feeling that there was something she could do about that. A part of her still felt angry, but not so angry that she would want to intensify her mother's discomfort, either. She sensed that this was within her power, too.

This is crazy, she thought. I can't do something like that. I could never do that, even if it was possible.

Maybe not, but that old *demon* inside you could, and we both know it, now don't we, Dani? Or is there a demon at all? Could it be that it's just you, Dani? Could it?

Shuddering, she turned and left her mother to her bad dreams.

Sam writhed on the bed. In her dream, she was being attacked by the doppelganger, who shifted forms as easily as a dancer might discard layers of gossamer veils, revealing something new each time. The creature had become her mother, dying and insane, her ex-husband,

133

dismissive and disapproving, and her daughter, willful and independent. She was crying out, clutching at the bed.

"Mom?"

The voice made her snap to sudden awareness. In a single, fluid motion, she reached beneath her pillow and drew the gun she had taken from the doppelganger, aiming it squarely at the chest of the creature wearing her daughter's face.

"Mom!" Dani screamed.

Sam realized where she was and that this was *not* a dream. Dani was wearing a robe. The bathroom door was open, the light on. Her hair was damp. The shower drain was making gurgling noises.

Sam jerked the weapon back at once. But it was too late. Dani stared at her in disbelief.

"Mommy?" she whispered, betrayal evident in her voice.

Sam dropped the gun to the bed and held out her arms. "Come here, baby."

Dani shuddered and retreated into the bathroom with a small, animal cry. She sounded as if she had been wounded on a primal level.

"Dani, wait, I'm sorry!" Sam shouted as she bounded from the bed and hurled herself at the door. She was too late. Dani slammed it shut and threw the lock as Sam reached the door. She heard her daughter break into sobs on the other side of the door, and she felt an intense pain rush through her at the sounds.

"Dani, come out, please," Sam called. There was no response other than the light, wracking sobs that had come moments before. "Honey, I'm sorry, I just got confused, I thought —"

She cut herself off. What could she say? She thought that her own daughter was a monster that had come to kill her in the night. That was the truth.

"I was having a nightmare. I didn't know it was you. I'm sorry. Talk to me, Dani. Please."

Silence.

"Oh God," Sam whispered. "Honey, please. Open the door. Or just talk to me. You're okay, aren't you?"

A soft, mewling cry. Nothing more.

"I love you, honey. You're my whole life. Don't be angry, please." She realized that was an unrealistic expectation. "Just talk to me, okay?"

The silence chilled her.

"Dani?"

No sounds.

"Dani, are you okay in there?"

Nothing.

Sam rose and tried the door. She knew that it had been locked, but she had hoped that rattling the doorknob would cause Dani to say something. At this moment, even a curse would have been welcome.

There was no reaction.

Terrible thoughts came into her mind, unbidden. What if the doppelganger had found them, disposed of her daughter, and taken Dani's place?

It couldn't know where they had gone, Sam reminded herself, not unless it had followed her from the parking garage, and she had been too careful to allow that.

What about the beach house? Dani's new friends? It could have followed Dani earlier in the day, then returned to the beach house to wait for Dani after it attacked Sam.

No, it was Dani in the lobby. The monitors had proven that much.

But it could have followed her. Waited until they were asleep. Taken Dani. Then made itself look like her again.

Jesus.

"Dani!" Sam shouted, throwing her full weight against the door. The door barely budged.

Images of her daughter trussed up by her ankles, hanging from the shower head, skinned alive, flashed into Sam's mind. She hurled herself at the door again and again. There was no sound from the bathroom.

The lyrics to an old song sprang into her thoughts: *Who do you trust, baby? Who do you trust?*

The door did not open. In a fit of desperation, Sam

raced to the bed and retrieved the gun. She slipped the safety off and shouted, "Dani, get away from the door, honey!"

She waited, then repeated the command. When there was no reply, she stepped back and squeezed off two shots, blowing holes in the door near the lock. After she fired the second bullet, the image of Dani, bound and gagged, her head placed directly before the lock, entered Sam's thoughts.

She thought that she might become ill, but she forced herself to push the door open, anyway. The doorknob on the other side fell off and struck the hard floor. There was no resistance.

Sam shoved the door open all the way and surveyed the bathroom. It was empty. Dani had gone. Directly across from her, she saw a door that had been left ajar. It led into the second bedroom.

"Oh shit," Sam said as she rushed into the bedroom and found it empty. A quick reconnaissance of the suite proved that Dani had run. She had left her clothes in the bathroom when she had undressed earlier and had obviously slipped into them and escaped the suite while Sam had been crying on the other side of the door.

Maybe the people at the front desk could catch Dani before she fled the hotel. Sam picked up the room phone and dialed the front desk. For a moment she could not remember the false name she had registered under. Then someone answered. A man.

"Front desk."

In a flash it came to her. "This is Rene Curtis in 2206. I'm looking for my daughter—"

"She just left, ma'am."

Sam hung up the phone. What little time she had to stop Dani from running off was quickly evaporating. She was wearing a sweatshirt and a pair of shorts, her running outfit which she had left in the car. She didn't have the time to bother with shoes. Grabbing her car keys she rushed from the suite and raced down the hallway.

She was halfway to the bank of elevators at the end of

the hall when she heard a gruff voice call out, "Freeze!"

Sam came to an abrupt stop. She knew that tone, having employed it many times in the past, and understood that she had no option but to reply.

"Set the gun down slowly!"

Sam suddenly became aware of the gun she still clutched in her hand. She could feel the sights of a security guard's pistol on her back, and so she slowly moved the gun away from her body and set it down.

All she could think about was Dani. By now the girl was on her way to the Ghia. She might even be pulling out.

The gun made a slight thump on the carpeted floor. Several people had opened their doors and were peering into the hallway.

"Step away from the weapon. Hands locked behind your head."

Sam complied as she heard the officer approach from behind. The tinkling sound of keys and handcuffs drifted to her.

"On your knees, then lay flat. Hands where I can see them."

Sam obeyed, laying on her stomach as the security officer swept the gun out of her reach. He was not some dumb bastard rookie, she thought in grudging admiration. Most rent-a-cops would have picked up the gun and destroyed any prints by now. Sam locked her fingers behind her head. She did not resist as the man roughly grabbed at her hands and cuffed her.

Then she heard him radio the front desk to call for the police.

Sam closed her eyes, realizing that by the time she talked her way out of this, Dani would be gone.

Eleven

Dani drove as if she wanted to get arrested. She changed lanes recklessly and pushed the Ghia to the top end of its limits. The image of her mother aiming the gun at her after she got out of the shower had been imprinted in her mind, and she could do nothing to force it away. Even thoughts of Bill and their incredible sexual encounter were not enough to banish the sight of her adopted mother brandishing the small caliber weapon and the look of murderous rage that had twisted her features. Dani had been lucky that her mother had not pulled the trigger. From the woman's expression, Dani was certain that she wanted nothing more than to empty the weapon into her.

The demon in her mind had cracked open the shell protecting her deepest fears. *She doesn't love you, you're nothing but a burden on her, she wants you gone, she wants you dead, she made a mistake eighteen years ago and she wants to blow you the* fuck *away—*

"No!" she screamed, changing lanes once again on the highway, cutting off a BMW.

The words of the demon were not true. She was certain that her mother loved her. But was this her mother? There was something wrong with the woman, terribly wrong.

Dani thought of a night ten years earlier, when her mother had thought that she was asleep. Sam's partner and occasional lover, a man named Paul, had been over.

138

Sam had confessed that the day was her mother's birthday and Paul had helped to get her thoroughly drunk. She confessed the way her mother had been driven insane by the disease that had ravaged her, and that her greatest fear had always been that she would go the same way.

Dani recalled the image of her mother leveling the weapon at her. Only the woman's years of training had kept her from squeezing off that first, deadly shot that had been perfectly aimed at Dani's heart. Dani felt as if she wanted to cry, but tears would no longer come. Shock and betrayal coursed through her, carried on the leathery wings of the demon in her brain that was not a demon at all, the demon that was what she had always been—the demon that she had always been denying.

Your Mommy loves you, honey.

Dani shook violently, as if to throw off those words from her childhood. Suddenly, she saw a dead man standing before her, laughing, bathed in blood. The image sliced across her consciousness with the speed and brutality of a butcher's knife, then it was gone. Dani shuddered. She knew the face. She knew the man. He was the trapper—the one who had awakened the demon. He was the one who had liberated her.

"Get the fuck out of me!" she cried, the Ghia nearly going out of control. She regained her senses, eased the car back from the narrow shoulder, and experienced images of the dead man two more times before she left the highway.

When she finally reached the beach house in Malibu, she saw that Bill's black Mustang was gone. Her heart shriveled. She needed him and she didn't even know his address or phone number. She had made love to him, given her virginity to him, released the demon and become a slut for him, but she knew little more than his name.

Running to the front door, passing the bronze lions, Dani reached for the door and found it locked. Breathing hard, she closed her eyes and tried to recall the sequence of numbers Bill had punched into the keypad beside the door.

Her mother had trained her to be observant at all times, and her training now paid off. Dani went to the keypad, punched in a series of numbers, and heard the click of the lock mechanism. She ran to the door and rushed inside, hoping to find an address book that might have had Bill's phone number.

The first phone she came to was an auto-dialer, with twenty-six numbers logged onto the memory card. None of them were marked with his name.

The phone rang, causing Dani to jump. She picked up the receiver. "Bill?"

"Hello?" A feminine voice. Dark. Sexual.

"I'm sorry, um, this is Madison's house." Dani realized that she didn't know Madison's last name.

"Dani?"

She suddenly recognized the voice. "Isabella?"

"Yes, Dani. What's wrong?"

Shuddering, Dani said, "Nothing."

"I take it Bill isn't there?"

"No. I came back here looking for him, but he was gone." No matter how hard she tried, Dani could not erase the tremulous edge from her voice. She knew that if she stayed on the phone, her speech would evaporate into a series of incomprehensible sobs. The tears were already gathering.

"Dani, did something happen with you and Bill?"

She thought of their incredible sessions of lovemaking and calmed slightly. Then an image of the dead man reaching out for her flared in her mind and she gasped.

"Dani?"

"No, nothing with Bill. He's wonderful. But I need him and he's not here. He's not here and I don't know where to find him. He didn't even give me his fucking phone number!"

There was the hysteria, she thought, right on time.

"Dani, I don't think you should be alone. Madison is here. She's staying with Angel and me.

Would you like to come over, too?"

She recalled Angel kissing the woman at the party and hedged. Then she realized that she couldn't go home, her mother would be looking for her there, and she couldn't stay here, either. Her mother had the phone number, and with that, she could probably find the address. The thought of another confrontation with Sam at this time frightened her even worse than the nightmare images that assaulted her.

Isabella's voice was on the line again. "I think I know where Bill is. I'll have Angel go and round him up. The two of you can meet here."

"Yeah, okay, that would be good," Dani said swiftly.

"Can you drive, or would you like me to come get you?"

"No, I can drive," Dani said. "Tell me how to get there . . ."

Forty-five minutes later, Dani found the two-story brick warehouse in downtown Los Angeles. If not for Isabella's vivid description, she would have thought she had the wrong place. There were no windows, and the building hardly seemed suitable for human habitation. There was a small alley on the side of the building and Dani found the door, which had been painted a rich blue. She knocked twice, and Madison greeted her.

"Come on in, baby," Madison said as she gave Dani a hug and led her inside. There were three heavy locks on the door and Madison threw each of them.

Dani was surprised by what she encountered inside the warehouse. She felt as if she had stumbled onto the set of *Alice in Wonderland* with Peter Max as set designer. Bright, garish colors rushed out at her. Rustling pastel veils hid soft lights that cast oddly beautiful tones upon the furnishings and upon her flesh. Winding staircases led to the elegantly appointed bedrooms on the second floor. Mobiles dangled from the ceiling and spun happily. The art-deco look extended to the furniture. Isabella was waiting with a glass of red wine for Dani, which she handed to the girl as all three sat on the oversized, luxurious couch.

"This place used to be a vault for one of the film studios to store their old prints. Then there was a fire and it all burnt up," Madison explained as she put her arm around Dani's shoulders and leaned into her slightly as Dani sipped at the red wine. It took Dani a moment to remember that she never drank. But the taste was sweet and it seemed to calm her, and so she held on to the drink.

"What's wrong?" Isabella asked, her voice lush and hypnotic. "You can tell us anything."

Dani nodded and began to relax, sensing the truth in Isbaella's words. She told them what had occurred after she left Bill at the Malibu house. When she described the moment she had emerged from the shower and her mother had pulled the gun on her, she burst into tears. Madison took her glass from her before she could spill what was left of the wine and Isabella took Dani into an embrace.

"She's all—she's all I've ever had," Dani sobbed.

"You have yourself," Isabella said.

"I've never been able to trust anybody except my mom," Dani whimpered. "Everyone's gone away, or they've hurt me."

Madison eased herself forward on the couch and rested her head against the back of Dani's neck, caressing her shoulders with her strong hands. "You can trust us. You know that you can."

And it was true, Dani understood. Resting her head against Isabella's breast, she felt an incredible surge of heat rise up from the woman's flesh.

"There's something more," Isabella said.

Dani quaked, but Isabella held her tight.

"Something you've needed to talk about for a very long time."

"No," Dani mewled. "It's terrible, what I did, what I am."

142

"We're the same," Isabella said. "And we love you. You have nothing to fear."

"We won't judge you," Madison said. "Tell us."

Dani suddenly felt a new presence in her mind, one that was powerful enough to keep the demon under control. She felt as if she were being immersed in a warm, clear running stream, a thousand delicate hands caressing her mind, easing her into a dreamlike state.

You must look fully into the memories that frighten you, a voice said in her mind. Isabella's voice.

Dani knew she should have been frightened by this. But instead, she was comforted.

It's the only way you can ever make your fears go away. Trust me. I won't let anything happen to you.

Dani felt her last vestiges of resistance fall away. She surrendered herself and the memories that she had been repressing finally broke loose.

Twelve

Dani had been walking home from the bus stop. There was only a two block walk to her house and the bus didn't go down her street. It was overcast and there was a chill in the air. She was sixteen, and she was dressed in khaki slacks and a white, bulky pullover sweater. Dark circles had formed under her eyes and her beautiful features were drawn up tight. She wore her sunglasses all the time.

Her best friend, Jami, had been found dead two weeks earlier. Jami's identical twin sister, Lisa, had gone into shock when news of her sister's death arrived. She had been hospitalized and a police officer had been assigned to her, in the event that the killer knew about the twin and wanted the experience of destroying his victim a "second" time.

Dani's mother had been working with the police to find the killer. Sam had warned her daughter to be careful and had wanted to send her away, but they had no relatives and Dani had refused to be separated from her mother. Sam had located one of the monster's burial grounds, where they had exhumed the bodies of two missing girls. His actual identity and the place where he had slaughtered his victims had not yet been established.

Unknown to Dani, she was about to learn the solutions to both mysteries. At the corner of the residential street where she walked, a red van had been parked. If she had noticed it sooner, she might have escaped.

As she approached the corner and passed the serviceman who had been digging up the main supply line buried next to the sidewalk, Dani realized that one of the van's doors had been left ajar. She heard a rustling sound from behind her and was about to bolt when she felt strong hands descend on her from behind. A damp, smelly cloth was pressed over her face. Dani had struggled, but the darkness had been inevitable.

When she woke, she was strapped to a chair in a nightmare-black room. There had been no hint of light, nothing for her eyes to adjust to. For a moment she felt a deep, resonant panic. Had she been blinded? There was no way to tell. She fought the urge to struggle in her chair. Whoever had taken her had not desired an unconscious victim. So long as her abductor believed that she was still asleep, she would be safe.

Suddenly a blinding light erupted in her face, burning her retinas, and she drew back, squeezing her eyes shut, screwing up her features as she stifled a scream. The light shifted from her face and illuminated a patch of floor instead. A man's voice came to her.

"Please, please, stay very calm, all right?"

Dani forced her body to relax. She nodded in a sharp motion.

"Okay, good," the man said. Dani saw that it was a flashlight in his hand. He raised the beam, pointing it at his own face. He was very handsome, with strong but gentle features and soft, empathetic eyes. His hair was slightly disheveled. "I know you're afraid, you don't have to be. Do you understand?"

Dani nodded, but she did not believe him.

"I'm going to show you something. I'm not doing this to scare you, even though I know it would scare me if I were in your position. I'm doing this to show you that you don't have anything to be afraid of. All right?"

"Yeah," Dani said, noncommittally.

The man aimed the flashlight at the far corner of the room. Dani saw a body lying there, facedown. A man wearing the same outfit as the serviceman who had kidnapped her.

"That's the man who was going to hurt you. He can't hurt you anymore. Now, I want to take off the tape and get you out of here, but I need to know that you're not going to go crazy on me, all right?"

"Yes."

"I've been all through this place, it's pretty scary. If you go running you might trip over something and hurt yourself. I don't want to see that happen, all right?"

"All right. Yeah."

The man nodded. "I'm going to put the flashlight in your lap, if that's all right. I'm not going to get fresh or anything, it's just that I need to see what I'm doing and there isn't any place else that I can put it, all right?"

Dani nodded. The man gingerly placed the flashlight in her lap. His awkwardness and his embarrassment did more to set Dani at ease than all his well-meaning blathering.

"This is probably going to hurt, and if it does, I'm sorry. But I don't think you'd want to be left down here, all right?"

"Yeah, go ahead."

The man picked at the edge of the adhesive tape. When he finally had a corner loose, he began to pull lightly at it. Small hairs were yanked from her skin and he grimaced as he pulled the tape loose and freed the first of her hands. Dani considered snatching the flashlight from her lap and beating the man's skull in — how could she believe that he was telling the truth — but something made her stop. Perhaps it was the way he flinched when she flinched, or the expression of sorrow in his pretty face. For whatever reason, she decided to allow him to free her other hand.

"Can you hand me that?" he asked, pointing at the flashlight. He did not want to reach into her lap to get it.

146

She did as he requested.

"Look, this is a pretty horrible place. That guy did some pretty sick things."

"I know," Dani said. "He killed my best friend."

The man nodded. "Let's get out of here, okay? I'll go first. Just stay real close and try to just — just watch *me.* Don't even look down if you don't have to. I'll tell you when we hit the steps."

"Yeah."

"Do you think you can stand up?"

Dani tried it. She was still a little dizzy and the man anchored her arm. The moment she raised her hand to indicate that she was fine, he released her and drew back quickly. Then he moved in front of her, exposing his back to her. They walked slowly, the dank cellar larger than she would have expected. She could see blood-stains on the walls. Chains dangled from hooks, leading to empty wrist cuffs. Taped to the walls were photographs, news clips, calendars, and magazines. The rapidly moving flashlight came upon something that looked like desiccated flesh, torn-open red meat with flies buzzing on it hungrily, then the beam whisked away. Dani knew that she was being guided through a charnel house. As her sense of smell returned, she tried not to gag.

Tentatively, she raised her hand and placed it on the man's back, training her gaze there as well. They came to the stairs he had mentioned, then climbed them carefully. He aimed the beam straight down and called out each step.

They reached the landing at the top of the stairs and the man shoved at the heavily reinforced door. A burst of light greeted them as the door swung all the way open and they raced out of the cellar, into a wood-paneled hallway.

The smells in the hallway were sweet, and the man slammed the basement door shut behind them. He shuddered and Dani could sense his fear. She looked at him and she managed a weak smile. He returned the ex-

147

pression, though his eyes were hollow and had obviously taken in far more than he was prepared to handle.

"Have you called the cops?" Dani asked.

He shook his head. "There wasn't time."

Dani watched him drop the flashlight and realized that he was shaking. An old sketch from *Saturday Night Live* raced into her mind. It was Richard Pryor talking about the movie, *The Amityville Horror* and how that movie would have been over in five minutes if it had been a black family that had moved in. The moment the faucets spat blood and a voice called, *"get out of the house!"* they would have been gone.

It sounded reasonable to her. She ran to the front door at the end of the hallway and found that it was locked. Glancing down, she saw that the door had several locks, and below them a keyhole. She flipped at the locks but they were all open. She tried the door again. It wouldn't budge. Only one of the dead bolts held the door in place — and there was no knob or lever, only that keyhole. It was the kind of bolt you needed a key to open from the inside.

The man behind her was approaching, asking what was wrong. She picked up a brass clothes stand from beside the door and drove it at the glass embedded in the door. It bounced off.

"Shit!" she screamed, and whirled with the six-foot long stand in her hands, holding it as if she was prepared to use it as a weapon.

The man held his hands up, his eyes wide with fear that she could sense was genuine.

"Get back!" she shouted.

"All right." He took several steps back.

"Is that the door you came in through?"

"Yeah," he said softly.

"Why's it locked?"

"I dunno. It shut behind me when I came in. I tripped. My foot accidentally smacked the stop that had kept it propped open. I mean, it closed, but it didn't lock. I didn't *think* it had locked." He shook his head.

148

"It must have locked. Some kind of automatic dead bolt. I dunno."

Dani crossed into the living room, slamming the head of the clothes rack into one of the living room windows. It bounced off. Systematically, she tried every window and door on the first floor of the house, but there was no escaping this place.

The man who had rescued Dani followed at a safe distance.

When they were in the kitchen, Dani had dumped the clothes stand and collected a handful of knives. She held one long butcher before her at all times and stuffed the others into the waistband of her jeans. The man had remained quiet and appeared frightened.

She considered the situation from his point-of-view — assuming he was what he appeared to be, and not the killer in disguise — and she decided that she would prefer to make an apology later rather than take the chance of ending up like Jami, raped, beaten, and burned to death. He did not try to talk to her until they had come full circle and once again stood near the front door. The house had been immaculate. There were no indications that a serial rapist/killer lived here. There were also no phones.

"Tell me something about yourself," Dani said.

The man nodded. "I'm Paul. Paul Greenfield."

"That's a start." Christ, she thought, I'm sounding like Mom. But I bet her hand wouldn't be shaking.

"I'm an insurance agent."

She examined the way he was dressed. Consummate yuppie, long sleeves rolled up, suspenders, tie, no jacket. She asked him about this last item. His ID would have been tagged to his jacket.

"I left it in the car."

She nodded and risked a quick glance outside. She had seen a car parked on the drive before. "Memory test. What kind of car do you drive?"

"A silver Cavalier."

"Ten points. License number?"

He gave it to her. But it still didn't mean anything. The killer could be an insurance agent, this could be the killer's car. After all, he didn't make a living killing little girls. That's what he did to unwind. That's how he had his *fun*.

The man was starting to run out of patience. "Look, I know that you're frightened, but I'm not the one—"

"Shut the fuck up!" Dani screamed, brandishing the knife. The killer would do anything to confuse her. Her mother had taught her to trust no one. Despite her racing heart and her trembling hands, she was not going to forget what she had been taught.

The man frowned.

"I want you to empty your pockets."

"What for?"

Just do it, she wanted to scream, but a knife wasn't as great a threat as a gun. For her to use the knife she would have to allow him to come very close, and if he took the weapon from her, even after she stabbed him, it would be all over. Her mother had taught her that the body could survive one hell of a lot of trauma. Stabbing victims were often struck a dozen or two dozen times, and it was generally shock or loss of blood that killed them, unless the heart was pierced or the throat cut.

"If you want me to put down the knife and believe you, then you'll do what I'm asking. I think you might have a key that unlocks this door."

Suddenly it all became clear to him. "You think I'm the one who took you. That I dressed up that body down there to fool you."

"It's possible."

He nodded and removed the contents of his pockets, turning them inside out to show that he wasn't hiding anything. Then he kicked his key ring to her. It skittered across the floor and she picked it up. Without taking her gaze from him she tried each of the keys. None of them worked.

It didn't mean a thing, she realized. If he was a real sicko he could have taped the key to his balls or jammed it up his ass. Or it might have been hidden somewhere else in the house. She hadn't tried the upstairs yet. The stairway leading to the second floor spilled out six feet from the front door. The corridor the man stood in was off to the left of the stairs.

Jesus, she thought, just like in the *Psycho* house at Universal. She hadn't made the connection until just now.

"Do me a favor, all right?" the man said. "I can see why you're afraid. I'm a little scared, too. I'm not exactly sure how we're going to get the hell out of here."

She nodded, urging him to go on.

"Tell me why I would have let you go if I was that bastard lying downstairs."

He was growing more confident, she noticed. He had used the words "hell" and "bastard" close together. He had been censoring himself fairly heavily up to this point.

"How should I know? Maybe you like to play games. You might have done this with Jami. You let them out of the basement, let them think they're getting away, then you close the trap. Maybe it's just fun for you."

The man slumped against the wall. "What can I do to convince you that you're wrong?"

You can't, she realized. Even if she looked at his driver's license and his name was correct, it wouldn't have meant anything. And for him to be able to prove that this wasn't his house with the address listed on the license, she would first have to know where in the hell she was, and at the moment, she had no idea.

"We're stuck," she admitted. "Tell me what you're doing here, what happened downstairs."

The man relaxed somewhat. "I was driving past and I saw this red van parked outside. A man was carrying something out of the back, it looked like a rug. Then I saw a hand slip out. I was lucky I didn't have an accident."

Yeah, right, she thought. This guy's been eluding the police for six months and he carries his victims inside in

151

plain daylight, trussed up in a rug? Give me a break.

"Then what?" she asked.

"I didn't want to let him know that I had seen him so I kept on going."

"Did you call the cops?"

"No."

"Why not?"

"I was — I dunno. I didn't think. I circled around and I saw that the door was still open on the back of the van. The front door was open, too. It was stupid, but I just came inside. My foot hit the doorstop and I grabbed at the door, caught it and let it close quiet, so that son of a bitch wouldn't hear. My heart was beating so loud that I guess I didn't hear the dead bolt.

"Then I heard something downstairs, tape ripping, this guy grunting, and I came down. I saw the way he was taping you up and something snapped. I was in the navy for two years. He wasn't expecting someone that would fight back. We struggled, he hit his head on something, cracked it open. I checked for a pulse and there wasn't one."

"So he's dead."

"You want to go down and check yourself?"

The prospect did not entice her. She surveyed his clothes. There was no blood on them, very little filth.

"I know you don't trust me," he said, keeping his hands where she could see them as he walked closer. Dani drew back, careful not to press her back against the door.

"You're right, I don't."

"But we have to work together if we're going to get out of here."

"Maybe."

Suddenly she heard a creak. A foot on a loose stair. She thought of the killer in the basement. A hundred horror movie clichés flashed through her mind.

Gee, I thought *he was dead. Guess I was wrong.*

Yeah, and I "tought I saw a putty-tat," she thought, forcing away a terrified giggle. Suddenly, she heard the telltale chu-click of a round being squeezed into the barrel of a shotgun and she looked up.

Wrong set of stairs, she realized. The killer wasn't on the basement stairs coming up. He was on the stairs leading from the second floor, descending rapidly. He was a middle-aged man dressed in jeans and a white T-shirt. A shotgun was in his hands. Dani had never seen him before.

As Paul turned to see what had distressed Dani so much, the man on the stairs pointed the shotgun at Paul's chest and pulled the double trigger. Paul's chest exploded in a hailstorm of gore and blood as he was thrown back against the wall like a rag doll. He sank to the ground, his mouth open, his dead eyes staring at her, his hands laying at either side of his body.

Chu-click!

Dani turned and faced the man on the stairs. There were two of them, she thought. Paul had told the truth. He had killed one of them downstairs. This one looked as if he had been taking a nap, waiting for the fresh meat to be trussed up and prepared for him. Had the sounds Dani had made while trying to get free of the house woken him? Or had he come downstairs to see Paul freeing Dani? Had he seen the light strike the other killer's body and heard Paul's words? Maybe he had locked them in and went back upstairs, smiling as he let them race around, rats in a fucking maze, ready to gnaw each other's faces off. Then he got tired of the game and came down to finish it.

It all made sense. The horror of it struck Dani full on. Her mind wanted to shut down. A single thought raced through her head:

Two of them! Holy mother of God, two of them!

And suddenly the world of her memories crumbled and fell away, like the myriad shards of a shattered mirror.

In the brick warehouse, Dani shifted uncomfortably

153

in Isabella's arms. Madison held her hand.

Don't shy away now, Isabella said in her mind. *This is the moment.*

I don't remember. I don't want to remember.

If you release it, the pain will go away. The fear won't control you any longer.

Release it? Release what?

Just think. Remember. How did you feel when you saw Paul die?

I was angry.

What else?

His eyes. His good, kind eyes. He had only been trying to help me.

What did you see in his eyes when the bullets hit him?

Betrayal.

You felt ashamed.

Yes.

And you felt angry?

God, yes.

You did something about it, didn't you?

Yes! Dani cried in her mind. *Yes!*

The elusive images of her memory reformed.

She was standing at the base of the stairs. The man with the shotgun had leveled his weapon at Dani's chest. She was no longer afraid, and that angered him.

"You better scream, you little devil cunt. You better scream 'cause I'm gonna send you up without the benefit of purification. I'm gonna throw you into the hands of the almighty with all your blood on your hands and He's gonna smite your fucking ass down, you better fucking believe it, cunt! He's gonna make you burn in hell for what you've done to my brother!"

Dani was barely listening. Something was happening in her head. The hatred she had felt for this man was coalescing into an angry black mass that smoldered and churned as she stared at him, the black pits of her eyes blazing with shining streaks of gold.

The barrel of the shotgun lowered slightly. He could feel her hatred. It reached across the distance separating them as if it had black, tentacled arms, with razor-sharp claws for fingers and ravenous mouths filled with sharp, pointed teeth in its palms.

Dani urged it on. She wanted it to touch him. She wanted it to clamp itself on his soul and tear him into bleeding, quivering strips of meat.

"You murdered my best friend, Jami, you piece of shit." Her lips were pulled back in an animal smile. Many times in the past, when she had been angry or hurt, she had felt the presence of the creature she had called the demon. Its murderous rage had infused her, but until now she had always resisted its call. She knew that it wasn't real, that it was nothing more than her own bitterness and her own hatred.

On the stairs, the murderer shook and cried, "Demon!"

"That's right," Dani said with a laugh. It was a demon that lived within her, all right, but it was also much more than that. This evil, alien thing was a part of her, with just as much right to exist as the part of her that loved her mother and always forced her to be a good girl. That was over now. The demon empowered her. With a cry of delight, she let it loose on the murderer.

He screamed in mortal terror, his shotgun falling from his hands and landing on the step beneath him as he fell back and clutched at his head, writhing like a preacher at a Baptist revival. Dani expected him to speak in tongues at any moment, and with perverse satisfaction, she realized that she could make him do exactly that; she could make him do or say anything she wanted him to. She had no idea how this was possible, and she did not care, either.

The murderer's fear raced toward her and she consumed it greedily, a sexual fire spreading through her as she tasted the varying shades of his terror. With his fear, came his memories and his reasons for the acts he had committed. It came in the form of a sermon. She heard the killer's voice, and that of his brother, raised to the heavens.

The cunts, the little devil cunts, we've got to redeem them.

Hear, hear.

We've got to rescue them from Satan, purify them, then send them to the arms of the Lord.

You betcha, brother. Amen.

We gotta tear their little hidey-holes first. Gotta do that with our holy spears.

Shit, yeah!

It's distasteful, I know, but they got to bleed, they got to give themselves all the way over to sin before they can be redeemed.

Brother, you said it, you bet.

Then we got to beat the devil out of them. We gotta make them confess the evil they've allowed into their bodies, and when that's over, we gots to burn them.

Got the propane in the corner.

Better they suffer the purifying flame here, a few precious hours of suffering as we burn it away, burn it all away. But not the face. Don't burn the face. Do that and good lord'll have trouble recognizing them.

Ay-yeah! You bet!

They got to suffer. They got to!

Brother, you know it! You know it!

Dani absorbed their thoughts and whispered, "Oh baby, I wish I had your brother with us, too. You're just going to have to pay double. You hear what I'm sayin' there, reverend? That's what you think of yourself as, isn't it? A reverend? A warrior for God?"

The murderer writhed and screamed.

"*A redeemer?* Well, what's say we give you a taste of what's waiting for you? Just a little feel of what you made my friend go through before she died, you fucking animal!"

Dani laughed as the demon ate the murderer's soul.

Slowly.

"The propane's in the corner," she said, ten hours later. "Let's go down and get some. And take the shotgun. You're gonna need it."

The zombielike creature that had been the murderer Jacob Willis bowed his head and dutifully obeyed. Together they descended into the hell of the cellar.

Dreamland fell away once more.

In the warehouse, Dani shook herself awake. "Oh, Christ, oh, I didn't, I didn't — "

"It's all right," Isabella said.

"It's not all right. It's not all right." Suddenly she remembered that Paul had always been using that phrase. She felt as if she was going to be ill. Isabella and Madison held her down. From the corner of her eye, she saw two figures approaching.

"Bill," she screamed, tearing herself loose from the two women as she launched herself into his arms. "Oh my God, oh my God. . . ."

"There's nothing to be ashamed of," Bill said.

She pulled away so that she could see his kind, loving face. But there was something cool and distant in his metallic blue eyes. Was it disapproval, she wondered?

"I'm a freak," she cried. "A monster."

"No more than any of us." Bill smiled as he gently caressed the side of her face.

She couldn't understand what he was saying. She had held out her secret heart for all to see. From his expression, Bill had obviously arrived in time to hear the worst of her confession. He didn't seem repulsed by her. None of them did. The three women gathered close, touching her, soothing her. She felt a wonderful burst of reassurance.

"What happened in the cellar, Dani?" Isabella asked.

Dani nearly shrieked. She wanted to forget this. She did not want to be hated for what she had done.

"Tell us," Bill said. "You have nothing to be afraid of anymore. You're home, Dani. You're with your own kind."

She shuddered at the words, then hung her head and told them the rest. She described the way she forced the murderer to commit vile acts upon his brother's body, then burn it beyond recognition. These acts had tortured him worse than anything else she had done to him and she had delighted in the pain and the fear that powered out of him. Finally, she ordered him to swallow the shotgun and squeeze the trigger. His head exploded and she gloried in a bath of his blood and brains.

The demon, sated and happy, withdrew into her mind and the savagery of what she had done came to her. She tried to follow the demon, retreating into the depths of her subconscious, but she did not have the courage to go beyond the superficial layer of her being. Suddenly she had sensed that it was vulnerable, and the part of her that had been disgusted by her acts, the part that had been afraid, walled up the demon. When it had regained its strength, it had railed against its captor, and so she had forced herself to forget everything that had happened; to remember would have been to give the demon life and freedom, something she did not want to do.

"It was horrible," she whispered. "It wasn't human, what I did."

"No," Bill said, his smile becoming even warmer. "It wasn't. Because you're not human, Dani."

She looked up at him slowly.

"And neither are we."

Thirteen

"Now that you know this much, it's time you learned it all," Bill said. "Do you trust me?"

"I love you, but I'm scared."

He waited for an answer. Angel, Isabella, and Madison caressed her. Each touch of their flesh upon her brought a sizzling charge of energy.

"Yes," she said at last as she leaned up and kissed him full on the mouth. "I trust you. Tell me."

She held him so tightly that she could feel their hearts beating in perfect rhythm. The thunder of his heart and the dizzying rush of blood as it was pumped through his veins consumed all other sounds. The perfect blue of his eyes became her world as she once again allowed herself to be intoxicated by his presence and whispered, "Tell me everything."

Bill nodded, and as he spoke, their world was swept away and replaced by another. "The first of our kind lived almost two thousand years ago. He was a Centurion in the Roman army. He had been present at the crucifixion of Christ. As the life was slowly bled from the Savior, the guardsman took a golden chalice and positioned it to catch the man's blood as he writhed in agony, reopening his wounds. His fellow guardsmen took very little notice. They did not realize that he had formed beliefs of his own, and that he was certain that this man *was* the son of God, the first true immortal.

"After Christ was dead, an accomplice of the Centu-

159

rion stole away with the chalice. They had been angry and felt betrayed. Both were certain that the hand of God would smite those who had inflicted such torment upon His only begotten son, and that Christ would escape his bonds and prove his claims. But he died, as would any man. The Centurion cursed God and kept the chalice, hoping to sell it to one of Christ's fanatical worshipers.

"Three days later, the body of the Savior disappeared and rumors of the Resurrection started to spread. The Centurion's accomplice had lined up a wealthy buyer for the chalice, a man who had been fascinated by the myths that had sprung up concerning this 'savior.' Brooding over the upcoming transaction, the Centurion decided that he wished to keep the chalice. An argument ensued, and the Centurion murdered his accomplice. The murder had not been thought out, and his actions were quickly discovered.

"The Centurion eluded his fellow guardsmen long enough to reach the hiding place of the blessed object. He now prayed to the god he had cursed; he prayed for forgiveness, he prayed for deliverance. The chalice still contained the blood of the lamb, the blood of Christ. When the Centurion's prayers were not answered and he heard the pounding of the vengeful guardsman at the door, he committed a desperate act: He drank of the blood in the chalice. He took the blood of Christ into his body, hoping that he too would become an immortal.

"The Centurion died horribly. When his fellow guardsmen succeeded in breaking down the door and entering the hovel he had chosen as a secure home for the chalice, they were sickened by what they had seen. It was said that smoke poured from the Centurion's mouth and that his innards had been boiled away, as if he had downed a cup full of acid. What became of the chalice is unknown. It may have eventually made it into the collection of the wealthy dealer, it doesn't matter. What matters is what occurred three days later.

160

"The Centurion woke from the sleep of death. His body had been heaped upon a mass grave. Several other corpses had been dumped over his. He climbed out and escaped. He had no idea of what had happened to him, or that he was still transforming. From the fused and twisted mass that had been his guts, he felt a terrible hunger. He tried to consume human food, but it made him ill. There were other concerns. He needed money. He had to find a place to stay and he had to escape the city before he was discovered.

"Fortuitously, he came upon a wealthy traveler and his wife. His need was great. It was not until he had attacked them that he understood the nature of his hunger. The woman started to scream when his teeth extended, becoming wolflike incisors — as he and his accomplice had descended upon the Savior like ravening wolves, so too would they bear the teeth of the animal. He tore out the throat of her husband, drinking deep of the blood that spurted from his severed artery. He lapped up the blood like an animal.

"The woman had been paralyzed by fear. The Centurion was sated, and so he did not kill her outright. Besides, he still needed shelter and gold. He commanded her to stop shaking and get to her feet. To his surprise, she did precisely as he requested. He found that he could influence her thoughts, that he could make her perform any act he so desired. The Centurion forced her to help him, and together they stripped her husband of his belongings and took him to the mass grave.

"Miraculously, they were not seen. As the Centurion later came to understand his condition, he knew that it had not been a miracle at all, it had been his own need that had shadowed his presence from the minds of the guards. Soon he sensed the encroaching presence of the dawn, and his instincts forced him to run. The woman took him to the villa that she and her husband had rented, and as the sunlight came, the Centurion started to burn. Then he was inside, safe, and he kept to the shadows, the woman pressed close to him.

"The day passed slowly, and he had considerable time for reflection. With no one to guide him in this strange, new life he had embarked on, he was forced to draw his own conclusions. He had desired eternal life above all else. The dictates of God's child had never truly interested him, only the rewards that Christ had promised his faithful. The Centurion decided that God had indeed turned His face away when the Centurion had cursed Him, but the soldier's pleas had been heard by another, by the fallen angel whose name was Lucifer. The Centurion decided that his present state had been Lucifer's jest on his maker. Lucifer had taken the blood of Christ's son and created with it a child of his own. A monster who would live forever, so long as he consumed the lives and souls of others.

"As the days passed, the Centurion did not let the woman out of his presence. He learned that he did not have to feed very often, he could subsist on the fear that he inspired in her breast. After a time, he came to experiment with his newfound power, and he learned that he could control the perceptions of others, he could make them see whatever they wished to see. And so he took the place of the woman's husband, eventually convincing even her that he was her husband.

"The Centurion, whose name was now Antonius, found that although he no longer required human food, there were other base hungers that had not subsided. He took the woman, making love to her with a savagery that he forced her to admire. Within a year, they had conceived a child."

"No," Dani said abruptly. "That's not right. In the movies, they're always impotent, they can't — "

"This isn't the movies," Bill said impatiently. "This is real. This is our lives. Do you want me to stop?"

"No," Dani said quickly. "I'm sorry."

"Tell her the rest," Isabella said.

"Hold nothing back." Angel restrained a giggle.

"There's not that much left to tell," Bill said. "Antonius fathered six sons. Each of them was born human,

162

but as they matured, their power began to develop and make itself known. They were called Initiates. Their father sensed this and by sharing his blood with them, by releasing the mask of humanity that hid their secret selves as he took them on the hunt and initiated them into his ways, they became like him. Shunning the sunlight was a small price to pay for immortality, they agreed."

By sharing blood, Dani thought. That's why the demon wouldn't let me think about protection when Bill and I made love.

"Finally, there was a seventh child, a daughter. Antonius was enraged by this. He was certain that his wife had betrayed him with another, as his seed could only produce fine, strong sons, and so he murdered the woman and her child. But that baby was not the last of the females born to Antonius or his sons. A few of them were allowed to live, as an experiment. They grew to be as wild and savage as their brothers, but with a single, crucial difference: They could not bear children. Neither the seed of human or immortal would bear fruit in their bodies. They were shunned.

"Throughout the ages, little has changed. Antonius himself was said to have been murdered by one of his sons, for reasons that remain cloaked in mystery, though it is rumored to have been over a female child that Antonius wanted destroyed. But his blood remains strong in his ancestors.

"We are those ancestors, Dani. We are the bastard children of the Dark Angel."

Dani shuddered. She could not bring herself to believe all of what she had been told, though a part of her knew that it had been true. "What do you mean, nothing's changed?"

Isabella stroked her arm and said, "We were all like you, Dani. Abandoned, left to die. Our true mothers killed because they bore a lowly female. We are shunned by others of our kind. All of us. We have survived by finding one another, by teaching each other and ourselves that we have become what we were born to become. Immortal."

Angel nodded. "We want to share our gift with you, Dani. We will never betray you. And we understand."

Dani looked to Madison. "Then you're like me. An Initiate."

"That's right, sweetheart. And tomorrow's my night to be turned."

Shifting her gaze to Bill, Dani saw an image in her mind of her mother aiming the gun at her heart.

"Will you come with us?" he asked.

Overcome with her love for him, needing desperately to make peace with the demon that had been nothing more than her blood, her heritage, Dani allowed herself to be enfolded in Bill's arms.

"I will," she whispered.

Bill kissed her, and held her as she began to weep.

Fourteen

Sam had found Detective Sergeant Edward Pullman to be somewhat less paternal in their second meeting. She had spent the night in the lockup, realizing that there was no one she could call at such an hour. The only person she would have trusted was Allen Halpern, and his home phone number was unlisted. She hadn't learned Rosalind's last name and calling Martell was out of the question. The officers on duty refused to call Pullman at home, despite Sam's urgent pleas. As the hours had stretched before her, she knew that the doppelganger had probably taken Dani by this time and there was nothing she could do about it.

If that had happened, however, the creature would not harm Dani. It would keep her alive and safe until it could contact Sam. All Sam had been able to do was sit tight and refuse to give the officers a reason to ship her to the nearest psychiatric hospital for evaluation. In the morning, the burly, white-haired homicide detective had visited her.

"So what were you doing with the gun, Ms. Walthers?" Pullman asked.

She told him that she had taken it from Mark Smith's killer when the man had attacked her earlier that night. There was no sense in muddying the issue with the truth. If she had given him another story about the doppelganger, she was certain that a seventy-two hour period of observation would be ordered and that was not acceptable; she had to get back on the street as quickly as she could.

"Why didn't you come to us?" Pullman asked.

"I was scared."

Pullman frowned. "From what I've seen and read about you, Ms. Walthers, you don't scare easily."

He took a folded-over magazine from his jacket and threw it on the table. It was a six-month-old copy of *People*.

Christ, she thought. She had forgotten about this.

"It says here you're a real go-getter. You like to work outside of the system."

Sam shrugged. "Actually, I just thought there would be more money in private practice."

That brought a small smile to his lips. It faded quickly. "So what were you shooting at in the hotel?"

Sam explained that she had reason to believe that Smith's killer was in the bathroom with Dani. When the girl wouldn't respond to the pounding at the door, Sam shot the lock. That part of her story checked out, at least.

"But your daughter left the hotel alone."

"I know that now." She shook her head. "I made a mistake."

Pullman shook his head. "I forgot to pick up rolls for my wife on the way home last night. That was a mistake. This is one major-league fuck-up. But I'll see what I can do, anyway."

Later, Sam was allowed out of holding long enough to work with a computer sketch artist in compiling a likeness of the "man" who had attacked her. It wasn't until quarter to five in the afternoon that Pullman returned and Sam was released.

"I've been in and out of court all day," he explained as they walked out of the precinct house together. "I didn't tell you the worst of it."

"And what's that?" Sam asked.

"The gun you had. It used to belong to a cop who

166

went nuts and shot his family three months ago."

"Jesus," Sam muttered.

"Tell me about it."

"Did they find him?"

"Yeah. But he had done himself in a bathtub, all the blood drained out of him. Never found the gun, until now."

Sam nodded. Within seconds, the cab that Pullman had called for her arrived. Sam thanked Pullman, told him that she would make her court dates, and promised that he wouldn't regret helping her.

"Sweet Jesus, I hope not," he said. She gave his arm a friendly squeeze and turned from him. She saw him watching her as the cab pulled away. He seemed sad and a bit angry, as if he knew that letting Sam back on the street was the worst thing he could have done.

Sam had no time to be coy. She assumed that the cab driver was an undercover cop; if not, he or his controller would be under orders by the police to report the location to which they had taken her. There was no time to worry about it. She considered having the driver take her to the airport, which would send her pursuers into a dead panic. Once there, she would have booked a flight to south of the border, used her substantial on-hand cash to bribe a woman of her general description to trade clothes with her and take the flight, then taken a series of cabs until the scent had been completely thrown off.

But it was no good. Ultimately, she needed to get home. There was a chance that Dani had returned there, or that the doppelganger had come and gone, leaving directions for her to follow. If she saw evidence that her place was under surveillance — and she knew exactly what to look for — she would adopt her plan to confuse the police long enough for her to pick up her daughter's trail.

She had the cab driver leave her at the hotel, where she picked up her car and went home, only to find that her house had been tossed. Pullman had not warned her about this. The police had done a decent enough job in returning items to their original positions, replacing the contents of drawers, leaving the scene the way they had found it — a mark would never have caught the intrusion. But once again, she had performed such tasks many times in the past, and she knew what to look for.

While she was upstairs she changed into a more suitable outfit. She slipped into a torn pair of jeans, pulled on her Air Jordan pumps, found an old, tight black pullover with sleeves, a pair of fingerless black gloves, and her favorite black leather jacket. Then she used a cord to tie back her long hair so that it could not be used against her, found her car keys and her mirrored sunglasses, then dug around in her closet until she found a black, featureless travel bag. Going through the house, she stuffed a collection of items into the bag that she could use as weapons against the doppelganger.

As she made her rounds of the house, she thought about the reasons for the strong interest that the police had shown in her. The mystery of the dead cop's missing gun had obviously been enticing enough to make the police wonder if their man had been helped along in his suicide, the perp taking his gun with him. More likely, of course, was that he hid the weapon somewhere in the city, a vagrant found it, turned it in to a pawn shop. But even she had problems with that theory. The owner should have filed off the serial numbers if he had been down for this, or checked the numbers and called the police if he wasn't. That lent weight to the first theory, that the man had not killed himself. Going with that for a moment, she realized that they could also put forth the possibility that the cop wasn't the one who did his family. Any department would jump at the chance to restore a dead cop's name and honor, provided they performed the investigation quietly; they wouldn't want any mention of their activities unless they were able to acquit their man and nail someone else. She hoped they didn't like her for this.

A new possibility came to her: Perhaps the doppel-ganger killed the cop's family, then set the cop up to take the blame. The creature could have performed the mur-der, appeared to witnesses as the cop, then taken the of-ficer somewhere and played with him until he finally died. How many lives had this thing destroyed, she won-dered.

The phone rang, making her start. The possibility that the phone was wired for a trace came to her as she answered.

"Hello?"

"Sam, this is Alex."

Alex Wren, the company's resident hacker.

"Are you at home?" Sam asked.

"No, I'm still at the office."

"Stay there," she said in a commanding voice as she hung up the line then raced from her house. Ten minutes later, she was at a pay phone outside a convenience store in West Los Angeles. Alex picked up on the private line.

Before he could start blathering, Sam told him what she needed. She had the number from the beach house memorized. It took him a few minutes, but he came back with the address in Malibu that she required. She thanked him, then hung up before he could start asking questions.

Soon she was heading toward Malibu, forcing herself to observe the speed limit. If anyone had been following her, they were better at this than she was. And if they were that good, she wasn't going to turn away their help once she reached her destination.

Thirty minutes later, Sam found the beach house. The Ghia was parked in the drive, along with a marked police vehicle. But how, she wondered. She had not called from the house, and the pay phone couldn't have been tapped.

Then she considered her phone answering machine at home. Dani's outgoing message with the phone number for the Malibu house had not been erased. The police had taken the number, ran the address, and come out here. But why were they here now? They should have come and gone hours ago.

The image of Dani lying dead on the floor of the beach house, a group of investigators going over her body came to Sam and she brushed it off. Pullman would have told her if anything had happened to her daughter. This was not the last remnants of a crime scene investigation. Her baby was all right.

Fine. Then what the hell was going on? Sam carefully left the GT-S and approached the police car, the travel bag slung over her arm. The driver's side window was partially open, the radio was curiously silent. Suddenly it squawked into life, causing Sam to gasp. She listened to the calls, noted the car's number, and waited to hear an inquiry on the unit's whereabouts. No such call came in. Sam knew where the heavy artillery would be kept, and she considered breaking in to get the double pump, but first she checked the car's hood. It was still warm.

Glancing in the direction of the Ghia, she saw that there was a slight buildup of oil underneath the car. It had been parked there since last night. She looked past the pair of bronze lions and saw that the door was slightly ajar. She could have slipped inside easily. Nevertheless, the prospect of entering a house this size with at least one, possibly two, jumpy cops did not seem appealing. The idea that the cops would be nervous was a logical one, provided there had been even a whisper that cop killers were involved in this situation. Even if everything was exactly the way it seemed, Sam could get her head blown off by trying to be coy.

Walking back to the police car, she opened the driver's side door and leaned on the horn. After a minute, a lean, short-haired man in uniform appeared. Sam eased off the horn. The officer's gun was in its holster, not in his hand. That was a good start, anyway.

The man approached, somewhat vexed, and Sam

170

looked at the upper windows of the house, hoping to catch movement. If the man's partner had been with him, she would have felt better. To the best of her knowledge, the doppelganger had been alone.

The officer came closer, not even attempting to force a smile. Sam liked that, too. She would have been cautious but polite in his position, nothing more. The doppelganger probably wouldn't have known that. And the creature acted alone. Sam had convinced herself that it was the only one of its kind, whatever the hell that meant.

Where there's one, there's usually more.

Sam was snapped back into a sudden, embarrassing memory. There had been five men in her life since she had adopted Dani. One had been a one-night stand that she had instantly regretted, another had been her partner, the other three had arrived during a brief period when she had been convinced that Dani needed a father.

Two of these had been good men, men who might have been up to the requirements of "the job," but Sam had come to realize that she hadn't truly loved either of them. The man who had said the words that had flashed into her mind was named Richard, and he had been an exterminator. She hated bugs, always had, and he teased her by telling her the secrets of his trade. One form of extermination involved leaving a substance that would stick to the roaches' legs as they walked on it. The poison was sweet to them, and they would lick their legs clean. The roaches had enough life in them to return home before they died.

Richard had been trying to make love to her, and all she could think about was cockroaches licking their legs. She never told him why she had asked him to leave and never returned his phone calls after that night.

Christ, she thought, that's a pretty fucking weird thing to be thinking about now, isn't it?

But maybe it wasn't. She had often thought about the way people died. She would come across their bodies and picture them getting up in the morning, racing around, arguing with their spouse or making love to them, playing with the kids, feeding the cats, taking a few moments to choose what they were going to wear — never realizing that they would never perform those tasks again.

Shocked from her revery, the cop came a few steps closer, and she understood why she had been thinking about Richard, and making love — something she would probably never get to do again.

The officer wore Richard's face.

It was the doppelganger.

The creature could only make her see people that she had already encountered, or, in Mark Smith's case, people whose photographs and videotaped interviews she had seen. Sam decided that the doppelganger had drawn a face from her more distant past so that it would not frighten her away, so that it could come right up to her before she was alerted to its true nature. By that time, of course, it would be too late for her to run.

Sam waited for the doppelganger to draw down on her and blow her head off, but the moment never came.

"Ma'am," it said respectfully.

Sam's mind reeled at this. The creature was playing a game and it wanted her to participate. It had obviously slaughtered or subdued the officer assigned to this car. Sam guessed that a team had been here earlier. They would have gone over the house, spoken to the neighbors, then left. Most likely, a neighbor had seen something that appeared suspicious and had called in to report it. This car had been sent to follow up.

"Good afternoon, officer," Sam said, immediately falling into the solicitous role of a concerned parent. "That car belongs to my daughter. Have you seen her?"

The officer shook his head. "No, ma'am. There's no one inside."

Sam frowned. "Do you mind if I have a look around?"

172

"Certainly, ma'am." The creature turned his back on her and walked briskly to the house.

Sam followed closely. The officer's strap was still over his gun. If not for that, she could have torn the weapon from him and cut him down before they reached the house. Sam would have to stay with her original plan, drawing the creature into tighter quarters where there might be objects that she could use against the monster. Out here, in the open, she would have been killed before she could reach her car.

The situation was mutually beneficial, Sam realized, as the doppelganger would not have wanted to take her in the open, exposing itself. Before her, the doppelganger opened the door and went inside.

Sam was already in motion as she stepped over the threshold. The receiving room was beautiful, and the mirrors lining the walls took away any doubt that Sam may have had. The doppelganger's true image was revealed in the reflection. Sam's hands had gone to the travel bag, which she had left open. When they emerged, she held an aerosol spray can in one hand and a cigarette lighter in the other. The creature spun in the large receiving room and raised its arm as Sam pressed the button on top of the can and flicked the lighter. A tongue of flame reached out as the doppelganger leaped away, the fire singing its arm and face. It changed as it rolled out of the way, its features shifting so rapidly that Sam could not recognize who or what it was becoming.

The doppelganger was a female, Sam could see that much in the mirrors. It had been wearing a tank top and jeans. That explained why its sleeves hadn't caught fire; Sam had burned its flesh directly. The receiving room was twenty feet square, devoid of furniture. The doppelganger had fallen with ten feet separating it from either of the two doorways branching off to the rest of the house. Its image wavered. For an instant, Sam could see it directly. It was a woman, crawling away, her wild hair covering her face.

173

There was no gun. Sam resisted the urge to look back to the open doorway leading outside. She was fairly certain that there had been no police car, either. The creature wasn't armed. Sam knew that she had it. All she had to do was bear down on it and hit the creature a second time and the thing would burn, but suddenly that was not a possibility.

It had become a she. *It* had become human. Destroying *it* would have been murder.

The doppelganger seemed to sense her conflict. With an inhuman burst of speed, she lifted herself from her feet and bolted into the next room. Sam raced after her, but when she entered the neatly appointed living room, the doppelganger had vanished.

"Shit," Sam whispered. At least she knew that the doppelganger could not become invisible. If that had been the case, she would have done so. But she was fast when she needed to be, faster than anything Sam had ever seen.

Sam knew that she could not afford to let the doppelganger escape. Her adversary would no longer worry about subtlety. Sam had hurt the doppelganger, and the creature was going to want her dead at any cost. And it had the advantage of being able to become anyone that Sam had ever met. It could wait a month, a year, then strike. But eventually, it *would* strike. That was a certainty.

Holding the makeshift flamethrower before her, Sam cautiously crossed the living room and found the small alcove where the bar had been set up. She set the aerosol can and the lighter down for an instant as she grabbed an ice pick and slipped it into her bag, then took a wine glass, wrapped it in a towel, and smashed it. Then she tied the ends of the towel into a slipknot and dropped the weapon into her bag.

The sound of footsteps treading carefully on stairs came to Sam. She pictured the doppelganger, wounded and weakened, dragging itself to the second floor.

174

Bullshit, she thought, her hands starting to shake. You want me up there. You're ready for me. Or you think you are.

Sam passed through the room whose walls were plastered with photographs, and cautiously peered through the doorway, expecting to see the doppelganger standing at the head of the stairs, another stolen pistol leveled at her. After all, there had to be something upstairs that the creature could use.

The stairs were empty. There was no one waiting.

Of course not, Sam thought. I can still retreat. If it were me up there, I'd wait until my prey was midway up the stairs, then make my appearance. Shit.

"Forget it, you bitch. You come to me," Sam hissed.

Sam took a step back, trying to think of a way to draw the doppelganger out, when it occurred to her that the murderess could have made her *think* that she heard the sounds on the stairs, when in truth, the creature was still waiting below. Sam turned to check her safety area a moment too late. The doppelganger plowed into her from behind, sending her face first into the stairs. Her forehead struck the lowest step and she lost her grip on the aerosol can. Her sunglasses flew off her face, cracking as they struck the corner. The can hit a step two thirds of the way up, bounced upward, and came to rest two steps before the top of the stairs. Fighting the horrible ache in her skull and the sudden nausea that had risen in her, Sam flipped over, onto her back, and raised the lighter.

The doppelganger grabbed at Sam's arms a moment too late. Sam ignited the lighter and ground it into the creature's face. If the monster hadn't snapped back so quickly, Sam would have burnt the doppelganger's eye. Pressing her advantage, Sam reached out, grasped the doppelganger's ankles, and yanked them forward, pitching the creature back. Sam had not been able to see more than a glimpse of the woman's face. She felt a slight surge of satisfaction when she heard the doppel-

175

ganger's head crack upon the hard wood floor.

Sam tried to rise and a sudden vertigo stuck her down. The blows she had received to the head in the elevator had been aggravated, and she felt as if she were about to pass out. The doppelganger lashed out with her feet, kicking Sam squarely in the gut. Sam was driven back to the stairs, where she winced with the pain of impact as her back struck the hard, serrated flats of the steps. The doppelganger leaped at Sam and she reacted instinctively, drawing up her own feet, catching the weight of the doppelganger, and flipping her up, over her head. Sam had not expected the maneuver to work, but the creature seemed lighter, and more frail than she had before. Sam tilted her head back and watched in disbelief as the doppelganger literally flew three quarters of the way up the stairs, gripped the edge of a step with both hands, and performed a modified handstand, flipping high into the air and twisting before she came to rest on the landing.

Sam had dragged herself from the steps and was holding on to the wall to keep her watery legs from collapsing altogether when she saw the doppelganger's image quiver and change. Suddenly she had taken on the likeness of Sam's mother. She was dressed in a white hospital frock, broken glass in her hands, blood dripping from her mouth, staining the frock.

"I'm proud of you, honey. You've grown up just like me. Do you want to know what's really happening? What you're really doing? You're hurting your poor little baby —"

"Bullshit, you aren't real," Sam said, shuddering.

"I had to die because you wouldn't have taken care of me. Because you would have been so goddamned selfish. You wanted your own life, you didn't care what happened to me. You were glad when I was gone. It was a relief, wasn't it?"

It's just punching my buttons, Sam thought. None of this is real.

176

"You were relieved! You were happy! You wanted to have a party, admit it!"

But she had admitted it, and taken the shame and the guilt that went along with the admission a very long time ago. In a way, she had been happy for both of them. The *insane thing* had not been her mother; her mother had been loving and kind. In her rare, lucid moments, she had tried to kill herself to end the horror. She wanted release. She wanted the freedom of death. When it came, she had been at peace, and had told her daughter that it was for the best and to never mourn.

Sam had forgotten all of that until this moment. In attempting to expose her weaknesses, the doppelganger had found Sam's greatest strength.

"Yeah, and your little dog, too, you bitch," Sam said. She suddenly felt the way she did when she was watching one of her daughter's horror films. The gore and the creatures were so obviously divorced from reality that they had no deep, emotional impact on her, they inspired a flash of revulsion, and nothing else. "Come on, let me see what you really are. Or are you too fucking ugly for that?"

"Why don't we see what *you* really are?" the doppelganger said, refusing to drop the persona of Sam's mother.

She's weak, Sam realized. That little trick she just pulled really took it out of her. She's stalling. In a burst of adrenaline, Sam raced up the stairs. The doppelganger's image of Sam's mother flickered, then the creature darted away from the stairs, out of view.

Dammit, Sam thought, but she remained quiet, coming to a stop just before she reached the top of the stairs. She collected the aerosol can, saw that it had been dented, the top release broken, and wondered if the doppelganger had noticed that. Probably not, she decided, and so she resumed her earlier stance, holding the makeshift — and utterly worthless — flamethrower before her. She hoped to corner the creature and keep it at bay until she was able to call the police herself.

Sam checked the view around the corner, onto the hallway corridor, and saw nothing but a series of closed doors. Wonderful, she thought. More games.

But that fear would not prove to be justified. Sam heard a gasp and she looked up to see the doppelganger clinging to the ceiling. There was no time for conscious thought, no time to question the absurdity or the impossible nature of what she was seeing. Sam dropped to her knees, allowing the lighter and the aerosol can to fall from her hands. She heard a rush of air from above as the creature descended. Sam dug her fist into her bag, felt her fingers close over the ice pick, and yanked it out. Both of her hands closed on its base as the doppelganger fell upon her.

Sam was thrown back by the impact. The doppelganger's body no longer felt light and ethereal. The woman cried out as the ice pick pierced her chest with the familiar slap of steel slicing into meat. Impaled, she struggled to break free and only managed to wriggle the cold steel inside her body, worsening the damage.

"You whore!" the doppelganger screamed as she fastened her hands on Sam's throat and began to squeeze. The ice pick was buried in the creature's chest at a ninety-degree angle, and Sam released her grip on it as she tried to force the doppelganger from her. The creature's hands were incredibly strong. Her neck would snap at any moment. She reached into her bag, withdrew the towel containing the shattered glass, slipped the knot, and jammed a handful of glass into the creature's wound.

The doppelganger released Sam as it threw its head back and wailed. Sam kicked herself free of the monster, her bag sliding from her shoulder in the process. The doppelganger lunged at her, the creature's hand closing over the bag. Sam pulled away and suddenly felt an icy stab of pain in her mind.

Why don't we see what you *really are?*

Sam felt as if her conscious mind were being peeled away. Her vision dimmed, then gave out completely. In contrast, her sense of smell became so acute that her world was suddenly consumed with the odors of blood and cooked flesh that the doppelganger radiated. From somewhere close, she could hear the tentative footfalls of the doppelganger as it came toward her, slowly, relentlessly.

"I know what scares you," the doppelganger whispered, this time in her daughter's voice. "What's happened to Dani, that scares you."

Sam fought the initial waves of panic as she pushed her body to respond to her wishes. She recalled where she had been before her vision was blotted out and she scrambled ahead, toward the door that was three feet to her left. Her head collided with the door and she felt her teeth rattle. Then her hand was closing over the doorknob.

The door was locked.

The doppelganger was upon her, straddling her from behind, yanking the cord from Sam's hair, and wrapping it around Sam's throat.

"I could tell you everything, but I won't you stupid cunt," the doppelganger snarled. Sam grabbed at the cord, managing to close her fingers around it before the doppelganger could pull it tight.

"You're afraid, aren't you?" the doppelganger asked. "You're afraid of failing your little girl. But you've already done that."

Sam forced away her terror at the doppelganger's words. She knew that if she gave in to her fears, the creature would have her. At any moment she expected the doppelganger to describe the manner in which it had murdered her daughter. Then it made a critical mistake.

"She's one of ours, now," the murderess said.

Dani's alive, Sam thought, repeating the words in her mind as she fought to keep the doppelganger from strangling her.

179

You have to save her. You have to save your little girl.

It was still possible. No matter what had happened, Dani was alive and Sam could get her back. But first she had to get away from the doppelganger. The creature leaned in close, so that it could whisper its next words in Sam's ear, and Sam abruptly released her right hand's grip on the cord, took hold of the murderess's hair, and yanked the woman forward with all that was left of her strength, sending the doppelganger's head into the door. The pain was not enough to stop the creature, but the moment of surprise was sufficient to cause the doppelganger to loosen her grip on Sam's body and mind. Sight returned to Sam as she broke free and rolled away from the doppelganger, struggling to catch her breath.

Sam forced herself to her feet, her hand reaching out for support. She was surprised as her fingers closed over a doorknob. Turning it automatically, Sam was relieved as it opened. The doppelganger, still wearing the ravaged form of her mother, rose up and lunged at her. Sam made it inside the bedroom and slammed the door on the creature. Before she could even look down to see if the door had a lock, the door burst open, sending Sam spiraling back until her leg struck something and she fell back, onto a bed. She was in one of the master bedrooms. The doppelganger stood in the doorway, chest heaving. Sam looked for anything she could use as a weapon.

Suddenly she realized that the sheets were stiff. She chanced a look downward and saw the blood stains. She was on the same bed where her daughter had lost her virginity, she understood, and anger flared inside her.

On the nightstand, beside the bed, lay her daughter's mirrored sunglasses. The doppelganger launched herself at Sam as she reached over, grabbed the glasses, and propped open one of the metal arms. The creature reached Sam and she stabbed with the glasses, driving the six inch long sliver of metal into the monster's eye.

180

The doppelganger screamed and writhed, beating and clawing at Sam, who was finally able to throw the creature off and leave it to die on the bed. Finally, it ceased in its agonies and Sam collapsed in a nearby chair, her heart thundering.

Sam waited until the pain in her head and chest subsided somewhat, then slowly made her way to the bed. She had been tempted simply to get the hell out of the house. There was no way she was going to be able to sell Pullman on this woman as the perp. But she had nowhere to go, no idea where Dani might have been taken, or by whom.

That was not true. The doppelganger had known about this place. She had gotten around in it with ease. That meant she was connected to Dani's new friends. In some twisted fashion, it was all connected.

Sam steeled herself and finally managed to examine the corpse. A part of her had been certain that the body would spring to inhuman life at any moment, but the rational, calming side of her nature reminded her that she had seen enough death in her time to know when a body was going to stay down. This one wasn't going anywhere.

The doppelganger had fallen on her stomach. Sam brushed the wild, tangled mass of hair from the woman's face and gasped. The doppelganger had been female, but she wasn't a woman, not yet. It was a child, fifteen at best.

"Oh Christ," Sam whispered, trying to reconcile the young, vulnerable girl lying on the bed with the creature that had tried on two separate occasions to murder her and had nearly succeeded both times. She barely made it to the small, adjoining bathroom before she became ill. When she was through, Sam stood at the foot of the bed for a time, staring at the body.

"What the hell are you?" she asked the dead girl, knowing that she would receive no reply. Then she saw that there was a wallet stuffed into the back pocket of the girl's jeans. Sam withdrew it carefully and began to search through its contents. There were five one hundred dollar bills, an assortment of tens and twenties, and a ream of credit cards.

When Sam saw the name on the credit cards, she recoiled. She feared that her perceptions were still untrustworthy. What she had seen was impossible. Then she forced herself to look at the lettering on the Visa Gold card a second time.

There had been no mistake.

A cold, angry fist closed over her heart as she pocketed the wallet, and fought the urge to race from the beach house. She looked at the body and knew what had to be done. Dani was in terrible danger, but she would not be able to help her daughter if she was being hunted for murder.

Sam took a shower, found a pair of gloves, then proceeded to mop down the house, erasing all evidence of her battle with the doppelganger. She found a strange, steel door in the kitchen with a security padlock beside it, similar to the one outside. Fortunately, the door was open. Sam returned to the bedroom, wrapped the body in a sheet, and carried the body downstairs.

The basement was more like a bomb shelter. The walls were heavily reinforced, with concrete floors and walls that Sam guessed were at least three feet thick. Some eccentric with a nuclear holocaust phobia had built it, evidently. Sam carefully laid the body in the far corner, then did what she could to camouflage it.

There was a pair of lockers near the stairs. Sam couldn't explain why she felt drawn to them, but she found a crowbar and forced the lock from the first one. Inside, she found a small arsenal. Handguns, pump-action rifles, automatic weapons, grenades, hunting knives, and more. Some of them appeared to be brand new, others had the look and smell of antiques. Sam thought of the officer who had owned the gun she had taken from the doppelganger in the parking garage the night before and wondered what stories she might find attached to each of these weapons.

A weapon from this batch was supposed to kill me, Sam realized. And I nearly used it to shoot my baby. Christ, what was I thinking?

Sam had been reliving those near fatal few seconds in her mind since the incident occurred. She could not block out her daughter's expression, the girl's wide, golden eyes and trembling lips as her shock turned to anger and betrayal.

Can't think about that right now. Can't think about it.

By training her attention on the cold facts, Sam attempted to turn her mind from what had happened with Dani and her murder of the doppelganger. She surveyed the guns more closely.

There were several nine-millimeter automatics. Sam recognized two as Beretta 92Fs. The military had replaced the Colt .45 with the nine-millimeter as the standard military sidearm in 1985. The Berettas were faster and more accurate, bordering on competition with the .357 Magnum. The gun held a fifteen round magazine, weighed two and a half pounds fully loaded, and was eight and a half inches long. Mel Gibson had used one of these in *Lethal Weapon*. There was an entire cache of Parabellum ammo with the weapons.

Images of the dead girl crowded before Sam. She took a series of deep breaths then turned to another weapon, a submachine gun. The moment her hand touched the weapon, Sam was overcome by an image of Dani crouched before her, hands raised, as the machine gun suddenly discharged, slicing the girl apart.

"The M76," Sam said shakily, determined to proceed professionally. Recalling the weapon drills she had endured during her professional and private training, Sam rattled off a litany of facts, praying that if she said the words aloud, her mind would focus fully on the cold, austere details, and would not torment her with further devastating and frightening images. She *had* to find a way to calm down. "The M76 uses the same ammunition as the 9mm. Selective fire capabilities with a full-auto cyclic rate of seven hundred and twenty rounds per minute. Folding steel stock. Weighs approximately nine pounds with a full thirty-six round magazine. This is good."

She selected a shotgun. "Remington 870P. Police action. Semiautomatic. Twenty-one inch barrel, seven round mag standard. Twelve gauge."

Sam flinched as she remembered the sound the sharp metal frame of the glasses made as they sank into the girl's head.

"Concentrate, goddamn you, this is for Dani!"

Sam inventoried the other weapons. The most interesting find was a pair of flamethrowers. She examined the room more closely and realized that it had been built not to keep someone out, but to keep someone in. They probably used this place to stash their victims until they were ready for them. Remove the weapons, shove someone down here.

Had Dani been held here? No, Sam decided. There was too much dust. The weapons hadn't been moved recently and they couldn't be stupid enough to put someone down here with all this for them to find. Besides, they didn't need to treat her as a captive, she had gone voluntarily.

"Fuck," Sam said, busying herself with the weapons once more. Sam spent an hour checking the weaponry, cleaning one of the handguns, then loading each of them with the copious ammunition she found in the second locker. Then she wrapped them in blankets she found in the hall closet upstairs and loaded them into the trunk of her car.

It was night by the time she was ready to leave, and there was one last task she needed to perform. She examined the doppelganger's body more thoroughly and came away with a set of car keys.

184

The doppelganger.

The *creature*.

Sam hated herself for her weakness in continuing to label the creature as such, but when she thought of the monster as a dead, fifteen-year-old child that she had killed, the world would begin to spin and she would fall to the ground, shuddering. She drove the girl's car, a brand new cherry-red Porsche, three miles down the road and left it. Then she walked back, removed the loaded Beretta from her newfound weapons stash, and headed for the address she had found on the fake ID the doppelganger was carrying.

Fifteen

Dani was free. She had never felt so alive. The flickering lights of Los Angeles looked surreal as she sat in the back of Angel's classic Thunderbird. Bill and Isabella flanked her. Angel drove and Madison sat beside her. The windows were open. The cool night air rushed in as they barreled through the streets. Dani howled in delight, along with her companions.

"Stop there," Bill said as he pointed to the corner. "I want to show Dani something."

Angel slowed the car and yanked it over to the side of the street. They were in a terrible section of downtown Los Angeles, near the entrance to a strip club. Bill opened the door and hopped out of the car before it had come to a full stop. He was wearing a long, black leather trench coat, black pants and shoes, and a fishnet shirt that revealed the lean muscles of his chest. All the girls dressed in what Dani would have once considered "slutty" attire. A week ago she would have been horrified at the thought of standing in the privacy of a dressing room, trying on clothes like the ones she had borrowed from Madison. Tonight, she was boldly strutting around in public, wearing the sexiest clothes she had ever seen outside of a Victoria's Secret catalog. She wore thigh-high black leather boots, a black micromini, and a satin and lace top revealing her generous breasts and the narrow U-shaped cleavage between them. The sunglasses had been left behind so people

186

would notice her eyes. Dani felt a need for them to stop and stare. She flushed with excitement at the thought of the desire they would radiate when they saw her.

Dani leapt from the car and followed Bill past the strip club, to the corner.

"What are we doing here?" she asked breathlessly.

"You'll see. Generally it's best not to draw attention, but tonight's a special occasion and I feel like indulging."

They turned the corner and Dani realized what had caught Bill's attention: A man and a woman were arguing. They had drawn a small crowd. Powerfully exciting waves of emotion radiated from all those gathered. Dani shuddered with pleasure. She wondered how Bill had detected them. He couldn't have seen them from the car. Had he sensed the woman's distress, the man's anger, at such a distance?

"If you rely on your eyes alone, you will be blind," Bill Yoshino whispered, confirming her suspicion.

Dani nodded, realizing that in this, as in so many other things, she was the student and it was best for her to quietly observe. She studied the scene before them. The woman was dressed as a prostitute. Dani restrained a laugh. So was *she,* for that matter. The woman had on a Day-Glo orange bra, a white skirt, and a pair of white stiletto heels. She was black and busty. Her ghost-white hair looked like a wig. Sunglasses with green lenses obscured her eyes. Her lips were large, split open, and bleeding. The man had her pinned against the wall.

"Greetings and salutations," Bill said as he effortlessly parted the small crowd of watchers. They were mostly women, scantily dressed. He caught the attention of the man who had given the prostitute a bloody lip.

"What do you want?" the man asked. He was a white man with a slight build. Dark hair spilled into the dark, evil pits of his feral eyes. A shit-eating grin ripped across

187

his cadaverous face, deep-set lines forming around his eyes and mouth. He wore a bomber jacket, a white T-shirt, and tight blue jeans.

Dani turned her attention to the woman, trying to understand why she cowered against the wall, enduring his abuse.

"Can't you see that we're busy?" the man said, begging for a confrontation.

Bill opened his hands in a solicitous gesture. "I just wanted to ask a favor."

"Yeah? What's that? You and your girl need a friend for the night? Patsi and Charice aren't doing anything except standing around diddling themselves."

Dani felt two women in the crowd draw into themselves at the mention of their names. Images of each woman receiving beatings crowded into Dani's mind, along with the exquisite fear accompanying the memories.

Bill turned to Dani. "She'll tell you."

Dani tensed. "But I —"

"Anything you want," Bill said. "You have only to ask."

A shudder ran through her. Though she was high on the woman's fear, she had the clarity of mind to understand what Bill was getting at: Even as an Initiate, she had great power. She could manipulate this man in any way she so desired.

The smell of the prostitute's blood drifted to her. She wanted to glide across the space separating them and lick the blood from the woman's lips, then plunge her tongue down her throat.

Christ, what are you thinking? Dani shouted in her mind, snapping out of the blood haze that began to suffuse her. She looked at the prostitute and saw that the woman was grinding her thighs together and caressing her breasts. Dani was both frightened and pleased to know that it was because of her. She gathered her thoughts and attempted to ease the intense sexual need

188

that soaked the air. Within seconds, the prostitute fell back against the wall, removed her sunglasses, and rubbed at her eyes, trying to prevent her shame-ridden tears.

The man in the bomber jacket looked away from the prostitute in contempt. He shook his head, then regarded Bill. "So your girlfriend's got a request. Does she have any money?"

Dani watched him, amazed at how brazen he was. He was a pimp, the woman one of his whores, nothing but property to be beaten and whipped into shape according to his standards. He was completely open about it. *Here's the going rate. You interested?*

In Tampa, a man like this would have been paranoid about undercover cops. But this man made no secret of what he was and what he had been doing to the woman. He liked the attention. He loved the fear his words and actions generated.

"I don't think you were listening too well," the man in the bomber jacket said quietly. "I hate repeating myself."

"We don't *need* money," Bill said. "We've got something better than that."

"There's nothing better than money." The man's attitude was changing, his limited patience was at its end. For an instant, Dani was certain that she could see blood red flashes surrounding the man. Dangerous hues. The uncomfortable sensation of ice-cold steel upon flesh came to her. The man was armed. Thoughts of escape flooded into her mind. The man grinned, sensing her fear. He may not have been one of their kind, but he was a born predator. He subsided on fear just as they did. The man laughed and turned back to his woman.

Anything you want. You have only to ask.

There was something she wanted. It wasn't rational. It wasn't in keeping with the mandates of their kind as she understood them, but at that moment she did not care. She fought the temptation to make him hurt the prostitute again so she could feel the woman's fear and shame. Instead, Dani lashed out with her thoughts, staggering the man. He dropped to his knees and several women in the crowd gasped.

The prostitute sank against the wall, realizing how close she had come to being struck again. She shook with gratitude and relief. Dani sensed that the woman was thanking God for whatever had caused the man to fall away from her. The thought made her laugh.

On his knees, the man in the bomber jacket flung his head back and forth, trying to regain control of his body. Dani was too quick for him. She forced him to turn and crawl toward the prostitute. Her relief faded instantly, her fear returning as she wondered what he was going to do to her. Dani made him lower his face to the black woman's white, stiletto heel.

Kiss it, Dani thought.

The man obeyed. The prostitute nearly laughed with nervous tension. She tried to draw away and the man caught her foot. His touch was not rough, it was tender, reverent. She relaxed somewhat.

Take the heel into your mouth and suck on it, Dani commanded.

The man did as he was told. A wave of jittery laughter broke from the crowd.

You love it. It's making you hard. Dani whispered in the narrow reaches separating her from her victim as she sent her thoughts to the mind of the kneeling man. His hips began to move rhythmically. *Suck like you were sucking a dick, you bastard. Try and make it come. Just like you're going to.*

The man's hips jerked spasmodically and a stain appeared on his jeans. Roars of laughter and waves of taunts issued from the crowd, from the men and the women whom this man had held in thrall. At the center of the crowd, the man rolled on his back, whimpering with shame.

"I'm sorry," he blubbered. "I've been bad. I didn't mean to be."

He deserves to be punished, Dani thought, sending her will through the crowd. *Punish him.*

The prostitute with the split lip kicked the man. Tentatively, at first, then with great venom and joy. Several others broke from the crowd and joined her, racing past Dani as they closed over the man, beating and kicking him.

Dani felt the man's fear, intensified it, and fed from his terror until he was plunged into unconsciousness by a kick to the head. The sensations faded and Dani quivered.

Bill took Dani by the arm and led her back to the car. "How did that feel?"

The experience had not been as satisfying as Dani had anticipated. She had expected to feel the rush of gratitude, the worship of those she had liberated, but those sensations had been empty and hollow. It wasn't until she had inspired abject horror in the heart of the man in the bomber jacket that the delicious rush came back to her.

"There's nothing like fear," Bill said as he opened the door for her and allowed her to slip inside.

"Nothing except *desire*," Isabella purred, correcting him as she placed her hands on Dani's shoulders and gave the girl a light hug.

"You know it," Madison called from the front seat. Stoically, Angel nodded her head. The Thunderbird pulled back into traffic. Several minutes passed before anyone spoke. Dani felt relaxed and happy. Isabella smiled approvingly. Madison's eyes sparkled as she regarded Dani from the front seat with a grin. Bill took her hand and held it.

"Is anybody hungry?" Bill asked.

"But I thought you said that human food was — distasteful to our kind," Dani said.

"Listen to her," Angel chortled. *"Our kind.*

You always did move fast, Bill."

"Shut up, Angel," Bill spat. The woman shrugged and fell silent. "And we're not going there for human food, anyway."

Bill gave Angel directions to an elegant restaurant up the coast. They drove in silence, Dani taking in the sounds of the night, her senses heightened to an impossible degree. Isabella lightly stroked her hair as Bill held her tight. They left the city and the rush of nearby waves moved through Dani. Her pulse quickened as she recalled the sublime taste of fear she had coaxed out of the man in the bomber jacket.

Something troubled her, but she could not tell exactly what, and so she surrendered to the comfort of her companions' sweet caresses. When Isabella kissed her neck, Dani did not feel threatened or repulsed, only excited. Isabella's kisses burned her flesh with a cold, beautiful fire. As they sped along the highway, Dani felt as if they might take to the air at any moment. The ride was that smooth.

She fantasized about soaring high above the earth in the comfort of her friend's arms, the doors of the T-Bird spreading open like wings as the car transformed into something from an old James Bond movie. Dani had never flown in her dreams. She had read accounts in psychology texts when she had been in school. A part of her had always wondered what it would be like to experience such freedom.

Sliding deep into the cradle of Bill's arms, Dani allowed herself to be swept up on the wings of a magnificent dream: She was flying above the Thunderbird, arms outstretched, the wind softly caressing her. Pirouetting in the air, she allowed herself to falter slightly and found that she was sailing beside the rear passenger door of the car. Looking in, she saw her physical body asleep in Bill's arms. Isabella continued to stroke her shoulder and kiss her neck, the woman's long hair brushing against the exposed flesh of Dani's breasts.

192

Angel caught sight of her. With a frown, the woman floored the T-Bird.

Dani lifted higher and raced the Thunderbird for a time. Soon it became clear that she was faster than the blur of a vehicle beneath her, she was beyond the capacities of any man-made object. She was a creature of nature, wild and free, wondrously alive and one with the night.

Dani broke off and flew up into the clouds. She rose so high that her exhilaration momentarily gave way to fear and she almost lost control. Suddenly she was bursting through the cloud layer, looking out on a pillowy vista of soft white clouds, her control once again absolute. The moon was before her, full and bright, its light almost blinding. She flew into the moon, its light consuming her vision.

For the first time in her life, she was at peace.

Sixteen

"Dani?"

The voice called her back. Madison's voice. Dani shook herself awake and found that the light hadn't abated. A flashlight was being shined in her face. Recalling the manner in which she had woken in the trapper's home, wrists taped to the chair, the glare of a flashlight in her eyes, Dani felt a sudden surge of panic. She bolted upright in the backseat, hands flailing.

"Calm down," Madison said with a laugh, averting the beam of light.

Dani settled as she reoriented herself. She was the only one left in the Thunderbird. Madison stood outside, holding open the rear passenger door. Dani looked around and saw that they were in a parking lot across the street from a posh, well-lighted restaurant. Valet parking was available at the door.

"Where is everyone?" Dani asked.

"Waiting for you."

Nodding, Dani hauled herself from the car. Her hair had been blown into mad tangles. It must have been the open window, she told herself. And Isabella's constant playing with it.

The others waited under a streetlight some fifty feet away, heatedly discussing something. They quieted as they saw Dani and Madison approach. Dani realized that they were not dressed for this restaurant. Men and women in formal wear were gathered near the door.

"They're never going to let us in, the way we're dressed," Dani said as she took Bill's outstretched hand.

"That depends on how they see us," he replied.

"What do you mean?"

"You know. You can make them see us any way you like."

Dani yawned, immediately raising her hand to cover her mouth, her eyes wide. "Sorry. Look, I can't do that. I don't know how."

"You have to learn sometime."

Dani finally caught on. She was being given an education into their ways. Though she understood that what he was proposing was indeed possible, she had no idea how to influence the manner in which their group was perceived. "All right, professor. Tell me what I need to know to pull this off."

"All you need to be is a good listener," Isabella said as she took Dani's arm.

"I don't understand."

"Listen with your heart and your mind. Try to feel. Reach out —"

Angel cut the woman off. "You sound like a long-distance ad. All you have to do is *this*."

Dani watched as Angel's form shimmered and changed, suddenly becoming the mocking twin of the friend she had lost to the trapper and his brother. "Jami!"

Bill advanced on Angel and slapped her hard. The image of Dani's dead friend fell away, and Angel raised her hand to her cheek.

"You can be such a bitch," Madison said.

"And you love it," Angel replied.

Madison was silent. Dani stared at her new friends,

forcing away the dual shocks of seeing Jami and also bearing witness to Bill performing an act of violence. Glancing at the crimson welt on Angel's face, Dani had to restrain a smile. She was coming to loathe that platinum-haired tramp, anyway.

Bill rested his hands on Dani's bare shoulders. At his touch, the incredible sexual energy of the previous night flooded into her. She wanted nothing more than to press his face against her breasts and feel his hands spider across her body.

"You have to be calm and focused," Bill said, his voice laced with impatience. His face suddenly became hard. As if she had been slapped into awareness, Dani forced her attention away from her sexual daydreams. She did not want to disappoint Bill. She loved him with all her heart.

His expression softened. "Just try."

Nodding, Dani allowed her eyelids to flutter closed. She tried to find an image they had both shared. The sound of Bill's laughter accompanied by a few startled gasps caused her to open her eyes.

Bill had changed. He was no longer Japanese-American. He wore a suit that was half a century out of date, and his features were rugged and dashing.

He was also totally devoid of color.

Any color.

He was Laurence Olivier in *Rebecca,* a film shot in glorious black and white by Alfred Hitchcock. She raised her hands before her face. They were gray and white. There was no doubt in her mind that she had become Joan Fontaine, the heroine of the picture.

"Well, my dear?" Bill said in Olivier's perfect voice.

Dani released her hold on the illusion. It fell away and she saw Bill smiling at her.

"God, that's wonderful," she said with a laugh.

"We can play later."

She nodded. There was a hint of devilishness in his

196

voice. She imagined taking on the images of movie stars as she made love with Bill, kissing Olivier and Redford, looking up into the straining face of Mel Gibson as he pounded into her. Then she frowned. Of course, that *seemed* like an amusing idea, but she wanted Bill to desire her for herself, not for a fantasy image of her. And she did not need any of those other men. She loved only him.

"Try again," Bill prompted. "Reach out to the man at the front desk. Find someone who would be familiar to him."

Dani bit her lip as she attempted to use her power. There were so many people in the restaurant. All she received was a confusing jumble of images.

"Focus," Isabella urged, taking Dani's hand.

Dani trained her attention on a couple standing just outside the open doors of the restaurant. They could see inside, where the man at the front desk waited. Straining, she could see through the woman's eyes. Suddenly, she had a perfect view of the man Bill mentioned. He was tall and handsome, with layered brown hair and rich green eyes. Dani forced her perceptions to hop the distance from the woman looking at the man at the front desk to the man himself. Then she was in his mind, sifting through the images she found there.

She discovered that he had been an embezzler, an agent of corporate America who stole from his employers. They let him go quietly, to avoid embarrassment, but he had not been able to find work in his field again. This job, as a restaurant host, was the best he could find. He had become used to the position, even happy here. There was very little pressure and he was approached by women constantly.

Dani tore the images of several regulars from his mind. She learned the names and habits of a wealthy, sophisticated couple and three beautiful young women. He had dreamt of having the younger women in bed, all at one time. To see them together would be a treat. Dani retreated from his mind, stealing away on the bright, silver thread that had connected their consciousnesses.

Previously, she had viewed her power as a dark, amorphous blob with talons and teeth. Now she recognized the sleek, powerful beauty of her ability. When her perceptions cleared, she saw that she and her friends had become the wealthy couple and their three lovely guests.

"Shall we?" Bill asked. He was now close to forty, with salt-and-pepper hair and a generous smile. Even his voice was alien.

"Yes," Dani said in a voice that startled her, but to which she would soon became accustomed. Each of the girls wore designer originals. At first, Dani could not tell which of the three women was Isabella. Their assumed shapes were totally different from their true forms. When they spoke, their voices did not give them away, but their patterns of speech revealed them instantly. Dani gravitated toward Isabella.

They went into the restaurant, secured a table without apparent difficulty, and were seated. The restaurant host commented that he was unaware that Mr. and Mrs. Dvorak knew Elise, Lorraine, and Thessila, the women whose forms had been stolen to cloak Madison, Isabella, and Angel.

"We met in Versailles," Bill said. "On vacation."

Madison smiled at the host, leaning forward slightly to ensure that he would have a perfect view of her cleavage. From his expression, the gesture was not unappreciated.

"He's coming with us," Madison whispered as the man vanished into the restaurant.

"Not tonight," Bill said, unable to take his gaze from Dani, who adored the attention.

198

"But tonight's supposed to be *my* night," Madison said with a slight pout.

Dani recalled suddenly that this evening was meant for Madison to be turned from an Initiate to a full vampire. The thought dampened her romantic, playful mood.

"It is," Bill said reassuringly. "It's the night for both of you."

Dani shuddered as she recalled the story Bill had told of Antonius and his sons. She was enjoying the night so far and she didn't want to see it ruined by what she guessed was involved in the "turning ceremony." Thus far, she had been able to convince herself that she belonged to a race that held magic in its breast, not murder. Even if that was an illusion, she needed to hold on to it for a bit longer.

"Don't worry," Angel said coarsely, "Bill won't rush you."

"That's for sure," Madison said. "I've been waiting forever." She frowned. "This is my night and I should get to pick."

"Stop whining," Angel complained.

Bill only laughed. "Don't worry, Madison. We'll let you pick, but not here. We're here for a different reason."

Madison sighed. "But, my God, what a tush that guy had. I would have loved to have sunk my teeth into him."

"There will be other opportunities," Isabella said reassuringly.

Dani relaxed and suddenly realized that she was hungry. She hadn't eaten in more than twenty-four hours and her stomach growled. The waiter arrived and Bill ordered for everyone. When their meals arrived, Dani and Madison ate ravenously, Bill, Angel, and Isabella picking at their food.

When Dani was finished, she eyed Bill's dish and allowed him to feed her from his plate. It was a wonderfully sensuous experience and it reminded her of her dream from the other night. Suddenly she thought of where she had been when she had the dream, of her mother and her other life. Sadness washed over her.

"What are you thinking about?" Isabella asked.

Dani knew that she could not lie to Isabella. The woman would know instantly. "My mother," she said in a small voice.

"That life is finished," Isabella said, gentle, but firm. "We are your family now."

Bill kissed her unexpectedly, and all thoughts of her mother, particularly the disquieting image of Samantha Walthers aiming a gun at her only daughter, fled from Dani's mind.

"I love you," Dani whispered. Bill kissed her again. Harder this time. She knew that he felt the same way about her, but she wanted to hear the words.

Her need must have been evident, because he took her hand in his and whispered, "Soon. Very soon."

She thought of what had awaited her the last time he said those words: They had made love. She contented herself with the knowledge that there was more to come, much more.

"What we did tonight," Bill said abruptly, releasing her hand, "was vulgar."

Dani flinched. "What are you talking about?"

"On the street, before we came here. The procurer. The man you hurt."

"I didn't hurt him."

"But you *caused* him to be hurt." He shrugged.

Dani suddenly felt defensive. "But you told me—"

"He deserved it, of course. I'm not denying that."

"All right," she said warily.

"But there are other ways. I want you to learn them."

Dani ran her napkin over her face. Her appetite

waned. She wanted more than anything to please Bill, but his expression frightened her. He was not giving her a choice in this. "What do you want me to do?"

"Look there," he said, nodding casually toward a table less than twenty feet away. A handsome man sat at the table with his date. Though his manners were impeccable in every other regard, he had a nasty habit of chewing and swallowing the crushed ice in his drink.

His date was a rather plain girl who had purchased the finest clothes but did not have the innate grace to wear them well. She wore too much makeup. Her hair had been set in the style made famous by a recent actress. On this woman, it seemed ridiculous. The cumulative effect was overkill.

Dani recoiled as the woman's perfume drifted across the restaurant to her. It smelled of pain and death. Curling her lips in disgust, Dani realized that it should have been impossible for her to detect a single scent over such a distance. Inhuman.

That's right, kiddo. That's what you are, she told herself. And you're okay with that, right, Dani? You're just fine. So why are your hands shaking, Dani? Why is that?

Bill touched her shoulder. She looked at him sharply.

"Tell me about them," Bill said.

Dani looked toward the other women, who watched her expectantly. "Yeah. Yeah, okay."

Reaching out with her mind was much easier for her this time. The silver thread extended and she gently leeched away the woman's secret fears and desires.

Dani shook violently. What she had seen was painful and dark. Isabella took her hand, steadying her.

"Her name is Rikki. She's tried to kill herself twice," Dani said shakily. "Both times over him.

Dominick. He has no idea. He's totally wrapped up in himself."

"Get it from both sides," Bill said. "No guesswork."

Dani extended the silver thread and entered the man's thoughts. She shook again as she withdrew.

"Bastard," she hissed.

"You can tell us," Angel said cruelly. "We're your *friends*."

"Stop that," Madison chided. "This is our night and you're ruining it."

Angel looked away, muttering an apology.

"Go on, sweetheart," Madison said. "I know this is important. What is it about this man that makes you so angry? What did you see?"

Dani drew a deep breath, trying to compose herself. She had encountered such a dark collection of memories within Dominick that she wished she had not delved into his mind.

"It would be better if you talked about it," Isabella said.

Dani felt her resistance easing. "Dominick's a hustler, though he doesn't admit that, even to himself."

"Good," Bill said.

"He hasn't worked a straight job in six years. He models sometimes and he's even done some pornos. That's just for pocket money. Everything he owns, even his place, is bought and paid for by ladies like Rikki, who fall in love with him and give him anything he wants. He's a user."

"Scum, I agree," Bill said drolly. Isabella shot him a look. "Tell me more."

Dani watched Dominick chew on the crushed ice in his drink. "He hurts women. He likes it. He likes to tie them up and do things to them. But only if they consent. Only if he can persuade himself that they really like it. Sometimes he can persuade them, too. Sometimes he doesn't have to."

202

She focused on his perfect teeth, closing over the ice.

"And that's bad?" Bill asked.

"Yes."

"That makes him a bad man, doesn't it?"

"It does," Dani said. "Yes."

"And we all know what happens to bad men."

"We do." She stared at Dominick. Saw his perfect lips. Perfect hair. Perfect teeth. Perfect face. The ice in his glass glittered in the restaurant's candlelight.

Glittered like so much broken glass.

Suddenly, the man shoved against the table, dropping his drink. Dani saw blood on the water glass. Pink liquid swirled through the water. The glass hit the table, fell off, and broke on the floor. The man clutched at his mouth, gobs of blood trailing from his fingers. Rikki, his companion, screamed.

Incoherent cries came from Dominick as he opened his jaws wide, revealing shards of glass poking from his cheeks. His tongue had been cut to ribbons. His throat worked furiously to dispel the unwelcome stream of glass slowly making its way down his windpipe, to his stomach, where it would rip his guts apart.

He was dying and he knew it. The pain was incredible. His mind wanted to shut down, but Dani was there with him, experiencing his terror, and she would not allow his consciousness to retreat and deny her the animal pleasure of his last thoughts.

Dani sat at the table, her body shuddering as she devoured his fear. She felt as if she was enduring the electrifying aftershocks of some terrible explosion. The man's fear went nova.

Suddenly, a second, even more powerful series of shocks wracked Dani's body: Rikki, the woman who had been obsessed with Dominick, and had attempted to end her life twice because of him, was confronting

203

the ugliness of his death and the lonely void that would be waiting for her when he was gone. Her fear lit up the room for Dani. The restaurant seemed to be engulfed in bloodred flames.

"Oh God, no, no!" Rikki screamed. The woman tried to deny the evidence of her senses, but Dani would not allow it. Dominick was dying. His blood was on the tablecloth, on the fine silk dress she had bought this afternoon, everywhere.

Dani suddenly noticed that no one else in the restaurant was paying any attention to the dying man and his screaming girlfriend. The emotions she had ripped from Rikki and Dominick crested. She found herself coming back to full awareness. Bill and the girls displayed signs that they had shared in the experience. Dani looked back to the table and saw that Dominick and Rikki were sitting at the table, staring at one another in horror, but they were fine. Dominick had not been hurt. There was no blood.

Understanding came to Dani. She had exposed each of their fears. Dominick had been terrified of losing his only true asset, his handsome appearance. Rikki had been frightened beyond all reason at the idea of losing her lover. On a stage that existed solely in their minds, she had made the couple act out those fears. Dani knew that if she had pressed on, she could have shattered either of their sanities perhaps even stopped their hearts with the fear she had inspired.

It was horrible. What had made her do such a thing? Punishing Dominick for being a prick seemed like a good idea at the time. The experience had been incredibly satisfying. But she had also played with Rikki, an innocent victim. What kind of monster was she to hurt such a fragile creature?

But no *true* harm had been done, and a hunger that Dani had barely been aware of had been sated, at least for now.

"Come on," Bill said with a grin. "We're leaving."

As they rose, Dani glanced at Rikki and Dominick. They were chatting pleasantly, the color returning to their faces. Dani believed they would never talk about what had happened. She hoped, however, that Rikki would smarten up and see Dominick for what he was. She toyed with the idea of dumping some of Dominick's unsavory memories into Rikki's head, but she knew that she had done enough damage. The woman's mind may not be strong enough for any more shocks.

Dani turned away.

They passed the restaurant host on the way out. Bill used his power to convince the man that they had already paid, and Madison lingered near the man until Angel hauled her away. They returned to the Thunderbird and Dani was amazed that the illusion she had cast before they went in had not fallen while she was in the throes of the psychic meal she had consumed. Isabella smiled and their false appearances vanished. She had been helping Dani.

They got in the car and drove back in the direction of the highway. "What I did in there," Dani said, "I thought it was really happening."

"That's the first stage," Bill said.

Isabella stroked her arm. "If you believe it, they'll believe it."

"But I got caught up in it. I should have known that it wasn't real. I was making it happen."

Bill shrugged. "You'll learn to separate yourself. It comes with practice. Don't worry about it, you did very well."

"So where are we headed?" Angel said as they approached the turnoffs.

"I'd say it's time to get *fucked*." Madison said with a holler. Then she turned in her seat and cautiously peered over the rim at Bill. "If that's okay with you."

"Anything you want. It's *your* night," he said.

Dani felt an odd pang of jealousy at this exchange. She recalled her earlier conversation with Madison concerning the girl's relationship with Bill. They had been lovers, but Madison swore there was nothing between them anymore. The thought of Bill with another woman—any other woman, let alone a friend—made Dani seethe.

You're being ridiculous, she reminded herself. Bill treats Madison as if she's a child. He treats you like a woman. He respects you. Get over it.

She turned her attention to Madison's unusual request.

"What's she talking about?" Dani asked nervously, picturing a visit to a whorehouse.

Isabella gave a slight laugh. "It's not what you think. It's a club. One of Angel and Madison's favorites."

"I still prefer the Sit 'n' Spin," Angel said.

"Well, it's not *your* night," Madison replied in her petulant, little-girl voice.

Angel laughed and shoved at her friend roughly. "At least we're dressed for it."

Dani suddenly became conscious of her provocative clothing and wondered exactly what kind of club they were going to. It occurred to her that both of the men she had hurt tonight could easily have been of their kind. One inspired fear, the other desire. They subsisted on the strong emotions they generated.

So what makes us any different? What makes us any better?

She felt a sudden, stabbing pain in her gut. The hunger was back, worse than ever.

I'm empty, a vessel that needs to be filled. The more you put into me, the greater my need the next time.

The voice of her hunger. Christ, she thought. Life as a vampire seemed to be like living each day on Chinese food. You could eat like crazy and never get filled up, never be fully satisfied. Her appetite for fear was returning.

She would have expected the emotions she had tasted in downtown L.A. with the pimp to have been enough for one night, but they had only awakened a deeper appetite. Would the experience in the restaurant prove to be nothing more than a precursor to a more frightening and deadly need that she would not be able to control so easily? The gnawing hunger in her soul seemed to confirm this.

"Bill," Dani said, "you gave me the idea that L.A.'s crawling with our kind. Are we going to see any of them at this club?"

"It's always possible," he said. From his expression, he obviously did not find the idea to be an appealing one.

They continued the drive in silence.

Seventeen

The T-Bird stopped in Silverlake. They entered a bar that, for tonight, had been converted to the underground *Club Fuck!* The Fuck! was a dance club catering to every homophobic's worst nightmares: Leather bound go-go boys flogged one another with whips raising glaring red and white welts on their flesh. Half-naked men and women walked past in fishnet and leather corsets, rings hanging from their nipples, bizarre tattoos covering exposed flesh from head to foot. The music was hard and loud, a mix Madison identified as "thrash." To Dani, it was a discordant mess. Somehow she was not surprised when, to the delight of the crowd, the drummer of the live band broke out a chain saw and went to work on his instruments.

Bill and Isabella drifted off and Angel threw herself into the "mosh pit" before the band, where the audience became participants in what Dani thought of as the night's debaucheries. Some dancers flung themselves against one another, while others duck walked, stomped, and thrust with knees high and elbows pointed. A knot of what had been humanity swelled into a frenzied mass of sharp, violent movement as the industrial sounds of FBI—Freebase International—piped in from above. The music had a repetitive, programmed beat, techno-chords slashing against a backdrop of thundering, dull, heavy bass. A distorted blanket of buzzing electric fog hung, enshrouding the sounds.

Angel danced with a woman whose bare breasts exposed twin pierced nipples. On a chain threaded between them hung a heavy, inverted crucifix. Angel and the woman flung themselves against one another with abandon. Dani grabbed Madison's arm and attempted to find a quiet corner.

"What are we doing here?" Dani asked, alarmed.

"Prey," Madison said, her tongue darting from her lips.

The word epitomized Dani's fears. She tore her gaze from Madison, hoping to hide her revulsion, and saw that Angel was kissing the woman with whom she had been dancing. Their tongues fluttered out and Dani realized that the other woman's tongue had been pierced. Dani averted her gaze, but everywhere she looked, she saw men wantonly sliding against other men, their bodies greased with sweat and desire, and pairs of women grinding and mashing their bodies together.

The music of Nine Inch Nails flooded through the club. Dani shuddered as the lyrics assaulted her: *"Head like a hole, black as your soul, I'd rather die, than give you control!"*

Isabella came up behind Dani. "Let's dance," she whispered in Dani's ear, pressing herself close.

"No, I couldn't," Dani said, staring at the crowd. Despite her protests, the feel of Isabella's bare skin brought the stark, electrical charges she often felt at the woman's touch. "I don't know how to dance."

"I'll teach you," Isabella said. "Come with me."

Dani found herself powerless to resist. If Angel had proposed this, or even Madison, she would have turned them down. But as Isabella led her to the dance floor, Dani felt a comforting haze descend on her. Dani's heart slammed in time to the music.

"No one's watching," Isabella said as she began to sway. "It doesn't matter what we do."

Dani stared at the woman. In the red, throbbing lights of the club, she was even more beautiful than Dani had realized. She was unaware that her body had begun to move in time to Isabella's; all she saw were the woman's eyes.

Reaching out to Isabella, she was delighted to find that the woman did not resist her. Dani's hands gripped Isabella's hips and drew them closer. Her own hips gyrated, her body flowing with the same casual grace she had possessed when she had made love to Bill. She threw her head back as she swayed from side to side, her breasts bouncing slightly as she ground her lower body against Isabella's and bucked with the pulse of the music. As she flailed to the music, her hair whipping back and forth, she started to moan with pleasure.

"Feel it," Isabella screamed over the thunderous noise. "Feel what they're feeling!"

Dani needed no further urging. She opened herself to the protesting rants that she tore from the dancer's minds. *We're freaks. We're not like you. We don't* care *what you think*.

"Yes," Isabella murmured. "That's right!"

Dani took it in, the alienation, the rage that had been so much like what she had felt when she had been growing up, when she had known that she was unlike anyone else and tried to deny that she was all the better for the differences. The demon had known, the demon had tried to tell her, but she had quieted the demon. No more.

Grinding her crotch against Isabella's leg, Dani moaned and gasped, feeling the call of an orgasm fast approaching. Dani allowed her hands to trail upward, over Isabella's breasts. She took the woman's face in her hands, bringing it close to her own as her probing tongue escaped her lips.

No, sister-love. Isabella's husky voice penetrated the recesses of Dani's rapidly clouding mind. *You would not respect me afterward, nor yourself.*

Isabella released her power, gently easing Dani back from the tremulous brink she had been approaching. A surge of conflicting emotions passed through Dani: anger, joy, hurt, and gratitude. It was all burned away by the expression of perfect love that Isabella held in her eyes for Dani. They finished the dance, then held each other as the music crashed to a stop. Dani almost cried.

They do love me, Dani thought as she felt Isabella's thundering heart against her chest. They do.

Will you trust me? Isabella asked, her words softly biting into Dani's thoughts.

Yes. Totally.

Isabella pulled away from Dani and nodded to a corner in the back. "Look there."

Dani did as she was told. She saw Bill and Madison talking with a beautiful, statuesque woman who was not dressed for the Fuck! as they had been. The woman's honey-blond hair cascaded to her shoulders. She wore a white silk jacket, a white frilly blouse, a short white skirt, white lace panty hose, and white high heels. There was a drink in her hand. As she spoke to Bill and Madison, her stance seemed to change. Dani thought it looked as if the woman's spine had suddenly been yanked from her body. The woman's pose relaxed, then she started to falter. Bill grasped her arm, lending his strength to hers. Madison rescued her drink and found a place to set it down.

"What are they doing?" Dani whispered.

"Don't you know?"

And suddenly Dani *did* know. The knowledge

211

made her ill. "She's the one. Madison's going to be turned tonight and she's the one who has to die."

"It's the natural order," Isabella said. "A part of who and what we are."

"I don't know," Dani said.

"What don't you know, Dani? If you want to be a part of this? That's a decision you have to make. But even if you left us behind, even if you ran away, you could never travel far enough to get away from *this*."

Isabella's hands shot out, her fingernail brushing across the back of Dani's hand. A tiny red line, no more than an inch across, appeared, followed by an intense burning. For an instant, Dani felt angry and betrayed. Isabella had *hurt* her!

With amazing tenderness, Isabella lifted Dani's hand to her lips and slid her tongue over the tiny cut. She kissed Dani's flesh, long and hard. Dani felt her heart thunder, and a brief surge of phantasmagoric images entered her mind. Breathtakingly beautiful arrays of color exploded before her eyes. They faded, and Dani felt Isabella release her hand.

The cut had vanished.

"We are marked by our blood, sister-love."

Dani blanched, trying to understand what separated her kind from the violent madmen who had raped and murdered her best friend and would have gladly killed her, too, if the blood of immortals had not run in her veins.

"To deny what you are is to invite madness," Isabella said. "We do what we must to survive. The wolf doesn't mourn its kill. The wolf respects it. We are the animal, Dani. We are the beast. Its mark is upon us and for that we are grateful."

"That's not who I am!" Dani railed. "That's not who my mother raised me to be!"

"Your mother wanted to kill you last night."

Dani had no reply. She lowered her head and said softly, "I don't want to be alone."

"You don't have to be. Not ever again."

Dani looked at Bill, Madison, and the beautiful blonde. They approached her and Isabella went to retrieve Angel. It was time to leave the Fuck! and get on with the night's business.

As they left together, Dani realized that they were not walking toward the Thunderbird. They went to the other side of the parking lot, where a white, stretch limousine was parked.

"What are we doing?" Dani asked, turning to Bill.

"Therese here is the driver for Alexis Devlaine, a retired porn actress who made a killing as a producer and publisher," Bill said flatly, as if he were reading her bio from a card. Dani felt chastised for opening her mouth. Bill's sudden distance upset her. She saw Bill glance at Isabella and frown. Dani's trepidation lifted. Was he jealous of Isabella? That was ridiculous!

Dani suddenly recalled the way she had been dancing with Isabella and decided that it was not so ridiculous after all. She would have to work hard to make him realize that he was the only one she loved, at least in *that way*.

"If we had stayed a little longer, we could have seen Alexis getting spanked and shaved," Bill added. There was a cruel edge in his voice that bothered Dani. She wondered if it had always been there.

He turned his attention to Therese. Fear was evident in the woman's pretty eyes. "Get in. You're driving."

The woman complied.

"Hunters say that fear spoils the meat. For our kind, it makes the kill all the more sweeter," Bill spat.

They're not meat, Dani wanted to say, they're

213

people, they have lives just like we do. This is wrong, we can't do this!

Dani wanted to run. She considered bolting from her friends, but something held her back. The demon.

There is no demon, it's just you, Dani, you, afraid to accept what you are. Think about what you did to Willis. Think of how it felt. How much you enjoyed it.

Dani thought about it and got into the car with the others. She sat between Bill and Madison. Angel and Isabella sat across from them. As they pulled out of the shopping complex, Dani felt a certain amount of confusion. If the blond woman was to be their victim, why was she driving? And why did they leave their car behind, at the club?

Voicing these questions brought a chortle from Madison. "The T-Bird was stolen. Where better to leave it than the Fuck!? And since we were going to need a new car, why not get a driver, too?"

Reluctantly, Dani admitted that it made sense, but she was still nervous about what the final fate of the driver would be, and what Bill and the others wanted from her.

"Just be yourself," Isabella said, reaching over and patting Dani's hands. "That's all any of us want for you."

The limousine driver took them back in the direction of L.A., but she avoided the main highway and took a series of back roads. Through the smoked-glass windows, Dani could see rolling, desolate stretches of land.

Dani thought about the stolen cars and Madison's "rented" beach house—which she was now certain the girl had acquired in a dark and terrible fashion. She thought of Bill's slight trace of amusement at her disgust for Dominick, the man at the restaurant.

214

They were no different from that "bad man." They existed by living off the emotions, the wealth, and the lives of humans. Because they were different, because they were set apart by their blood, they convinced themselves that it was right, that theft and murder were justifiable.

The lucid moment passed as Dani recalled the feel of Willis's blood as it washed over her two years earlier, and the feel of his life being crushed by her will, her desire. The voice of the demon spoke in her mind:

We are not like them, any more than a wolf and his prey are alike. They exist separately, and come together only to satisfy the natural order of things. Every creature must feed, Dani.

But not like this, she thought. Not like this.

Then you will wither and die, sister-love. You will wither and die.

Dani looked up sharply, driven from her thoughts by the telling reference. She stared into Isabella's hard eyes and knew that it had not been the demon speaking to her, it had been Isabella.

"If you want to say something to me, say it like this," Dani thundered. "Don't try to fool me. It's not going to work."

"No, it's *not*, is it?" Isabella asked, her smile widening to a frightening degree. "That means you're learning."

Dani flinched, but she remained silent. Isabella's meaning was clear: Dani's powers were developing at an alarming rate.

Isabella continued. "You see, Dani, you have to choose this. No one else can make the decision for you."

"I need time," Dani muttered.

Bill shifted uncomfortably beside her. "That's the human in you talking."

"I am human," Dani snarled.

Madison turned to her. "Not any more, sweetheart. I know it's hard, but — "

"What the hell do you know?" Dani snapped. "This is tailor-made for you."

Madison recoiled at her friend's words. Then she relaxed and said, "Actually, it is."

Bill regarded Angel and Isabella. "I think it's time."

Mournfully, Isabella lowered her gaze. Dani saw this, and fear shot through her as she tried to react, tried to say something, but her immortal companions were too fast for her.

Bill reached over Dani, grabbing Madison's hair. He yanked the woman back with a savage tug of his hand. The back of her head ended up in Dani's lap and she squirmed as Bill curled his fingers into a claw and ripped at her neck. He carefully avoided the jugular, but it was a deep and bloody gash anyway. Madison's hands flew up, clawing at Dani and Bill. Angel and Isabella reached over and grasped for her flailing limbs.

Dani, too stunned at first to try to help the girl, surprised Bill by shoving him back, away from Madison. He slammed into the door and rebounded. Madison sat up and reached for the door handle. Her hand found it as Angel and Isabella caught her. Madison struggled desperately with the car door, but it was locked.

"Stop it!" Dani screamed. "What are you doing!?"

Madison wailed incoherently as the girls held her in place. Bill grabbed Dani from behind, pinning her arms to her side as she struggled. She became aware of the intoxicating odor of Madison's blood and she knew at once that Madison was not one of them after all, the girl was *human*.

That didn't make sense, Dani thought as she des-

216

perately recalled the first time she had met Madison in the dress shop and what occurred later. Her car doors had been locked, but Madison had somehow gotten into the car and placed the package with the dress inside, leaving the car locked once again. Dani had convinced herself that she had left a door unlocked, but deep down, she knew that wasn't true. When she learned of her true blood, she assumed Madison had used her powers as an Initiate to pull off the act. And when they had taken on the carload of gang members in the street, Madison had provoked them believing she had the power to control the situation.

Dani tentatively reached out with her silver thread, tapping into Madison's thoughts. She withdrew instantly. The explanation had been horribly mundane. Madison had bribed the attendant to break into the car for her and help her plant the package. In the car, that next day, Madison had been deluded. Dani had saved them from her foolishness.

Her light brush with Madison's mind had caused Dani's hunger from earlier that night to return tenfold. She felt her reason slip away as she saw Madison looking over her shoulder at Dani, her eyes wide and pleading, like those of an animal about to be butchered.

Dani felt an odd change begin to take place in her body.

"Please!" Madison cried, her body shaking as she slowly slid down into shock. "You said I was an Initiate. Please!"

They want to make me into one of them, Dani thought. They want me to take blood, to kill Madison. This is the moment. Dani recalled the last time that phrase had come into her mind: It had been only yesterday, when Bill had made love to her. He had torn through her body's defenses, made her a

217

woman, not a child, and that had been the first step to becoming a true immortal. Dani had chosen to sleep with him, as a human might. She had been an unwitting partner in her own conversion. But this was different. Then she had not known all the facts. Now she did. The hunger slammed into her, making her gasp. *Could* she turn away from this?

And did she really want to?

"Don't hurt me, please!" Madison cried.

Dani knew from Madison's eyes that the girl understood what was about to happen. Fear and betrayal danced in her eyes. But even without looking at her, Dani would have known what the girl was feeling. She could sense every emotion as it passed through the young woman. Hating herself, she licked at the fear Madison was emitting and found that at the first taste, her hunger had spiraled out of control.

"Make her want it," Bill said.

"What?" Dani murmured, swimming in a blood haze.

"Let her still be afraid, but make it so she needs it," Angel said coarsely.

"You have the power to be merciful," Isabella said. "But you must not kill the fear. If you do that, there will be no point to any of it. You will not change."

Dani stared into Madison's eyes. She knew how simple it would be. She felt desire in her own breast and all she had to do was reach out with the silver thread and alter the woman's perceptions.

Mercy, Isabella had said. What use did their kind have with mercy?

Dani shuddered, as the changes she had sensed in her body began to manifest. Her skin became clammy and cold. Her vision shifted, and she could see strange, Day-Glo colors emanating from Madi-

218

son, Isabella, and Angel. Streaks of primary colors lashed out from the women, followed by more subtle varieties from the secondaries.

No wonder they decorated their place like a bad acid trip, Dani thought drunkenly.

She felt her teeth starting to grow, and with this sensation came a rush of panic. Dani shook and kicked in Bill's arms, but he held her effortlessly and seductively kissed her neck. He was easing his desire into her, she realized. She tried to force his strong emotions from her, but a part of her welcomed them. The feel of his lips upon her skin made her weak.

"Stop it," she whispered, but she didn't mean the words and they both knew it. Bill reached around and lightly caressed her breast, sending an explosion of pleasure into her brain. She rocked with it, sailed to the brink of orgasm, then felt the sensations shorn off an instant before she went over.

—as he and his accomplice descended upon the Savior like ravening wolves, so too would they bare the teeth of the animal—

The legend of Antonius, the first vampire.

Dani could feel her own wolflike incisors reaching down from her upper jaw and she was suddenly afraid to close her mouth, terrified that she would bite her own tongue off. A giggle came from her. She could not restrain it.

She looked up and saw that Isabella and Angel had extended their razor-sharp teeth. Their eyes were blazing. From her reflection in the smoky glass beyond the women, she could see that hers were, too.

She closed her eyes, fighting the sensations. "I can't do this. I won't. Not yet."

Bill plunged his tongue into her ear, causing her to squirm in his arms. "Then we'll leave. You'll never see us again. You can be human. You can age and

219

die alone. You have to choose."

"Not now, not tonight," she begged.

"Yes," Bill demanded. "If you love me, then do it. It's the only way we can be together. All your life you've been a child, standing in that window you described, staring out, watching the living go by. Take my hand. Be alive with the night. I can help you."

Madison was quivering like a frightened animal. "Dani, please help me. I'm your friend!"

Dani nodded. Madison was correct. She had been Dani's friend. The girl was going to die here tonight. If she did not kill Madison, one of the others would. It was over for her. She could not be saved.

So let it *be* someone else, Dani. Why does it have to be you? The blood scent rose and overwhelmed her, as if in answer to her plea.

"Help me. . . ." Madison's piteous cry.

There was something Dani could do for her friend.

Mercy, Isabella whispered in Dani's mind.

Yes, she thought, reaching out with the desire that Bill's less than tender ministrations had provoked. Madison's head fell back slightly as the thread reached her. She parted her lips, gasping slightly. The fear did not leave her eyes.

Dani knew then what she was going to do. Moving as if in a dream, she reached forward, then felt herself being violently yanked back by Bill. His hand squeezed her breast with such fury that she cried out in pain, but his action had only been a diversion, calling her attention away from his actual agenda. Her eyes fluttered and she saw him in the reflection in the passenger window, saw his ivory teeth reaching from his mouth. An instant later they plunged into her neck.

Had it all been a lie, she briefly wondered. Maybe they had been playing with her the same way they had been playing with Madison, confusing her senses, altering her perceptions to make her believe that she was one of them, a god, an immortal. But she knew that was nothing but a fantasy, wish fulfillment. Better to die here, with Madison, as a human, than live like one of them. But she was like them. So very much like them.

Bill allowed Dani to feel the pain of his teeth in her neck, though he held her perfectly still, not allowing her to writhe and tear open the wounds he was creating in her flesh. The orgasmic fugue-state returned in a burst that left her shaking. But this time she understood what she was experiencing, and that made the sensations even more powerful.

Suddenly, she was blind to everything but her own need. This is what she must do to be loved and wanted, to finally belong. And the need to consume, to slake her inhuman thirst, and ease her painful hunger, was becoming even more pressing. Bill's fangs sank deeper into her flesh.

As the vampire's blood mixed with hers, Dani allowed her canines to stretch. Angel pushed Madison back, into Dani's grasp. Taking a handful of Madison's hair, Dani eased the girl's head back, exposing her soft, sweet throat. Madison's neck was already covered in blood. Dani licked at the blood, tentative at first, then lapped it up greedily. Her mind was awash with Madison's fear and desire, which mixed together like the soft colors on an artist's palette.

The pleasure she felt as she sank her teeth into Madison's throat was indescribable. Suddenly she was an animal, free to hunt, free to *kill*. She was answerable only to herself, only to her needs. Blood poured into her mouth and sank down her throat. Madison projected a mad euphoria, like that of a drowning victim an instant before his death. Dani felt as if she could drown in the river of emotions that flowed from her victim.

She curled her hands into talons and plunged them into Madison's chest. Ripping the girl's chest open, Dani moved from the pulsing, spurting throat of her friend and buried her face in the girl's wildly beating heart. Her teeth closed over the organ as she severed two major arteries and was blown back by the fountain of blood that sprayed in her face. Dani laughed and screamed as she swallowed all that she could bear. Howling for her friends to join her, Dani tore at the body in a mad frenzy, ripping it apart the way a mad wolf would devour its prey.

And for a brief period of time, Dani Walthers ceased to exist. The demon held sway.

When it was over, Dani realized that Bill had released his fangs from her neck long ago. Her perceptions were sharp and clear, she felt like a god.

"Welcome, Dani," Bill said as he licked the blood from her lips, their tongues briefly entwined. Isabella and Angel kissed her too, licking at the blood. "Welcome forever."

The limousine sped through the night.

Eighteen

Sam parked the GT-S several blocks from the estate and made her way back on foot. A high wall surrounded the mansion and its grounds. Sam paused at the gate, considering her options. She saw no indications of security cameras or motion sensors. Getting over the walls would not be difficult, but there might be dogs prowling the green, and Sam knew that even with the 9mm she carried, she would be lucky to stop one, or perhaps two, before they reached her and ripped her throat out.

In this case, the direct approach seemed her best option. Sam found the call button on the concrete post next to the main gate and leaned into it for close to five minutes. Lights shined in the mansion, cars were parked in front. An instant before Sam was about to give up and rethink her strategy, a crackle sounded from a metal grid above the call button.

"Yes?" A man's voice. Sam recognized it instantly.

"Samantha Walthers," she said, her voice stony, unyielding.

After a slight pause, a loud, metal clank sounded beside her as the lock mechanism was released. The gates swung open a few inches. Sam looked at this suspiciously.

"Dogs?" she asked.

"No," said the bone-weary voice in reply. "Not anymore."

What the hell is *that* supposed to mean? Sam thought. Before she could ask, there was another crackle and the voice cut out. Sam was left wondering if she could trust the owner of that voice. She had done so before and had come to regret it. The winding road leading to the house, beyond the spacious gardens, was a five hundred yard stretch. Sam turned from the gates, went back to the GT-S, and returned with the car. Her headlights were on high as she nudged the gates open with her front bumper, then drove to the front of the Victorian-style mansion, where she propped the door open, thrust out her leg as bait, and waited for the rush of the animals. Finally, when she was convinced that there were no dogs, Sam left her car and hurried up the front steps, to the door, which had been left ajar.

Drawing her weapon, sliding the safety off, Sam entered the mansion. She instantly felt as if she had fallen into a segment from *Lifestyles of the Rich and Famous*. The floors were teal marble, the hard wood walls covered in fine art. She was in the vast receiving hall, staring up at a pair of winding staircases that led to the second floor. A huge, crystalline chandelier hung above her.

The sound of leather striking meat and a soft groan came to her; the noise echoed mercilessly throughout the mansion, making it impossible to pinpoint its location. Sam reconnoitered the entire first floor and found every room brightly lit but deserted. Climbing the stairs to the second floor, Sam came to the landing, then entered the hallway and followed it to the left. After making a turn at the end of the hall, she saw an open door and found what she had been looking for.

Sam crossed to the door, peered in anxiously, and

saw a four-poster bed, a full-length mirror, elegant rugs, and a few paintings. It would have been a catalog-perfect image if not for the naked man hanging from the ceiling in gravity boots. She could only see him from behind, but she knew his identity instantly. His flesh was crisscrossed with ugly red welts, a small pool of blood had formed on the floor. The crack of a whip sounded and the man flinched. His tormentor was on the other side, striking at his chest and legs.

"Allen," Sam called.

The beating stopped suddenly. An older man dressed completely in leather stepped around his victim. He wore a mask with a zipper across the mouth. He appeared unarmed, except for the whip.

"Allen, take off the mask," Sam said, the gun at her side. The figure before her nodded and complied. The gracious, fatherly features of Allen Halpern greeted her.

Sam felt her anger drain away. She had hoped that she would be wrong about this, but there had been no mistake. Halpern crossed the room and opened a cabinet. Sam leveled the gun at him, afraid that he would pull a weapon. Instead, his hands fastened on a tray bearing a bottle of champagne on ice with two crystal chalices. He opened the bottle with the skill of a connoisseur, the elegance of his deliberate movements a stark and almost comical contrast to the manner in which he was dressed.

Sam crossed the room and stepped in front of the wounded, naked man. Pete Martell hung there, slack-jawed and glassy-eyed. He stank of his own urine. His face revealed several days worth of stubble. Sam shoved the gun into the waistband of her jeans, released the gravity boots, and awkwardly got Martell to the bed. Animal noises came from his parted lips. His expression revealed fear, laced with

225

desire. There was no hint of reason about him. His mind appeared to have been shattered.

Sam had despised this man, even feared him for the power he had exerted over her, but now all she felt was pity. She checked his breathing, decided that he was in no immediate danger, and turned from him. Allen Halpern stripped off his leathers, changing into a pair of camel-hair slacks and a short-sleeve shirt that revealed his expertly maintained physique. He was anything but a frail old man.

He carried the serving tray in both hands and nodded toward the open door. They went downstairs, to the study, where Halpern stoked the fireplace and sat cross-legged before the flickering, warming fire. Sam joined him, accepting a glass of champagne from his steady hand. She could not take her gaze from his eyes. They were dead and cold, despite his friendly smile.

Sam kept a tight rein on her emotions. She wanted answers, she wanted to know where her little girl was being held, and she wanted to beat the information out of this man with the butt of her gun. But she stayed in control.

"How much do you know?" she asked.

"More than I should," Halpern replied casually.

Sam closed her eyes, swallowing hard. It was all she could do to keep herself from slapping the chalice out of his hand.

"You're not touching your drink," he observed.

"The fire's enough for me," she said, dancing around her concern that her glass might have been lined with some powdered drug. This man was still dangerous, as far as she was concerned.

"More's the pity. It's very good, and I hate to drink alone."

"I'll still have to disappoint you. What can you tell me about my daughter?"

226

"Very little, except that she is almost as beautiful as her mother."

Sam shuddered. This man made a career out of charming his enemies into lowering their guard so he could slit their throats. She would not fall prey to it. Watching his eyes, she knew that his verbal seduction was a halfhearted effort, in any case.

"Your girl is dead," Sam said, carefully gauging Halpern's reaction. His body tightened for a moment, then he lowered his head and nodded.

"Yes, I know," he said. "I could feel it when she died. She wasn't in my head anymore." He paused. "I don't like being alone."

Christ, Sam thought. How powerful was this thing she had killed? The doppelganger had been able to establish a link with Halpern that she maintained even when they were separated. It was as if she had bitten him on the neck and made him a slave. Sam shuddered. When this was over, when Dani was safe and at home with her, where she belonged, Sam was never going to allow her daughter to watch another of those cheesy horror movies of which she had been so fond. The damn things were striking too close to home.

"Her name was Miss Tory, by the way," Halpern said.

Sam nodded gravely. She decided to start at the most recent, most vivid memories, and work her way back. "Why were you torturing Martell?"

"I thought you would have enjoyed that," Halpern said evasively.

Sam shrugged. "You weren't doing it for my benefit. You weren't expecting me here. Tory was supposed to kill me. Was that your idea?"

"No," he said quickly. "I like you."

The muscles in Sam's hard-set face quivered at the smoldering ember of desire she saw in his eyes.

227

"Then whose idea was it?"

"Hers. She wanted it done."

"Why?"

"I don't know. I didn't ask questions. I just gave her what she wanted."

That wasn't true, Sam thought. He was still protecting her.

"Did she know my daughter?" Sam asked.

"They met, once. A year ago. She told me that much."

Sam frowned. "We were still in Tampa a year ago."

"I was in Orlando on business. Miss Tory came along. She wanted to visit Epcot. Your daughter was there."

It came to Sam in a sudden burst. Dani and Lisa had gone to Orlando with Carlotta. When they returned, the rift between Dani and Lisa had widened. Dani had been quiet and withdrawn for a week. She had acted as if she had been frightened by something, but she maintained that nothing had happened on the visit. Carlotta swore that she had kept both girls in her sight at all times. She confirmed that there had been no unusual occurrences.

"Did Tory approach my daughter?"

"No, she didn't have to," Halpern said. "Miss Tory could sense that Dani was like her. She tried to make contact —"

Sam could not take any more. She threw the glass into the fire, where it shattered, the drink causing a tiny burst of flames. Her hand edged toward the gun as she screamed, "My daughter is not *like* that piece of shit!"

Halpern recoiled from this and Sam understood the full measure of her mistake. But she could not take the words back, and once given voice, her anger could no longer be hidden away.

Tell me what you know, she wanted to scream, but she held herself back. "My daughter is *not* like Tory."

"Miss Tory felt otherwise," Halpern said, the light of betrayal and fear flickering and dying in his eyes. He was once again a dead man walking. The observation made Sam relax slightly, though the man's allegation irritated her terribly.

She switched tacks, hoping to force away the frightening possibility Halpern had brought up, that there were others like the doppelganger and Dani was one of them. "What was Tory, exactly?"

"An Initiate. A failed Initiate, at that."

"I don't understand."

"A half-vampire."

Sam could not restrain a slight, nervous giggle. The mention of the word brought bizarre, ridiculous images to her mind. A scene from a bad TV movie that she had watched with Dani years ago came to her.

Gee, Inspector, bite marks on the neck, body drained of blood, third one this week. You don't see a pattern, do you?

"It's not what you think," Halpern said. "And you've seen things that can't be explained away, haven't you?"

The images dissolved at once, replaced by memories of Tory clinging to the ceiling and flying up the stairs. Sure, that could be explained away, Sam thought. I could be going out of my fucking mind after all. But I'm pretty sure that's not the case.

It had been Halpern's name on Tory's credit cards. They had obviously shared some strange, symbiotic relationship. He provided her with cash, clothes, and a place to live in comfort and elegance. But what need did she fulfill for him? Sex? She was just a child, or so she had appeared. He had called her

229

an Initiate, a half-vampire. Vampires were supposed to be immortal. Could the doppelganger have been older than it seemed, older than either of them, perhaps?

Sam exhaled a ragged breath. "All right. Tell me exactly what happened in Orlando."

Halpern tilted his head warily. "Miss Tory sensed Dani. She tried to reach out to her, but Dani pushed her out. Dani was very strong, even in her state of denial. She knew what she was, but she couldn't accept it, and so she had forced the knowledge down deep where she hoped it would never be heard from again."

"And you're saying my daughter is what? An Initiate?"

"Yes. The blood of Christ tainted by Lucifer, the Dark Angel, runs in her veins."

Sam buried her face in her hands. She wasn't sure if she wanted to laugh or scream.

"Think what you like. It doesn't alter the reality of the situation. I can explain it to you, if you like. The way Miss Tory explained it to me."

"All right," Sam said, and forced herself to listen patiently as Halpern told her the story of the Centurion who became Antonius, first of the vampires, and of his descendants. In a way, all that he said made sense, provided she was willing to make the leap into believing that such creatures as vampires truly existed, and that they were clever enough and powerful enough to live in the human world while escaping detection for almost two thousand years.

"Not all of them like what they become. Some go Wildling."

"What's that?"

"They go crazy. They turn on their own kind, slaughter other vampires. The Parliament convenes for them, generally."

"The Parliament?"

"A group made up of their most powerful. But there is a force behind the Parliament, the Ancients."

"Why did Tory tell you all this?"

He looked down. "She was very lonely. She had been rejected by her own kind."

"Why? What did she do?"

"She had been turned. She had shared blood with a full vampire, she had killed while under his influence. But when the time came for her second kill, which had to be made before three nights elapsed, she could not bring herself to do it. There was still too much of the human in her. She could not kill on her own."

"This is new," Sam said, trying to keep up with Halpern. "You're telling me that they have to kill *twice* before they make the leap and become full vampires?"

"No, they become vampires after the first kill. But if they do not make the second kill, they revert. They become more powerful than they had been as Initiates, but far less powerful then they would have been as Immortals."

Sam was grateful that Halpern had become so animated while discussing the myths that Tory had pumped into his brain. Somewhere, in all that he was telling her, she would find something that would be of use in saving her daughter. She was certain of it.

"You don't believe me, do you?" Halpern said, his slight excitement fading. "Miss Tory told me what they did to her that third night. Shall I tell you?"

"All right," Sam said, allowing Halpern to relate the story in full detail. It involved another, more terrible use for the concrete room beneath the beach house.

231

"Why did you bring us to Beverly Hills?" Sam asked, hoping to divert the emptiness that she could see returning to Halpern's eyes as he drew himself in and prepared to shut down.

"Miss Tory *wanted* it," he said crossly. "I told you that."

"I still don't understand—"

"Your daughter was an offering," Halpern said sharply. "Miss Tory wanted to get back in Yoshino's good graces."

"Who's Yoshino?"

"Bill Yoshino. The Immortal who tried to turn her the first time. She disappointed him, and afterward, she wanted another chance. But he was not willing to give her one. Then she thought of your daughter."

"Jesus."

"She had known Dani's name from her look into the child's head, and she knew that Dani lived in Tampa. That was all she knew. I hired an outside investigator to find you. When he did, it turned out that you had led a fairly public existence. All the pieces were there. All I had to do was bait the trap, offering you this position, which you could not afford to turn down."

"Why was Tory trying to kill me?"

"Because you're Dani's closest link to her humanity. If you were gone, there would be nothing for her to hold on to."

"Then why didn't she just kill me when she had the chance, at Smith's house?"

"It wasn't that easy. Dani could still love you after you were dead. They didn't want to make a martyr out of you. The ideal scenario would have had Dani killing you herself, irrevocably cutting her ties to humankind. But when they had both of you here, when they saw up close the bond you shared, they

232

knew that it was too dangerous to let you live. Miss Tory was going to force you to take your own life in your office after you dictated some wild, rambling last words to your daughter. You would have blamed her for everything that had gone wrong, you would have cursed her and said that your only regret was that you weren't taking her with you, demon child that she was."

"She would never have believed such a thing," Sam said angrily, her heart thundering at the pain her daughter would have suffered, pain not unlike her own.

"I think she would have. The call of blood is very strong for their kind. She would have believed it because she would have *needed* to believe it. It would have been the only way."

"But I'm not dead."

"No, you're not."

"And Tory is gone."

Mournfully, he closed his eyes in acquiescence.

"Tell me where they've taken my daughter."

"I can't. I don't know."

"But Tory lived here, with you."

"My niece," he said sourly. "That's what we told people. She didn't invite her friends over, and I wasn't asked to any of their little parties, though I paid for many of them."

"One more thing. Why were you torturing Pete Martell? How did he fit into all of this?"

"He didn't. That was the problem. He was messing things up."

"In what way?"

"He was trying to get you fired. That couldn't be allowed."

"You were the one who hired me. What could he do?"

"Go to the board of directors. I had kept most of

the bad things from them." Halpern swallowed hard. "If action had been taken against you, if you had left here and taken Dani with you, it would have spoiled everything. Besides, he pissed me off with what he said on that tape. And Miss Tory liked the sound he made when I hurt him."

Sam stared at him, trying to decide if the man was ignoring her question, or if she was losing him to the enormity of the doppelganger's death.

"Martell was going to shoot you tonight," Halpern said.

Sam froze.

"Then he was going to go home, write out a confession, and blow his brains out. You had ruined him. He hated you."

She understood. Tory had planned on killing Sam, then setting up Martell to take the blame. Clean and simple.

Watching Halpern's cold, dead eyes as he stared into the fire, Sam decided that she could trust leaving him behind as she went in search of some clue among the doppelganger's belongings. Reaching the doorway, she heard a drawer slide open and turned to see Halpern lifting a large caliber weapon from the drawer. It seemed to be a magnum. She went for her own gun and had drawn the weapon when she saw that he was not pointing the magnum at her. With a weak smile he jammed the gun into the underside of his jaw and pulled the trigger.

She watched in horror as his head exploded in a geyser of blood and gore, then his body toppled to the ground.

Jesus, she thought, her grip on her own weapon suddenly loosening as she fell to her knees. She would have vomited, but she couldn't remember the last time she actually ate something. After suffering through a series of wracking, dry heaves, the tremors at last subsided and Sam lifted herself from the floor. Turning away from the mass of gore that had been her employer's head, Sam stumbled into the hallway. The smell of feces and urine had been too much for her to voluntarily endure.

"Damn you, you fucking coward," she screamed. "God damn you to hell!"

She knew that her rage was irrational, but she had wanted Halpern alive. As he had pointed out, she had seen too much to blithely discount all of what he had told her as an old man's mad ramblings. She would have to proceed as if the people who had taken her daughter shared his beliefs. That didn't mean that *she* would have to accept them as fact. The day would never come when she would believe her daughter to be a monster, capable of acts such as those the doppelganger had performed.

Looking at her watch, Sam debated. It was possible that the shot had not been heard by the neighbors and would not be reported. If that were the case, she could take all night searching the house. But the roar had been deafening and if she was caught in this place, with Halpern dead and Martell tortured out of his mind, she might never have a chance to rescue her daughter.

She gave herself ten minutes. Finding Tory's room turned out to be very easy. It had been adjacent to the bedroom where Martell had been beaten. The room looked like that of any teenager, with posters of rock stars on the wall, makeup everywhere, clothes strewn around. Nothing that would help her. She realized how foolish she had been to think she would find a diary of some sort that might hold answers to where her daughter had been taken, but the assumption had seemed reasonable at the time. According to Halpern, the girl was very lonely. She spoke to him, of course, confided in him, but she had known that he wouldn't really understand. A diary would be a perfect place to hide her secret fears and desires.

Sam examined the large, walk-in closet and found that one of the walls sounded hollow. She found a small niche hidden behind a false stretch of paneling. In the niche was a cardboard box filled with videotapes, letters, and a black leather diary. She nearly screamed with triumph.

Checking her watch, Sam hefted the box into her arms, raced downstairs, and left the mansion. She hurled the box into the GT-S and pulled away from the estate. Sam was several blocks away, driving at a comfortable speed, when the first of the police cars sped past her in the opposite lane.

Nineteen

The limousine was parked in a deserted field, the doors open, the vampires gathered around the car. They stared into the backseat, at Madison's remains. If not for the scraps of clothing that hung on the body, it could have been mistaken for a butchered side of meat. The sight was strange and unreal to Dani.

"It's really going to be hell to get all this shit out of the upholstery, you know," Bill said.

Dani almost laughed. Then the enormity of what had occurred threatened to close over her and she chased it away, concentrating instead on the adoring looks she was receiving from Bill and Isabella. She knew that she should have been sickened and repulsed at the sight of Madison's ruined body, but she convinced herself that she wasn't bothered in the least. It was just meat, after all.

Still entranced, the beautiful, blond-haired driver was busy following the orders Bill had given her. She had removed the spare canister of gasoline from the trunk—in her line of work she could never afford the risk of running out of gas—and was spilling the liquid over the interior of the car and the open hood. A small metal door sat open on the side of the limousine and a gasoline-stained cloth had been stuffed in the open mouth leading to the gas tank. When she finished with the canister, she gave it one last shake, then tossed it in the backseat.

Dani turned to look at Bill. His electric blue eyes shined in the darkness, his leathers slick and glistening. Though they had spent considerable time licking the blood from each other's exposed flesh, their clothes were soaked through with gore. Bill's ardor had been roused by the event and he had taken Dani savagely after they left the car, throwing her down on the hood. They rutted like animals while Angel and Isabella watched. Isabella was silent, but Angel offered a steady stream of rude, but encouraging comments. All pretense of romance was gone. The experience had been gratifying for them both, a needed release, nothing more.

Dani angled her head in the blond's direction. "What about her?"

"Whatever do you mean?" Bill asked brightly.

"Only this," Dani said as she casually extended the silver thread to the mind of the driver. Effortlessly she projected an image of being trapped in a flaming car into the blond woman's mind. The driver recoiled in shock, fell back, and started scrambling away. Angel caught her and held her.

"That's cruel," Bill said, loving it. He turned to the driver. "What's your name again?"

She couldn't speak at first, fear constricting her words. Finally, she said, "Therese."

"Madison's departure *has* left us with an opening to fill."

Angel touched the underside of the woman's jaw with her sharp nail. "what do you say?" Angel whispered. "Would you like to live forever? Pretty and sexy like this for all time?"

"Yes," Therese whispered. There had been no hesitation.

Bill crossed his arms over his chest. "Make her believe it, Angel. Make her yours."

At will, Angel's red-flecked canines extended and

238

she bit into Therese's neck, tasting her blood, as she filled the woman's mind with dreams of immortality and godlike power. Therese bucked against her, trembling and moaning, then fell to her knees on the soft earth. Angel began to step away and Therese reached out to her, grasping anxiously at her legs, resting her head against the woman's thighs like a lover.

Angel's eyes sparkled with crimson as she reached down and caressed the driver's face. "This one's mine, Bill. To do with as I see fit. Understand?"

"Of course," he said.

Isabella was ignoring all of it, her gaze fixed on the horizon. Dani noticed the woman's solitary position, but she ignored it for the moment. She was still looking into the backseat.

"Shouldn't we bury the meat somewhere else?" Dani asked. "We don't want an investigation."

Angel slapped at the back of Therese's head. The woman stood up and tossed her purse beside the car, where it would remain safe after the car had been torched.

"They'll think it was Therese who died," Angel said as she kissed the other woman. "We don't want them looking for our new love, now do we?"

"But the police will come anyway," Dani said. "Homicide will be called and—"

"You worry too much," Bill said as he hefted the cigarette lighter he had taken from the driver. "Look at Isabella. She's found something for us to *really* worry about. Haven't you, Isabella?"

"You could view it that way, I suppose," Isabella said casually.

Dani turned and shifted her gaze to the horizon. In the distance, tiny slivers of blue and pink sliced across the earth. Dani felt something uncoil in her stomach, like a snake. The first tremors of fear rumbled through her.

"The sun can kill us, can't it?" Dani asked, breathless.

Isabella smiled. "That's right."

"If we burn the car, then we won't get back to shelter in time," Dani said, panic overtaking her. It couldn't end like this. Not for such a stupid reason as they had forgotten to look at their damned watches. Why was everyone being so casual about this, she wondered.

Bill laughed, flicked the lighter, and touched it to the gasoline-soaked rag near the gas tank. Then he backed off and broke into a dead run. "It's a game we play, Dani. It's called *run* for your *eternal life.*"

Dani froze at the first glimmer of bright yellow peeking over the horizon. Then she felt the cold touch of Isabella's hand as the woman yanked her out of her sudden paralysis and dragged her away from the car. Angel's control of Therese was absolute and the woman raced behind her mistress. The vampires ran at an incredible pace, their human companion quickly lagging behind.

Behind them, the gas tank of the limousine ignited and the vehicle exploded, a cloud of flames sending an angry fist into the early morning sky. There was a growl and a boom similar to that of a shotgun blast. A wave of force slammed Therese to the ground. The vampires withstood the deafening blast and its aftershocks.

"Angel!" Therese screamed, her words tinged with mortal fear.

"Don't worry, sweetheart," Angel called. "We'll be back for you."

The vampires ran across the field, Angel and Isabella flanking Dani. They ran so quickly that Dani recalled her dream from earlier that night, of spreading her arms and taking flight. Her surroundings became a blur.

"We're going so fast I feel like I can *fly!*" Dani

screamed, her hair trailing behind her, whipping in the breeze. Her body barely registered the strain of her pace.

"Then do it!" Angel howled as she took Dani's free hand. "Isabella, now!"

Dani gasped. The impossible once again occurred with the casual grace she had come to associate with her new, inhuman condition. Isabella and Angel kicked off the ground, their bodies suddenly parallel to the horizon, but they did not fall and their pace did not diminish. They tugged at Dani's hands as she watched them in disbelief.

They were flying.

For the love of Christ, they were actually *flying!*

"Yes," Isabella called, "now!"

Sensing that they were about to lift her into the air with them, Dani shouted, "No, don't! Wait, please!"

The women laughed and Dani's attention was suddenly fixed on a billowing, black shape that took to the sky ahead of her. It was Bill, rising high, leaving the earth behind as his jacket spread out behind him, like dark wings. He looked over his shoulder at her and winked.

There was no warning for Dani as Angel and Isabella tightened their grips and yanked her high into the air. She tumbled and floundered, her heart threatening to explode as the ground became a blur under her wriggling legs. The wind sliced into her and she turned her face away, unable to breathe. She squeezed her eyes shut, felt a steady, urgent tug, and opened them again to see that they had gone even higher. They were now close to thirty feet in the air.

"Holy shit!" Dani screamed, but there had been a burst of laughter mingled with the scream.

"It's wonderful, isn't it?" Isabella called as they rose even higher. Dani felt as if she was riding the currents of air.

Angel threw her head back and closed her eyes in

rapture. "I *came* the first time I did this on my own."

As if on cue, Angel and Isabella loosed their hold on her hands.

"Jesus!" Dani cried as she clawed at them, the ground now more than a hundred feet below. But they sailed away from her, spinning and performing incredibly complex acrobatics in the air. For an instant, Dani's attention was so drawn by their antics that she forgot the danger she was in. Suddenly it came to her that she had not begun to fall. Dani convinced herself that she was being carried along by her own momentum and she would falter at any moment. She couldn't possibly be doing this on her own.

Angel back-flipped before her and came to a stop, suspended in mid-flight. She wore an expression of exaggerated concern as she placed her hands on either side of her face and screamed, "Wendy, think happy thoughts! Happy thoughts!"

With a cackle, the vampire rose out of the way as Dani barreled through the spot Angel had occupied only seconds before.

Isabella dropped back into view, sidling up next to Dani as she said, "No one is helping you now, sister-love. This is all because of you!"

Dani relaxed slightly as she realized that she was not going to fall to her death. Nevertheless, she *had* to come down sometime, and the sun was rising at their backs. She could feel its uncomfortable warmth stealing over her body.

Looking over her shoulder, Dani saw the bloated red orb of the sun. It had risen a quarter of the way over the horizon. The sight made her gasp.

Fly high, fly high, let's go, let's go! a voice called in Dani's mind. Bill's voice.

"We can't go higher, we're going to burn up!" Dani screamed.

Nevertheless, she followed her friends as they rose toward the clouds. Behind them, the sun gradually took hold in the sky. Dani felt an uncomfortable, painful warmth seep into her skin. The soft morning light stung and she felt as if her flesh was being scraped away by razor blades.

"We're not going to make it!" she screamed.

Suddenly, Bill turned and angled back toward her, his mouth open in a silent scream.

Well then, we better give up, he called within her mind.

Without warning, he lost his ability to fly and tumbled from the air. Angel and Isabella followed his lead, their arms floundering as their legs kicked and pistoned. They clutched at the air, looking for handholds, and spiraled downward.

Frightened to remain on her own, Dani carefully adjusted her flight, bringing herself around in a graceful arc as she changed direction and angled downward. Far below, she could see the hard, unyielding surface of a massive lake. Mists clung to the blue-green waters.

The vampires tumbled like sky divers whose chutes had not opened, hollering and reaching up toward Dani to save them. They fell from a thousand feet in the air.

A thought flashed in her mind: why had she retained control of her abilities when the others had lost theirs?

She was newly turned. That couldn't be it; vampires became more powerful with age. She had fed more than the others. Perhaps. Then it came to her: The older vampires were more powerful in some ways, more *vulnerable* in others. Her body had changed, of course, but it was still used to the sunlight. For a time, she would have more resistance.

Dani realized suddenly that perhaps she could save them, or one of them, at least. If she could in-

243

crease her speed and overtake one of them, she might be able to catch them in her arms before they struck the steellike surface of the lake and were mashed to a bloody pulp. Then she would have to pull out of her dead-fall before she hit the lake.

That couldn't possibly work, she thought. Maybe in a comic book, but not like this.

Why not, kiddo? Because things like that just don't work in real life? You're flying. You're a fucking vampire. Get over it!

The taunting voice in her head was correct. She *had* to try. Judging from the distance and their rate of descent, Dani understood that she could save only one of them. Angel was no use to her. The girl could splatter for all Dani cared. Isabella had been loving and kind. She did not want to see Isabella die. But it was Bill that she raced toward.

For a few moments it seemed that her plan might work. She ignored the biting pain from the rising sun and put out of her mind thoughts of how they would still face death by fire after she rescued him. All of her attention was focused on the desperate plight of the man she loved.

I'm not going to make it, Dani realized. Bill would strike the waters before she could reach him. Her heart thundered painfully as she wailed his name in pain and grief.

Suddenly, Bill ended his free-fall. He adjusted his body, aiming himself like a long sliver of glass at the hard waters. The pose was one of an expert diver. Angel and Isabella followed his lead, gracefully rising up from their undignified descents to fall into position beside Bill.

They were going right through, Dani thought in alarm. They're going into the waters!

She watched the surface of the lake and knew that there was no time for her to pull out of her own rapid plunge. Imitating the pose of the other vam-

244

pires, Dani watched as Bill, Angel, and Isabella sliced through the waters and disappeared below. Screaming as the glasslike surface of the water approached, Dani closed her eyes and felt her hands cut through the waters. Suddenly she was through, sinking into the murky depths.

A hand clasped hers and she found herself yanked down as she opened her eyes and saw Bill next to her, smiling broadly. He opened his mouth and allowed a burst of bubbles to escape his lips. Dani had been holding her breath. She anxiously tried to shake off his grip and claw her way to the surface, but her lover tugged her back in the other direction. They sank a few feet and Dani became aware of Angel and Isabella swimming casually toward her. Above, the sunlight sliced away the light covering of mist that had formed on the surface of the lake. Blinding white, sparkling diamonds of light glittered above. Their brightness made Dani's eyes hurt and she turned away from the sight.

The waters were becoming slightly warmer. Dani felt her lungs start to ache. Angel drifted before her, mouthed the word "sorry" and curled her hand into a fist. Dani attempted to wriggle her body out of the way, but Bill gripped her from behind. The blow sank into Dani's gut with considerable force, despite the water blocking it. Dani coughed as the fist connected and she expelled the lungful of air she had cautiously been hoarding. Water filled her mouth and she swallowed inadvertently, feeling the cold sting as the liquid filled her lungs. She fought desperately, twisted and kicked, but it was to no avail. They held her easily.

They're trying to kill me, Jesus Christ, I'm gonna drown!

The harder she struggled, the quicker her lungs became suffused with water. She tried to breathe, but it was impossible. Her mind rebelled at the thought of death, and she wondered if she would experience the euphoria that her mother's textbooks claimed a drowning victim undergoes just before death.

But the others were not drowning, and she was like them.

There's nothing to be afraid of, sister-love.

Isabella's voice, calm and soothing.

Relax and trust that we would allow no harm to come to you. The sun has risen and the surface would provide only death, not shelter.

Dani barely listened. She had finally noticed the lascivious smile that had spread on Angel's face. The woman rushed forward, took Dani's face in her hands, leaned in, and kissed her. Dani felt the woman's tongue snake into her mouth and she tried to bite down on it, but Angel retreated.

Dani saw the blond-haired vampire pinwheel away from Bill's outstretched fist. She realized that his grip had loosened on her arms. With a sudden, final burst of desperate energy, Dani ripped herself loose from her captors and swam upward, toward the light. She knew that the sun would burn her, but that did not matter at this moment. She needed air to breathe, she was about to drown!

From the periphery of her vision, she could see Bill and Isabella following. Her arms and legs pumped with wild abandon, but she had the sense that they could have overtaken her if that had been their goal. The light, she realized, they were terrified of the light.

The waters became scalding as she climbed higher. A thought occurred to Dani moments before she would have broken the surface of the waters: She had stopped breathing and she had not died. Hesitating, Dani held herself in the boiling, blistering waters near the surface of the lake, and sent her silver thread deep within her own body. She could feel her heart slowing, and sensed that her physiology had changed in unfathomable ways. She recalled a movie she had seen, *The Abyss,* in which humans breathed in oxygenated water. The idea took root in her and she began converting the elements of the liquid surrounding her to a substance that it could utilize for survival.

Dani sank back, into the depths. The waters became dark and cool, and she found Bill, Angel, and Isabella waiting.

Isabella caressed the side of Dani's face, which had been sunburned red. *We are yours, sister-love. We would never harm you.*

Dani could sense the strength draining away from the other vampires. They were becoming drowsy, finally reacting to the change in their bodies that was keeping them alive within the waters. The water in her lungs was a slightly uncomfortable sensation, but there was no pain.

She reached out with her thoughts and asked, *What do we do now?*

Follow us, you'll see, Bill replied.

Angel winked at her. Dani had not forgotten the stolen kiss, nor forgiven it. There had been little of the sensuous charge that she had felt when Isabella had touched her. This girl seemed to loathe her, for reasons that Dani could not even begin to guess.

They swam downward, to the soft earth at the floor of the lake. Bill dug his hands into the ground, ripping up a section of earth. Angel and Isabella followed suit. Dani watched what they were doing and realized uncomfortably that they were digging their own graves. She joined them, finding a patch of ground on the floor of the lake that gave easily with her newfound, inhuman strength. The graves were only a few feet deep and each took several minutes to excavate.

Bill finished first. He took Dani's hand, pulling

her away from the ditch she had been digging. The thought of burying herself here, alone in the wet earth, had terrified her, but she had not let on to the others that she was afraid. Bill pulled her close and kissed her. The sensation was pleasing, but thoroughly without the earlier fire that had marked their couplings.

You came back for me, he said in the confines of her thoughts. *It's* me *that you love.*

She saw an odd look pass between Bill and Isabella, who turned away. Bill eased her back, from her feet, and together they sank into the grave he had dug. Dani threw her arms around him, quaking with fear. He lightly stroked her hair as Angel and Isabella shoved the earth upon them, burying them alive.

For an instant before sleep came to her, Dani felt the urge to cry. Then she tightened her hold on Bill, and they drifted together into the comfort of oblivion.

Twenty

Sam had been afraid to go home. She knew that she was being paranoid. There was no reason to believe the police would be waiting for her at her rented house in Beverly Hills. But there had also been no reason for her to suspect the police of tossing the place the day before and keeping quiet about it. She was on the brink of exhaustion and she needed a place to rest.

It was just after sunrise. She had driven thirty miles down the coast from the Halpern estate and pulled her car into the deserted parking lot behind a seafood restaurant, where it would not be spotted from the street. She had checked out the building and found a lunch menu posted on the wall. People would probably begin to arrive before long. She would have to leave soon.

Where could she go? Hotels were out of the question. If the police really wanted her for questioning in relation to Halpern's death, that was the second place they would begin to look — after her rented home. She could disguise herself, check in under a false name, but she could not disguise the car. If she were to leave the GT-S at the airport and rent another vehicle, it would simply provide a trail. The only other option was dumping the GT-S and stealing a car, and that was risky. If the police weren't looking for her, they would be looking for the stolen car. She would have to keep her car and that meant she would need a place where she could keep the car enclosed, away from casual inspection.

Sam ran down the list of the people she had met in California and only a few names came to mind as people who might provide shelter for her. There was Rosalind, the receptionist at the firm, and Alex Wren, the computer genius. She could phone Alex, beg for his help, and he might even come through. On the other hand, if the police had placed a tap on her phone, as she suspected, they would have already heard her speak his name, and they may have gotten to him already. That left only Rosalind, and Sam could not assume Rosalind would be willing to help, either. She wondered briefly if Martell's place would be open, but the police were bound to go there at some point.

She had already paged through the phone book and had been unable to find a listing for Alex. As for Rosalind, she still didn't know the woman's last name. That meant that she would have to show up at the office or phone there to learn anything more. Sam put the GT-S in gear and pulled out of the parking lot. She cruised down the highway for several miles, then took an exit at random. Before long she was driving through one of the many beach towns along the coast, and she found what she was looking for without difficulty.

The video arcade was packed with kids who had stopped off on their way to school. Sam found a teenager hanging around outside, looking forlorn and broke, and she made her pitch. He followed her to the pay phone and waited as she quickly wrote out his script. She had him read it back to her, then she checked the time. It was seven forty-five. The office would officially open at eight. Sam had the feeling that Rosalind would answer before that. If not, she was certain the kid would risk getting to school late for the twenty Sam had waved in his face.

Rosalind answered.

"Hi, this is Nino with AKO Florists? I have a delivery here for a Rosalind Peters and I needed directions."

"Well, I'm the only Rosalind here, but my name isn't Peters, it's Avery."

The kid made a "thumbs up" sign to Sam and said, "In East L.A., right?"

"No, I live in Santa Monica."

"2205 West Lake?"

"No," Rosalind said, her annoyance growing. She was clearly not going to give away the final bit of information. "Who is this again?"

Sam ran her hand over her throat.

"I'm sorry, I must have made a mistake," the kid said. He hung up the phone and Sam handed him the bill. "Thanks lady!"

"No problem," Sam said as she ran back to her car, then headed for Santa Monica. When she arrived there, she stopped and found a local directory. Rosalind was listed. She bought a map and found the address without difficulty.

Rosalind lived in a small house overrun with greens. There was a carport with no vehicles in evidence. Sam parked the car six blocks away and doubled back. There was no home security system, no prying neighbors, and no indications that Rosalind shared the house with anyone. Sam used the lock-pick set that she had secreted in her black bag and was inside the house within two minutes.

The furnishings were unremarkable. Sam looked around enough to see that her assumption had been correct, Rosalind lived alone. A gray cat came up to Sam and brushed against her leg. It mewled piteously and led Sam to the kitchen, where Sam noticed that its food and water dishes were almost empty. The remnants in the food bowl were hard, they had been there from the previous day. Rosalind left in a hurry and had forgotten to feed the cat.

"Oh shit," Sam growled, causing the feline to edge away. "All right, I'll feed you."

The cat brushed up beside her then leapt to the kitchen counter as Sam opened the doors, found two dozen cans of the same cat food, then went to work feeding the cat as the animal nudged at her arm, licking her, trying desperately to nibble at the food before Sam could get it in the bowl. The food stank to high hell and made a loud slurping noise as it dropped into the bowl. Sam took a knife, smoothed it out some, then set it down as she filled the water bowl and set it next to the cat on the counter. The cat dug in, forgetting to thank her.

Sam commented on this, but the cat ignored her. She stared at the cat and felt her entire body begin to tremble.

This is a *normal* life, she thought. Feed the cat, go to work.

A normal life was something that she had never known. Christ, it would have been so nice to have been bored once in a while. To just sit back and relax. To settle down.

Tears started to form in Sam's eyes and she chased them away. She couldn't think about that now. Dani was in trouble. In the handbag slung over her arm were Tory's videotapes. The diary had been worthless. Sam had read it in the car. All it contained was endless reams of mindless, erotic poetry.

Sam turned from the kitchen and hunted out the VCR. She found it in the bedroom. The machine was a high end, four-head stereo high-fi model, perfect for what Sam suspected she would need.

There was a tape in the machine. Sam ejected it and set it on the bed. Last week's *L.A. Law*. She dug into her bag and loaded the first of the videos she had taken from Halpern's mansion.

Her mind recoiled at the sight before her. She saw Tory bathed in blood, reciting her dreadful poetry as she sliced a bound and gagged man to death with a

252

razor.

The strap on her arm suddenly dug into her flesh. She felt as if she were carrying the butchered remains of a murder victim. Shrugging off the dead weight, Sam allowed the bag and the tapes it contained to fall to the carpeted floor. Her fingers grazed the stop button, then fell away. She was not interested in watching a home video snuff film, but the scene unfolding before her had a sense of familiarity to her. She watched a few more seconds of tape, then shut it off, dug into the bag, and loaded in another tape. The scene unfolding was similar to the last. There were five other tapes. On the second to last she found what she had been looking for. The man who was being murdered in this video was lying in a tub. Tory wore a uniformed officer's blue shirt, cap, and holster over her skinny, naked form.

Sam had no doubt that this was the officer who had previously owned the gun Tory had attempted to use against her, the gun the police had taken from Sam at the hotel. She stared at the final tape for several minutes. The gray cat came into the bedroom and curled up at her feet.

"God, I dunno," she whispered as she looked at the black, unlabeled tape. She did not want to view another of these scenes, but she had not been able to find anything that would lead her to her daughter. She *had* to try the last tape. Plugging the tape into the machine she hit "play."

The scenes on this tape were different. They were very grainy, shot at night, from what looked like the back of a van. The camera had been aimed at a warehouse sitting across the street. There was an alley beside the building. A car was sliding into the alley as the tape began. Sam decided that this was not a professional surveillance job. A pro would have left the camera running at all times. An amateur would think that they could wait until their subjects were in range before throwing on the recorder. Tory had probably shot the footage herself.

The car vanished from view and there was a rough, in-camera edit. The time and date counter revealed that it had been close to four in the morning, five months ago, when the video had been shot. Sam watched anxiously as she saw several figures emerge from the darkness where the car had been hidden. The camera zoomed in abruptly, taking a medium view of the figures.

A handsome Japanese-American wearing a long, leather coat walked before two other women. They were dressed in "Club MTV" style clothing: leather-studded bras, boots, short skirts. One had bright blond hair, the other dark spiky hair cropped short. The blonde carried a bottle in a paper bag and she had her arm around the other girl. They talked and laughed, even sneaked a kiss while the man's back was to them and he unlocked the side door.

The blonde said something to her companion which made the girl panic. She tried to run, but the blonde held on to her effortlessly. The girl started to scream, then she stopped as her attention was captured by something high and out of frame.

The camera jerked suddenly. The image careened wildly to the left as the shooter pulled out to a wide shot and held the camera steady as something materialized out of the darkness high above the women's heads and sailed toward them.

"Holy shit," Sam cried as she watched the blond woman shove the girl with the spiked hair from her, so that the dark-haired girl was now in line with the door. The girl turned her head and issued a startled cry as the creature that had emerged from the shadows caught her. The Japanese-American at the door darted back, out of the way, as the flying creature slammed into the spiky-haired girl and barreled her into the warehouse, out of the camera's view. The image shifted to a tight shot of the blonde and the man as they laughed and went inside, pulling the door

254

shut behind them. When he laughed, his lips pulled back to expose razor-sharp canines, wolves' teeth.

Sam stared at the screen, slack-jawed, as the tape ran out of control track. The image became a blur that evaporated into gray and white snow.

"No fucking way," Sam said as her head struck the bedpost and she realized that she had been backing away from the television. Sensing her fear and confusion, the cat had left the room.

She sat there, shaking, and finally gathered her courage to watch the tape a second time, then a third. Finally she examined the last section frame by frame. It had been a woman who had wrested herself from the darkness and flew at the spike-haired girl. She had long, flowing dark hair and her mouth was filled with ugly, sharpened teeth. Her hands had stretched out before her like claws, her fingers long and sharp, resembling talons. When she caught the spike-haired girl, she had lifted her from her feet and flew her into the warehouse.

Sam left the machine on a freeze-frame of the dark-haired woman, eyes blazing, claws and teeth glinting from the moonlight instants before she struck.

This was not a human being. Sam could rationalize the doppelganger's existence any way she liked, as memory was a tricky thing and her perceptions easily distorted. But this was real. This was cold, photographic evidence.

Attempting to deny what she was staring at, Sam wondered briefly if the footage could have been faked. Flying harnesses were common in Hollywood productions, and the fangs and claws could have been prosthetics.

But the woman had gone inside the warehouse and the door had closed behind her. If lines had been securing her, they would have been snapped by the door. And she could see in the earlier shot that there was no such apparatus in view.

It was real. Everything Halpern had told her had

been the truth. Vampires existed.

She forwarded the tape to the Japanese-American. Yoshino, Halpern had named him. Sam had no doubt that this was the man who had seduced her daughter.

But there was something that Sam didn't want to think about, couldn't begin to believe. She tried to force the thoughts away, but they would not be denied.

If what Halpern had said was true, then Dani was like the others. She was a monster, like them.

My little girl.

An abomination, a creature whose sole purpose for existence was to spread fear and misery. An inhuman thing.

My baby daughter.

Sam would not believe it. She knew what was in the girl's heart, and she clung to that thought.

I love you, baby. And I won't ever leave you the way my mommy left me. You can count on it.

That was true, and for now, it was the only truth Sam needed to worry about. The clue she had hoped for was on the tape. The warehouse had been Yoshino's refuge only a few months ago. There was no reason to believe that he had moved since then, and if he had, the warehouse itself might hold a clue as to where he had gone, where he had taken Dani.

Sam rewound the tape and started at the beginning. She couldn't understand how Tory had managed to take this footage. According to Halpern, the vampires could sense one another, and an Initiate was far less powerful than a creature who had been turned. But Tory had been turned once. She was caught in the middling world between the Initiates and the vampires. Her powers were extremely developed. It was possible that she clouded the perceptions of the others to mask her own presence. The vampire's blood-lust would have helped her in this. After all, they were just about to make a kill.

"All right," Sam whispered, "think about this logically. Where in the hell is this warehouse?"

But the thoughts would not come. She had a terrible headache and she had seen far too much, discovered far too much. She was exhausted, barely able to function. Her mind was on overload. Sam stared at the screen for a time, then got up and curled herself into a ball as she lay on the bed. She reset the alarm on the nightstand to allow her two hours of sleep.

The cat returned and curled up with her. Tears flowed from her as she gently stroked its flank and faded into unconsciousness.

She woke with a start less than a minute before the alarm was set to go off. She reached over, killed it, and reset the time. Then she raced into the bathroom and splashed cold water on her face. There was some Gatorade in the refrigerator and a collection of candy bars. She took a swig of the orange Gatorade and stole a few Cadbury bars. She felt alive and awake, and cursed herself for her earlier weakness. Two hours could mean the difference between saving her little girl and losing her forever.

She ran the tape again, trying to find a street sign, a number, anything that would give the location away, but there was nothing. It was just another building, presumably in downtown Los Angeles, considering the graffiti in the alley, and on the next building over.

She froze.

Sam screamed in delight as she realized what was wrong with the warehouse, what set it apart from the other buildings: There was *no graffiti* on its walls. There were no homeless people lying in the alley. The street was dead. It was the middle of the night and the street people were avoiding it as if it was the house of the devil himself.

Sam collected her videotapes, plugged Rosalind's *L.A. Law* back into the machine, and considered the cat's bowls. She checked them and the food bowl had been licked clean, the water half empty. It would be drained by the time Rosalind returned home. The woman would never know that Sam had been there, not unless she took an inventory of her candy bars.

Peering out cautiously, Sam checked to ensure that her departure would not be seen by the neighbors. Then she left the house and walked at a steady, relaxed pace as she went back to the GT-S. She got in the car and took off, anxious to begin her search.

Twenty-one

"Mom?"

Dani stood in a small, black interrogation room with a table and two chairs. A glaring, white hot light hung from the ceiling. There were no doors, no windows. Dani was not alone. She was sealed in tight with a deranged woman who sat in one of the two chairs, her feet up on the table. The woman tossed a gun back and forth from one hand to another. She wore mirrored sunglasses and a nasty smile.

"Mom?" Dani repeated.

The creature wearing Samantha Walthers' face and form laughed derisively. "You know better than that."

Dani recognized the voice. The figure sitting before her was the demon incarnate.

"What do you want?" Dani said, her back against the wall. Her fingers searched for a crack in the marble that might indicate a door, a window, anything. There was no way out of the small, black room.

"Have a seat," the demon said.

"I'll stand."

"Go on, do it," the demon implored. "I'm not going to bite you. *Not unless you want me to.*"

The words stung Dani. They were very close to

those Madison had used when she had first coaxed Dani into using her power. The vampires had deceived Madison. They had played with her perceptions and made her believe that she had powers, too, but that had been a lie. She had not been an Initiate, she had been *prey*. Meat. Nothing else.

Nothing except Dani's friend, that is.

The demon set the gun down on the table and let its borrowed hands drop to its borrowed lap. "I'm not going to ask you again."

Dani sat down, across from the demon. "Am I dreaming?"

"I'm wondering about that myself. The acid test for me has always been, if you're aware of the concept of dreaming, you can't possibly *be* dreaming. But I'll give you that one. Sure, you're dreaming. Reality is whatever you want it to be."

"What do you want?"

"What do you *think* I want?"

Dani shook her head. She had no idea what this abomination desired of her.

"Why do you have to look like that?" she asked, trying to change the subject. She shifted her gaze from the demon whenever possible.

"You don't like the way I look? This is upsetting to you?" The demon laughed. It was dressed exactly the same way Samantha Walthers had been dressed the night she had drawn her gun on her daughter.

"Yeah, it bothers me. Do something. Make yourself look like something else. I dunno."

"But I like it this way, Dani. I'm comfortable. And besides, losing this form would make things easy on you, and you've been taking the easy way out for too long now."

"What do you mean?" Dani asked in a weak, frightened voice.

"You know *exactly* what I mean."

"I did what you wanted," Dani said, leaning forward, gripping the edges of the table. "You wanted to be let out. You wanted to be in control. I let you."

The demon shook its head and chortled. It reached up and played with Samantha's hair much the same way Samantha would. "But you didn't, Dani. Not really. All you did was buckle under."

"You're full of shit," Dani said. Suddenly, she reached forward and snatched the gun from the table. The demon looked on with an amused smile.

"What are you going to do?" it asked. "Shoot me?"

"I might."

"You really think you can—with me looking like this?"

"Maybe."

"That I'd like to see."

Dani shuddered. "Tell me what you want. Get to the point. What do you mean I'm buckling under?"

"Exactly that. You dreamed of love, you dreamed of romance. You wanted passion and uninhibited sex. But you told yourself you were a good girl and you wouldn't do anything about what you wanted. Then the first time an opportunity came up, you couldn't wait to rip your panties off."

"I'm not going to apologize for making love with Bill," Dani said. "I thought that you of all people would approve."

"I'm not a person. I'm you, a part of you. You'll never come to terms with what you are . . . unless you accept me fully."

"I know what I am." Dani's wolflike incisors suddenly sprang from her jaws. "I'm more than human. I'm immortal."

"No, you're not. Not yet. There's more. And your friends, or those people you think are your friends, aren't telling you everything. You can sense that much, can't you?"

Dani's finger closed on the trigger. She stared at the face of her mother and slowly put the gun down. "I don't understand any of this. You should be enjoying yourself."

"But I'm not. I'm not really free. So long as you do what the *pack* tells you to do, so long as you blindly follow, I will never be free."

Maybe that's just as well, Dani thought. The demon shrugged, and Dani realized that even her thoughts were available to the creature. That made sense. After all, it had admitted to being nothing more than a product of her mind.

"You're taking the easy way out of this," the demon snarled. "The truth is staring you in the face and you don't want to look at it."

"What do you know about the truth?"

"I know everything you know, Dani. And a hell of a lot more. I know everything you're not willing to admit to yourself. Everything you refuse to see is painfully obvious to me."

"Is it really?"

"Samantha Walthers raised you. She gave you everything. She loved you without conditions, without restraint. And she never lied to you."

"Bill loves me," Dani said.

"Has he ever said it?"

Dani had no reply.

"Has he done anything but show you that he's willing to say anything and do anything to accomplish his own ends?"

"That doesn't —"

"It doesn't what? It doesn't matter? You know it matters, Dani."

The demon's voice was changing, taking on a tone that was similar to that of Samantha Walthers. Dani now understood why the demon had chosen to appear to her in this form.

"I've got to wake you up, Dani. There's so little

time."

Dani heard a pounding on the walls, outside the small room.

"Remember when you were in Willis's house? Remember the way you thought? You were in danger and you looked at the situation the way your mother had trained you to. You have to do that again. You have to look at things from every angle, Dani."

"My mother wanted to kill me!" Dani cried. "She was crazy. She was —"

Dani broke off in mid-sentence. She was about to start crying. The demon swung its legs over the side of the table and came to her. It knelt before her.

"Your mother told you of a *doppelganger*. That's what she called it. A creature that could make a human being see it however it wished to be seen. Does that sound familiar, Dani? Does that sound like what you are? And who was that girl that Bill had a bad relationship with, six months ago? Who was that, Dani?

"Didn't it ever occur to you that maybe Bill has more friends than just the ones you've met? Didn't you ever think there were more like you, that the entire world is crawling with beings like you?"

The pounding on the walls grew louder. Dani could hear Bill calling her name.

"You've got to wake up to reality, Dani. Before it's too late for both of us. You've got to —"

WAKE UP.

The words rang out in a different voice. A man's voice.

WAKE UP.

Bill Yoshino's voice.

Dani reached down and tore the sunglasses from the face of the demon, the borrowed face of Samantha Walthers. The eyes were not those of her mother. They burned with the fires of damnation. Dani turned away before those fires could consume her.

263

WAKE UP, DANI!

"Think about what I've said," the demon whispered.

Dani nodded once, then the walls imploded and she woke from the dream.

Dani opened her eyes, expecting to find herself in the watery grave where she had been laid to rest at dawn. Instead, she was standing on the shore of the lake, Isabella and Angel holding her up. She looked down and saw her dangling feet grazing the muddy earth. In a burst of awareness, she found that she could not breathe, her lungs were filled with water. Panic flooded through her and she started to cough, expelling the water in a torrent. When it had drained from her, creating a small puddle at her feet, she shrugged off the strong hands of the vampires and sank to the ground, her knees sloshing in the mud. Dry heaves ripped through her until finally she was able to relax and breathe normally.

A pair of boots sank into the earth before her. She looked up to see Bill towering above her, his expression bereft of compassion. He offered his hand and she took it, but not without a moment's hesitation.

"We couldn't wake you up," Bill said. "There's a lot for us to accomplish tonight, you know."

Dani looked around and saw that night had fallen. It seemed very odd to exist without the sunlight. She would get used to it, she supposed.

"Are you all right?" Isabella asked.

"Yeah, fine," Dani murmured as Bill lifted her into his arms. He took her in a comforting embrace and kissed her softly on the lips. There was no passion in the kiss, and very little of the explosive charge that Dani had felt when she had first been touched by him. His lips were cold. She felt as if she were kissing a dead man. He was not the brooding,

264

romantic figure of her dreams. She felt as if she had been asleep for days, and she was only now waking up.

"There's a little disorientation," Isabella said. "That's normal."

The dark-haired woman touched Dani's hair, brushing it away from her neck. Isabella's lips lightly brushed Dani's skin and the girl felt energized, her every nerve ending suddenly alive, the warmth suddenly returning to her cold, wet body.

You are safe, sister-love. We are with you in these frightening times.

Dani nodded as relief flooded through her. Isabella understood what she was going through; she had obviously experienced the guilt and the inner conflict that raged within Dani, and she had emerged perfectly content, and serene, like a goddess.

Angel, who had been standing off to the side, said harshly, "We need to hitch a ride. We can't hang around here all night. You know what will happen if we do."

"There is time," Isabella said. "Don't worry."

"Someone better," Angel said darkly, then she turned and started walking.

"Why don't we fly?" Dani asked, recalling the rapture of the previous night's experience. "It would be faster."

Bill shook his head. "Flying drains us. It's a pleasure best reserved for after a kill . . . How do you feel?"

"Well, pretty tired," Dani said truthfully.

His dispassionate manner was beginning to unnerve Dani. She felt as if she were back in school. What would this have been, she wondered, Vampirism 101?

She didn't appreciate being treated like a child. She had been turned, she didn't need them anymore.

If she chose to, she could walk away at any time.

Dani's shoulders slumped. Big talk. If only it were true. A part of her needed their encouragement, their joy at her accomplishments, their unrestrained love. She was hungry for it. Still, the hunger was one that she could control, for now.

Without a word, Dani turned and followed Angel, who was a dozen yards ahead of them. Bill and Isabella caught up quickly, flanking her.

Dani surrendered herself to the subtle rhythms of the night. From somewhere far distant, she could sense humanity. A town of some sort. It would be teeming with life, with prey. The ache in her stomach which she had been ignoring suddenly sharpened. She hoped it was from the water she'd expelled from her lungs, but she knew it was more than that. There was a physical need that was just now making itself known, a frightening wellspring of desire for the thrill of the hunt and the sweet taste of fear and blood. This made no sense. Bill had told her that a full vampire rarely needed to kill. Strong emotions, fear and desire, were proper sustenance for them. Why then was she feeling these terrible pangs of hunger?

Bill and Isabella regarded one another. A strange, unfathomable look passed between them. Bill gave a slight smirk and turned away. Isabella looked down and refused to meet Dani's gaze.

After a few minutes they came to a road. Angel took a position on the road's far side. She shrugged off her leather jacket, exposing her strapless studded bra and ample breasts.

"I don't think a lot of cars come this way," Dani said. "It looks pretty deserted."

Bill shrugged. "There's a town that we could get to before morning and take a room, if we need to. But I'd like to avoid that."

Dani didn't have to ask why. She was certain that

if her blood thirst grew more intense, she would have a difficult time restraining herself in the company of humans. She pictured herself surrounded by armed humans, a bloody victim at her feet. The *pack* could not afford to be exposed. Dani shuddered and looked at the others. As she had feared, her need had been apparent to them. Angel had felt disgust at Dani's weakness, Bill amusement, Isabella sadness.

"Don't worry," Angel said. "All I need is one shot and we'll have a ride."

Several minutes later they saw headlights in the distance. Dani, Bill, and Isabella crouched on the opposite side of the road from Angel, who arched her back and set her hand provocatively on her thigh as she raised her thumb.

The car breezed past without slowing. Angel watched it go, her eyes wide, her mouth set in an cartoonish O. A few seconds passed before a stream of raging obscenities started to fly from her. She kicked at the ground, then squatted, slammed at the black pavement, and broke a section off. With a wild scream she hurled the block of pavement over her head. It landed nearly a thousand feet down the road, exploding into a shower of rubble when it hit.

"Motherfucker!" she screamed.

By this time, the other vampires had not been able to restrain themselves. They laughed at Angel's fury, and the blond-haired vampire turned on them, leaping into the air and sailing for them. Dani had joined in the laughter, and her amusement abruptly faded as she realized Angel's trajectory would cause the vampire to barrel into her at any moment.

"She's pissed, use it against her," Bill whispered as he stepped away from Dani.

"Don't laugh at me!" Angel cried. "No one fucking laughs at me!"

Dani wished she could come up with some taunting reply that would have made Arnold

Schwarzenegger smile, but all she could do was hide her fear and hold herself rigid as the vampire closed in. At the last moment before Angel would have slammed into her, Dani sidestepped the flying body and grabbed hold of the vampire's outstretched arm. She caught Angel's ankle in her free hand and was captured by the momentum. Suddenly feeling like a participant in a woman's wrestling match from hell, Dani pirouetted, playing "airplane" with Angel until they were turning so quickly they became a blur. Then vertigo threatened to overcome her, and Dani finally released Angel, sending her twenty feet across the road, where she crashed to the ground and rolled, picking up speed and again taking to the air, only to falter once more and collapse.

Dani's world was spinning and she fell to the ground until the sensation ended. When the dizziness passed, she found herself smiling, and saw Angel picking herself up from the dirt on the other side of the road.

"You bitch!" Angel screamed. "I'm gonna make you fucking pay for that."

Isabella took a step forward and was about to speak, but Dani stopped her. "Wrong, asshole. I still owed you for that kiss from this morning, remember?"

Angel hesitated, the fight beginning to drain from her. She tottered slightly, as if she were punch drunk, then bit her lips and said, "You didn't like it?"

Dani said nothing, and soon, Angel's mask of hatred fell away. The vampire grinned. "All right, we're even. But you should try this if you think it's so easy."

"No problem," Dani said, shrugging off her own jacket and handing it to Isabella. After thinking a moment, Dani decided to remove her satin and lace top as well as her micro mini. Since she hadn't been wearing underwear, she now stood there, naked in her thigh-high black leather boots.

"That should get someone's attention," Dani said as she took up Angel's position. The blond vampire passed her, shaking her head and smiling.

"Watch out, you're gonna get me hot," Angel whispered. "Then I'm gonna want to get me some."

"Yeah, you wish," Dani replied. The thought of making love to another woman did not repulse her as it once had, but she had no interest in Angel. Isabella was another matter. Even from across the road, Dani could feel the flush of desire that the sight of her naked body had elicited from Isabella. She basked in the sensuous pleasure and consumed Isabella's sexual need as if it was an appetizer for a rich dinner. Isabella shuddered, but she didn't seem to mind Dani's intrusion.

As before, Dani's hunger did not subside. Once whetted, it increased. Turning her inhuman senses to the town in the distance, Dani could almost taste the succulent array of petty fears and desires waiting to be stolen away by one of her kind. And more importantly, she could sense the blood.

Dani shook violently as she felt something new. Prey was about to arrive. The rush of a beating heart filled her senses.

"A car is coming. A man is driving it," she said.

Seconds after she spoke, a pair of headlights appeared in the distance. As the car drew closer, Dani extended her silver thread and retrieved a few random images from his mind. She witnessed several scenes of the man with his family, laughing and playing. The images might have been culled from a series of Hallmark ads. Then she suddenly felt angry when she realized the family was playing in the *sunlight*. She wanted to rip those picture-perfect memories to shreds.

"This is going to be sweet," Dani said dreamily.

Across the street, crouching so they would not be seen, the vampires waited. Dani could sense their anticipation. It matched hers.

Soon the headlights were close. Dani stepped into the middle of the road. She slipped a finger into her mouth, wet it, then touched it to the soft patch of fur between her legs. The car's headlights turned her into a brilliant white wraith and its brakes squealed like a frightened animal as it came to a stop inches before striking her.

The road had been winding, with small hills and dips. The car's brights had been on. Dani could see nothing of the car or its driver. But she could sense the enthusiasm of her companions wane slightly. She heard a door open. Stepping around from the front of the car, beyond the blinding headlights, Dani saw that she had stopped a police cruiser.

Twenty-two

Dani was mortified.

Her hands went to her breasts, covering them quickly. Her fear bottled up in her heart and threatened to explode within her. All her life she had been taught to respect police officers. Taking one of them as *prey* would be like murdering her own mother.

And why should that be so difficult? sang the voice of the demon in her brain. *She's just meat. Just like the others.*

Dani wanted to warn the officer, she wanted to use her power to force him back into his vehicle. She could do that, she knew. She could make him go away and not even remember seeing her. But when she tried, she found that she could not focus her inherent power. The man shook, his mouth set in a frown. He seemed embarrassed, but he did not relent. Dani's fear had caused her to lose control of her abilities.

"Ma'am, can I ask exactly what you're doing out here?" He unsnapped the strap of his holster.

If Dani had been alone, she could have extricated herself from the situation with ease. She could have played the victim, gained his sympathy, and, when she was calm, sent him along, all mem-

271

ory of the incident removed from his thoughts. But she was not alone, and the unpredictable nature of the vampires, Angel especially, had unnerved her, making her unable to react in a proper manner.

"I was hungry," Dani said. Her body became rigid. She wondered why in the hell she had said *that*. Because it had been the truth, she realized, and her mother had taught her to tell the police the truth.

"I'm sorry?" he asked, tilting his head as if he had not heard her correctly. The police officer was young, just under thirty, with an athletic build. He seemed like the type who would be kind, but firm. His eyes were hazel, drifting lazily between green and brown. His hair was short and he had a midwest twang in his voice.

"Not born around here, were you, officer?" a voice called from behind the man. To the officer's credit, he drew his gun quickly, turning in the direction of the voice. The ugly crack of shattering bones filled the night as Angel slapped the gun out of his hand. It slammed on the roof of the car. The police officer resisted the urge to grab at his wounded hand. Instead, he reached for the nightstick on his belt. Bill surged forward, grasping the man's wrists and pinning him against the side of the car.

"Hay-yah, ah'd say we got us a fine little philly here," Bill said, his country-boy accent almost as disturbing as his wolf's teeth, which gleamed in the light from inside the cruiser. "You ah—you didn't have time to call this one in, now didcha?"

The police officer said nothing, his attention riveted on Bill's rapidly elongating fangs. He was fighting his fear well, but he would have to give in sometime.

"Oh, Dani was right," Bill said, dropping the

phony accent. "You're going to be a tasty morsel."

Dani stood off to the side. "Let him go."

Bill shot her a glance that made her cringe. She looked away and walked to Isabella, who held out her clothes.

"Our little Dani thinks we should let you go, officer," Bill snarled. "Now what do you think the likelihood of that is, hmmmm?"

Angel ripped the officer's belt from him, taking the nightstick, his vial of mace, and his handcuffs. "I think we can have some fun with these."

Dani watched as Angel licked the shaft of the nightstick, up and down. The officer shifted his attention to her display and became aroused, despite himself.

"Fun and games, officer," she whispered. "We live for fun and games."

Dani took a step forward. Isabella put her hand on Dani's arm. "This has gone too far," Isabella said. "It can't be stopped."

Dani knew Isabella was right. She could feel the blood lust radiating from Bill and Angel. Allowing Isabella to help her into her clothes, Dani felt the cool night air bite into her flesh. The woman's hands trailed on her skin a few instants too long. The sexual energy that was transferred to Dani through her touch helped the girl to take her mind from her fear, and concentrate on what she could do to help the officer. She sensed that the only merciful act she could perform would be to take his gun from the roof of the car, aim it at his head, and pull the trigger. He was not going to survive to see morning.

Grief suffused Dani and she allowed Isabella to hold her.

"Come on," Bill said, "it's time to motorvate."

"You know it," Angel replied.

Dani watched them and understood for the first time exactly how alike those two had been, even though she had thought they were worlds apart when she had first met them. At least Angel was honest about who and what she was. Bill hid his cruelty beneath designer clothes, GQ hair, and a perfect, loving smile that held no true compassion.

I loved you, she thought. *I gave my heart to you. How can you be like this?*

"We have to go, we can't remain out here," Isabella said softly.

Dani nodded.

"You drive," Bill said, glancing absently in Dani's direction. "Therese is down the road, about a mile. We'll pick her up, then head for home."

A strange sensation came to Dani. She was suddenly aware that her fear had caused her bloodthirst to lessen. It had also made her unaware of Therese's proximity. But now, as she extended her senses in the direction Bill had indicated, she could feel Therese. The woman's heart was thundering in anticipation at the thought of her reunion with Angel.

"Why don't we just wait for her?" Dani said.

"You don't want to miss out on the action, do you?" Angel said with a laugh. "All right, let's wait. But get the cruiser off the road and kill the lights, in case anyone comes by."

Dani followed the vampire's commands. As she climbed into the cruiser and pulled the car to the shoulder, she thought of her strange dream, her meeting with the demon. Had the demon been right? Were its accusations correct? Was she no more than a slave to these people, as Therese had become?

No, Dani thought firmly. *They're my friends. We're the same. They've come to grips with what*

274

they are, that's all. In time, I'll be just like them.

That thought, meant to comfort, caused her to shudder.

Angel reached out with her thoughts and ordered Therese to run the remaining distance. Soon the former limousine driver was at their side. As Dani got out of the car, Angel gave Therese a fleeting kiss. The blonde sighed and sat down in the driver's seat. Dani wanted to stay with Isabella, but Angel grabbed her arm and hurled her into the back, quickly sliding in beside her as Bill shoved the police officer inside and crammed in beside him.

Isabella sat in the front, beside Therese. A wire mesh grill separated the front and back seats.

"This isn't going to do," Isabella said as she tore at the mesh, yanking it from its moorings and hauling it from the cruiser. Then she returned to the car and reached over the backseat to take Dani's hand. "Much better."

"Let's go," Bill said impatiently. "I'm starved."

The car pulled out, and Angel commanded Therese to turn off the radio. Its incessant squawkings seemed to be getting on the vampire's nerves.

"Leave it on," Dani said.

"Why?" Therese responded dully, as if she had been drugged.

"Because we'll need to know if this unit gets a call. If he doesn't respond, they could get suspicious and—"

"I can fix that," Angel said, narrowing her gaze.

Therese jerked in the front seat and handed the radio's handset back to her mistress. Angel snuggled up next to the police officer, who had somehow managed to disconnect himself from reality. He radiated no emotions.

Dani had been equally impressed and frightened

275

by the change that had come over the police officer. While she admired his lack of fear, she felt her blood rise to the challenge, along with that of the other vampires. She wanted to make him afraid, she wanted to taste his terror. Most of all, she needed his blood. Her hunger was back in full force, and she felt her reason slipping away, slowly succumbing to the animal desires coursing through her.

She pictured her mother sitting between the vampires and that made it worse. The hunger did not abate and her sense of guilt became overwhelming. It was her fault this man had been captured. But if it had not been him, it would have been another. She wondered if the vampires could recall the faces of their victims over the years.

Another thought occurred to her. How old were these creatures? They spoke of immortality. They might well be the ages they appeared, but there was a sense of otherworldliness to Isabella, and Bill spoke as if he attended the premiere of Olivier's movies in the thirties and forties. Somehow she knew it wouldn't surprise her if he had.

Her thoughts froze when she saw Angel push the handset into the officer's face.

"I can make you do anything I want," she said. "I could bite your damn dick off, then make you eat it. And I promise, I could make you have fun with it. Of course, you'd know what you were doing. You'd *feel* everything, the lack of blood, the shock. But I'd keep you around, I'd keep you aware. Face it, sweetie, you're mine."

The man spasmed involuntarily. Dani knew this was every cop's worst nightmare. She wondered if the officer's gun was still on the roof. They hadn't bothered to retrieve it and she hadn't heard it fall. It could have been wedged up near the cruiser's bank of red and blue lights. Had he considered that? Was he secretly clinging to that one hope for salvation?

Dani knew that she could be cruel and tell the vampires to stop long enough for her to see if the gun was there and discard the weapon if she found it sitting there, but she had no desire to do so. Let the man keep his fantasy. Besides, his mind might collapse entirely if he had no hope left.

Angel was continuing to play with her food. "You're going to do exactly what I tell you to do or I'm going to skin you alive."

"You'll do that anyway," the man said, making the mistake of acknowledging them.

"It speaks," Bill said. He immediately shifted to the mock-southern accent. "And here ah thought cotton had lost his little voice. Come on now, boy. Why don't you just tell us *whut* makes you tick, hear? Less'n you want us to have the fun of finding out ourselves."

Dani stared at Bill in contempt. Gazing into his cold, merciless blue eyes, she could not find the man she had fallen in love with. She was no longer even aroused by him.

Angel reached up and gripped the back of the man's head with her hands, holding him by his short hair. She moved the handset near his mouth. "Tell them you had a flat and you're fixing it. It's gonna take you a while. Then you have to cruise by home. You've got a situation there you have to deal with."

"They'll call his house," Dani said. "When he doesn't sign back on, they'll call his house."

"Let them," Bill responded. "We'll be way the hell out of here by then. They won't know where to look."

"Hell, by the time we're done with them, they won't even know what they're looking at," Angel said with a cackle.

Isabella watched them from the front seat, quiet and serene. At last she said, "You're wasting time."

Bill frowned and turned to the police officer. "Do it."

The man was silent. He refused. Dani stared at him and decided that the vampires had made a mistake by showing their teeth. Their very being was so alien, so beyond the normal scope of this man's perceptions that by reveling in their strangeness they had made themselves unreal to him, they had made the situation unreal. He had somehow convinced himself that this was a nightmare, and eventually, he would wake up.

Angel snuggled in close and licked at the side of his face. "Do it or we'll stay around town after you're dead and find out where your family lives."

This jarred him into action. He had to protect his family. He could not afford the luxury of disbelief any longer. Clearing his throat, the officer nodded. Angel pressed the call button and he recited the words she had dictated to him. There was only a slight tremor in his voice. He said nothing that could be interpreted as a code, a signal that he was an officer in distress. Apparently he had hoped the situation itself would be so unusual that red flags would be thrown up in the dispatcher's mind. If that occurred, there was no indication. His words were accepted, and he signed off.

Angel tore the handset loose and pitched it to the floor.

Dani stared at the man. Suddenly she sensed a low, reverberating pain emanating from him. Bones had been broken in his hand when Angel had swatted the gun from him. He had said nothing, he

278

had not even allowed himself to feel the pain. But now, the pain could not be denied. He focused on it instead of his fear.

The officer was not going to beg for his life. He was not going to give them that satisfaction. But they had already found his weak spot, his family, and he would have to pretend that his wife and children did not matter to him.

"What's your name?" Angel asked.

The man apparently thought this was a good sign. Dani recalled Bill's warning about being a captive and having your kidnappers depersonalize you because it meant that they were about to kill you. The man evidently believed that he now had time, and with time, he could find a way to escape.

"Hal Jordan," he said.

Dani almost giggled.

"What's so funny?" Bill asked, amused by her reaction.

"Nothing," Dani replied. She had read a lot of comic books when she was younger. Hal Jordan was the name of Green Lantern's secret identity — Green Lantern, a comic book super-hero born without fear. The police officer wasn't giving in to them, she realized. He had given a made-up name. A flush of admiration for this man and his courage welled inside her.

She had never known her birth parents. Occasionally she would fantasize about them. The idea of a mother other than Sam was ridiculous to her. But somewhere she had a father, and when she pictured him, he would look very much like the police officer who was about to be savaged by her companions.

Angel rested her head on Jordan's shoulder and stroked his chest. The familiar, loving gesture was a horrible mockery, and Dani wanted the vampire to stop; but Angel was not about to stop, not for her, or anyone else. Dani could feel the bloodthirst rising within her companions, and it pulled at her own hunger, her own need.

"Hal, Sweetie, why don't you tell us something about yourself," Angel said in a low, husky voice.

"There's not much to tell."

"Oh, come on. I mean, they all say that, in the beginning. But before we're through, we're gonna know everything about you. So might as well save us all a lot of bother and just answer me."

Jordan thought about it for a moment, then nodded gravely. He could sense the truth in her words.

"I'm a cop."

Bill rested his arm against the windowsill. "No shit."

With a grin, Angel said, "Just like your father before you, I imagine? And his father before him?"

"No," he said. "My dad was a dentist. He hated the idea of my being a cop. He tried to stop me."

"But you're big and strong so you didn't let him."

"No, I did what I wanted to do."

"That's good," Angel said soothingly. "What about your daddy? Is he still alive?"

Dani watched as Jordan looked down. The throbbing pain in his hand had become worse. She could feel it. His attempt to concentrate on his pain, to move away from the memories of his father—which Dani could sense were painful—did nothing but delay the inevitable. She surprised herself by easing her silver thread to his mind, just far enough to give him a tiny push and help him to let down his defenses.

He shuddered, a tear suddenly falling from his

280

eye.

Angel spun, angrily. "Don't you fucking touch him **again**," she spat, then caught Isabella's warning glare. Angel turned back to her prey. Isabella reached back and stroked Dani's hair.

Dani felt the fluttering of wings within her thoughts as Isabella's voice penetrated her consciousness. *There's nothing you can do, sister-love. And nothing you should do. You hunger. A feast is at hand. Give yourself to it.*

Dani cleared her mind and made no reply. She watched silently as Angel caressed the officer's face and urged the man to tell her more about his father.

"He died a few years ago," Jordan whispered.

"And you miss him."

The officer set his jaw. The muscles in his face twitched. "Yes, I miss him."

Bill and Angel laughed. They could tell from his furtive manner that this was a lie.

"What did he do to make you glad he was dead?" Angel said, gingerly picking up the officer's wounded hand. When the man did not reply, Angel kissed his hand and sent a dagger of searing pain into his consciousness. He bucked in the seat and Bill held him down.

The officer grimaced. "He broke the law."

"Oh, tried and true, ranger blue, he got a sad song for me and you," Angel said with a sigh.

Dani felt nothing but hatred for the vampire and her vicious tactics. "You fucking bitch," she whispered.

Angel lazily turned to Dani, sensing the wave of strong emotion rushing out of the girl. "I'm only doing what you're afraid to do. I've been gentle up to this point, out of respect. You're new. This is hard on you. I know that. I went through it, too.

281

But if you get out of hand, so will I. And you know what I'm capable of doing."

Dani felt a sudden explosion of panic erupt in the officer at Angel's words. Her dispassionate view of what she was about to do made it seem terrifyingly routine to the officer and horrifyingly real. He had spent time in the company of killers who matter-of-factly recited the graphic details of their crimes as if they were reading their grocery lists aloud. He understood that the people who had taken him could kill him and feel absolutely no remorse.

With his fear came a sliver of memory: When Jordan had been a teenager he had worked in a slaughterhouse. He hated the job, but he stuck it out for an entire summer. In the small town where he had been raised, the slaughterhouse was the only business hiring. He needed the money if he was going to have his own car. He bought the car, but somehow he couldn't seem to get the smells of the slaughterhouse out of the interiors. They remained until he sold the vehicle. It took him a long time to realize that the smells had been a part of him, not the car. They hung about him, suffocatingly strong.

To the officer, the vampires had that smell. Fear burned through him as he pictured himself as nothing more than a helpless animal being marched to his own demise. Despite herself, Dani tasted his fear and found it sweet. Her heart thundered in excitement, her lips quivering at the thought of the pleasure that was yet to come this night.

"Go on," Dani whispered, hating herself for the words.

Angel turned to the officer, whose face had become pale. "Parents are always embarrassing their children. Here you are, a danger ranger, and your daddy was a criminal. What did he do? How exactly did he break the law?"

When the officer did not reply, Angel tweaked up the pain he had been feeling. Jordan cried out in agony.

"Jesus!" he screamed.

"Yes, Hal," Angel said. "Tell us about Jesus. Then we'll get back to your daddy."

The officer bucked in the grip of the vampires and the searing pain they inflicted. Shards of memory rocketed from him and Dani experienced them, her thighs grinding together as the familiar sexual heat that accompanied her hunger abruptly returned.

Though Hal had been a regular churchgoer, he had never truly come to grips with the idea that God might have been anything more than a popular myth created by the weak. A fiction for people who needed a higher power to take responsibility for their lives because they were not willing to do it themselves. When he moved to California, he had fallen in with a group of Wiccans—witches. A girl he had dated revealed herself to be involved in a coven, and due to his wild craving to get into her jeans, he allowed himself to be talked into attending one of their meetings. He was surprised by what he found there. The Wiccans didn't believe in predestination. The concept of a vengeful God or a crafty, plotting Satan was irrelevant to their beliefs. They were in control of their own lives. They were free.

He slept with the girl that night and stayed with her for several weeks, but then he met the woman he would eventually marry and have children with, and he left his girlfriend for her. His wife was a devout Catholic, and he had no difficulty in resuming the role of the devout worshiper.

But at this moment, he was sitting in the back-seat of his cruiser with the children of Lucifer, and he had no choice but to believe in their reality. When he tried to deny them, they would send their tendrils inside his mind, causing him pain and pleasure, torturing him in ways no human could. They would not even allow him the peace of insanity, or the dulling of his reason.

Dani found his fear succulent. He might have been prey, he might have been an animal compared to them, but he was a magnificent animal, and he would not give himself to them easily.

Angel slid her hand to the officer's crotch. "So you don't believe in God, huh, baby? That's all right. He probably doesn't believe in you."

Hal was silent.

"I mean, where was God when your daddy was off committing crimes? Was He protecting your daddy's victims? Was He protecting you?"

"Stop," the officer said, his voice wavering.

"Yeah, in the name of love, Sweetie. Come on, if God gave a damn, people like you and me wouldn't exist. That's what you're here for, isn't it? To pick up the slack? To serve and protect?"

"Yes."

Angel splayed more of his memories for her companions to view. Hal had lived by a simple code, to cause no harm to others, unless there was no other choice. He had always dreamed of becoming a police officer because he had wanted to protect those who could not protect themselves. When he had been a boy, he was constantly befriending the smaller children who were being targeted by bullies.

"You are *so* noble, Sweetie-Pie." She stroked his erection through his pants, her hand moving faster now. He was hard and straining, repulsed at his body's reaction to Angel's ministrations.

Without warning, Angel burrowed deep into the officer's mind, scouring through the memories he had kept hidden, even from himself. The fear he radiated at the thought of these memories being unearthed was both tantalizing and repulsive to Dani. She didn't know what she was supposed to feel. She was sorry for the officer's agonies, but they brought her pleasure and a release from the horrible *need* that was welling up inside her.

"Your daddy was a very naughty dentist, wasn't he? He was old and he wasn't getting any, so when the young pretty girls came in, he put them under gas and diddled them, didn't he? That's what he did."

Dani watched them in mute horror. She was watching this noble man being destroyed, and a part of her was loving it.

"Yes," Jordan replied finally, tears forming in his eyes. "That's what he did."

Twenty-three

"You knew all about it, didn't you?" Angel asked.

Hal did not respond. His entire body was rigid with resistance. These memories were buried deeper than the rest. His most powerful fear would be pried from him only if these memories were released.

God help me, Dani thought. I want it. I want it so goddamned badly.

"Give it up," Dani whispered in a wanton tone that shocked her.

Angel grinned. "You heard the lady."

The officer fought to hold back the words, but it was hopeless. In a halting manner he said, "There was a girl when I was in high school. Her name was Mary Ann. She came to me one day. She was upset."

"And she started talking trash about your daddy, didn't she?" Angel asked.

The officer's heart was racing. "Please," he said.

"Can't stop now," Bill said.

"This is humiliating," the officer cried. "Stop."

"Nope," Angel said. "Not in this lifetime. Now tell us all about poor little Mary Ann. It sounds like she got a poke, and she didn't want it."

"Please," the officer begged, tears streaming down his face.

Dani felt her illusions about the man begin to slip away. The realization that he was just a man, possessed of a man's weaknesses, angered her. "Tell her!"

The man shook as if he had been slapped. Biting his lip until it bled, he finally said, "She knew me. She thought maybe she was going crazy, and she needed someone to talk to."

"About your daddy and what he did to her."

"Yes."

"What did she tell you?"

"That he put her under. She was asleep, and then she found herself coming around. The mix must have been off. Her dress was bunched up around her waist. She wasn't a virgin, she had been with two other guys. She thought she was dreaming at first. But it was her dentist over her, pushing his thing inside her. That's what she called it. *His thing.* She started to fight him, tried to get away, and he gassed her again. When she woke up, the nurse was with her, and she convinced herself that it had been a dream, a really bad dream. But she wouldn't go back to him anymore. She wouldn't explain why to anyone. She just stayed away.

"Then one afternoon, she was in the A & P and she saw my father staring at her. He had this expression on his face that scared her. At first, she couldn't remember where she had seen that expression before. Then it came to her: It had been in the dream, when she had woken up and saw him inside her. That's when she knew that it wasn't a dream, it had really happened."

"What did you do?"

"I hit her. I'd never hit a girl before, and I've never hit one since. She was a goddamned liar. A fucking little slut. I told her that if she ever repeated a word of what she had said to me, I'd beat

287

the shit out of her. And I would have. But I didn't have to. She kept her mouth shut."

"You liked hitting her, didn't you?"

"No," he said. It had been a lie.

"You'd enjoy hitting me right now, wouldn't you?" Angel asked.

"I'd fucking kill you if I could," he hissed. The vehemence in his delivery surged pleasantly through the vampires. His passion was contagious.

"But you can't," Angel said, tweaking up his rage. "No one can."

The officer's fear returned.

Angel laughed. "So little Mary Ann chose the wrong person to cry to, and a part of you knew *all along* that she had been telling the truth. That's why you stopped doing what your daddy told you to do. That's why you moved away."

"I don't know," he muttered.

"I know," Angel said. "I know you better than you know yourself. And you're nothing but a piece of shit."

The man nodded and before Dani's eyes, he fell apart. She watched him with loathing. His self-image had been nothing but a lie. All the good he had done in his life was simply to assuage his guilt, because he had *known* that the girl had been telling the truth about his father. He had done nothing with the knowledge except run away and cloak himself in illusions.

Something within Dani snapped. A lifetime's worth of hatred, frustration, and betrayal surged in her, overpowering her reason. The man was like everyone else who had ever hurt her, and exactly the same as the one person who had wounded her most deeply.

"Son of a bitch!" Dani screamed as she lunged for him, her wolf's teeth, sharp and glistening with her spit, growing instantly. Angel turned and caught her, holding her back. The man's fear intensified. Suddenly, he was nothing but a frightened animal who had seen the eyes of his executioner. "He's just like her! They're the same! Fuckers just the same!"

Isabella whispered something to Therese, the driver, and the cruiser pulled off the road. They drove down a small dirt drive protected by a canopy of trees.

"Get them out of the car," Isabella said, a touch of regret in her voice. The patch of woods was deserted and quiet. Bill hauled the officer out of the cruiser. Angel kicked the passenger door open and pulled Dani out the other side, kicking, screaming, and biting.

"He's just like her, just *like* her," Dani wailed hysterically as Angel held her.

Bill threw the cop on the hood of the car. "Kiss your immortal soul goodbye, motherfucker. Death is coming."

Bill nodded, and Angel guided Dani in the officer's direction. "Hey, look!" Angel called. "He peed in his pants!"

Therese sat behind the wheel, her eyes glazed and unseeing, though she had a perfect view of what was about to happen.

Isabella stepped in front of Dani and Angel. They were within six feet of the officer.

"What the hell is this?" Bill snarled.

"This isn't the way," Isabella said.

"It goes down however I say it goes down," he replied. "She has to kill on her own. You know that. Look at her. She's ready for it."

"No, Bill. She has to make this decision herself, not because you and Angel sent her out of control."

"It works either way."

"Only for a while. Then you know what happens. She could go Wildling."

"I don't care. I want it. I want to see it. I've waited a long time for this."

"Dani," Isabella said as she reached out and placed her hand on the side of Dani's face. Dani nearly bit her palm and Isabella drew her hand back, to the amusement of Bill and Angel. Isabella narrowed her eyes and reached out with her power.

DANI!

The girl shuddered, and some of the wild energy that had overtaken her started to fade.

Sister-love, listen me.

Dani's struggle's ceased. She stared at Isabella through a blood haze. Isabella stroked her hair, and Dani began to calm down.

"What do you mean, 'He's just like her? They're just the same?' Are you talking about the Walthers woman?" Isabella asked.

Dani nodded sharply. "They're so full of shit. All of them. My mother—"

"She's *not* your mother."

Dani recoiled. She tried to hang on to the anger that had suffused her, but it was quickly slipping away. Samantha Walthers had worn the mask of the loving parent, but she had come within a breath of shooting Dani. Hal had put across an image of compassion, he was a champion of the weak, but this too had been a lie. Dani hated the man. She hated both of them for their betrayals, for not living up to the images she held of them. But her emotions were weak and in her heart she knew that her reasoning was faulty. The situations faced by Samantha Walthers and Hal Jordan had been far more complex than she could ever appreciate.

290

"She *is* my mother," Dani said with an abrupt turn, a trace of defiance in her voice.

"Her blood's not in you. Ours is. She betrayed you. You must forget her."

Dani looked to the officer. She could feel his terror. It was enormously appealing. Then she pictured her mother in his place, wearing his uniform, her lover holding the woman against the car. Her desire faded.

"I can't forget her."

"She's part of your old life. She would kill you if she knew the truth."

"I don't believe it. That's not true."

Bill slammed the officer to the car's hood. The man's head was thrown back to the metal and he slid forward, falling in a heap at Bill's feet. The vampire gestured at Angel, who released Dani. The blood rage was gone from her. He turned his back on the officer and took a few steps in Dani's direction. Isabella was at her side.

He pointed accusingly at Isabella. "Do you know what it's going to be like for her, come morning, if she doesn't feed tonight?"

Dani felt a gnawing fear at his words. Beside her, Isabella smiled. Dani glanced at her and attempted to draw strength from the woman's defiance. She smiled, too. Enraged, Bill set upon Dani before the girl could dart out of the way. He caught her face in one of his strong hands, his fingers and thumb digging painfully into the hollows beneath her cheekbones.

"This is *not* funny, Dani. You've seen junkies before, haven't you? At least in the movies or on TV. You've heard the Walthers bitch describe what they go through, right?"

Dani could not deny his words. Nevertheless, the sight of his violence directed toward her was nearly as jarring as the image of Samantha Walthers pulling a gun on her. Apparently sensing this, Bill eased his grip and caressed the side of her face. He looked down, his hair falling into his eyes. Isabella stood beside them, chest heaving, her eyes narrowed in rage.

"I'm saying this for your sake, Dani. The newly turned need blood every night. Without it, you can become something terrible."

Wildling, they had said earlier. But what in the hell was a *Wildling?*

Dani stared into his face. The love she had felt for him was gone. His words were hollow, the compassion in his face a well-maintained illusion, a Hollywood facade. He wasn't saying any of this because he wanted to spare her pain, he had other reasons. Dani wished she knew what Bill Yoshino wanted from her, but she was afraid to ask.

Sensing the sudden change in Dani, Bill released her and backed away. He gestured in the direction he had left the cop lying on the ground. "Kill him."

But the officer was not where he had fallen. Dani saw that Hal was on his feet, his back turned to them, his hand reaching toward the bank of lights sitting atop the car. A sudden burst of wild energy coursed through the man as his hand closed over the object he had been searching for.

The gun, Dani thought. He had managed to keep it from his surface thoughts, but he had also guessed that the gun had been wedged on the roof.

The officer turned and began firing. The first shot whistled past Dani's face, the second tore a hole in the open flap of her leather jacket.

Dani leaped and was upon him. The officer had taken the gun in his left hand, which accounted for his lack of accuracy, despite the girl's close proximity. She wrested the gun from him and hurled it into the woods. It struck a high branch several hundred feet away and fell to the ground with the sound of a falling corpse. Dead weight.

"You would shoot at me?" Dani screeched. "You would fucking shoot at *me?* Don't you know what I am!?"

The officer's fear returned. He trembled and sobbed as Dani bared her fangs. The animal need that had been with her all evening redoubled in force. Suddenly she became attuned to the rhythm of the man's wildly beating heart, the rush of blood through his veins, and the swirl of images crowding into his consciousness. Reaching out with her power, Dani ravenously fed on the sights and sounds that played out within his mind. He was experiencing the same euphoria that had overtaken Madison before she died, the brain's final response to the inevitable horror of death.

A kaleidoscope of images played before her: She saw the officer with his family, one of his children walking for the first time; his wife reaching out to him as they made love, stroking his face, moaning that she loved him; and a football game in high school when he scored a touchdown, the crowd exploding, his father in the stands, cheering him.

Along with the memories, she could feel the emotions accompanying them. Best of all was his encompassing fear that he would never see those he loved again. His memories became warped and metamorphosed into bizarre, nightmarish images.

Dani watched as he found himself back in the slaughterhouse; now he was the stupid animal being marched to slaughter, and his wife and children held the hammers that would be used to beat him into oblivion. Then he was in a soft leather chair, a dentist's chair, a bright light shining in his face. He

293

was not alone in the chair. Mary Ann, the girl he had struck, was sitting in his lap, and his erect penis was inside her. Her eyes were closed, and Hal's father lifted and dropped her onto his son, who was strapped into the chair, a bit stuffed into his mouth.

Time to make you into a man, boy. Time to show you what real men do with their little sluts after we put them to the gas!

The officer was screaming, bucking wildly in his dementia and in reality, but Dani felt no sympathy for him. She delighted in his agony and held him tight. As she yanked his head back and exposed his throat, she heard a snicker of laughter from behind her. Bill's laughter. It made her hesitate. Suddenly, more recent images flowed from the officer's mind. Dani viewed herself through his eyes. He saw her as a ravenous, wolf-like creature with blazing eyes and dripping teeth that existed only to take pleasure for itself, to perpetuate its own existence at the cost of human life. She was nothing but a predator, an animal, wild and out of control.

Don't you know what I am!?

"NO!" Dani screamed, tearing herself away from the officer and from the overwhelming array of sensations crowding upon her. The need was terrible. It wracked her body and clawed into her guts, which felt as if they had been set on fire. She shuddered and Isabella ran to her, gathering her into a comforting embrace that eased the girl's suffering, at least for the moment.

Angel, who had been standing off to the side, her arms folded over her breasts, rushed forward and caught the officer while his delirium continued to hold. Bill looked on in disgust.

"Just let me finish it," Angel said as the officer's

head lolled back, exposing his throat. Her fangs were extended.

"No," Bill said as he approached Dani and Isabella. Dani's tear-drenched face angled toward him. Isabella stroked her hair. "You have to learn. By sunrise you're going to understand the difference between humans and what *you* have chosen to become. I know it's a hard lesson and I'm sorry, but you have to learn."

He nodded to Angel, and she dragged Hal back to the cruiser and dumped him inside. Bill turned to Isabella.

"Dani rides in front, with me," Isabella said.

"Play your games all you want," Bill replied. "In the end, there's only one way for this to come out. We both know that."

He reached into Dani's jacket and gave her breast a painful squeeze. "You know it, too, don't you?"

Dani drew on Isabella's strength as she whipped her freed hand around and slapped Bill's face. The blow connected with such impact that he snapped back, teetering on the balls of his feet. Then he recovered and turned back to her. There was blood on his face. He had been so surprised by Dani's reaction that he had allowed one of his long, razorsharp teeth to puncture his cheek.

Running his fingers over his bloody face, Bill forced a slight smile. Then he offered his redstained fingers to Dani. He held them within an inch of her trembling lips. She fought off the urge to try and bite them off his hand, then felt the hunger rise up in her, causing a flare of sexual heat to rise from her moist center. Hating herself, she allowed her tongue to slip past her lips, grazing his bloody fingers. Then he withdrew them and laughed.

"There might be hope for you yet," he said. "Put her in the car and let's get out of here."

Dani stared at him as he turned from her and got into the backseat, next to Angel and the officer. She wanted to hurt Bill Yoshino. She also wanted to be taken by him, she wanted to open a slight wound on his throat and feed from him as they made love in the open.

The contradiction was terrible to her. She had no idea what she really wanted. But she knew her only chance of salvation was in breaking from Isabella, breaking from all of them, and running free into the night.

"I won't stop you, sister-love," Isabella said, sensing her thoughts. "If you so wish it, I will hold the others here long enough for you to get away."

Dani considered it, then felt the gnawing hunger, the blossoming pain that reached through her entire body as if cold steel had been poured into her veins. She knew that she could run the length of the world and never escape the call of her own blood. Weakened by her hunger, she fell against Isabella, who helped her into the car.

In moments, they were gone.

Twenty-four

The lights of Los Angeles were blinding to Dani. She found a pair of sunglasses in the glove compartment and put them on. Streetlights and neon streaked past. Glaring headlights wavered. She settled comfortably in Isabella's embrace and caught sight of the image displayed in the rearview mirror: The officer in the backseat sat motionless between Bill and Angel. Though he was wide awake, no thoughts took root in his mind. The mad tangle of emotions he had experienced earlier had completely drained away. Whether his mind had been irrevocably shattered or not would only become apparent with time.

Dani watched the man for a time and felt a touch of her earlier admiration return. It was possible he had retreated so far into the depths of his subconscious that he had found a hiding place where even they could not follow. Whatever the case, he had managed to deny the vampires his fear, and they were sullen and angry over this turn of events.

As they drove through downtown Los Angeles, on the way to the converted warehouse, Dani felt safe in Isabella's arms. The woman stroked her hair and whispered kind, loving words to her, as Sam had done when Dani had been a frightened child.

They had left the woods hours ago, and Dani was surprised to realize how far they'd traveled the previous night. Then she recalled the brief time when she'd been asleep and dreamed of flying. She'd slept far longer than she'd realized. Dani thought of the dream, and the time later, when the dream had been made into a reality. In many ways, her new existence was a bright, shining adventure. She was incredibly powerful. The ability to fly was hers. Her body could adjust to horrible conditions. Dani sensed that if she surrendered herself fully and obeyed the dictates of her blood—avoiding fire and sunlight—she would live forever, young and beautiful.

That had been the most shocking revelation of all: She *was* beautiful. Even when she had seen herself through the eyes of the police officer, she had seen her own inherent beauty. She was a woman now, no longer a child. She had Bill to thank for that much, anyway. When they had made love, she had been a goddess. And now, sitting quietly in the police cruiser, she was aware of far more than her primitive human senses had ever revealed to her in the past. She could reach out and feel the presence of humans for blocks around. With hardly any effort, she could read the surface emotions of men and women several blocks away, out of the range of her vision. The experiences were intoxicating.

Dani felt a sharp pain and her momentary elation retreated. The hunger was once again making itself known. Dani allowed a ragged breath to escape her. For all she had gained there was a blood price. She wondered what would happen to her if she was unable to pay.

"Don't be afraid," Isabella whispered. Each

touch of Isabella's gentle hands brought a sizzling charge of energy to Dani's skin, warming her. "In time, the hunger will not be so demanding. You will be the one who is in control."

"I want that," Dani said.

"Good."

They passed a bank with a signpost displaying the time and weather in glowing orange lights. It was eleven fifty-six, four before midnight.

"Mind if I smoke?" Therese asked.

The words stunned each of the vampires. Therese had been lifeless the entire evening. Dani had barely paid any attention to her, as the woman had been only slightly more aware of her surroundings than the police officer in the backseat. Angel had been keeping Therese thoroughly under control, letting the woman draw upon her skills as a driver while all other aspects of her personality had been muted.

Bill shot a disdainful glance at Angel, who shrugged and said, "What are you looking at me, for? You're the one who's got her lighter."

"Sure," Bill said warily as he dug his hands into his coat and withdrew the lighter. He flicked it a few times, amazed that it would work at all after getting wet. He handed it over the seat, to Therese. She thanked him absently and took out a pack of cigarettes. Therese put one of the cigarettes in her mouth and was about to light up when Dani told her to crank open the window.

"No problem," Therese said as she opened her window all the way. A burst of cool air rushed in, along with the sounds of the city at night. They pulled up to a light. Therese lit the cigarette with her left hand, slipped the lighter into her pocket, and took a few puffs before she exhaled in the direction of the window. She took the cigarette from her mouth and held it outside the car with her left hand.

Bill reached over the officer and grabbed Angel's arm roughly. "What is this?"

Dani understood his concern. So long as Therese was nothing more than a department store mannequin with a driver's license, the woman was no threat to them; she was also not a temptation. By easing her grip on Therese's mind, Angel had opened the door to the beautiful, blond-haired driver's thoughts and feelings. That was especially dangerous tonight considering Dani's fragile condition. Dani laughed bitterly and wondered if that was why Angel had brought Therese around. She could already feel some of the woman's emotions swimming up toward the surface of her consciousness. Anger, fear, and desire radiated from the woman, arousing Dani's insatiable appetite.

"Put her back under or I'll do it for you," Isabella said forcefully.

Angel shifted in her seat. "Bill, you promised I could do anything I wanted with this one."

"I remember what I said. Now you remember what I told you when Isabella and I first found you, picking your kills like an amateur. There was a city-wide manhunt for you, remember? But we fixed that. We convinced everyone that John Dorron was responsible, even made him believe it."

Dani found the name John Dorron strangely familiar. She tried to place where she had heard it before. Suddenly it came to her. She had read about Dorron in one of Sam's old textbooks. He had been a serial murderer in the early fifties.

Christ. That meant Angel was at least *sixty years old*. How much older were the others?

Bill continued. "And after that we taught you how to be safe. We told you so long as you followed the rules, we would always have a place for you."

"There are other places for me to go."

"You have that option," Bill said coolly.

"The Parliament would have me. I could work for the Ancients. You know what I'm capable of."

"All too well. But you have no discipline. One day you're going to get all of us killed if you don't stop playing around."

"But that's what this life is about, Bill. Playing. Being free. You also taught me that. It's not my fault you and the *noblewoman* over there can't keep up."

Isabella rankled at the taunt, but she kept her gaze focused on the road ahead, forcing away the sudden fury that had risen in her.

Dani tried to keep up with the conversation, but she was lost. The Ancients had been mentioned before. The Parliament was new. Both of these groups were enigmas to her and she still had no explanation for those the vampires had dubbed *Wildlings*. And why had Angel called Isabella a noblewoman? She couldn't be that old, could she?

Dani pictured Isabella in clothing centuries out of date. It was not a difficult image to conjure.

Another thought came to Dani as she noticed the anxious, sidelong glances Angel was giving her. The vampire was jealous and afraid, though she hid her feelings well. Dani suddenly felt empowered. She carefully reached out with her silver thread to Angel, who severed it brutally.

"Don't try to scour *me,* you little bitch," Angel snarled, her tone lacking its earlier conviction. "I'll push you so far back into your head you'll think you're back in that basement, about to get fucked and charred into oblivion!"

"Right," Dani said respectfully, though, for the first time, she was not afraid of Angel. She wondered if she was being cultivated to take Angel's place. But what that meant exactly was still a mystery to her. All she had been able to guess about the pack was that they had found safety and companionship with one another, and that was why they stayed together. She suspected there were other reasons and wished she could find out what they were.

A man's voice came out of nowhere and said, "Hey, you're a little out of your jurisdiction, aren't you?"

Dani's head whipped in the direction of the open window. They were parked at a light and another police car had pulled up beside theirs. The salt-and-pepper-haired officer in the passenger seat of the other car had spoken before he had taken a good look at who was behind the wheel of the car, and the condition of the vehicle itself. The vampires were about to muster their power, to deal with this new threat, when the officer sitting between Angel and Bill suddenly came to life.

"Officer down, officer down!" he wailed as he leapt forward, attempting to claw his way over the backseat.

Dani watched as the officer in the car beside them reached for his handset. She could feel Isabella's power coiling as the woman prepared to strike. A terrible panic seized up inside her. An entire scenario flashed before Dani: The vampires would reach out with their power and take control of the new police officers. They would command the officers to follow them. The group would come to a deserted parking lot, abandon their vehicles, and the two new cops would either be slain or taken hostage. Images of her mother years ago, in uniform, leapt unbidden to the forefront of her thoughts. Those men had sworn to the same pledge her mother had taken, to serve and protect. They were exactly like her. That meant she should hate them.

Before she was aware of what she was doing, Dani reached into Therese's mind and released a bolt of fear. The woman slammed her foot on the accelerator and the cruiser's tires squealed as they pulled out into traffic, heading northbound toward a pair of vehicles passing east and west. The cruiser's side scraped the rear bumper of the eastbound car, but they managed to barrel through the opening and make it safely through the intersection.

"Fuck!" Bill screamed.

Dani sensed that while it was still *possible* for one of the vampires to reach back and seize control of the officer's minds in the other car, it was too late to prevent the cops from calling in a warning that a fellow officer was being held hostage. A description of their car would also be issued. In his rage, Bill apparently was not considering claiming the minds of the pursuing officers. They had been exposed. Their true faces may have been seen. Bill was furious. He needed a convenient vessel upon which to vent his anger, and he found it in the hysterical form of Hal, the officer they had abducted.

"Officer down! Officer down!" Hal continued to scream.

"Lights *out,* motherfucker!" Bill shouted as he forced his hands to change into talons and commanded Angel to seize hold of the officer.

"Don't!" Dani screamed. "We might need him as a hostage!"

But Bill Yoshino was beyond such considerations. Dani could sense the rush of blood within him, and she knew her words had not even been heard by the vampire. She felt sick. She was about to witness a vampire savaging his prey. It had been different when she had been an active participant, her perceptions warped by her blood haze. This time she was outside the event, a voyeur, and there was no erotic thrill as there had been with the other acts of violence they had committed; this was a painfully stark look at murder, and Dani could do nothing to prevent what was about to happen.

With a blurred motion, Bill drew his taloned hand across the officer's throat, slicing deep. A spray of blood struck the back of Isabella's head and she turned instinctively, opening as blood rained upon her face. She swallowed greedily.

"No!" Dani hollered. The sight of Isabella surrendering her inherent grace to the beast within was pushing Dani to the edge. Still, the part of Dani that knew hunger was envious of the feeding. Shocking herself, she grabbed Isabella's face and kissed her full on the mouth, the sting of blood excited her into a passionate frenzy as she licked every drop of blood from Isabella's face.

"Shit!" Bill screamed, and Dani turned to see Bill draw his other hand back and slap at the shuddering form of the dying police officer, striking him under the jaw with enough force to tear his head from his body. The head spiraled back and was caught in the angle between the rear dash and the window. It was wedged in tight, facing away, the officer's expression of fright visible to passing motorists.

The headless corpse spouted blood. Bill and Angel took great gulps and washed themselves in the hot crimson liquid. Isabella restrained herself. Dani stared at the red torrent. She wanted it. God, she wanted it more than anything in the world. The blood she had tasted only whetted her appetite. She felt an overwhelming urge to jump over the seat and join the animals in their feast.

No, Goddammit, no! she screamed in the confines of her thoughts. *That man is dead because of you! Dead, just like Madison, just like Jami!*

And your Mom, too, Dani, the demon added. She might as well be dead to you, the way you've ignored everything she spent a lifetime teaching you. Dead and buried, it wouldn't make any goddamned difference to you, would it? All you care about is getting what you need. Always has been.

Not true, Dani wailed, *not true, not true, not true!*

But she could not force away the faces of the dead. She could not forget the pleading expression, the hurt, anger, shock, and betrayal in Madison's eyes.

Dani turned away, the hunger causing an intense pain in her skull. She felt as if a pick had been driven deep into her brain and she wanted to scream with her agony, but she held her pain inside. The nerves in her teeth caused shooting lines of fire to reach upward as her canines extended. The world became a bloodred blur; she nearly lost consciousness.

"More for us, more for us, the stupid bitch," Angel said as her senses were overrun by the blood fugue accompanying the feast. The vampire

305

screamed with delight and lashed out with her hand, which she punched through the roof of the car. Her howl was ear piercing.

Dani was certain that she could take no more. It was Bill's fault. He was the one who should be made to suffer. He had drawn Madison into the pack, he had manipulated her from the beginning. But a part of Dani loved him, despite all he had done. She turned her attention to Angel. She had no such conflict with that platinum-haired cunt.

The anger welled up in her. She would leap over the back of the chair and attack Angel. She didn't care that Angel was one of her kind, she hated what she had become. They were *monsters*. Her thoughts became scattered, chaotic. There was no beauty in them. How could she have kidded herself? She didn't care, she didn't care. She wanted to see that creature scream as her own blood shot at the roof. She didn't care. She was hungry and she needed to feed and she didn't care!

DANI, STOP!!!

She felt as if she'd been yanked backward, restraining hooks sinking deep into her flesh and her mind. Comforting waves of pleasure eased into her brain and soon her blood haze cleared. A high, sharp, and entirely human scream pierced Dani's muddled thoughts, abruptly bringing them back into sharp focus. She looked around and saw that Therese was screaming. For the first time since last night, their driver was in full control of her senses and was unable to believe what was happening to her.

In the backseat, Bill and Angel were nearly finished with the corpse. Their reason had been dulled by the blood, but they were coming around. The situation had somehow moved completely out of their control. Bill and Angel had become distracted by their feast, while Isabella had been occupied holding Dani back, keeping her from the brink of madness. No one had been left to control the chauffeur. Therese drove erratically, shifting lanes, sideswiping cars, angling ever closer to the opposite lanes of traffic.

Isabella was about to reach out and assume control of the woman, but she had been too slow. With stunning ferocity, Bill climbed halfway over the seat and grabbed at the wild, blond mane of the driver. Therese had time only to gasp before Bill threw her to the left with his incredible strength, forcing her out of the driver's seat. Angel screamed as Bill pushed Therese through the open window and out of the car. Dani and Isabella watched helplessly as Therese tumbled into the cold night wind. Behind them, a collision sounded as two other drivers tried to keep themselves from striking Therese's crumpled body. The stolen vehicle careened out of control. Bill sank into the driver's seat, slamming his foot down on the accelerator.

"Stupid fucking humans!" he screamed. "You *never* trust stupid fucking humans!"

Dani realized that her betrayal had gone unnoticed. Bill believed that Therese had struck the accelerator of her own accord, that it was Angel's fault because she had released her control of the driver.

"You promised!" Angel squealed. "You fucking promised, you son of a bitch!"

"We'll get you another one," Bill hissed.

Dani jumped as she heard a window burst behind her. She turned in time to see Angel smashing the rear passenger window. The vampire

307

crammed the headless corpse half in, half out the window, and began to laugh hysterically as she watched its arms flopping in the breeze.

Dani was not about to put up with this desecration of Hal's body. She reached back and shoved the officer's body from the car, into the street. At least he was beyond Angel's reach. She didn't care that she was inviting Angel's wrath. The vampire swatted at Dani, who darted out of harm's way.

"That's enough!" Isabella said in a commanding voice. Angel calmed down and sank into the seat, her arms crossed over her breasts. She looked like a pouty child. Nevertheless, Dani was afraid to turn her back on the vampire. Angel seemed to sense this, and it made her grin.

Sirens pierced the night. Bill found the control for the flashers and the car's sirens, both of which he activated. They approached a light and the traffic parted for them.

Dani was still looking back, but she focused beyond Angel and saw a police car behind them. She couldn't tell if it was the same car that had first discovered them. It didn't matter. Putting her fear aside, she turned and looked ahead to see four police vehicles careening to a stop at the intersection ahead, forming a barricade. The vampires had been shepherded into a trap. Bill cut the wheel sharply to the left, hopped over the divider, and collided with a car barreling down from the other direction. The impact shook the vampires. The front fender of the cruiser had crashed into the driver's side door of the opposing vehicle, a small, white Volvo which collapsed under the onslaught. The driver hadn't been wearing a seat belt, and he'd been thrown face first into the passenger foot rest area. Dani couldn't tell if he was alive or dead. There was blood on his windshield, and she assumed he'd been killed on impact. A half dozen other cars skidded to avoid the Volvo, creating a pileup that forged a clear path for the vampires.

Bill threw the cruiser into reverse, disengaged their car from the Volvo, threw it back in drive, and floored the accelerator. Miraculously, the cruiser shot forward. The police car behind them had also hopped the divider. It raced toward them, its driver trying to cross in front and block them off. They outdistanced the car by inches and flew through the street. The pursuing officers moved in an arc, crossed before the backed-up mess of piled cars, and hurtled toward them.

Of the four cars that had formed the barricade, two remained behind to help with the wounded. The other two followed the first car.

"Fucking humans!" Bill screamed as he pushed the cruiser through the streets of Los Angeles. They came to a traffic jam and Bill skirted around the cars, hopping the divider and throwing on the cruiser's brights. They were within a few feet of another collision when he cut the wheel sharply to the right and drove up onto the divider, then crossed back to the proper lane at the light and sailed across four lanes of traffic to make a right. He checked the side view mirror. The other cars were gone.

Bill let out a whoop of joy that was contagious. Angel screamed and bounced in her seat. Even Dani felt a wild surge of relief. This nightmare was over. They would find a place to abandon the cruiser, then make it back to the warehouse on foot, if necessary. Isabella squeezed Dani's hand and smiled.

Suddenly, a blinding pool of light struck the

front window and the car's bloodstained hood. Bill jerked the car sharply to the right, out of the pool of brilliance, but the light swept in their direction and targeted them once more. Bill's mood immediately darkened. From somewhere close, Dani heard the steady whipping of the air that could only be made by a helicopter.

"Fuck!" Bill shouted as the light struck him full on. The helicopter had moved ahead so they could shine their spotlight directly in his face, blinding him.

"*Stop!*" a tinny voice called from a loud speaker above. "*Stop or we will fire on you!*"

Bill turned to Dani. "You're the expert. Will they do it?"

She was trembling. "I dunno. I can't believe they're doing *this*. It's reckless endangerment."

"I can't see a fucking thing," Bill shouted.

"There should be ordnance in the trunk," Dani snapped. "A shitload of guns, at least. Tear out the seats."

Stunned at Dani's sudden take-charge attitude, Angel spun and ripped apart the backseat with her talonlike hands. Dani hated Bill and Angel, perhaps enough to see them dead, but she didn't want Isabella to die with them. Dani turned back and tried to roll down the window on her side. When it wouldn't go fast enough she panicked and punched at the window, shattering the glass. Then she hauled herself out the side, leaning out far enough to see beyond the glare of the spotlight. She screamed directions to Bill, helping him to avoid a collision with another blue and white.

The spotlight suddenly shifted at her, blinding her. But so long as it struck her, Bill was able to see the road. The beam shifted back and forth,

310

then settled on Dani again. The officers could fire on her at any moment, and Dani considered reaching out with her power to cause them to crash the helicopter. Madison's face flashed before her.

How many more like me are you going to make? she seemed to ask. Hal appeared behind Madison, his dark eyes beaming with accusation.

The vision faded, but it had brought with it an odd serenity. Smiling grimly, Dani closed her eyes and waited for the first of the bullets to tear through her.

Twenty-five

Dani heard a terrible explosion of gunfire and flinched. She expected to feel the burning pain of bullets ripping through her, but she felt nothing. The explosion came again and the spotlight veered off, the helicopter flying high and away. Dani turned and saw Angel leaning out the window behind her, a smoking twelve-gauge pump-action shotgun in her hands.

Angel had saved her? Why in hell had she done *that?* Dani had been ready to die. She had wanted it.

Bullshit.

Perhaps in that single instant she had embraced some bizarre, noble ideal of self-sacrifice, but now, she was actually grateful to Angel for saving her life.

From inside the car came a scream. "Get in!"

Bill slammed the brakes and sent them into a vicious spin. Dani caught a glimpse of two police cars skidding to a stop in front of them and heard the squeal of tires from behind. Leaning out the window, she was almost thrown from the car, but a pair of strong hands gripped her from behind, anchoring her. Isabella. Angel was not so lucky. She was thrown from the car, the pump-rifle tumbling from her flailing hands. One of her hands reached toward Dani, who surprised both of them by grabbing hold of Angel. The car spun in its arc. Angel laughed as she spread her arms and legs wide, creating an X with her body as she sailed only a few feet over the pavement. The car ground to a sudden stop and Dani lost her hold on the vampire. Angel flew over the hood, bounced twice, then came up in a standing position in front of the car, the headlights making her appear ethereal.

Dani quickly surveyed their situation. Two police cars sat to their left, another behind them. The police officers were getting out of their cars, taking positions, preparing to draw on the vampires. The stolen cruiser faced the divider. Across the street lay a shopping mall that appeared to be open, catering to late night shoppers.

"Fuck it," Bill snarled as he gripped the wheel.

Standing in front of the car, Angel seemed to sense what Bill had planned. She nodded, and he floored the cruiser. Angel rose straight up, avoiding the front grill of the car, and dove toward the car's roof as it passed beneath her. Her fingers sunk into the metal roof as if it were made of clay and she aimed her head at the rear window. She struck with incredible force, the top of her head and shoulders crashing through the glass as she released her hold and fell into the backseat. The cruiser raced across the opposite lanes of traffic. Miraculously, it wasn't struck by oncoming cars, though a BMW sliced cleanly through the space they had vacated only seconds before.

Inside the car, Dani *thought* she knew Bill's plan. She thought they were going to ride the sidewalk, like the *bad guys* in a seventies action film. But that hadn't been his intent at all.

The department store window loomed up before them. Dani tried to scream, but there was no time;

the front end of the cruiser plowed through the window as if it were made of Hollywood candy glass. There was an impossible sound, like a thousand mirrors shattering at once, and a glittering rain of razor-sharp shards fell upon the cruiser. Then they were through the frame, inside the store.

"Holy shit!" Angel cried happily from the backseat.

Dani realized the store was not deserted. She was vaguely aware of posters proclaiming a special ALL NIGHT SALE!!! and giddily thought that the people who ran the store were never going to try a promotion like this again. The cruiser mowed down a window display, sending the splintered arms and legs of well-dressed blond, tanned mannequins into the air. Or maybe they were native Californians, she thought crazily. Who could tell the difference?

The cruiser sideswiped a glass case that overturned as it broke apart, a collection of watches flung haphazardly across the floor.

Bill glanced over at Dani. "Prepare yourself, my dear. It's going to be a *bumpy ride*."

He had said it in his best Bette Davis impression. It made her think of their common love for old movies. She shuddered at the thought of all they had shared. There was no further time for conscious thought. All she could do was react to the sights stretching before her.

To one side of the car Dani saw wooden displays with elegant men's clothes, and a sign reading, POLO — RALPH LAURENT. Beyond it lay a cornucopia of ties, sweaters, and jackets. Directly before them lay a wooden gazebo with displays for men's suits. Bill smashed through the gazebo. A chunk of wood rose up and slapped the cruiser's

314

front window, opening a spiderweb crack around the point of impact. The rest of the fractured gazebo was thrown out of the way, some pieces bouncing off the hood. The white, featureless head and torso of a mannequin wearing a pink shirt slapped the window near Dani, making her start, as she watched the styrofoam head burst apart on impact.

Bill cut the wheel sharply to the right to avoid a perfume counter, then angled sharply to the left to escape a sturdy-looking ivory pillar. A grand piano was to their left, a large glass elevator and an escalator beside it. Bill made another right and suddenly they were racing through a gauntlet of perfume counters, one on either side of the car. The alley between them was very narrow and filled with people who either dove over the counter, or were struck by the cruiser. A man in a brown leather jacket was sideswiped by the cruiser. He performed a mad series of pirouettes, spinning like a Warner Brothers cartoon character, bouncing off the car's passenger side until he was flung clear. Two women went over the front end, one flying up and over the car, another holding on to the hood for a few seconds before she fell beneath the car and was crushed.

Dani watched the scene as if it were a bad T.V. movie. It all seemed frightfully unreal. Behind the counters were a collection of Robert Palmer video girls, their dark hair slicked back. They wore too much makeup, identical suits, and interchangeable attitudes. The women hollered, screamed, and leaped out of the way like seasoned athletes. The pretty female customers with light, porcelain skin—so much like the ones who had once tormented Dani—set their hands on the sides of their faces and froze as if they were posing for the

Home Alone poster. One of them was thrown over the car, where her head struck the front windshield. There was a horrible crack and a smear of blood as her lifeless body fell away. The car's rear tires lifted as Dani heard the bump and knew they had run over the dead woman.

Through it all, Isabella sat quietly, her hands folded in her lap. A perfect state of serene repose. She wore an expression of annoyance as the car lurched from side to side, braked, accelerated. She looked as if she were sitting in a theater, enduring a film to which she had been dragged and would have walked out on, if she could. The screams of the shoppers and the wail of the cruiser's siren had alerted enough people to clear a path for the runaway vehicle. Up ahead were a series of display cases. Some of the tables holding the cases were plastic, others metal. Racks of flashy earrings and cheap beads sat above the glass, with skeletal trees bearing costume jewelry. The tables were struck with sufficient force that each one of them was lifted up and over the front window, raining glittering cheap accessories over the hood.

Only the last of the cases proved to be a problem. It struck the window and came through, into Isabella's lap, as shards of glass sliced into the vampires. Dani had raised her arm in time to protect her face, but a hail of glass was embedded in her arm, despite her leather jacket. Vials of foul-smelling liquid spilled upon them, making Dani gasp and wheeze for breath. The car stank of blood and perfume. The pain and loss of her own blood made her feel weak and forced her to once again recognize the burning hunger coursing through her. Isabella pushed the display, hurling it through the shattered window frame, and out of their way.

"There it is!" Bill screamed, and ahead lay the mall entrance.

Dani looked back and saw Angel's face covered in blood. A small shard of glass jutted from her forehead. She swatted at it then plucked it out and tossed it to the seat. Her platinum blond hair was marred by blotches of crimson. She was busy watching herself in the rearview mirror, primping her hair as if the blood were mousse, when she saw Dani staring in her direction.

"What the hell are you looking at?" Angel spat.

"They're coming!" Dani screamed, focusing beyond the vampire to point at the preposterous sight of two police cars continuing to follow them, crossing into view as they emerged from a section of the store under construction. The cars passed between skeletal wood support beams, tearing apart the plastic covering stapled to the wood.

"Shit!" Bill said, obviously angry with himself for not seeing the safer, easier route to the mall entrance. A couple ran ahead of them, trying to reach cover before the cruiser hit them. Laughing malevolently, Bill aimed the car directly at them. They screeched and ran while cutting looks over their shoulders, the man keeping a tight grip on the woman's hand. He yanked the woman toward a shoe display with blue luminous back lighting. The cruiser plowed into them. There was an ugly crunch of bone as both humans were scooped up onto the hood. The man flipped over the roof and fell to the carpeted floor behind the car. The woman struck the frame near Dani then fell to the side of the car, where she vanished.

"A double!" Angel hollered. *"All right!"*

Dani looked ahead and gasped. They were dangerously close to the frame of the mall entrance.

Bill veered off at the last possible second, grinning.

They spilled out into the mall, the vampires in the stolen cruiser, two police cars following closely behind. Dani tried to reach out with her power, praying she could influence the driver of at least one of the pursuing cars to stop before they were forced into confrontation, but her adrenaline was flowing, and her fear and perverse excitement were making it impossible to properly focus her power.

They sideswiped a display for a florist shop, sending red and yellow roses into the air and young lovers leaping for cover. Dani thought of the flowers she had never received from her dates, and the fact that she would never be on dates again, that her life would never be normal again.

Not unless you want it to, honey.

Madison's voice. Poor, dead Madison, who had believed the vampires' lies. She thought she was one of them. Her life had been the price for her foolish trust.

You're beginning to see, aren't you? the demon whispered in her mind. But you're forgetting one thing. You killed Madison. *You* did it.

Dani turned these thoughts away, shuddering. She'd done what she had to do to survive. If it hadn't been her, it would have been one of the others. There had been no choice. None at all.

Let me know when you believe that, the demon whispered.

Dani focused her attention on the chase. She wondered why the police had not simply shot their tires out. She heard the screams of mall goers ahead and had her answer. One stray shot and an innocent could die. But the way Bill was driving, more would die anyway. She was grateful the sirens on their stolen cruiser had not failed them. At

318

least people would have some warning. But as they raced through the mall, that warning didn't seem to be enough for everyone.

There was a craft show at the mall. Out of town artisans. Tables and wall hangs ran down the center lane of the mall's wing, leaving only a narrow gap to each side. Bill steered to the left and struck a chair that had been occupied moments before by a woman in her fifties. The bumper slapped a wall hang containing ceramic plates with serrated edges that looked like buzz saws. The plates, which had been painted with repetitious scenes of a snow-bound log cabin, fell to the ground, shattering.

The cruiser raced past a phone mart, a toy store, and a *GQ*-style men's clothing shop, both police units still directly behind them. Ahead, to the left, were marble benches sprinkled through a rest area. Some were bolted into place, others seemed to spring up organically from the ground. Bill avoided these expertly, though the cruiser continued to slam into the edges of wall hangs or bring down displays at the front of stores.

They tore past a table where Dani saw dozens of finely crafted glass objects, clocks, lamps, and paperweights containing nature scenes with the perfectly preserved and enhanced remains of butterflies. In the speeding car, stared at with fear and fascination by the mall goers, Dani felt like one of those butterflies under glass. Painted and beautiful, but lifeless and without hope. She had no control over what was happening to her. None.

Bill crossed right as they hit the food court. He hit the brakes as he spun the wheel, causing the vampires to grab the dash for support. Dani's hand closed over the window frame beside her. She heard the crunch of glass and felt a sharp, hot sting. It couldn't be avoided. Isabella jammed her legs and feet against the dash. Angel was thrown around in the backseat.

The hunger ripped into her brain. The number of humans surrounding them in the food court was suddenly too much to bear. Each had been satisfying their hungers, stuffing themselves with submarine sandwiches, pizza, chicken, muffins — anything they so desired. Who were they to deny Dani her hungers? They ate the flesh of animals. To her kind, *humans* were nothing but animals.

But killing them was wrong, wasn't it?

Dani's mind was swimming. She fought to remain in control as they sped past a group of partitions displaying a series of wood placards inscribed with dainty, new-age messages of hope and love. Her hand shot out and grasped the wall hang, yanking it down upon the people who had been too slow or too afraid to dart out of the way.

She wanted to scream. She wanted to ask Bill what business he had taking them here. Didn't he realize if the police captured them, they would be forced, sooner or later, into the daylight. They would burn.

"Too much. Too fucking much," Bill muttered.

Dani swung her gaze to see what had captured Bill's attention. They were dangerously close to a fountain, and beside the fountain lay a cart filled with hundreds of cute stuffed bears wearing sailor suits, pink frilly dresses, and smoking jackets with pipes. She stared into Bill Yoshino's perfectly sculpted, godlike face and saw that the man had gone insane. Blue flames flickered in his eyes. He aimed the car toward the cart and floored it.

"Don't!" Dani screamed, but the single word was all she had time to release. The cruiser smashed into the cart, sending a cloud of teddy bears into the air. Bill laughed hysterically at the sight. Then the front axle of the cruiser caught on the cart's heavy frame and ripped loose. Suddenly the stolen police car jackknifed and slid on its side.

Dani had a vague impression of television monitors, a dozen or more, alternating between comprising one large picture and several individual ones. Signs proclaimed, THOUSANDS OF TITLES, ALL BRAND NEW! The cruiser crashed into the glass window of a video store. Dani was on the bottom, pressed against the passenger door, which was skidding across the ground. Isabella had fallen upon her, anchoring herself to protect the girl from the shower of broken glass. The car struck a wall and Bill was thrown through the cruiser's shattered windshield. He sailed deep into the crowd gathered there. Angel was pressed against the rear passenger door, holding on. The siren mercifully shorted out.

Dani heard nothing but the rapid beating of her own heart. Other sounds intruded. From somewhere close, another siren approached, growing louder. Tires squealed as one of the other police cars stopped nearby. A door was opened and a pump rifle was made ready with the same telltale *CHA-CHUKKK* Dani had heard in Willis's home two years ago, when the killer had descended the stairs and prepared to blow her head off.

Within the stolen cruiser, Angel was the first to recover. She climbed out of the backseat, over Isabella and Dani, and exited through the shattered front window. Then she hesitated, frowned, and turned back.

"Come on," she hissed, offering her hand to the other vampires.

Isabella grasped her hand and allowed the vampire to haul her from the car. Dani pulled herself up and scrambled out behind her.

321

Looking around, Dani saw a police car set in a right angle to the store, the officer taking cover behind the door of his vehicle. There was only one man. She glanced at the store and saw a crowd wedged deep within the video store, huddled against each other to avoid the bloody form of Bill Yoshino. He lay near the cash registers, moving groggily, trying to clear his head.

"They'll see us," Dani said in a harsh, frightened tone. "They'll see what we really look like!"

"They'll see *something*." Angel said with a grin made all the more monstrous because of her bloody face. Dani understood. Angel had been utilizing her power, sending it before her like a shield to alter the perceptions of the police officers and the human spectators.

"All of you, on the ground, now!" the police officer, a dark-haired man with a mustache, commanded. "I said now! You won't get a second chance!"

Dani saw they were in the man's direct line of fire. If they could get to the other side of the car, it would shield them from gunfire. But there was no time.

In the video store, Bill rose to his feet, shook his head once, then darted into the crowd and grabbed the first human he saw, a teenager with an amber shirt and teal, pleated pants. The boy wore a name tag and looked as if he worked there. He yelped as Bill lifted him into the air with both hands. The teenager flailed, but he was held firmly over Bill's head.

"You want to really believe a man can fly?" Bill shouted, hunching his shoulders as if he were going to hurl the teenager at the police.

There were no warning shots. For an instant, Bill's chest was exposed as he held the teenager

322

high. The police officer fired a carefully aimed barrage that lifted Bill off his feet and slammed him back into the store. The teenager flew from his arms and landed in a heap with the thunderous crack of broken bones and Bill fell, knocking down a Freddy Krueger stand-up.

"Bill!" Dani shouted in disbelief. Minutes ago she had decided she hated the vampire and would have gladly killed him herself. But the sight of his chest exploding in a cloud of blood had shocked her into the sudden awareness that no matter how much she despised him for what he had done to her, a part of her would always love him.

Impossibly, Bill Yoshino's body began to twitch. Dani felt a flood of relief that soon turned to dread. Bill leapt to his feet with the panache of a vaudevillian, spreading his hands and tilting his head with an ingratiating smile, as if he had just performed a complex tap number and was ready for the appreciative applause of the crowd. His jacket had been torn to pieces by the shotgun blast and his chest was a bubbling, bloody mass of rapidly fusing skin.

Dani looked back to the police car and saw the officer scrambling with shaking fingers to reload his gun. Bill crossed to the police officer, gesturing at his bullet-riddled chest. "You think that kind of crap is going to kill *me,* you pencil-dicked little puke? Sunlight and fire, asshole. That's it!"

The officer was able to load one round into the chamber of his gun. Bill slapped the man's hand away and the gun went off, wounding a human in the crowd. Screams erupted as people fled the store. Bill's left hand fastened on the man's head, lifting him up by the hair, while his right transformed into a talon and sliced across the officer's neck like a scythe, gouging a ragged tear in the man's throat. Bill tore the man's head from his shoulders, then leaned down and gulped from the geyser of blood spraying from the headless corpse. His healing process was accelerated, a thin layer of flesh weaving itself over his chest to hold in the blood he consumed.

Blaring sirens alerted the vampire to the advance of two other police cars. He flung the body away.

"Bring them on!" he screamed in his blood-induced frenzy. "Bring them all on!"

"No!" Isabella screamed.

He spun on her. "But this is *fun!*"

"It's gone too far. We have to go. Now." She nodded upward and the other vampires followed her gaze. One hundred feet above their head was a beautiful, domed, stained glass skylight.

"You go if you want," Bill snarled.

Isabella's eyes narrowed. "The blood of the Ancients, Bill."

"What the hell are you talking about?" he screamed, but there was fear in his eyes. He seemed to understand exactly what she was saying.

"Remember what I told you when I first came to you?"

He flinched, cutting a sharp, pained glance at Dani. She stared at him in openmouthed wonder. Isabella had been the one who had turned Bill. *She* was the eldest. Her will was law.

"Damn you," he spat, but he said nothing else to contradict her.

The police cars screeched to a stop, forming a right angle around the other police car and the jackknifed cruiser, cutting them off. The officers were out of their cars in seconds.

"Now!" Isabella shouted. The vampires needed no further urging. Angel and Bill were the first, spreading their arms and throwing their heads back as they ascended. They looked like souls captured in a beam of light, ascending to the heavens. The sight was so incredible it left the officers on the ground momentarily stunned.

Dani was terrified. She had only flown once. She had no idea if she could do it again, especially while her hunger was siphoning her strength.

"You have to," Isabella said, rising into the air, gripping Dani's hand. She allowed herself to be pulled along, but she knew she would only slow the woman down. They were a dozen feet in the air when Dani tore her hand free and poured all of her desire and will into the task of remaining aloft, and rising upward. To her amazement, she did not fall.

"Jesus Christ," Dani whispered, feeling as if her body had suddenly become hollow, like a reed. Of course she could fly. The currents of the air rushed through her, carrying her along. This was natural.

Yes, sister-love. Yes!

Isabella's familiar, comforting presence eased into Dani's mind, making the task even less strenuous for her. She threw her head back and raced upward, toward the stained glass. Isabella was three feet above her and Dani was covering the distance separating them without difficulty. Bill and Angel brought their hands up, balling them into fists, instants before they struck the glass.

Gunshots sounded and Dani felt a horrible, burning pain in her leg. Her perception of the world slowed as she saw Bill and Angel shatter the stained glass. The shards fell in her direction and she looked down and away to shield herself. On the ground, eighty feet below, she saw the police officers. Tiny yellow bursts of flame leapt from their hands. Something struck her back like a fist, and she found she couldn't breath. Her lungs seized up.

DANI, NO!!!

Isabella screamed in her mind, but Dani was overcome by a sudden delirium. She heard the crackle of falling glass, felt a rain of shards on the top of her head and back, then saw the glass fall to the ground, glittering from the moonlight in a beautiful display of red, violet, amber, and green. It was mesmerizing, inviting.

Dani saw another burst of light and felt something slap against her ribs. She looked down to see a slight trickle of blood erupt from her flesh where a black, charred hole had been burned.

Oh Christ, she thought with sudden, painful awareness. I'm shot. Oh Jesus, God, I'm shot!

She understood where she was, suspended almost ninety feet in the air, her body a thing of weight and substance, impossible to hold at this height. She couldn't fly, she wasn't lighter than air, she had been insane.

God help me, I'm gonna die! Dani thought, then another bullet tore through her, this one snaking through her arm.

"Help me!" she screamed, her hands reaching out as she abruptly fell, her head thrown back as she cried out in fear. Her fingers grazed those of Isabella. The vampire looked at her sadly, then turned and flew after the others, who were already out of the skylight, hovering in the night sky above. Dani tumbled in the air, her view alternating between the skylight, through which Isabella and the *pack* vanished, and the roof of a police car, fast approaching.

She gasped for breath, found her lungs would not work, and felt a horrible, searing pain in her leg and back. Dani clawed at the air, looking for the sturdy currents that had bouyed her up earlier, but it was over, and she knew it. There was no last-minute rush of euphoria, only a deadening sense of regret, a final blinding spell of fear, and a crush of pain as her body struck the roof of the police car with a bone-splintering crack. The metal gave beneath her, tearing like paper, she felt her skull collide with the steering wheel. She heard the short burst of a horn, then her head snapped back so forcefully she was certain her neck had broken.

Agony screamed through her, and she waited for it to vanish as her brain overloaded and ceased to register the impulses. But that didn't happen. Trembling, her body racked with agony so frightful Dani had never dreamed such pain existed, she tried to lift herself up and succeeded only in turning herself over, so that she was staring upward, toward the skylight.

For a moment she thought she saw a trio of figures high in the night sky, gods she had once been like. A red haze covered her vision as blood leaked into her eyes, mingling with her tears. Her body convulsed twice, then she was still.

Twenty-six

Dani was not dead.

Nevertheless, she was not entirely certain she was grateful to find herself alive after the punishment her body had endured. Her eyes flickered open. She was still lying within the police car on a blanket of shattered glass and ruined metal slick with blood.

Her blood.

She tried to move, found she could manage to lift her arms a few inches, then allowed them to fall to either side of the metal cavity in which she was resting. They dropped with the cold certainty of dead flesh. There was no feeling in her hands.

"Holy Christ, it's moving, guys it's moving—"

Dani froze, becoming perfectly still. She closed her eyes, hoping to present as pitiful and non-threatening an image as she could muster. Her world was darkness. She didn't dare open her eyes again, or attempt movement. In any case, she wasn't certain she would have the strength.

Footsteps came to her. Thick shoes crushing glass underneath. Weapons cocked, safeties thrown back. Heavy breathing. Underneath it all, warm, delicious *fear.*

Dani waited and soon she felt the cold muzzle of a weapon touch the hollow of her cheek. It nudged her. She remained perfectly still.

In the crowd surrounding them, people shifted

uncomfortably. Dani felt their fear and excitement. Forcing down her ravenous hunger, she fed tentatively, daintily, absorbing their emotions, allowing their fears to eat away at her own.

"Leave her alone, she's just a kid, for Chrissake!" someone shouted.

Dani wanted to smile, but she controlled herself. How long had it been since she had been *just a kid?* A few days? A week? She couldn't say. It all ran together in her mind.

"That guy's right. Look at her. She's dead."

A second voice. A man. One of the other officers.

"She isn't dead. She's breathing. Look."

Silence. The gun was removed. She sensed the presence of a man's face close to her chest. Dani fought off the temptation to bare her fangs and tear out his throat.

Right, she thought. She couldn't even raise her hands more than a few inches, and she was going to take this man's life. The image made her laugh. It came out as a short, hacking cough. She heard the man withdraw quickly.

"Shit!" he said. "Right in my goddamned eye."

Silence. Discomfort. The man wiping blood from his eye. Blood that had come when she had coughed. Christ, how badly was she hurt? Dani felt the panic come upon her like an overwhelming tide, and she forced it down, forced herself to be still.

"How in the hell could she be alive? Look at her!"

Dani knew she could reach out with her power and see through one of the officer's eyes, but she didn't have to. Now that her initial panic had subsided, she had a fairly clear idea of the damage her body had suffered. She was amazed to feel so calm and detached from what had happened to her, but she had been swept up in the absolute belief that no matter how terrible the damage had been, she was not going to die. She would be well once again.

The pain was horrible and intense. She had inflicted this kind of suffering on Madison. This and worse. But that was the nature of what she had become. Hunter or prey. Killer or victim. Mankind had dressed itself up, cloaked itself in illusion, but at its heart, it was vile, animalistic, no different from those it proclaimed monsters.

For a time, Dani had worried that her race was no better than the human killers, like the men who'd killed Jami and would have raped and murdered her, too, if she hadn't used her survival abilities. Now she saw that humans and her kind were not the same. There was no malice in her heart for her victims, only need. Humans existed to satisfy that need. That was all.

Pain swept through her and she threw her head back, biting down hard to stifle a scream.

Christ, what a load of shit, she thought. *She was human. Her mother was human. She wasn't a monster like the others.*

But if that's true, why am I still alive?

Dani had no answers. She suddenly remembered the feelings that had coursed through her when she had emerged from the bathroom in the hotel room and saw her mother aiming a gun at her chest, an instant away from firing.

But she did *not* fire, an insistent voice urged in her mind. *Your mommy loves you.*

Dani forced the voice away, holding on to the seething anger that had enveloped her the night she left the human world forever. Another image replaced that of her human mother betraying her: She saw Isabella, Bill, and Angel fly up through the skylight—*without* her.

Damn them, she thought. Last night, when they had been tumbling from the sky, headed toward the lake, Dani had been willing to risk her own life to save Bill; she honestly believed she loved him. As their time together wore on, however, she came to realize she barely knew him, and the more he revealed of his true face, the more her love had turned to loathing.

Why should she be surprised that he'd turned his back on her. Angel had no reason to help her and every cause to desert her. But Isabella had been her true friend. Isabella had called her *sister-love* and had taught her to dance. She had protected Dani. How could she have gone away and left Dani wounded and helpless for the police?

Anger flared in Dani's heart. She had no idea why her only friends had betrayed her, but a part of her was grateful, because they had taught her a valuable lesson: She could trust no one but herself, depend on no one but herself. One day she would find the vampires and she would pay them back for the knowledge they had imparted; she would pay them back in *blood*.

Voices ripped through the comforting veil of unconsciousness that had almost fully descended upon her. Dani moaned and opened her eyes. One of the police officers was near her, eyeing her suspiciously, his gun drawn. Thoughts of revenge would have to be set aside. For now, she had to find a way out of this situation. Dani felt a tear roll down her cheek.

"It hurts," she whispered softly, allowing her eyes to flicker open.

"Goddamned right it does," the officer said, his voice stony. He was a handsome, ruggedly built black man in his mid-thirties. He had obviously seen the remains of the officer Bill had ripped apart. There was no sympathy in his eyes.

"I didn't hurt that man," Dani said, slowly gathering her power and focusing it on the officer. He flinched as she reached out with the silver thread

331

and connected gently with his mind. His surface thoughts came to her. The man had a daughter roughly her age. He had been staring at Dani's ruined body, thankful his own daughter had been a good girl and had never gotten involved in any of the bad shit he saw on a daily basis. Dani planted an image in his mind, a vision of his daughter taped to the killing chair in Willis's basement, the murderers railing at her about purifying her soul by raping, beating, and burning her flesh. Then she changed the identity of the girl in the chair to herself.

The man's eyes softened. He turned away suddenly, and looked back at her, first with suspicion, then with a grudging compassion. He lowered his gun, then holstered it.

"The ambulance has already been called for the innocent bystanders you helped injure. The EMTs will be here soon. They'll help you."

"I'm really afraid," Dani said in a high, little girl voice. "I can't move. I can't feel *anything.*"

That was a lie. She could feel pain. Incredible pain. She had been shot in the back, thigh, arm, and ribs. If she had been human, she would not have survived the trauma of the wounds she had sustained while aloft, which had been compounded by the shattering impact she endured when she fell. But she was not human. All four bullets had passed through her clean, thank God, and the damage they had caused would heal.

Dani gasped. She had overlooked something crucial.

"What's the matter?" the officer asked. His name tag read "Leonard."

Dani bit her lip. She had been unconscious for a time. The officers had seen her real face. They would have to be dealt with.

"It *hurts,*" she said again. The tone she had

332

achieved was one calculated to make her appear small and helpless, a victim, not a predator. She smiled inwardly and wondered if she could muster the strength to do what needed to be done.

From outside the mall, sirens wailed. The ambulance was arriving. There was very little time left. Dani reached out with her power to the crowd gathered around the crime scene and felt a growing wave of excitement laced with fear. Her body was inside the car, her face hidden from view. The only people who had seen her were the police officers. They would be difficult to manipulate, but the task was not impossible. She thanked God no reporters had been here with their cameras. It would be over for her, then.

Dani felt a tinge of amusement. That had been the second time since she had woken that she had expressed her gratitude to God. Well, why not, she decided. There was a lot to be grateful for. Without the blood of His only son, her kind would never have existed, and she would not currently possess the strength to save herself.

Dani turned her thoughts back to the task at hand, realizing the pain she felt was nearly enough to sink her back into the pit of delirium if she wasn't careful. Though it was going to be unpleasant, perhaps even shocking, she had to see herself the way the officers had seen her; she had to risk looking through the eyes of Officer Leonard.

"Sir?" she said in a weak, frightened voice. She caused the officer to hear her words in the voice of his own daughter.

Officer Leonard shuddered. Dani took advantage of his distraction and extended her silver cord into his thoughts. She was able to see her own body through his eyes and she instantly withdrew. Squeezing her eyes shut, Dani forced away her own terror and recalled the image she had seen: Her flesh had been savaged, blood was everywhere. She looked as if she had been shot to death then resurrected. That may not have been far from the truth, she realized.

Despite the ugliness of her ruined flesh, she was gorgeous, startlingly beautiful. Her earlier perception had been correct, she was not a little girl anymore, she was a grown woman with a haunting sensuality. Even bloodied, bruised and broken, her loveliness could not be denied.

Dani coiled her power, absorbing the fear and excitement of the crowd, then lashed out at the police officers. She stripped away their memories of her true face and supplanted them with visions of girls her age they had encountered on the streets. It would be much later, if ever, when they got around to comparing their memories of her. By then it would be too late.

There were five officers in all. One of them, Harry Marks, had been the partner of the first cop who had reached the pack. The sight of his partner's headless corpse had sent Harry into a blind, killing rage. He had been the first to fire on Dani. The sound of his gun had woken the others from the stupor caused by the sight of the vampires rising into the air. Shaken from their paralysis, they had drawn and fired. Dani had no idea who had hit her and who had not. Officer Leonard may have fired the shot which struck her in the back, bringing her down. She had no idea. Strangely, she harbored no malice for their actions. They were doing their job, fulfilling their oaths to serve and protect their own kind. Even if she *had* been angry, there were others more deserving upon whom she could vent her anger.

Recalling her power, Dani sank back in exhaustion. She heard the EMTs approach and wondered what story the police would tell. They couldn't expect anyone to believe she and the others had

334

flown. The sight would have to be written off to mass hysteria. The broken skylight was not a problem, the gunfire could have shattered it. But there was still Dani to consider, and the dent she had left in the cruiser when she had landed on the car's roof. And why would they have believed the criminals were flying in the first place? Had the perpetrators used grappling hooks, wires, or some advanced technology? It was all pretty farfetched, but it was *humanly* possible. Dani planted this thought in one of the other officer's minds. Suddenly, an emergency medical technician in his mid-twenties came to the car and dutifully restrained his urge to cry an obscenity at the scene waiting for him.

Dani sensed he wanted to know how in the hell this had happened, but the EMT remained silent and appraised the situation. His partner arrived. She was in her late thirties and had beautiful auburn hair. They glanced at each other and made a tacit agreement to keep their curiosities in check. They could read about it later. For now, there was a life to save. Together they bandaged Dani's wounds. Her stomach and back each had a pair of entry and exit wounds. The same with her arm and thigh. She had lost an incredible amount of blood. They worked a hard board and a harness beneath Dani, secured her for movement, and lifted her out of the car with the help of Officer Leonard.

Dani was set in a stretcher. Several IVs were run into her left arm, which had been cut by ground glass earlier. They had removed several chunks of glass from her flesh and had worried openly that slivers could be lodged deep inside her, like shrapnel. Dani had not been comforted by this suggestion. Her free hand was set at her side, then strapped into place. Blood flowed into her from the IV. Her body sucked it up greedily, but it was not enough, and it was not the same as if she had taken it from a victim. Nevertheless, it would sustain her.

Dani was amused by the irony of the situation. They were unwittingly giving her what she would have killed them to take. The metal hand brakes were taken off the stretcher and the EMTs raced her from the incident scene, Officer Leonard following them.

They went down a long corridor, past a stretch of stores. Dani heard them talking and learned several other units had been dispatched to the mall, most of them concentrating on the department store. The press had been summoned, but the police were keeping the reporters and camera crews back.

"They drove *through* the mall?" the female EMT asked incredulously.

"Crazy bastards," Officer Leonard muttered. "Never seen anything like it. Hope I never see anything like it again."

"But the others got away," the EMT said.

"We'll get 'em," Officer Leonard said without much conviction. They came to a collection of doors leading to the outside, and the ambulance. There was a harsh glare of lights. Barricades had been set behind the ambulance and the door, volunteers and off-duty officers holding back the curious. Dani could sense the presence of cameras outside. She could not let anyone photograph her face.

The EMTs opened the doors. Dani reached out with her power, forcing Officer Leonard to rip free the sheet on his side of the stretcher and use it to cover Dani's face.

"What are you doing that for?" the male EMT asked.

"Little girl deserves some privacy," he said sluggishly. There was no time to argue with him. Beneath the sheet, Dani felt the heat of intense lights

336

and heard the whirr and clicks of shutters. The loud, indignant cries of reporters came to her. She smiled, happy to cheat them out of their front page photograph.

Dani was loaded into the ambulance, the sheet removed once the door was closed behind her. She released her hold on Officer Leonard, who looked at her angrily. Though he had no conscious idea why he should have felt violated, that exact feeling raced through him.

"Shoulda handcuffed the bitch," he muttered, running his large hand over his sweaty brow. The woman with the auburn hair and compassionate eyes stayed in the back with Dani. The male EMT slid into the driver's seat. Officer Leonard climbed into the back, his attention riveted on Dani's face. She had been pretending to slip in and out of delirium.

"Is she gonna make it?" Officer Leonard asked the auburn-haired EMT. A part of him obviously wished she would not.

"Let's hope," the woman replied. "She seems to be stable."

Officer Leonard ran his hand over his face. Dani looked at him, sensing his thoughts. He was angry at himself for not following procedure. The first thing he should have done when she came around was try to probe her for information about her associates. But he had been too rattled to think so logically. It took a lot to make a man of Officer Leonard's training and experience disregard standard operations, but the sight of the vampires rising into the air had been just enough to accomplish the task.

"I need to ask you some questions," the man said, pulling out his notebook. He turned to the female EMT. "Is that all right?"

Dani's head lolled back and forth. He wasn't going to get a damn thing from her, she decided, but there was no reason to make him think she was purposefully withholding.

"Her vital signs are very strong," the auburn-haired EMT said with a heavy degree of surprise. "She should be able to understand you. She's not in shock, though she should be, after what she suffered."

Dani could feel her flesh mending and fusing under the bandages. It was an odd sensation, ticklish. She wanted to giggle. Then her hunger seized up and she convulsed, causing the EMT to seize her shoulders and hold her down.

"Grab her," the woman said.

"I've got her." Officer Leonard took the EMT's place.

Dani saw the woman ready a syringe. She imagined herself lying in bed, sedated, strapped down, possibly handcuffed, as the sun rose through the nearby window, its fiery hand stealing across her body, setting her ablaze as she cried and screamed.

"Hurry up with that!" Officer Leonard cried. Despite his terrific strength from his daily workouts, he found holding the teenager down a nearly impossible task.

Dani's head whipped about sharply, her golden eyes blazing with her hunger. She tore her left arm free of the restraints, shoved the officer away from her, and reached out to tear the IV from her flesh. Officer Leonard struck the other side of the narrow walkway inside the ambulance and somehow kept his footing. The auburn-haired EMT held on to the syringe and grabbed at Dani's flailing arm, hoping to sedate her. Dani's hand curled into a fist and slammed into the woman's stomach, driving the wind from her. The EMT collapsed to her knees, the needle grasped in her hand as she tried to take in air.

338

"What the hell's going on back there!?" the driver called in alarm.

Officer Leonard advanced on Dani once again, his hand reaching for his weapon, but he wasn't fast enough. Dani sat up and ripped apart the restraints holding her legs as if they had been made of tissue. Her wounds had not completely healed. She continued to feel weak, but she had to get free of the humans and find shelter before the dawn.

Dani leapt from the stretcher, head down, and barreled into the officer, slamming her shoulder into his ribs. He coughed and went down. She felt a hand on her leg and turned to see the female EMT on her knees, about to plunge the needle into her exposed thigh. Whirling, Dani kicked at the woman, driving her up from her knees. The woman's arms pinwheeled and she lost her grip on the syringe. The ambulance lurched and the EMT fell back, cracking her head against the metal rail of the stretcher.

The driver strained his head, looking back, and gasped at the sight.

"Drive!" Dani screamed, lashing out with her power. She felt the familiar hunger return as her razor-sharp teeth burst from their housings. "Do it!"

Twenty-seven

The driver whipped back in his seat as if he had been struck, then he recovered and turned his attention fully upon the road, all other thoughts forced from his consciousness.

Dani heard Officer Leonard moaning softly. She turned and saw he was sitting on the floor of the ambulance, his face pale, his leg twisted up underneath him at an unnatural angle. He had a radio in his hand. It had been attached to his belt, but she hadn't paid any attention to it before now. Suddenly she recalled the police cars that were parked on the other side of the street from the ambulance. Dani had learned all about police procedure from Walthers; it should have occurred to her earlier that there would be another car behind them, an escort. She considered utilizing her powers to see if that's who he was trying to signal, but she was already keeping the driver in thrall, and she was too weak to divide her concentration. It had to be a backup of some kind.

Officer Leonard's finger was on the call button, holding it down. "She's—"

Tearing the radio from his hand, Dani screamed, "She's had enough of your shit for one night, that's what!"

Dani finally noticed the drawn pistol in his other hand. She drove her boot over his wrist, pinning his gun hand to the floor, and felt tempted to leave the radio on as she slowly tore Officer Leonard to pieces, forcing him to scream and wail for the audience.

Her hunger nearly overpowered her reason.

First his face, watch it all come off, bite it off, give him a mirror, let him see himself—

"No!" Dani screamed, forcing back the insanity brought on by her blood-need, which had been worsened by her injuries.

Officer Leonard stared up at her incisors and her burning, yellow eyes. "What the hell *are* you?"

Dani stared at him. A part of her wanted to scream she was human, like him, but she knew that was a lie. No matter how much she longed for the simple life that had once been hers, she knew now there was no turning back.

Why then, couldn't she bring herself to kill the officer? His fear was palpable. Her need ripped through her painfully, urging her to take him. Somehow, none of it mattered. All she wanted was to be left alone, and if she died, it would be in a manner of her choosing.

She crushed the radio, then tossed it onto the stretcher where she had been moments before. Crouching, she took the gun from him, then gathered him up by his shirt and hauled him to the other side of the ambulance, near the unconscious form of the auburn-haired EMT.

"Hush," she said in a voice that was completely her own. "Just be quiet and you won't be hurt. Just be quiet. Don't say *anything.*"

Officer Leonard nodded, and Dani turned her back on him. Her wounded leg was weaker than her undamaged one, but not by much. Drawing a breath, she took the safety from the officer's weapon and kicked open the back doors of the ambulance. A rush of night air blasted into the ambulance. For a moment Dani thought that she had been wrong, then she saw the car following them and aimed the weapon.

Maintaining her control of the ambulance driver, Dani ordered the man to change lanes, giving her a perfect view of the police car's driver's side.

"No!" Officer Leonard shouted behind her.

Utilizing her enhanced senses for guidance, Dani squeezed off two shots. The front and rear tires of the vehicle exploded and the car went into a tailspin, screeching to a stop as the ambulance sped on. She turned to face the officer, who had a perplexed expression on his face.

"It's not going to be long, is it?" she asked. "Before others come after us?"

"No, it's not," he said, his eyes wide with wonderment, his fear momentarily subsiding.

She nodded. The helicopters would pick up the ambulance quickly, then it would all begin again. Dani hurled the gun from the open back doors of the ambulance.

"Go another two blocks, make a right, then stop," she said to the entranced driver. The effort of keeping him under control was beginning to show on her. She leaned against the side of the stretcher and saw that her bandages were soaked with blood.

Officer Leonard slowly shook his head. "I don't understand."

She gave a nasty half-laugh. There was much that both of them did not understand. She had spared him when her need had commanded her to do otherwise. Laying in the cruiser, she had set herself above humanity. But she had just proven that she was still vulnerable to them. Perhaps it had been the memory of Leonard's daughter that had helped her to curb her violent impulse. Dani had been without a father all her life. She didn't want to be responsible for inflicting that pain on another.

You're going soft, Dani, a taunting voice called in her head. But maybe that's not so bad.

The ambulance veered to the right. Dani stared at the officer's face, and thought of those upon whom she truly wished to vent her rage. She decided that sparing the officer had not been a noble gesture after all. She had merely been denying herself so that she would not be fat and bloated with blood when the confrontation with the vampires came. Unfortunately, her anger only served to stoke her hunger. She clawed at herself and cried out as a dozen burning pokers were thrust into her stomach and her brain.

She needed blood. She needed it to heal and to survive. Without any further conscious thought, she advanced on the downed officer, her vision clouded over by a crimson haze.

I have to control this, she thought. I can't be a slave to this. Oh, Jesus, please, don't make me do this!

She drew closer, unable to stop herself. The officer saw the sudden change in her eyes. He tried to defend himself, but he was defenseless against her inhuman strength.

My mother used to wear that uniform! My mother, *for God's sake. Please!*

Dani hooked her hands under the man's arms and lifted him up. He struggled, shoving at her face, trying to hold her off, but he might have been a child wriggling in his mother's arms for all the good it did him. His fear drifted from him, falling upon Dani like a gentle sheet of rain in the middle of a desert. The sweet touch of his fright

343

made her shudder with ecstasy. She delighted in the confusion and betrayal in his eyes.

I don't want to do this! she wailed in her mind, a prisoner of her body's all-consuming hunger. Dani opened her jaws and felt the hot, sweaty flesh of his neck, heard the thunderous call of his pulse as his artery throbbed wildly.

Yes, I need it, I need it—

Something crashed against her back, causing her to stumble forward, dropping the officer. He cried out as he fell upon his twisted leg. Dani enjoyed his agony. She turned and saw the driver, a large red canister hefted in his hands. She had lost control of him when the blood-need had taken her.

"Don't!" he screamed, raising the canister as she advanced on him. She slapped it away and shoved him back, against the stretcher, the guard rail jammed into his back.

Good, she thought. He'll do. He'll do just fine.

"Any port in a storm, sweetheart!" she cried, holding him down with one hand. She curled her free hand into a talon and brought it up above her head. With a scream she sent it downward, aimed to tear his heart from his chest.

Her hand stopped centimeters from his white shirt. Dani trembled with uncertainty, then threw her head back, screaming wildly as she fought the hunger. The EMT screamed as well, and for a moment, his terror bloomed in her mind, a blinding white explosion that filled her and gave her the strength to push her blood-need away. She released the man, backing away from him, and nearly fell from the ambulance. Her hand caught the doorjamb, and she saw Officer Leonard's face as he watched her. His lips quivered as he held back an expression of disgust and nodded to her.

Her entire body trembled. She bit down hard on

her lip and felt as if she were going to cry. Turning, she leapt from the ambulance and ran through the streets of downtown Los Angeles, thoroughly unafraid of the inherent dangers of the area.

She ran several blocks, losing herself in a twisting series of alleyways. When she found that she could run no more, she collapsed against a wall, near a pile of trash.

Dani sobbed openly, clawing at her stomach and her head. The blood-need was not going to leave her alone. This was going to be her life until time itself came to an end, and she was powerless to do anything about it. Eventually she would kill someone else. She knew that now. And next time, she would find it a little easier. After all, Madison had been her friend, and Dani had killed her. How hard would it be to take a stranger when the need was fully upon her?

One day she would be no different from Bill, Angel, and Isabella.

But that didn't *have* to be the case, she reminded herself. She could just sit here, in the open, and watch the sunrise. That's all it would take.

God, she wished that she could see her mother one last time. She pictured herself at home, sitting on the floor working on a report for school. No matter what kind of day Sam had endured, her face would always light up with happiness and pride the second she walked through their door and saw Dani. There were times when Dani had waited all day, looking forward to seeing that expression on her mother's face. Sometimes it was all that got her through her dark, lonely existence.

She hated the woman, wanted to kill her.

Her friends. Lisa. If she could only phone Lisa. The past wasn't gone, it wasn't dead. She would

345

know that for certain if she could only talk to Lisa.

She'd be terrified of you. She knows what you are.

Bill had made love to her. He had helped her to fulfill a lifetime's worth of erotic daydreams. He had held her even as the silence of a watery grave had descended on them.

He's an animal, filth. He lied to you, used you.

Isabella had been her friend, she had given her kindness and warmth. The woman had loved her and protected her. She had made Dani see herself as beautiful.

She ran off and left you. Just like they all did.

"STOP IT!!!" Dani screamed. The voice in her head trailed away, leaving her to shiver and quake in the perfect silence left behind. Dani sat, her back against the wall, her blood-need simmering within her, slowly eking away her reason. She entertained fantasies of slaying the first human who entered the alley, regardless of who they might be, young or old, it made no difference. But when a couple cut through the alley, she held herself even tighter, forcing herself to ignore the wild pounding of their hearts and the rush of blood as it pumped through their veins. They had walked past her without noticing her, or sensing how close they had come to death incarnate.

That's what she was, she realized. That's what all of her kind were. Death dealers. Fear merchants. Their task had been to spread misery, to give the human race a heightened sense of tragic drama, to bring out the beast in all of man. Or maybe they were just a sick joke conceived by a fallen angel with a lousy sense of humor. She would never know. It didn't matter. She was spiraling toward delirium.

346

Dani absently wondered what time it was. She would have to make a decision soon. The police would be looking for her. If she was going to find a hiding place, she would have to do it before long. And if she was going to kill herself, she would have to find a better place for it. Death had always terrified her, but now she saw it as a release. Her only condition for giving in to death was that she do it on her terms, not as an animal, locked in a cell, chained up and unable to face her end with dignity.

Dani stood up and heard a rustling sound. She spun, surveying the alley, and saw no one. She was afraid to reach out with her power. It would cause her hunger to flare once again, and whoever she had detected would not be safe from her. The blood-need was worse than it had ever been. Every conscious, rational thought was a chore to bring about, each step a bitter trial.

The rustling came again, accompanied by a whisper. Her name, spoken in a tone that was soft and warm.

"Mom?" Dani asked.

In a way, sister-love.

Dani looked up sharply. Isabella hovered a dozen feet up, the glow of an exposed, orange bulb casting her voluptuous form in silhouette. Dani's initial urge was to launch herself at the woman, to tear into her and take the blood she needed from this woman who had so grievously betrayed her. Her anger flared briefly, and was replaced by a deep, abiding sadness.

"Get the hell out of here," Dani said. "Leave me alone."

"I can't do that," Isabella said. She reached out with her arms and slowly descended to the ground, like an angel. "You're not safe here."

347

"I know that. I don't need *you* to tell me. I don't need any of you people."

"That's not true," Isabella said in a level tone, though Dani's words obviously caused her pain.

"Just get away from me!" Dani shouted as Isabella touched the earth and stood before her. She turned her back on the woman.

"I'm sorry, Dani. I had to get the others away. There were cameras. We would have been seen. That can't happen. You'll understand, in time."

"Fuck you," Dani said, wondering why in the hell she hadn't attacked Isabella when she had the chance. Her anger had certainly been strong enough. She wondered if Isabella had done something to calm her.

"I know you don't mean that," Isabella said patiently.

"Yeah, you know everything about me. You've been pulling my fucking strings from the beginning, haven't you?"

"No," Isabella said. "I have not." The woman hesitated. "Look at me, please."

Dani turned to face her. Anger and need swept through her. She shuddered.

"All I have tried to do—all of us have tried to do—is make you accept who and what you are, Dani. You cannot live in the human world ever again. You would go insane."

"What do you want from me?" Dani cried suddenly. "I'm not like you."

"You are exactly as I am. I found acceptance difficult, too. I nearly walked into the sunlight."

Dani rankled. Isabella had known what she was planning. She wondered if the woman had taken the secret from her mind or if she could see it in her eyes. It didn't matter.

"You went away and left me!" Dani screamed as

she hurled herself at Isabella. The woman gripped her arms and held her back easily. Dani struggled, then relaxed in the other woman's grip. She found that her tears had not played out entirely. Isabella took her into a warm, comforting embrace. The woman's power was intoxicating to Dani, who pulled away before she was overcome with desire. Shivering, Dani wiped away her tears, angry at herself for the display.

Isabella released Dani's hands and reached for the blood-soaked bandage taped to Dani's ribs. Before Dani could object, Isabella tore it free. The bullet wound was healing over. The ruined skin around the charred black wound had been replaced by a smooth covering of pearl-white flesh. Only a small puckered hole remained.

Dani backed away, tearing away the bandages covering the wounds in her arm and thigh. Her flesh had been restored.

"Omigod!" Dani cried as she turned from Isabella and stumbled to the wall. A series of dry heaves wracked her. Isabella bent down beside her, stroking her back. Dani shrugged off the woman's hand. Isabella was not so easily deterred. She placed her hand on Dani again, and this time, the girl surrendered to her touch.

"No, no," Dani said in a strangled cry. "I'm just a kid, this isn't fair. God, no. . . ."

"Sister-love, forgive me, but you must hear me out."

"No," Dani whimpered. Despite all she had done, Dani still felt human deep inside. A human blessed with wondrous abilities, to be certain, but a human girl, with time to make decisions, time for a life. The evidence of her flesh told her that her time had passed.

"Dani, you must make a second kill. You've

crossed the threshold. You cannot be human anymore. You must kill again, before three nights have elapsed. If you do not, you will die."

Turning to stare into Isabella's darkened face, Dani felt the greatest fear of her life. She threw herself into the older woman's arms, quaking in pain and grief.

"I can't," Dani wailed. "Don't ask me to, I *can't!*"

Isabella held her close, stroking her blood-soaked hair.

"I tried," Dani said, thinking of the humans in the ambulance. "But I couldn't bring myself to do it."

"You are still thinking like one of them. I know. I did it, too. But the time for that has passed."

"I couldn't."

Isabella kissed Dani's neck. The sensual current that passed between them caused Dani's flesh to tingle. "You did nothing wrong."

"I'm gonna die!"

"I pray not, Dani. There *is* time."

"I can't. Not tonight."

Isabella stroked Dani's skin lightly. "No, not tonight. Tonight you will rest. It will be all right. Trust me, darling one. Nothing will happen tonight."

Dani thought of the first officer, in the woods. She would have killed the man then, but Isabella had prevented it. She asked Isabella why she had intervened.

"Because it wasn't your choice, Dani. You were being manipulated into making a kill, influenced by Bill."

"But Bill said I wouldn't be worthy if I couldn't—"

"It's always difficult in the beginning. And *Bill*

forgets his place."

Dani stared at the woman. "You run the pack."

"Oh yes. Didn't you guess? It's always the quiet ones you have to look out for."

Dani let out a deep, ragged breath. "I loved him. He lied to me. Jesus."

"It's what he is. I shouldn't have allowed it. There were other ways."

Dani stared into her dark eyes. "You mean *you* could have made love to me. You could have been the one to seduce me."

"Yes."

"Why didn't you? Didn't you want me?"

"I did. I still do. But not the way you mean."

"How then?"

Isabella hesitated.

"You can't hide anything from me," Dani said with a bravado she did not feel. She had a sense that Isabella, the eldest and the most powerful of the pack, could withhold her secrets from Dani with ease.

Isabella looked directly into Dani's gold-flecked eyes. "I wanted what you once had with *her.*"

Dani felt as if she had been struck. She exhaled sharply. "My mom," she whispered.

The vampire nodded.

"But she tried to hurt me," Dani cried.

"She didn't know you, Dani. She's not one of us. She could never understand what you feel deep inside, what you always had to hide away from her. But you would never have to hide anything from me. I would never judge you. And I would live for all time, with you. I would love you for all time. That is something she could never do. Not even if she wanted to."

Dani collapsed into Isabella's arms, sobbing for the life to which she could never return.

351

"It's tearing you apart, isn't it, Dani? The fear. The blood. The need. It's too much for you."

"Too much," Dani whispered, her reason seeping away.

"Then take what you need from me," Isabella said, shrugging off her jacket to reveal her soft, creamy shoulders and long, delicate throat.

"I can't," Dani sobbed. "I'll hurt you."

Only an hour before she had wanted to kill this woman, but now all she desired was to have Isabella make good on her promise.

"Help me. Please!"

"I will," Isabella said, leaning forward and kissing Dani softly on the lips. Dani responded greedily, clutching at the woman's face as her world became a blur of confused images. She felt the hunger work through her body and this time she did not try to fight it off. There was an unbearable heat and wetness that rose up from her sex, and she took Isabella's hand and guided it toward her moist center. The vampire resisted.

"Not the human way," Isabella breathed. "Let me show you."

As they kissed, Isabella reached deep into Dani's mind, freeing her desires. Dani felt an explosion of pleasure reach up from between her thighs as she gasped and ground them together. She found herself in a continuous, impossible state of orgasm, her body barely able to contend with the incredible surges of pleasure. She had never felt anything like this before. Even her time with Bill had not been like this.

Dani threw her head back and allowed her incisors to extend from their fleshy housings. Her world dissolved as she assimilated the fears and desires of hundreds, even thousands of humans in the area, feeling their gentle touches, their angry

352

blows, hearing their soft words, their agonized screams. She was inside the head of a murderer, then his victim, tasting the rush of anger as a trigger was pulled, the final blinding flash of fear and pain as life fled.

She sunk her teeth into Isabella's neck.

"Yes!" Isabella moaned. "Take what you need, darling love. Take what you need."

Dani was engulfed in a final, crimson tide of blood and fear. The hunger abated and her world dissolved as she sank beneath the surface of a churning, scarlet sea.

Isabella watched as Dani collapsed in her arms, sated. She withdrew from the sensations that had nearly drowned her in a sea of unreason. Dani could have killed her with the feeding, her need had been that great. Isabella knew she should have been more careful, but she had needs of her own and they had almost gotten the better of her.

In the far distance, she heard the wail of sirens. Lifting Dani into her arms, the girl's head bobbing slightly, Isabella allowed the currents of night air to carry them upward. Flying while she carried another would have been a difficult task even if she had been at full strength. As it was, she had been left weakened and drained by Dani's feeding, barely able to send her power out around her like a cloak, altering the perceptions of any who might look up and see her take to the air. The dawn was not far off, and the burning light of the sun would accept no excuses. They had to get away.

Rising up a few feet, then finally to the level of the second-story window, Isabella felt like easing herself down again and hiring a cab. But that would involve humans, and that was always a risk.

"Mom?"

Isabella's heart leapt. She looked down and saw Dani's head lolling from side to side as they rode the night winds. The girl was suffering from a slight delirium, Isabella knew, but that did not detract from her joy at the word Dani had spoken.

"Mom?" Dani repeated.

"Yes," Isabella said without hesitation, her elation powering their flight as they took to the skies, rising above the filth-ridden streets of Los Angeles.

"Are we going home?"

Smiling broadly, the vampire leaned down to kiss Dani's cheek.

"Yes, Daughter," she whispered, "we're going home. . . ."

Twenty-eight

Samantha Walthers sat quietly in the GT-S. The brick warehouse Tory had videotaped was across the street. She was parked in roughly the same spot Tory had used to take her "surveillance" footage. Finding the warehouse had taken the entire day. Ultimately, it had been a homeless woman and her talk of the "devil house" that had guided Sam to the correct neighborhood. The homeless woman had slept outside the warehouse once and the nightmares visited upon her that night were the worst she had experienced in her life. Once Sam found the neighborhood, locating the lone building bereft of graffiti had not been difficult.

Sam wiped the sweat from her eyes and glanced at her watch. The night was almost over. She had been in the car for eleven hours. Her back was sore, her muscles felt locked into place. She wished she could get out and stretch, but that would be suicide. Two of the vampires were already in the warehouse. She had watched the Japanese-American, Yoshino, and the blond-haired girl with the punk hairstyle descend from the night like dark angels. Dani and the creature that had flown in the videotape had not arrived. Sam recalled the image of the dark-haired vampire sweeping their victim inside the warehouse—eyes blazing, razor-sharp teeth glinting, talons ready to slash—and wondered if she actually stood a chance against monsters like this.

Don't think about it too much, Sam thought. They'll sense the fear, they'll find you.

Christ, she needed some sleep.

Sam focused her thoughts. She had been out here for hours and had not been harassed by any locals. That was not entirely surprising. The GT-S was not in good shape. Sam had purchased several cans of spray paint and had desecrated the pure, expensive lines of the car. Dents had been applied with a sledgehammer. She had used one of the guns to blow a hole in the rear window, creating a spiderweb of cracks. Dark sheets of acetate had served as makeshift tinting to disguise her presence in the driver's seat. The car looked like a wreck. Only its tires gave it away. They were in perfect condition. There was nothing Sam could do about that. Fortunately, no one had stopped to strip the vehicle, despite its wretched condition, and so she had gone unnoticed.

The vampires had not detected her presence. They seemed to be in a foul mood when they had arrived, angry and distracted. Yoshino had slapped the blonde after she made a remark, then stepped into the warehouse without noticing the slight nicks around the lock that gave away Sam's other enterprise of the evening. She held the car's cell phone in one hand. Six numbers had been pressed.

Suddenly, a deep, soothing, electronic voice sounded from the phone as the line disconnected. "If you would like to make a call . . ."

Sam regained a dial tone, then struck the redial button. She watched the alley, her finger poised over the last digit.

Earlier she had broken into the building and rigged the place to blow when the phone rang and an exposed piece of wiring gave the necessary spark. Having investigated dozens of arson claims, Sam knew exactly how to torch the building using items she was able to buy from an all night Builder's Emporium. The vampires' phone had call blocking and so she programmed it to only receive calls from her current number.

She thought of all the things that could go wrong with her plan. The vampires could discover the explosives. Sam had been as careful as possible, but it had been a crude job. She discounted this possibility. They would have gotten the hell out of there if they suspected anything. Unless they had defused her setup already and were waiting to draw her out. Why bother? They could take her anytime. And even these ridiculously overconfident creatures would hesitate before attempting to unwire a bomb. Wouldn't they?

Her heart started to pound furiously.

Avoid the fear, dammit, forget how impossible all of this is, you have a job to do, Dani's in trouble and you have to save her!

Sam unwrapped another candy bar with her teeth. She was close to sugar shock. Over the course of the evening she had devoured close to a dozen candy bars. She needed to stay wired and awake. Yawning, Sam forced her eyelids to remain open, though they fluttered and fought her. She bit down on the Milky Way as if it were her salvation.

The sugar pounced on Sam and she shook violently. Keep thinking, she reminded herself. Keep straight. What other problems do we have?

The vampires would be surprised, perhaps, that Tory was not waiting for them. That *could* put them on the defensive, but not necessarily. They might assume she was indulging herself at Sam's expense, or having a private party at the Halpern estate. Their arrival at the warehouse had been long after the evening news, and they probably had not learned of Halpern's death. In any case, there was no time for them to acquire a car and drive to the Malibu house or the mansion. Not tonight, anyway. If, however, Dani and the remaining vampire had settled somewhere else for the night, Sam would be screwed.

Tomorrow night, the vampires would see a newspaper or a television report of Halpern's death and they would make a point of checking the beach house. With their animal senses, they would find Tory's body easily. They would know she failed, they would be waiting for Sam to make a move against them. Sam could blow the warehouse at any time, killing Yoshino and the blonde. God knew, she wanted to murder that bastard. He had seduced her little girl, he had done things to her body and her mind. Christ, she hated him.

Sam's finger grazed the last button.

"If you would like to make a call . . ."

Relief flooded into her. She disconnected the line and hit the redial. Get a grip, she told herself. If she were to blow the warehouse now, the other vampire, the one with her daughter, would never come here. She could lose Dani forever. Her only hope was to trap the vampires inside the warehouse and arrange an even exchange, Dani for their lives.

Of course, if Dani were with them, she would have to be willing to sacrifice her daughter's life and her own if they gave her no other choice. She would die for the girl. She had known that in the emergency room at the hospital, eighteen years ago. But even if everything Halpern had said was true, even if her baby was one of these creatures, she wasn't sure that she could do something that would bring harm to the child, even if it were to spare Dani from a lifetime of horrors. So long as Dani was alive, there was always a possibility of her life turning around, of somehow saving her from monsters like this, or seeing her save herself.

That's not what Halpern said, she thought. Once they become full vampires, there's no turning back. They have to kill twice, first under the blood and influence of their "sponsor" and the second time, in less than three days, on their own. Had Dani been seduced not only into sex, but also into murder?

The thought made Sam want to cry, but she kept a tight rein on her emotions. The vampires could sense strong emotion. They might come out and find her.

God, the car was hot. For hours she had fantasized about rolling down the window, just a crack. The windows were automatic. She wouldn't have to start the car. Just turn the key in the ignition. The green ring around the ignition would light, with three other indicators on the dash. The vampire with Dani might see the sudden flash, despite the tinted windows, and everything could go to hell.

Yeah, but I could have done it a thousand times by now, she groused in her head. This is ridiculous. They're not going to show.

They have to show.

They're not, I'm telling you.

Sam smiled. She knew the owners of those voices from her memories. It had been back when she was on the force, and she had to do surveillance work. Jack, her male partner, hated this duty. He never believed that a perp would show. After they got drunk one night and became lovers, Sam dreaded surveillance. He would get bored and start suggesting things they could do to make the time go faster. Sam had been tempted. She would

sit there, reminding herself that she was a professional, that she would never compromise her prin-
ciples for a few moments of gratification.

Once, he took her hand and put it in his lap, so
that she could feel how hard he was getting, just
staring at her in the dim light. Christ, that had
been a turn-on, knowing that she didn't have to
do anything, just be there for him, and he would
get hard. She would feel his excitement leap forward, as if it were a palpable thing in the confines
of their car. It would make her breasts ache with
need as she squeezed her legs together and tried to
concentrate on her job. Most of the time, she had
not really minded when he stared at the swell of
her breasts or the curve of her throat. But there
was a difference between having an urge and acting upon it. The business with the hand was out
of line.

Sam was angry at him for acting unprofession-
ally and agitated with herself for wanting it, too.
In a cool, but *polite* tone, she informed him that
he had given her the tools to cripple him for life
with one healthy squeeze. Jack took her hand
from her lap and made no other untoward sugges-
tions. The next morning, after they were off shift,
Sam invited herself into his place and leaped on
him.

*You don't confuse work with pleasure. You
don't get emotional, you don't get turned on. You
stay clean.*

Not an easy lesson, but a valid one. What she
was doing here tonight was the same. She had to
disassociate to some extent. The goal was to save
her daughter. If that called for her to take the
lives of these inhuman abominations, no problem.
She recalled her days of training, with targets
painted on cardboard popping up. Some were rep-
resentations of criminals, guns drawn. Others were

360

women with children, innocent teenagers. Sam had scored one hundred every time.

I know the difference. I can tell the good guys from the bad.

But what if your baby's crossed the line? What if she really is one of them?

Sam shook herself free of that line of reasoning. She wasn't about to let herself get fucked up over this. She had a job to do and that's all there was to it.

Still, she couldn't remember the last time a man had looked at her the way Jack had that night. Their relationship hadn't lasted. Maybe she had been too hard on Jack, holding him up to an impossible standard. There weren't many men in her life after she found Dani, but she had walked away from each of them for the same reason: They wouldn't have made suitable fathers for Dani. Consequently, Dani had grown up without a father of any kind. Sam had assumed both roles. Thinking about her lovely and intelligent daughter, Sam had no complaints—although she would have liked to have made love one final time before she died.

Reality crowded in on her. The cell phone had nearly toppled from her hand. The recorded voice was speaking again. She coaxed a dial tone from the phone and hit redial.

God, she had almost fallen asleep. She checked her watch. Sunrise was at five-thirty. It was ten minutes after five. She cursed and twisted in her seat. The heat in the car was oppressive. Her hand was on the key when she saw movement from the alley. A shape was breaking from the shadows, descending with a matchless grace.

It was the dark-haired woman from the video, the one who had flown and attacked. She did not look the same as she had on the tape. In person, the vampire looked like a goddess, an elegant, beautiful woman who radiated serenity. She held Dani in her arms, carrying her the way Sam had done once, when Dani had fallen asleep in front of the television and needed to be put to bed.

"That's my job, you bitch," Sam whispered irrationally, the delirium she had been fighting off all night now threatening to overtake her. Dani was dressed in leathers and there was something on her face, arms, and legs. It might have been blood.

Sam tried to recall the disciplines she had learned. Stay calm, remain outside the event. Distance yourself from your emotions.

Fuck you, distance myself, that's my baby!

Sam shuddered. The hard, cold weight of the weapons she had strapped to her body in preparation for this event was becoming intolerable. She was seized by a terrible headache.

With an inhuman effort, Sam remained in the GT-S. She watched the vampire gently set Dani on the ground as she fished a set of keys from her pocket. She was obviously concerned that her knock would go unanswered, for whatever reason. The door was several inches of thick, reinforced metal. Sam hefted the phone in her hand, excitedly. The perfect opening had been delivered to her. She would blow the warehouse now. The door would fly from its hinges, crushing the vampire. Sam would collect Dani and they would drive away, safe.

She touched the last digit. Nothing happened.

A cold, metallic voice sounded. "If you would like to make a call . . ."

"Shit!" Sam screamed. The automatic disconnect had severed the connection. She scrambled to get a dial tone, then looked up to see the vampire walking from the partially opened door, toward Dani's inert form. By the time she finished the sequence,

Dani would be in the vampire's arms. They would both be struck by the blast.

Sam burst from the GT-S, screaming her daughter's name as she struck the redial on the phone. The vampire whirled in her direction. She was several feet away from Dani, but still in the direct line of fire from the warehouse. Yoshino, the Japanese-American, suddenly appeared in the doorway. Dani looked up groggily in the direction of her lover. Sam struck the final digit and an explosion sounded from within the warehouse.

The building was rocked by the force. Hairline fractures snaked across its exterior. Its reinforced walls somehow contained the blast. There were no windows, no outlets to vent the explosive fury of the fireball within the warehouse except the open doorway near the alley. A torrent of flame burst from the rectangular opening, engulfing the man who had stood there, unsuspecting. Yoshino would have screamed if he could, but the fires had incinerated him, leaving only a charred, twisted skeleton that danced as the fiery gusts blew him about.

The steel door had been blown outward, slamming into the female vampire, who had put up her arm and turned away in defense. The door smashed her into the far wall of the alley, where she crumbled into a heap.

Dani had been shocked into awareness. She had screamed as she saw Yoshino die, then scrambled back from the tongue of flames that scorched the wall before her.

Across the street, moving steadily, Sam opened the long, leather trench coat she had purchased to conceal the arsenal strapped to her body. She felt the shotgun bang against her ribs in its makeshift sling. The weight of the 9mm handguns taped around the thighs of her jeans and the automatic strung across her back comforted her. She tore one of the Berettas free and readied it. The fires were subsiding, and Sam walked quickly, the 9mm raised in case there were more of the creatures that the explosion had not destroyed.

Sam reached the curb and stepped into the alley. Smoke partially obscured Dani from her. Steam reached out and engulfed her flesh. She smelled burnt flesh and wondered if her daughter had been hurt in the blast.

Christ, she thought, oh God, baby, you've got to be all right. Please!

She found Dani crouched over the dark-haired vampire. The partially melted door had been lifted from the woman. Sam wondered if Dani could have done that. Isabella rose to her knees, shoving Dani behind her. Her eyes were blazing, her teeth sharp and wolflike. Sam aimed the weapon at the vampire's face and fired twice. The first shot tore through the woman's forehead, the second passed through her left eye. The vampire snapped back and fell at Dani's feet. The teenager screamed, and Sam grabbed her hand.

They had gone only a few feet when Dani wrenched herself free of her mother's grasp and screamed, "No!"

Sam spun, careful not to aim her weapon at her daughter, and was unprepared for the sight greeting her. Dani had changed. Her golden eyes were fiery and her open mouth revealed a collection of razor-sharp teeth and wolflike canines.

Don't feel, Sam thought desperately, don't be afraid, don't hesitate. Dani doesn't want this to be happening to her anymore than you want to see it. You've got to help her whether she thinks she wants it or not. You've got to!

Dani leaped at her. Sam was unprepared for her incredible speed. She tried to focus beyond the twisted expression of hatred on her daughter's face

364

as she brought the butt of the weapon around. Too late. Dani seized her mother's arms and threw her against the wall. Sam heard a sharp crack as the back of her skull connected with the concrete. She felt a rush of vertigo and struggled to hold on to consciousness. The pure, animal delight on her daughter's face was enough to shock her back into complete awareness. Sam's hands were free, though her arms were going numb from the twin pressure clamps of Dani's hands. She aimed the gun at the metal door and fired four times.

As Sam had expected, the explosive report of the weapon caused Dani to jump back instinctively. Sam was free.

"Dani, you've got to listen to me!"

The girl looked down, realized that she had not been shot, and snarled, "You killed them! They were my friends and you *fucking* killed them!"

Bloodred flecks were deeply embedded between Dani's canines. The fight drained from Sam as she saw them.

"Oh Jesus, baby, what did they make you do?" Sam asked.

"Nothing I didn't want to do," Dani said with a wicked smile. "Want me to show you?"

Dani advanced again, but this time Sam was ready for her. She brought the gun up in time and slammed it against the side of her daughter's head. Dani tottered and Sam struck her again. The sight of her daughter in pain was horrible to Sam. Knowing that she had caused that pain was nearly paralyzing. Dani reached for Sam and the older woman cracked her head a final time. Dani collapsed.

Jamming the Beretta 9mm into the waistband of her jeans, Sam noticed that Dani's face had relaxed in unconsciousness, she appeared human. Sam wasn't taking any chances. A pair of handcuffs were looped through the hooks of her jeans. She removed them and brought her daughter's hands behind her back. The handcuffs clicked shut with finality. Sam dragged Dani's limp form with both hands. There was no traffic, but the gunshots had drawn the attention of the neighbors. People were poking their heads out of windows, a few had gathered on the street.

"LAPD!" Sam hollered. "This is a bust!"

A few people ran at these words. They were quickly replaced. Sam hauled her daughter to the passenger side of the GT-S and loaded her in. Another set of handcuffs waited in the car. She secured her daughter's ankles with these.

"I'm sorry, baby, I don't have any choice," she whispered.

Dani moaned softly in response. Sam hurried into the driver's seat and jammed her key into the ignition. The engine turned over and Sam whipped the car into the street, scattering a collection of passersby who were gradually edging closer to the alley beside the warehouse. Sam had to get away before the police and fire arrived. She had smeared mud on the license plate of the GT-S, but the treatment the car had endured so that it would fit in outside the warehouse would now make it stand out in traffic. There was another problem, too. She looked in the rearview mirror. Soft streaks of pastel pink and gold hung upon the horizon. Hopefully the tinting would help Dani. She had a blanket in the back, too.

The streets slowly filled with traffic. Sam forced herself to drive at a normal pace. Keeping the GT-S unnoticed was a priority. She glanced over at her unconscious daughter. Dani was curled up like a small child, her head angled toward Sam and bobbing with the slight shocks of the road. The over-the-shoulder seat belt held her in place. Sam wondered if she had been hallucinating Dani's attack. This was her baby girl, this was *Dani,* for god's sake. Dani wouldn't try to hurt her.

Sam reached over to stroke her daughter's hair and drew back quickly as Dani's eyes flashed open and her savage grin returned.

"Didn't anyone ever tell you, Samantha?" Dani said as she shoved her legs apart, shattering the chain between the handcuff's bracelets. Her shoulders bunched and she did the same thing with the cuffs securing her wrists. *"Tricks are for kids!"*

Samantha, the woman thought, she called me Samantha.

Somehow that had even been more shocking than the sight of Dani employing her inhuman strength to break free of her bonds. Before Sam could say or do anything, she was jolted by the sound of something heavy dropping onto the car's roof. Sam floored the car, sending them barreling through a light. Pounding came from the roof. Someone was up there.

Some *thing* was up there.

Beside Sam, Dani was giggling. The sound was horrible. It cut through Sam, making her hands tremble. Dani shrugged off the shoulder strap. The high, sharp sound of metal being torn asunder came to Sam and she looked up to see bloody fingernails poking through the roof. There was a popping sound, uncomfortably similar to a can opener piercing the lid of a can, and a second set of fingers burst through from above.

"Jesus!" Sam hollered, fumbling with the Remington shotgun, attempting to bring it around. She looked straight up in time to see the roof of the GT-S torn back with a deep, sharp, rippling sound. She had heard that sound before, in auto accidents. The sky was suddenly visible, the deep black curtain of night giving way to a violet and gold haze. The daylight was coming fast and hard.

Isabella appeared over the massive rip she had torn in the roof, looking down with a twisted smile. The vampire's left eye was a bubbling mass of gray-white activity, as if a dozen gore-drenched worms were crawling in the empty socket. A black hole was visible in the creature's forehead. It leaked gray-white liquid.

"Mom!" Dani shouted in concern.

"I'm here," Isabella said.

The word Dani had used practically shattered Sam. Was this creature Dani's natural mother? Was that the reason the vampires had wanted Dani so badly?

No, Sam reminded herself. Female vampires were sterile. Only human women could carry the children of the damned.

Isabella reached down for Sam, the vampire's fingers lean and sharp.

I'm Dani's mother, I raised her, Sam thought as she aimed the Remington at the vampire's chest. Sam's finger curled around the trigger as Isabella's hand approached her eyes. "Fuck you!"

Sam felt something slam into her from her right side. The shotgun went off, the roar deafening. Thrown against the door, Sam lost her grip on the wheel. The GT-S careened to the left and grazed the divider. Another car rushed past.

It was Dani, Sam realized dully. Dani had saved the vampire. Her daughter's hands were clawing at her flesh, leaving deep, bloody furrows.

"Dani, the road!" Sam screamed. Her daughter looked up and Sam pushed the girl away. Dani fell back into her own seat as Sam reached for the wheel. The car veered sharply to the right and came within inches of plowing into a red Ford. Sam steadied the GT-S and heard a wailing scream from above.

The vampire was still with them, hanging on to the frame of the vehicle. Sam raised the Remington.

"Do it!" Dani screamed.

For an instant, Sam was convinced she had her daughter back. Dani wanted her to shoot the vampire. Suddenly, she felt a raking talon graze her throat and she understood that Dani had not been talking to her. Before she could fire, Dani gripped the stock of the shotgun. Sam pressed herself back into the seat and looked up, determined to stare her executioner in the eye.

Isabella was laughing, her head partially inside the car, when suddenly her expression changed. She twisted around, looking through the car's front window, fear etched on her once lovely face. Sam shifted her gaze to follow the vampire's and saw that they were speeding toward the passenger side of a pickup truck.

It can't end like this, it can't, it can't—

Sam hit the brakes, but it was too late. The GT-S squealed in protest as it collided with the truck. Dani had not been belted in. She was flung forward, toward the windshield, which she cracked open with her body. Sam felt the strap of the shoulder harness bite into her chest as the car struck with the high, grinding sound of ruined metal. She gasped, suddenly unable to breathe. From the edge of her vision, she saw Isabella fly over the top of their car, slam into the side window of the truck with a bloody crash that shattered the window, then flip over the top of the vehicle, vanishing from view.

The pickup had whirled in an arc, dragging the GT-S around so that it sat crossing the lanes of traffic instead of flowing with them. The truck's front bumper touched that of the GT-S. They were stopped.

Sam fought off the onslaught of shock. She couldn't breathe. Trembling, she clutched at her chest, wheezing, trying to draw a breath, and finally, one came. Tears of relief falling from her eyes, Sam drew a series of deep breaths, ignoring the pain in her chest and lungs. She turned suddenly, to the passenger's side, and felt as if a half-dozen knives had been driven between her ribs. Gasping with unexpected pain, Sam looked in horror at her daughter's body. The windshield was ruined, a spidery mesh of glass. She would have to kick it out to see where she was going. Dani was curled up in a fetal position on the dash, facing the glass.

Ignoring the red-hot, blinding pain, Sam freed herself from the restraining seat belt and reached for her daughter. She felt for a pulse and was relieved to find a strong one. Dani twitched and shifted in her position enough to prompt Sam to risk moving her. She shrugged off the harness with the Remington, afraid that the weapon would go off, and put the shotgun on the dashboard. Sam carefully pulled Dani back and set her on the passenger seat. Resetting the seat belt, Sam dragged the blanket out of the back and covered her daughter with it. Drawing her jacket over her face and arm, Sam punched the shattered windshield out of the car with the Remington. A few shards of glass pierced the girl's leather jacket. Sam gingerly plucked all that had fallen on her daughter's still form, then settled back behind the wheel.

For the first time, she could see the driver of the other car. He was out of the pickup, stumbling around. Sam looked at the hood of her car. It had been driven upward from the impact point, the chassis scrunched severely at the front end, on the passenger side. Steam was coming from the car. Sam noticed that the car was still running. Her need to escape was overpowering. She threw the car into reverse and found that the front bumper was locked with that of the pickup.

"Son of a"—Sam stopped, drawing a painful breath—"son of a bitch!"

"You miserable whore," a voice called from above. "If you've hurt her, *I'll kill you.*"

Sam did not need to look around to identify the owner of that voice. It was the vampire. Sam floored the car and heard an angry, shrill cry of metal grinding against metal, but the GT-S could not pull free. Sam looked up and saw the vampire circling overhead in wide, graceful arcs.

"Fuck!" Sam shouted.

Above, Isabella laughed. The woman seemed to be prolonging her attack, tweaking up Sam's fear as if she were feeding from it. Heart thundering, Sam realized that the vampire was doing exactly that. In a fit of desperation, she threw the GT-S into drive and plowed forward, slamming into the pickup, then went into reverse and felt the car shake free of the pickup, her bumper clanking to the ground.

Sam jumped as the Remington dropped into her lap. She forgot she'd put the weapon on the dash. There was a shrill, piercing cry, and Sam knew that the vampire was coming in for another attack. The Remington was primed. As she slammed the GT-S back, Sam stopped the car suddenly and threw on the emergency brake. She took the shotgun in both hands and found her prey by standing in her seat and twisting around. The searing pain made her wince and drove the breath from her, but she ignored her sudden agony and targeted the vampire. She heard Dani moaning, coming around again.

"Mom?" She squinted twice, looked up.

"I'm here, baby," Sam said in a hoarse whisper

as the vampire drove herself forward, sweeping down on Sam with the exact same motion she had used on the videotape. Sam watched the vampire's gnawing mash of teeth as the creature sailed closer, then Sam dropped down into her seat as the vampire clutched at the spot where Sam had been an instant before. Raising the Remington, Sam trained it on the vampire's midsection and fired.

Isabella was nearly blown in two. Her stomach exploded in a bloodred cloud, her legs pitching and floundering, veering to the left, her upper torso angling to the right. Her body flailed as it hurtled over their car and struck the ground hard, rolling until it sank to a halt.

"NO!" Dani screamed as she unhooked herself from the seat belt and scrambled over the dashboard, ignoring the glass. She leaped over the hood and faltered as she hit the ground. Taking a few steps, Dani fell once again, then half-stumbled, half-crawled to the spot where Isabella lay.

The woman's sole remaining eye was open and staring. She was not breathing. Dani saw an ugly piece of ivory bone jutting from her back and had to turn away as she vomited blood. She forced herself to look back at her friend.

"This can't be happening, it can't," she chanted, leaning down close to Isabella's face, kissing the woman. There was no response. She reached out with the silver thread and tried to make contact with Isabella's mind.

Nothing.

Wailing with grief, Dani picked up Isabella's hand and placed it on her hair. The caress Dani enjoyed as the dead hand fell away was an accident. Dani threw her head back and screamed until her lungs were raw. She did not hear Sam get out of the car, the blanket in her hands. It wasn't until she felt her skin begin to smolder that she thought to train her attention on the sky.

The sun was rising.

Hours ago, she had leaned out of the stolen cruiser and prepared herself for death. She thought that hers would be a noble sacrifice, she would die to save others, all her potential victims through the ages. That had been before she had actually been shot, and known the agony of having steel jacketed bullets tear through her. Again, there was a momentary urge to stand and wait for the sunlight to consume her; her true family was dead, after all. She had nothing to live for. An existence of killing others like Madison and Hal was all she could look forward to, and she would have to face it alone.

"Dani!"

She squeezed her eyes shut and did not look in Samantha Walthers's direction. She wasn't alone. There was another reason for her to continue.

Footsteps drew close as the heat from above became more intense, raking fingers of sunlight causing her skin to smolder, steam rising from her flesh.

"Dani!"

She sensed Walthers standing only a few feet away. Turning, she saw the woman holding out a heavy blanket.

"Please, honey," Sam cried. "You've got to come with me. You can't stay out here."

Dani smiled darkly. The woman was in terrible pain, both from the accident and from the realization that her adopted daughter was descended from a race of monsters. Nodding, Dani rose and allowed Samantha to drape the blanket over her. She pulled it tight over her face, like a shroud, leaving a slight crevasse through which she could see. The heat was becoming unbearable.

"Baby, you're going to be okay," Sam said, "it's all going to be all right. But you've got to come with me."

"I'll come with you, Samantha. I will."

Dani watched as her adopted mother flinched at these words, then nodded and stepped into the street. There was oncoming traffic in the other lanes, a few cars. Sam pulled the submachine gun and walked into the middle of the road, gun leveled at an approaching car, which screeched to a stop. A black BMW.

"Get out of the car!" Sam screamed at the driver. The man wore pinstripes and suspenders. "Now! Move it!"

The man nearly wet himself as he scrambled to comply.

"Keys in the car?" she asked.

"Yes."

"Then get the hell out of here. Run!"

He bolted in the other direction, nearly getting himself killed as he crossed the lane of traffic snaking around his stopped Beemer. Sam had already taken a large satchel out of the Toyota's trunk. She retrieved it and gestured for Dani to follow her. The girl ran to her side and entered the passenger side door. Her hand sizzled on contact with the metal handle, which was reflecting sunlight.

"Shit!" she cried. "Burned myself."

Sam got behind the wheel and handed the satchel to Dani. "There's gloves in there."

Dani unzipped the satchel and dug through the collection of weaponry and ammo Sam had stuffed inside until she found the gloves. A leather face mask, identical to the one Allen Halpern wore when Sam found him at home, was there, too. As Sam pulled the stolen Beemer into traffic, Dani slipped the leather mask over her head, keeping the heavy blanket over her at all times.

Sam looked over, disturbed at the sight her daughter made. But the girl needed the protection and these windows weren't even tinted. She wished she could have kept the GT-S, but it could have given out at any time and even if it hadn't, the police would have spotted it easily. Try finding a single BMW in this town, however, and you're looking at a shell game on wheels.

They drove for five minutes in silence. Sam pulled into a strip mall near a bar, where she pried the license plate loose from the BMW and switched it with a similar looking car parked beneath a deserted streetlight far from the closest store.

Oldest story in the world, she thought crazily, boy meets girl in a bar, he gets lucky and one of them leaves their car in the lot overnight. Well, whoever it was that wanted action is sure as hell going to get some once the cops find the stolen plates on their car.

She wasn't happy about this, but she knew it was necessary if she was going to get away and stay clean.

They drove for another ten minutes, Dani huddled under the blanket. It was heavy canvas, specially reinforced to keep out sunlight. Sam had found it with the weapons and guessed its use immediately.

They went through the streets, observing all speed limits, blending in with traffic. Sam anxiously checked the rearview mirror for police cars. They seemed to be clear. Sam prayed it would last.

"Good old L.A.," Sam said, forcing a wry tone as she inclined her head toward a Porsche dealership. "You wouldn't see one of those back in Tampa."

Dani grunted under the blanket, her voice distorted by the leather mask. She raised the blanket a few inches, allowing Sam to see her blazing gold eyes. Calmly, Dani said, "Samantha?"

"Stop calling me that. I'm your mother, dammit."

Beneath the leather, Dani laughed. It was a harsh, sarcastic laugh. "There's something you should know."

Dani's voice startled Sam almost as much as the use of her first name. She had never been anything but "Mom" or "Mother" to Dani, depending on the girl's mood.

"What is it, baby?" Sam asked with a tremulous voice. Tears gathered in her eyes.

Dani's eyes narrowed and became intense. "Samantha, the moment we get to wherever you're taking me, I am going to *kill* you for what you've done."

Twenty-nine

Sam drew a deep, sharp breath, as if she had been struck squarely in the chest. Tears fell from the corners of her eyes. The road before her blurred and Sam wiped away the sweat that was steadily descending. Her fingers groped for the AC, but she couldn't find the controls. To do that, she would have to look away from the road. Then she might have to see Dani's eyes once again. Those eyes had been filled with malice. They were not her daughter's eyes.

"Didn't you hear me, Samantha? I said that I intend to kill you."

"Don't say that, Dani. I know it's not true."

Dani smiled. She had told Isabella that she could never kill again. That had been before the Walthers woman had come back into her life and destroyed any hope she had of coming to terms with her inhuman blood.

"You think you know so much about me," Dani said contemptuously.

"I know *everything* about you."

"You do."

"That's right."

There was a pause. Sam watched the road. Dani could feel the woman's fear. She didn't need her silver thread for this. The emotions radiated from the woman in sumptuous waves. Dani consumed

377

them greedily.

"I've killed people, Samantha."

Sam shook violently, then calmed herself. "Who?"

"My friend Madison."

Biting her lip, Sam asked, "Only her?"

"You sound disappointed."

"Only her?"

Dani hated the woman's tone. "You haven't been listening to the radio. Because of me, maybe a dozen others are dead. Then there's Willis. I killed him, too. But that was a long time ago."

The muscles in Sam's face drew tight. She pressed her lips together, attempting to stay calm. The very concept of her baby growing up to murder someone horrified her. She had to somehow focus beyond her emotions. Dani wasn't in control of herself. She had been used by the monsters. You don't blame a loaded gun, you blame the person who picked it up and fired it.

"Madison is the only one you murdered," Sam said.

"Are you having a problem hearing me, Samantha?" Dani said angrily. *"Yes."*

Sam nodded. If what Halpern had told Sam was correct, her daughter could still be saved. An Initiate was turned with its first kill, while under the influence of its mentor. It took on all the characteristics of a full vampire, but would not remain as such unless it made a second kill, on its own, within three days of the first.

"When was it that you killed Madison?"

Dani told her. Sam felt her body stiffen. Two nights had passed since the murder. Tonight was all Dani had left.

"Honey, you've got to listen to me. There's still a chance—"

"There's no going back, Samantha. Even if there

378

was, I wouldn't take it. I'm happy like this. I like it."

"You don't mean that."

"Of course I do."

Sam swallowed hard. "You're still a human being, Dani. You're not like them. Not the way you think."

"Christ, are you in for a surprise."

"Maybe we both are."

Dani shook her head. "I'm not human, Samantha. I can get into your head. I can find out everything you know. I can see what scares you. You can't hide anything from me."

"I don't want to. Do it."

Dani was silent. "You don't get it, do you? I can make you do things. If I wanted, I could make you *kill yourself* and save me the bother. You could be just like your momma."

Sam restrained a pained cry. She thought of the doppelganger. It had planned to make Sam shoot herself, and it had used Sam's troubled childhood against her. Dani's behavior was not unlike that of the doppelganger.

They're not the same. My daughter's not like that thing!

No, Sam realized. Dani was more advanced than the doppelganger. The vampires had turned her. Body, mind, and soul. But there was still a chance to get her back. Sam clung to that thought.

"I love you, Dani. No matter what."

"You fucking liar!" Dani screamed. She lashed out with her hand, punching it through the window beside her. Glass flew outward and the sudden explosion of sound caused Sam to lose control of the BMW for an instant, then quickly recover it. Dani ripped the glove from her hand and held her hand out of the blanket's reach, where Sam could see sunlight falling directly upon it.

379

"Put the glove on, Dani!" Sam screamed.

"Why? I'm human. I'm just like you!" The flesh of her hand sizzled. The tiny hairs below her knuckles burst into flame. *"Isn't that right?"*

"Jesus, Dani, stop it!" Sam cried as she grabbed her daughter's hand and forced it back under the blanket. She could tell from the first moment of resistance that Dani's strength was amazing. Inhuman. Sam realized that the only reason Dani's hand obeyed Sam was because Dani had allowed it. Sam started to weep openly, unable to restrain her emotions.

"I don't know why you're upset, Samantha. Are you afraid I'm going to drag out your death? That I'm going to make you really suffer? That's reasonable. 'Cause that's what I'm going to do."

"Dani, please, don't you know how much I love—"

The girl shot forward, slamming Sam's head into the glass beside her. The BMW careened wildly. "Say it one more *fucking* time, and I'll rip your head off!"

They were about to sideswipe another car and Dani backed off, taking the steering wheel until she felt Sam's hands upon it once more.

"All right," Sam said with a ragged breath. "I won't say the words. But you know it's true. See for yourself, if you think I'm lying to you. I don't have anything to hide."

Dani settled back in her chair and drew the reinforced blanket around her. She was tired of people telling her what to do. Especially the Walthers woman.

Despite herself, Dani allowed her silver thread to tentatively extend to her adopted mother. She withdrew her power a moment too late to avoid the glowing rush of love that exploded from Samantha Walthers. The emotions were similar to those Isa-

380

bella had held for her, but they were stronger in Samantha, a burning nova rather than a tiny flame. The near constant, dull throb of her hunger abated for a moment. She could not risk using her power again. She would not be able to endure another brush with Samantha Walthers's perfect love.

"Dani? Are you all right?"

"Just drive the fucking car," Dani spat. She clutched at her temples.

Samantha Walthers's perfect love.

Ridiculous. Walthers had betrayed her and wanted to kill her. She had no understanding of what it meant to be one of Dani's kind. The blood of immortals did not run in her veins. Walthers loved the child she had molded and shaped. She didn't even know the *woman* Dani had become in the past few days. Dani regained the hatred she had nearly lost her tenuous hold upon.

"Dani, I'm serious. Is it the light? Are you—"

"Shut the fuck up and drive, will you!?"

Sam turned away.

Dani recalled her brief encounter with Samantha's thoughts. There had been something beneath the warm, encompassing layer of compassion and love. Dani had sensed an underlying current of anger, fear, and revulsion.

Anger at herself for not being there when you needed her, for making the mistakes she made. Fear that something terrible would happen to you, something she wouldn't be able to prevent. Revulsion for the blood-need clouding her daughter's reason, the painful addiction that made you refuse to see the truth.

You feel those things, too, Dani! You feel them!

Lies. All of it lies. She's angry at me for not being her fucking little girl anymore. Afraid of me

381

for what I might do to her. Repulsed by what I am, by what I've really been all along. She never wanted to see what I was.

"Pull off the road," Dani said. "I want to show you something."

Sam looked in her direction. Dani could feel genuine fear lapping off the woman in waves. It was delicious.

"Dani, if you do something to me now, you're not going to make it to shelter. You know that, don't you?"

There was something in the woman's eyes. Concern, certainly. But was her concern for Dani, or for herself?

Dani considered reaching out with her power, but she was afraid. It was pointless, anyway.

She came back for you. She wants to help you. Bullshit.

Walthers hadn't been motivated out of love. It had been fear. She was afraid that Dani and the others would come after her eventually. That's why she attacked them first. She could never have beaten them if they were ready for her.

"Come on," Dani said. "Pull off. I'm not stupid."

Sam nodded and drove the BMW to the shoulder. Cars whipped past them. Dani raised the blanket and Sam held it up for her. With a short, cruel laugh, Dani unzipped her jacket, exposing her chest and stomach. Her gunshot wounds were still healing, and her skin was puckered with small round holes where the bullets had entered and exited her flesh. She knew Samantha would recognize bullet wounds.

"Sweet Jesus," Sam cried, her trembling hands going to the wounds, touching them gently. "Tell me what happened."

"What do you *think* happened? I was shot, you

382

stupid bitch."

Sam flinched. Her daughter had never spoken to her this way. She hated it.

"I was shot four times," Dani said. "And I'm feeling pretty goddamned good, all things considered. So, do you still think I'm human?"

"What happened to you?" Sam asked forcefully.

"Do you mean how was I shot, or what happened to me in general? Since I'm not your pretty, precious little baby anymore?"

"How were you *shot?*"

Dani grinned beneath the mask. The smile dropped when she realized that she had sounded exactly like Angel.

Sam obviously had no knowledge of the slaughter at the mall, or that her adopted child had nearly been blown to pieces. Describing the event in meticulous detail, Dani watched the blood drain from her adoptive mother's face.

"Dani, you've got to listen to me. I can help you."

"You're the one who's not listening," Dani said as she zipped up the leather jacket. "I don't want anything from you. I don't want your help. I don't want your pity. I'm telling you, Samantha. I came with you for *one* reason. You killed my family. And for that, I'm going to kill you."

Sam squeezed her eyes shut. Dani wasn't going to listen to her. Turning away, she threw the stolen BMW in drive and reentered traffic on the highway.

"I can't stop you, Dani."

"Sure you could," Dani said, her words muted and distorted by the leather mask and her open hatred. "You could try, anyway. That'll make it more fun for me when I tear you apart."

They drove in silence.

Suddenly, Dani recognized the area. "Malibu.

We're going to the beach house!"

"Yeah, honey. That's where we're going. You'll be safe. There's a concrete cellar. Reinforced. Nothing can get through. No sunlight."

"That's very considerate of you," Dani said venomously.

Sam tried to force her jangling nerves to ease. "Are you all right?"

"What do you mean?"

"The sunlight. Your hand. Are you all right?"

"Uh-huh."

Silence. Sam concentrated on the road. Mist was burning off the greens to the side of the road. The burning amber at their backs had consumed the sky. The sun had risen.

For a moment, Dani felt concern that Sam might pass out behind the wheel. Her head was suddenly filled with images of cars flying off embankments and exploding into flames. Sam had sat with her daughter watching cop shows on television, laughing with her about this phenomena. It took a lot to blow up a car in real life, but on TV, you could sneeze on one and see it explode.

Laughing with her mother. Sharing. Perfect love, blossoming like an explosion of flames.

Suddenly she recalled her last sight of Bill Yoshino. He had been standing in the doorway of the exploding warehouse, a look of anger and surprise on his face as the fires wrapped around him from behind, like the arms of a lover. He had exposed her to all she had been curious about, he had released her true self from the prison of lies Samantha Walthers had constructed for her adopted daughter.

A second bloodred explosion rocked her memories. Sam firing the Remington, blowing Isabella apart. Dear, gentle Isabella, who had been there for Dani when Samantha had not been, who

384

would have been alive with Dani an eternity after Walthers was turned to dust. Isabella, who had loved Dani for who she was, not who the woman wanted her to be.

A third, shocking wave of sound and force. The warehouse shuddering, bricks flying from the walls, into the alley. Angel, the one she would have enjoyed watching die, had been taken mercifully and quick, somewhere near the heart of the blast, hidden from sight.

They were dead, all of them. Dani was alone, with no one who could guide her through her new life, no one to help her understand and survive. In a way, she was dead, too. But she had one last task to perform.

Sam reached over and touched her shoulder. She had evidently noticed the tremors raking through the girl.

"Honey, please. Are you okay?"

Dani slapped her hand away. "Are you out of your fucking mind? Am I okay? You think it's that simple? I was shot four times, and I'm still walking around. I killed Madison. I ripped her heart out of her fucking chest, for chrissake. I'm a vampire, you moron. No, I am not okay."

Sam was startled. This was Dani's first admission that she was anything but thrilled with her inhuman condition.

"Dani, let me in. I can help you."

"Give me a fucking break! I get high drinking blood. I can jump off a goddamned cliff and fly, if I want. If I needed to, I could probably lift this fucking car and throw it. Does that sound like I need help? I'm a god, for chrissake, and you keep treating me as if I'm still your little girl. That's all you think of me, isn't it?"

Sam would have cried, but her tears had been exhausted. "No baby. I think you're all grown up.

385

But I don't think you're done needing me."

"You're wrong."

They were on the last stretch leading to the beach house. Suddenly, the two-story structure loomed into view. Sam pulled into the drive, beside the Karmann-Ghia.

"We'll see," Sam said as she threw the car into park and killed the engine. "Wait here. I've got to take care of something; then I'll get another blanket, and we'll get you inside the house."

Sam didn't wait for her daughter to reply. She went to the back of the BMW, removed the stolen plate with trembling fingers, and switched it for the license plate on the Ghia. Then she put her old car in neutral and rolled it into the shrubbery, where it would be out of view. She looked back to the BMW and saw a shapeless, still form sitting beneath the blanket. Running inside the house, Sam found the second blanket in the basement, and turned to look in the direction of Tory's body. Approaching it fearfully, Sam lifted the body, hauled it from the basement, and hid it in the pantry across from the basement door. Pausing, she stared at the keypad security lock beside the door. She had spent time examining it before she left the beach house last time, and had learned its secrets. Taking a deep breath, she forced her hand to stop shaking long enough to key in a sequence of numbers.

When she was finished, Sam left the kitchen, where angry beams of sunlight sliced through the windows and created yellow-white blocks on the floor. Crossing through the house, Sam regarded every window as an enemy.

Returning to the car, Sam opened the door and held out the second blanket. "Ready?"

Dani burst from the car, Sam wrapping the second blanket around her. Together they ran to the front door, entered the house, and ran through. Beams of light struck Dani full on. There was a sizzle and the disturbing smell of cooked meat as steam rose from the blankets.

"Go, go!" Sam hollered, guiding her daughter through the house until they reached the door to the basement. "Step down. Careful, baby, careful!"

Dani hurried down the first few stairs, out of the light. She threw off the blankets, practically drinking in the darkness. Yanking off the gloves, mask, and her jacket, Dani allowed her hair to fall free on her shoulders. She turned suddenly, and saw her mother standing at the top of the stairs, her hand on something next to the door, just out of sight.

"You think you hate me, but you don't," Sam said quietly.

Dani heard a series of clicks. Lights came on in the basement. A generator kicked into life. Cool air blew from vents near the ceiling. It would be so easy for her to take command of the Walthers woman, to force her to come down and join her in the basement. She coiled her power, then let it drain away.

"I don't love you," Dani said. "I *can't* love anymore. That's why Bill could never say it back to me. It's impossible for my kind."

"I told you, you're wrong," Sam said as she stepped into the basement and yanked the door shut behind her. A series of electronic clicks and a steady humming sounded for a moment, then the mechanisms in the heavy steel door powered off and were still. "Now I'm going to prove it."

Thirty

Dani stared at Samantha Walthers in shock. "God, you're a stupid bitch. Those people you killed were my family. My *real* family."

"No. We're family," Sam said as she descended the stairs. "The only family that matters."

Dani stood rigid as Sam approached her. The woman gave her a wan smile, brushed past her on the stairs, then descended to the basement floor. Dani stared at her, incredulous.

Sam walked to the pair of weapons lockers and stripped off the guns she had been carrying. Cracking open the doors, she placed the Berettas on the shelf and hung up the Remington and the machine gun. The bag with the rest of her armament had been left in the stolen BMW. An amateurish mistake. Nevertheless, she certainly didn't have to worry about being left weaponless, the cabinets were filled. But there were still a half-dozen chocolate bars in the bag, provided they hadn't melted already. The basement had no food stores. The humans who had been trapped down here were all the vampires needed to sate their appetites.

Sam stripped off her watch and set its alarm. "This will go off at seven tonight. The sun will be down by then, it should be safe for you."

"I don't love you anymore," Dani said weakly.

"Yeah, maybe. I figure if I'm still alive when this

goes off, then maybe you do." She tapped the last button on the watch then shook her neck out. Her chest still burned where the seat belt had grabbed her, but so long as she made no sudden movements to either side, she was all right.

Across from Sam, Dani wondered why she hadn't attacked the woman yet. The human was walking with pain. She seemed to be exhausted. Turning in Dani's direction, Sam stopped suddenly, staring at her in wonder. "What?" Dani asked.

" 'Why Miss Jones, you're beautiful,' " Sam whispered, the words laced with pain.

Dani understood the reference. A movie she had watched on the late show with Sam many years ago. Michael Caine or someone like that, removing his secretary's glasses, noticing her for the first time, though she had been trying to get his attention the entire film.

"You really are all grown up," Sam said sadly. Her tone was that of a parent who had missed seeing her child's first steps.

"I've changed in a lot of ways," Dani said, suddenly aware of the dull, throbbing ache of pain in her stomach. Her hunger was starting to flare. "You want to know what I did to Willis, the son of a bitch that trapped me? You know, the one *you* couldn't protect me from?"

Sam closed her eyes and drew a sharp breath.

"I can tell you now," Dani said. "I remember it. I like remembering it."

Wearily, Sam crossed to the staircase and sat down. She winced with pain. "Sure. We've got twelve hours. Tell me whatever you want to tell me."

"It started coming back to me 'cause I was thinking maybe I'd do the same thing to you."

"Whatever."

The word infuriated Dani. She crossed to the stairs and slammed her hand into the concrete beside Sam's head. The blow connected with a sharp crack. Powdered rock filtered to the ground. Sam barely flinched.

"Don't act like you're not afraid of me!"

Sam looked up at her sadly. "I'm afraid *for* you, Dani."

"I'm not listening to this."

"You should listen to me, Dani. I'm your mother. Me. Not that *thing* we left on the road back there. Don't you understand that?"

"You're meat. You're prey."

Sam hung her head.

"You are going to *die!*" Dani wailed.

"Then I might as well tell you I love you."

Dani trembled.

"Just words."

"Find out."

Dani shook her head. She could have extended her silver thread, but she was afraid to learn the truth behind those words.

Sam left the stairs and found a rolled-up sleeping bag in the corner. "You don't hate me, Dani. But I think I understand why you're trying to convince yourself that you do."

"You don't understand anything about me," Dani said, the hunger swelling inside her.

Sam pulled the drawstring on the sleeping bag. "There's another one of these in that corner, over there."

"What are you talking about?"

"I'm tired, I'm going to get some sleep. Haven't you had enough for one day? I know I have. It's over, Dani. You're safe."

Dani hugged herself, restraining the urge to leap at the woman, and savage her. "Yeah? Well, *you're* not safe."

"Doesn't matter. You're okay. That's enough for me."

"You're full of shit."

Sam stripped out of her clothes, leaving on her T-shirt and panties. She laid out the sleeping bag and crawled inside, turning her back on her daughter. "Goodnight, Dani."

"You've got to be fucking kidding me!"

"I'm tired," Sam growled. Her tone was one that had always quieted Dani in the past. It achieved the same effect this time.

Dani watched her mother. She couldn't tell if the woman was faking or not. She must have been insane. Didn't she understand the risk?

Well, Dani, here's your shot, the demon whispered in her tortured mind. *Waiting for a sign from God or something? You wanted her dead, go over there and kill her. She's not going to stop you.*

Shut up, Dani hissed. She felt a slight burning in her stomach as the hunger moved through her, but Dani sensed that this was a *manageable* hunger. It had not been brought about by true need. The blood she had taken from Isabella would see her through, at least until nightfall. Her desire for blood had been spawned by the nearness of helpless prey.

So why not feed? Why not take the Walthers woman now, have done with it?

No, Dani decided. It would be better this way. Let her be afraid.

She reached out tentatively with her silver thread and found Sam sound asleep. Entering her dreams would have been simple, an adventure, even. She had never done that before. She was certain that she could leave nightmares for the woman. Dani could use the uncharted vistas of Sam's dream world against her.

But oddly enough, she was feeling sluggish. Her body was becoming acclimated to the natural cycles of sunrise and sunset. Though she was perfectly safe, her blood warned her that it was unnatural for her to be awake. She would be better off gaining some rest. Walthers was no threat.

Dani forced down her hunger, taking control of the need coursing through her. She found the sleeping bag her mother had mentioned and stripped off her ruined clothes. She stank like hell. Blood and piss. A shower would have been wonderful right about now.

Sliding into the sleeping bag, Dani curled into a fetal position, amazed at how much she desired her mother's touch. If she had possessed the strength, she might have dragged herself to where Samantha Walthers lay and slipped in beside her. But her strength had vanished and her hunger was a steady, annoying ache that faded as she surrendered to the darkness.

Isabella stroked her hair. The woman's hand was soft and comforting.

"Mom?"

"I'm right here, baby."

Dani sprang to full awareness. It had not been Isabella who had spoken. It had been the *other* Walthers.

She lay in the sleeping bag with her adopted mother. Sam was curled up behind her, stroking her hair. Dani swatted at her hand and scrambled away, cursing. Stabbing her hands through her hair, Dani sprang to her feet and walked into a wall. The pain she felt as she collided with the concrete was nothing compared to the ravenous fire snaking through her gut. The hunger had returned. This time it was not manageable. This time the need was real.

The alarm on Sam's watch went off suddenly, a series of high shrill beeps that made both women jump.

"Oh God," Sam said with a laugh as she fumbled to turn the alarm off. The beeps continued. The smile that had reached Dani's face faded.

"Turn it off."

"Yeah, I'm trying."

Dani's senses were more acute than they had ever been. The sharp tones emitted by the watch seemed to echo off the walls to her. Her head began to throb. She felt a reverberating pain in her gums with each tiny beep.

"I said, turn it off." Dani's voice was darker, menacing in tone. "I'm not going to tell you again."

Sam had taken the watch off and was tapping at several buttons on its side. With unexpected speed and ferocity, Dani crossed the room and snatched the watch out of her hand, smashing it to bits against the wall. She slammed the hand against the wall again and again, throwing her head back as her incisors sprang from their housings and her hands transformed into talons.

The hunger was her world, she was an animal, with an animal's needs, there was blood present and by God, she was going to have it.

No, no, no, please don't make me! the little girl who had been Danielle Walthers screamed in the body of the beast. But it was a small, pitiful wail.

The vampire turned, golden eyes blazing, and stopped.

The prey was holding a flamethrower, the gas jet lit. A tiny spark of flame erupted from the nozzle. The vampire took a step forward and the prey released a three-foot-long tongue of flame that scorched the air separating them. The monster withdrew, and Dani suddenly found herself in control, staring down at her naked body in horror and shame.

"Omigod!" Dani cried, turning away from her adoptive mother as she went to collect her discarded clothing. She dressed hurriedly, then turned to face Walthers, who was keeping the flamethrower aimed in her direction. Her fear suddenly gave way to annoyance, then anger. Who the hell was this woman to threaten her in such a manner?

393

"Dani, can you hear me?"

"I'm looking right at you," Dani snarled. "What do you think?"

"I'm wondering if I'm talking to my daughter."

There was a pause. "You never had a daughter."

Sam bit her lip. "I raised you, Dani. It doesn't matter whose blood is in you."

"It doesn't?"

"No."

"Then put down the flamethrower."

"I don't think so."

Dani tilted her head slightly to one side, like a wolf. Bill used to do this. It was disarming, in an evil way. "We both know you could never use it."

"Then it shouldn't frighten you."

"Who said that it did?" Dani drew a few steps closer. Sam backed away. Dani grinned, coming closer again. Sam moved back, edging closer to the weapons locker.

Beyond her mother, Dani caught sight of the vast array of ordnance inside the cabinet. "What the hell is that for?"

"You tell me."

"How the hell should I know, Samantha?"

"Don't call me that. You know who I am."

Dani laughed. The hunger had not left her, but it had not destroyed her ability to reason, either. An odd sound came from Walthers. Dani seemed perplexed.

"Stomach growling," Sam explained. "I'm hungry."

"Really?" Dani asked quietly. "Me too."

Dani could feel the fear and revulsion that radiated from the woman. It caused Samantha terrible pain to see her baby girl dressed like a whore, shot up and covered in blood and brains and piss. Dani reveled in the fear she provoked. Hungrily, she reached out with her silver thread, anxious to take more of the woman's fear.

Suddenly her world was replaced by another. With a startled cry she fell to the cold floor of the cellar, her eyes wide, her lips drawn back to reveal human teeth. She shuddered and moaned.

Sam set the flamethrower down and raced to her daughter's side. The pupils of the child's golden eyes dilated then shrank several times, as if the light was constantly changing, but the lamps hanging from the ceiling gave off a steady yellow-orange glow.

"Baby, what is it?" Sam begged.

"They had this room designed special," Dani whispered. "Tory had known about this room, never thought they would use it on her. She wasn't Wildling. How could they do this to her?"

Sam tried desperately to understand what was happening.

"Holy Christ, why did they do that?" Dani muttered.

"What are you talking about, Dani?"

"They turned her, just like they did me. Bill and Isabella. But when the time came for her to kill on her own, she couldn't do it, so they locked her in this room they had built in case they ever had to deal with Wildlings. What the hell are Wildlings!?"

"Vampires who kill their own," Sam whispered. She held her daughter as she convulsed.

" *'Why did Tory tell you all this?'* " Dani whispered. The voice Samantha Walthers heard in her mind was her own.

" *'She was very lonely. She had been rejected by her own kind.'* " Allen Halpern's voice.

" *'Why? What did she do?'* "

" *'She had been turned. She had shared blood with a full vampire, she had killed while under his influence. But when the time came for her second kill, which had to be made before three nights elapsed, she could not bring herself to do it. There was still too much of the human*

395

in her. She could not kill on her own.' "

Sam finally understood. Dani had gone into her mind and had witnessed one of her memories, a strong one that had been on the surface of her thoughts, her meeting with Allen Halpern. "What else do you see?"

"They put Tory down here with a human. The stuff from the lockers had all been moved upstairs."

Dani's pupils were expanding and contracting as if she were in a nightclub, exposed to strobe lights. Sam reached down and stroked her hair.

"It was the third night for Tory. They told her that if she didn't kill by the third night, she would die. But it wasn't true. They lied to her, just like they lied to me!"

"I've been trying to tell you, baby. You just wouldn't listen, I'm sorry. I'm so sorry. . . ."

"She became human again. They abandoned her. They turned their backs on her. They went away, oh God, they went away and left her all alone. . . ."

Dani was crying, wailing in grief. Sam leaned down and kissed her forehead. She felt a new wellspring of grief over Tory, the girl she had been forced to kill. The child had been a murderer, Sam had seen the tapes. She had also been lonely and frightened. In her mind, Sam had a difficult time reconciling the creature's dual nature.

"I won't leave you, honey," Sam said. "I won't ever go away, I won't—"

Dani's eyes suddenly focused. The hunger pulsed and pounded inside her. Her hand transformed into a talon, flicked up with a lightning-quick motion, and was jammed beneath Sam's jaw.

"Gotcha."

Sam issued a brief cry of surprise. She forced away her emotions. "Dani, what you just saw was real."

"How would you know?" Dani asked as she grabbed Walthers by her hair and slowly rose.

396

"I know all about Tory. I know how Yoshino was using her."

"I don't want to hear your lies."

"They're not lies, Dani!" Sam pleaded, wondering how she had once again lost control of the situation so quickly.

"Tell me. Make it short."

Sam related all she had learned from Allen Halpern and described what she had seen on the tapes. Forcing down her tears, she described each of her encounters with the doppelganger, including her fatal confrontation with Tory.

"Don't you get it, Dani? They set us up. Both of us. People like Yoshino don't do anything unless they have a reason. There was something they wanted from you, Dani. You must have figured that much, anyway."

Dani stared at her mother. Her mind was awash with confused images: Madison telling her about the "bad relationship" Bill had been involved in six months ago. That had been Tory. A blood haze descended on the memory. The sunset, Madison watching the sunset, the sky turning deep scarlet, red as blood, waves suddenly rising up before them, crimson waves that fell on them and consumed them.

Your blood, sister-love. You cannot deny what you are.

Isabella's words. An image of Isabella turning suddenly in the cruiser, more animal than human, opening her jaws to take in the steady stream of blood issued from Hal's spouting, headless corpse in the backseat. Isabella had lied to her. She hadn't been thinking about Dani, she had been thinking about herself. They had all lied to her!

Madison's face came before her again. Poor, trusting Madison. Dani thought of her dress, her beautiful dress.

Suddenly she was back in the basement, looking

397

into her mother's face, squarely set, determined not to flinch, not to look away. Dani's sharp nails had broken the skin beneath Sam's jaw, leaving a tiny line of blood. Dani's tongue flickered from her drawn lips. She wanted to taste the woman's blood.

"NO!!!" Dani screamed. She loosed her hold on Walthers's hair and scrambled back, turning as she vaulted to a standing position. She half ran, half flew up the stairs and slammed into the heavy steel door.

It did not budge.

Dani went wild, slamming at the door. Images of her mother and herself flooded into her. They sat on the couch, Sam crying even worse than Dani after the girl's first date went badly, crying so much that it became comical. Being held in the woman's arms. Running beside her. Graduation day. The look of perfect pride in the woman's face.

Dani's hands transformed into talons. She raked at the metal, pounding at the door, kicking it, screaming, "You've got to let me out. Got to let me out. You don't understand!"

"It's not going to open, Dani. Not for twelve more hours. That's what I programmed it for when we first came in here."

Dani wailed, throwing her head back. The hunger was flaring. It made every nerve in her body tingle with pain. Her need burned her flesh. It was a struggle for her to maintain her hold on her identity. She was Danielle Walthers. She was Samantha's daughter.

She was a *monster*. A murderer.

"If you want to be one of them, you're going to have to kill me," Sam said.

"Oh Jesus, you think I won't?" Dani screamed in anguish. She heard Samantha approach. The woman was at the base of the stairs. Dani did not have to turn to know that this time Sam had come with open hands. The flamethrower sat in the corner. The weapons locker was untouched.

It would be easy, so easy. Turn and fly at her. Rip her fucking head off, wash yourself in the healing blood, immerse yourself for all time.

"I love you, Dani. You're the only thing that's ever made my life worth living. I always knew that one day you were going to grow up and leave me. That's the way it should be. But now I know that if I have to lose you like this, then I might as well not have a life."

Dani slammed at the door, clawed at it, and sank against its cold surface as she started to cry, tears red as blood leaking from her eyes.

Thirty-one

The house was silent. Morning had arrived. Upstairs, a figure sat in the darkened pantry, staring at the metal door leading to the basement. The harsh glow of sunlight radiated from the kitchen windows, through a few cracks the woman had neglected to seal. But she was safe. The door would open soon. The waiting would be at an end.

Shifting uncomfortably in the chair, Isabella touched the quivering mesh of pale skin covering her stomach. Never in her existence had she been harmed so grievously. Others of her kind could never have withstood the physical and emotional trauma of such wounds. But Isabella's elegant, refined hands had rolled a finely woven carpet of centuries behind her. But for their kind, with age came strength.

She had died, yes. The process of death and rebirth was not one she looked forward to, but she had endured it several times in her long and trying existence. If the shotgun had been aimed at her head, there would have been no hope for resurrection. She had been fortunate. Her spine had been damaged, but not completely separated. Consciousness had returned to her shortly after Walthers had taken Dani away in the stolen car. She had felt the intense heat of the sun and had fought off the panic rising in her breast. Her flesh would burn and she would die without hope of rebirth. Reaching out with her power, Isabella had latched on to one of the spectators, who picked up her limp, shattered form and carried it to his apartment in one of the nearby tenements. As he hauled her away, Isabella projected a mental command through the crowd, sending into disarray their recollections of the event they had witnessed.

The man had been an amateur photographer. He took Isabella to his darkroom, where they spent the day together. She unleashed and satisfied his every desire, feeding from his emotions. At the climax of their encounter, she slashed his throat and took his blood. By nightfall, she had recovered well enough to take the man's car and drive to Walthers's house. No one was there. Then it occurred to her. The beach house. The cellar.

She had arrived in the middle of the night and found the stolen car parked outside. Sensing Dani's presence, Isabella entered the house, crossed to the kitchen, and found the door to the cellar locked. She cursed herself for never learning the codes to the security overrides. Technology was Yoshino's department. He had been fascinated by it. She had only learned to drive out of necessity; it was impossible to live in Los Angeles without a car, and there were times when she needed to be away from Bill and Angel.

The timer on the door had been set for shortly after sunrise. A search of the house had proven a waste of time. Walthers had not locked Dani in alone to wait out her final hours of hunger, she had gone in with her. Isabella felt she could almost commend the human for her bravery, but she had sensed how devastatingly strong Dani's need had become. She had no doubt what the night's outcome would be.

There had been no choice except to wait. Isabella sat at the kitchen table, staring at the clock. Dani's hunger reached out to her, flaring like a dying sun in its final, tormented moments. Then it subsided. Dani had fed. Walthers had been killed.

The sunlight was going to be a problem. Come morning, when the door unlocked, fatal light would be streaming through the windows like angry fingers of white flame. Dani would rush out of the cellar, driven mad with grief over her hours of confinement, and would enter the arms of the light, where she would die screaming. Walthers had, unwittingly or not, engineered the means of the child's destruction. Isabella had to prevent Dani from walking into the trap. She worked hard, tearing up sections of the rug. When she had gone into the pantry to find something she could use to secure the heavy rugs to the glass, she found Tory's body.

Isabella chided herself for not smelling the corpse, but her body had not fully regenerated. In truth, she was a mess. Bits of metal had lodged in her empty eye socket, making regeneration impossible. Several of her internal organs had fused, and her nervous system was no longer wired quite right. There had been enough heat and flame in the shotgun blast to ruin her body for good.

There had been plenty of time, and so she had taken Tory's body outside and burned it. Once, she had hoped Tory would be the one to fulfill her dreams, but the child was feral and undisciplined, worthless. Nevertheless, her remains deserved to be treated with respect. Shattering several wood planks on the back porch, Isabella spent the rest of her time creating the makeshift wall over the kitchen windows. Then she dragged her chair to the pantry and sat inside, waiting for the door to open and her daughter to appear. Once Isabella had Dani, she would seek out the Parliament, and through them, an audience with the Ancients, who might be able to help Isabella heal her devastating wounds.

There was time, so much time. Isabella looked the perfect image of serenity and utmost patience, but, in truth, she loathed waiting. She wanted to pound on the door until it leaped from its hinges, but it had been designed to withstand the frenzy of a Wildling attack. In her weakened state, she would do nothing but upset Dani, and that was something she wished dearly to avoid.

Suddenly, a series of electronic clicks sounded, along with a pneumatic hiss. Isabella leaped to her feet. The door opened.

Dani stood in the shadows of the doorway, dried blood caked around her mouth, her clothes soaked through with blood.

Isabella stood, her hands trembling. Dani's expression held out the promise the vampire had longed to see. In a harsh whisper Isabella said, *"Daughter."*

The girl took a frightened step into the corridor of dim light separating the pantry and the basement door. A stray beam of light fell upon her.

"Dani, no!" Isabella screamed, leaping forward, out of the darkness. She saw the child smile cruelly at the last second, then felt Dani's hands on her arms, clamping down hard. Isabella's momentum was used against her. She was flung across the kitchen, into the makeshift collection of boards, towels, and uprooted stretches of rug. Her body connected and glass shattered as the wood planks were driven forward, with her weight, through the windows. Isabella fell back, into the kitchen, tumbling down from the counter. She screamed as a large block of searing white light fell upon her. In horror, she saw that Dani was standing full in the light, squinting slightly, unharmed.

"What did you call me?" Dani asked.

Isabella could not respond. The sunlight had brought agonies upon her tender flesh that she hadn't endured in over a century. Screaming, she raised her hands before her face and attempted to stand. The sunlight struck the back of her head, burning away skin, causing a handful of long, black hairs to fall away. She dropped to her knees and crawled back to the base of the counters, where the direct sunlight could not reach her.

The sound of footsteps on the stairs came to her. Someone else was down there, coming up. She saw the Walthers woman appear at the doorway, a flamethrower in her hands.

"So you've made a decision," Isabella said.

At least it was my decision to make, Dani thought, but she said nothing. The sight of the once beautiful Isabella ruined and ugly had saddened her immensely.

"Dani, get out of the way!" Sam cried. Her daughter hesitated for an instant, then did as she was asked, moving off to Sam's side.

The sight of Dani's betrayal galvanized Isabella. The vampire rose up, ignoring the burst of sunlight that charred her flesh, then raised her hands before her face as she saw the Walthers woman strike the release on the flamethrower.

Too late, too late, Isabella thought.

There was a tiny, pitiful spitting noise, nothing else. The fiery burst of flames Isabella had anticipated did not arrive. She lowered her hands and saw Walthers desperately working the flamethrower, trying to discover what had gone wrong with the unit.

With a scream, she launched herself at the human. Dani moved between Isabella and her human mother, and the vampire barreled toward them. Flesh sizzling, intense pain streaking through her brain, Isabella opened her arms and gathered Dani to her, the momentum of her flight slamming both of them back, into her mother, who had been standing at the entrance to the basement. They were flung into the comforting embrace of the shadows, Isabella's momentary burst of flight ending abruptly as they fell down the stairs, tumbling in a mad collection of limbs. The flamethrower bounced on the stairs and fell to the semidarkness.

Dani twisted free of the vampire and fell over the side, gracefully landing on her feet. From the stairs, she heard the familiar and terrible crack of shattering bones. A human cry of agony. Isabella's triumphant chortle.

"Mom!" Dani screamed, turning to see Isabella crouched over Sam on the stairs, her mother's form deathly still.

Isabella looked up sharply. She could feel the tingling at the back of her scalp, where her flesh was attempting to regenerate. But she would need blood. With a cruel laugh, she hauled Samantha Walthers's limp form into the air and slammed it against the wall. The woman moaned, her eyes fluttering. The pained expression on Dani's face enraged Isabella. She held Samantha by the throat with one hand as she transformed the other into a talon. She ran her razor-sharp nails along the human's throat.

"This is what you want for a mother?" Isabella screeched. "Frail and mortal, aging and past her prime? Is this what you want to *become?*"

Without hesitation, Dani scrambled to the spot where the flamethrower had fallen. She grabbed the unit, tapped the trigger, and cried out in relief as a wide tongue of flame roared from the weapon. Rising, she aimed the weapon at Isabella. Even burned and wounded, the vampire was magnificent, a goddess. Samantha Walthers looked like a used-up child's toy. Memories of Madison flashed before her.

"Yeah," Dani said. "That *is* what I want! Put her down!"

"That seems unlikely, sister-love." She glanced upward, at the searing white light filtering in from the kitchen. "It's death for me, if I do. And you can do nothing to harm me. Not without hurting this worthless bag of flesh."

"She's not *worthless*," Dani said.

"To me she is."

"You lied to me, Isabella. You lied to me about everything."

The muscles in Isabella's face tightened. "You had to be made to see, you had to become true to your blood."

"I have," Dani said. "Put her down and I won't hurt you. You know I have feelings for you."

"Easily said, Dani."

Trembling, Dani hissed, "She's *hurt*. Let me get her to a hospital. Her life for yours."

They regarded each other. Isabella raised her head up, looking down imperiously. "I'd like to believe you, Dani. I would." She paused. Her expression softened, her eyes growing wide with need. "It's not too late, you know. You can be turned again. It could be me, this time. I would not leave your side, daughter, I—"

"You are not my mother!"

Isabella stared at the teenager, chest heaving. She tightened her grip on Sam's throat, squeezing until the woman shuddered and wheezed, her head lolling forward.

"Please!" Dani cried.

"Put down the weapon."

"Isabella—"

"Put it down or I will kill her." The vampire's voice was shaky, laced with emotion.

Dani forced down her panic. Think about what Sam would do if it was the other way around. Concentrate. "You'd do that anyway, Isabella. I've got to believe that you want to live a hell of a lot more than you want revenge."

"You can't *let* me live, Dani. You know I'd come back for you. For you and the woman, both."

"Maybe not."

"Please, Dani," Isabella said, her mask of rage dropping slightly, "think about what you're giving up. You will never fly again. You will age and you will die. And through it all, the need will never leave you. Never. You have touched the sky, child. You will never again be happy with life as a mortal, rooted to the earth."

Dani felt a fluttering at the gossamer borders of her consciousness. A wind rose up. A gentle, familiar touch grazed her thoughts. Dani was overwhelmed by beautiful images of flying over the city at night, piercing the clouds, laughing and crying with delight as she sailed with the power of a god.

No! She had risen above her blood. Her mother had held her, and had opened her mind for Dani to bathe in the perfect love she held for the girl. Dani had experienced dozens of her mother's most intimate memories, felt her joy at her daughter's triumphs, her pain and fear when the child had been missing. She would not throw that away, even if it meant that she would never take to the skies again.

Dani forced Isabella out of her thoughts.

"Then it's a standoff," Isabella said.

"No," Dani whispered, gathering the power that had been left to her as her blood right and turning it upon the vampire. Isabella had been totally unprepared for the attack. Dani slipped beyond her defenses. Before Isabella could react, Dani cast Isabella into the dark cellar of the serial killers, where Dani had woken years earlier, strapped to the chair. Isabella screamed in fear, strapped down, the flames of the killers approaching her flesh.

Dani lapped at the woman's fear, probing deeper, pressing her attack beyond the level of her conscious mind.

"Come on," Dani said, tasting the exquisite fear that radiated from the vampire, "let's see what makes *you* afraid."

A horrible, ugly face appeared before Dani, frightening her so much that she nearly withdrew. She looked at him again. A swarthy man, his face lined with sores, his hair black and wild, striking at her with a hand wreathed by rings that drew blood with the blows.

This man, this man had *harmed* Isabella. Deeper, go deeper.

Images flowed into Dani. She was walking through the streets of Florence, Italy. The year was 1619. Isabella walked beside her, smiling, happy as the sunlight washed over her, a lover's caress. Horses rode on the cobblestone streets.

Words tumbled from Dani's mouth in a voice that was not her own. The language was not English, but Dani understood it anyway. "You really must be married, Isabella. You know that mother thinks it's a scandal, and all her friends think you will be a dried-up old spinster."

"Indeed," Isabella said with a laugh. "At the ripe old age of eighteen."

"I was married much earlier."

"Well, I'm not you, sister-love."

Her sister, she thinks I'm her sister, Dani thought.

"I want to see the world, and write about what

I encounter. I can hardly do that if I'm—"

The scene changed abruptly, Isabella's words cut off. It was night and a soft orange glow reflected up from the rain-swept streets; lit torches rested in braziers fastened beside every door.

Dani stood in the dining chamber of a modest home, a tray in her hands. Isabella was staring at her father in shock.

"Married?" Isabella said in shock. "I don't even know this man!"

"Giovanni Vasari has made a sizable offer for your hand, Isabella. I will not have you embarrass me before him. If you like, we will discuss it at a more appropriate time."

"In other words, you'll beat your point into me." Isabella turned to Dani. "Mother, please!"

"Your father is correct," Dani heard herself say in a new, alien voice. This time, she was Isabella's mother.

"I'll run away. You can't force me."

Her father stood up. "By the law of church and society, you are my chattel, until I give you to a husband. Run away and I'll have you found and declared insane. The choice is yours. Marriage to a nobleman, or a life with the mad. Whichever you desire."

"To hell with you," Isabella said, rising. Her father's hand clamped down on her. He dragged her from the table, kicking and screaming. Dani sat quietly, waiting for the inevitable sounds of the beating to begin.

No more, no more, I don't want to see anymore, Dani thought, but the scene changed again. She was with Isabella in bed, seeing through the eyes of the vicious creature Isabella had been forced to marry, the swarthy man. A mirror propped in the corner confirmed this.

Helpless to stop the events that had transpired

centuries ago, Dani watched in mute horror as Vasari beat Isabella and used her cruelly, forcing her to perform abhorrent sexual acts. When Isabella struggled to maintain her dignity, despite his abuse, he dragged a candle to their bed and burned Isabella, burned her horribly while sparing her face and hands. Isabella screamed, trying to fight the man, but she could not keep him at bay. Her body was lined with burn marks, puckered, scarred flesh.

When it was over, he cried, "Three years! Three years of marriage and no children. You're a freak! Worthless!"

Isabella lay on the bed, crying. Dani, a weakening presence in the vessel of Isabella's husband, screamed in horror as the man rose from the bed and took a blade from a nearby dresser.

"Divorce me, I'll say nothing of what passed between us," Isabella pleaded as she saw the knife.

"I don't believe in divorce," Vasari snarled, "and I don't think you could keep your wicked little mouth from spreadin' lies about me, neither."

"They'll catch you, they'll—"

"I own them!" Vasari shouted, lunging at her. Something changed in Isabella during that instant, her blood took hold. The woman did not know that she was an Initiate, that her father had held that title by name only. Her power manifested and she took the man's life, reaching out with her anger and fear, snuffing out his mind with the merciful ease of blowing out a candle.

Dani was shocked from Isabella's mind. She found herself back in the cellar, the flamethrower dragging on the floor. Isabella had released Samantha, and the woman had crawled down the remaining stairs, dragging herself away. Her legs were twisted at odd angles. White-hot pain surged from her.

"Do it, Dani!" Sam was shouting. "Honey, do it now!"

I can't burn her, Dani thought. Not after what happened to her. The same thing almost happened to me in that trapper's cellar.

"Dani, hurry!"

Dani looked into Isabella's ruined face. The vampire was trembling, her lips curled up in anger at the violation. "You want it all? You want it all? *Fine!*"

Before Dani could raise the flamethrower, Isabella lashed out with her power, sending a barrage of images into Dani's head, driving her from her feet. She saw Isabella running from the land of her birth, ashamed and frightened by what she had done. Eventually, she came into the company of Alyana, a woman who ran with the shadows and was a lover to the night. A vampire. She taught Isabella the truth about herself, and became Isabella's mentor and friend.

Though Isabella had not wished to carry the child of the monster she had slain, she was crushed to learn that she was barren, as were all women of her kind, and she would never feel a life grow within her. It was Isabella's continuing sadness over this fact that eventually drove Alyana from her.

Through the centuries, Isabella collected a menagerie of others like herself. She adapted herself to the world, which raced on painfully oblivious to the existence of her kind. But she had never felt satisfied with her existence. Those vampires she took on as companions remained only that. The few she turned came to resent her and leave. Only Dani had held out hope of easing the need that had ravaged Isabella for centuries. This child could truly *be* her daughter.

Dani forced away the attack of memories.

411

Something lay beneath them, a secret Isabella had been hiding.

There, sister-love. Isabella wailed in Dani's mind. *There is the monster you wish to slay. There is the consummate evil you've chosen to hate. There, Dani. There!*

Dani knew that she was at the woman's mercy. Isabella could destroy her mind with ease. Instead, the vampire withdrew.

"I won't harm you," Isabella said, "I —"

Dani's second attack was as much of a surprise as her first. Isabella would never have believed the child to possess the strength to come at her a second time. The child tore apart the walls surrounding the single memory she dared not lay open to Dani. Before she could resist, the scene was exposed for both to experience.

Isabella lay with Bill Yoshino, Angel curled at the foot of the bed, watching them with amusement. The girl, the doppelganger, Tory, knelt at the bedside, frightened and expectant. Dani saw through Tory's eyes.

"All right," Bill said. "Here are my rules. I'm the one who turns her. If you can get Dani away from me, then you get to run the pack for another hundred years. But if she stays with me, if she chooses to become mine, then your power goes to me. Is it a deal?"

Isabella laughed. "Of course. But you'll never win."

"We'll see."

Dani rebelled at the sight. A game, it had all been a game! Tory had come to the vampires, told them of the Initiate she had found, and they had destroyed Dani's life for the sake of their own amusement.

A game, you fucking bitch! Dani screamed within the shuddering, vulnerable passages of Isa-

412

bella's mind.

No, sister-love, it may have started out that way, but when I met you, and grew to love you, I knew that you were the one I had been waiting for. You, Dani. I love —

Dani's anger exploded. She turned the full force of her power against Isabella, driving from the woman every fear she had ever endured. Isabella was strapped to the black chair, Giovanni Vasari searing her flesh with a torch, her father standing behind him, laughing. Alyana, the woman who had turned Isabella fully to their ways, turned and left the woman in disgust, a void opening in her life that would never be filled again. Dani, the child who might have been her daughter, had turned on her, plunging a silver, flaming dagger deep into her heart.

No! Dani screamed, attempting to withdraw. She was killing the woman. Dear God, she was killing her. She had wanted to hurt Isabella, punish her for her betrayal, but she did not mean for this to happen.

Isabella grasped at her, pleading like a child for her life. Suddenly, Isabella's world was consumed in a raging explosion of fire.

Dani was back in the cellar. Isabella had fallen in a heap, across the stairs. Sam had dragged herself to the floor and was pulling herself toward Dani.

"No," Dani whispered, "I'm sorry, I'm so sorry."

"It's alright, baby," Sam whispered. "I'm here. Mommy's here."

A sharp, feral hiss cut through the quiet of the cellar. Dani and Sam turned. The thing that had been Isabella rose, pulling back its lips in a feral snarl.

"Sweet Jesus," Dani whispered, suddenly aware of the flamethrower in her hands. "Isabella!"

The creature did not seem to recognize the name. Dani did not have to reach out with her silver thread to know that all vestiges of Isabella's personality had been destroyed. What had been left in their place was the beast, the raging animal that existed within each of their kind, its humanity stripped away. It looked up sharply, at the sunlight above, and drew back in fear. Then it focused its attention on the meat below. The woman on the floor was closest. Helpless. Easy prey.

Isabella crouched, preparing to leap at Sam.

"Don't!" Dani cried, but Isabella sprang. With an anguished scream, Dani raised the flamethrower and released a torrent of flames that snaked across the distance separating her from the monster, and engulfed the creature.

Isabella writhed, screaming in agony. She fell to the base of the stairs, clutching at herself, moaning in pain and despair. The flames wrapped around her without mercy.

Mercy.

You have the power to be merciful, Isabella had said to her once.

Pushing aside her fear of what her power could do, Dani once again reached out with the silver thread. She found the dark, animal mind, all that remained of Isabella, and forced a single image to replace the burning, horrible pain. Isabella and her sister, walking the bright streets of Florence, laughing and teasing, discussing their dreams.

Suddenly, there was nothing. A haunting, silent vacuum.

Isabella was dead.

Dani shook herself free of the woman, then scrambled back as she felt something touch her arm. She turned, heart racing, and saw the kind, loving face of her mother. With a strained cry, Dani launched herself into the woman's arms, holding her as tightly as she dared.

"It's over, baby. It's over," Sam said, stroking her daughter's hair.

"Oh Jesus, Mommy, I killed her, I killed her."

"It'll be alright, baby. You're gonna be fine."

"Don't hate me, please."

"No, baby, never. Don't even think that. I love you, Dani. I love you and I'll never go away again."

"I killed them both," Dani said, almost choking on the words. "Isabella and Madison. Oh God, what am I!?"

"You're my daughter, honey," Sam said as she brushed the tangled mat of hair from the girl's face and kissed her. "You'll always be my daughter, no matter what."

"*I love you*," Dani said, half-crying, half-laughing the words she had feared she would never be able to speak again.

"I love you, too, baby," Sam whispered, easing her daughter into her embrace. "I love you, too.

This time, when Dani cried, the tears that fell from her eyes were clear, salty droplets.

The tears were *human*.